HOLLYWOOD TOUGH

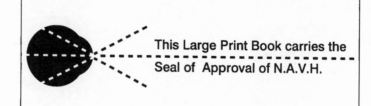

This Large Print Book carries the
Seal of Approval of N.A.V.H.

HOLLYWOOD TOUGH

STEPHEN J. CANNELL

WHEELER
PUBLISHING

Published in 2003 by arrangement with St. Martin's Press, LLC.

Wheeler Large Print Hardcover Series.

The text of this Large Print edition is unabridged.
Other aspects of the book may vary from the original edition.

Set in 16 pt. Plantin by Carleen Stearns.

Printed in the United States on permanent paper.

Library of Congress Cataloging-in-Publication Data

Cannell, Stephen J.
    Hollywood tough / Stephen J. Cannell.
      p. cm.
    ISBN 1-58724-416-0 (lg. print : hc : alk. paper)
    1. Police — California — Los Angeles — Fiction. 2. Divorced
women — Crimes against — Fiction. 3. Hollywood (Los Angeles,
Calif.) — Fiction. 4. Motion picture industry — Fiction.
5. Large type books. I. Title.
PS3553.A4995H65 2003b
  813'.54—dc21
                                           2003041138

This book is for two great, longtime friends.

Grace Curcio Without your help, friendship, understanding, and love, I would have talked much more and accomplished much less. You make me strong.

Jo Swerling, Jr. Your grace, diplomacy, and friendship have shown me how to stay calm and be secure, even when the ship is going down.

I love you both.

Mitigate the penalty, not the misconduct.

—LAPD Management Guide to Discipline

1

THE HOLLYWOOD
PARTY

Shane Scully sure didn't want to go to this
Hollywood party. It was way the hell out in
Malibu, and except for Nora Bishop, he and his
wife, Alexa, weren't going to know anybody
there. The party was to announce Nora's engagement to a movie producer named Farrell
Champion, whom neither of them had met.
Making it even worse, Shane and Alexa were
cops and would probably stand out like psychi-
atrists at a Star Trek convention. They didn't
understand movie people or Hollywood, with
its strange language and customs. So Shane
was more or less dreading it.

Alexa, on the other hand, could barely con-
tain her excitement. She had spent at least two
hours getting ready, which to tell the truth kind

of pissed him off. One of the things he prized most about his beautiful black-haired wife was that she never made a big deal out of her appearance. She could show up most places wearing a horse blanket and look better than anybody there.

But all afternoon she had dithered and fussed until it had made them hopelessly late.

"You think these earrings are too gaudy? You think this blue-and-red scarf is too much with the tan skirt . . . ?"

"No, looks great . . . love it . . ." But it didn't matter what he thought, because she would just wrinkle her nose and stare at the clothing on the bed, then pull out a new ensemble.

Shane had dressed quickly, showering and combing his short black hair with his fingers. He glanced at his rugged angular face in the mirror. He was in his late thirties and his bony cheeks and hard, deep-set eyes reminded him of an over-the-hill, beat-up street fighter. It always surprised him when someone described him as handsome. At least, he marveled, he'd been lucky enough to jump the many hurdles required to marry the most beautiful woman on the LAPD.

They finally got in his Acura at five-thirty, left Venice, California, and headed toward Malibu. They were almost an hour late when they passed the old Getty Museum, then the Malibu Pier. Shane drove while Alexa chattered nervously.

"That last guy Nora dated, remember him, Shane? The one who traded futures on the stock exchange?"

"Yeah. Bill something, with the dimple in his chin . . ."

"That fucking dimple was a surgical add-on," Alexa growled. "Boy, was I glad when Nora gave him the old flusheroo."

"Yep. Bill was sleaze."

"And remember Paul Bennett? Remember him? How on earth Nora ever decided to get entangled with Paul Bennett, with his polo ponies, which everyone thought he owned but it turned out he just rented, and the rented Ferrari . . . he should've rented a personality."

"Yeah, Paul was definitely toe-jam. A skunk."

She turned and looked at him. "Are you humoring me, buddy?" She smiled.

"I agree Nora's been flying in a bug storm, but we don't know anything about this new guy either, except that he has a great press agent. He's in almost every national magazine."

"Whatta you mean we don't know? I've been talking to Nora about Farrell Champion since she started to decorate his Malibu house last year. He's the real deal — A-list all the way — and she's so happy, Shane. At last I think she's found Mr. Right."

"Yep, yep . . . pretty exciting." God, he was dreading this party.

When they passed the Serra Retreat, the former mansion of the woman who once owned

9

twenty miles of California coastline, Shane slowed the Acura and picked up the expensive invitation. It had a slightly corny Hollywood theme. On the top of the embossed card it said: "It's a Wrap on Farrell's Bachelorhood." There were some old-fashioned drawings of 35mm movie cameras, underscored by the inscription: "Come Help Us Celebrate Farrell's Biggest Epic Yet . . . It's a Love Story."

He flipped it open to the map that showed where Farrell Champion's house was located behind the Colony gates in Malibu.

"I hate being late. Maybe we should just call in sick," he suggested, grinning.

"Nothing doing, you coward. Besides, I want to see the stars. I hear Julia Roberts is going to be there. Farrell produced one of her movies last year, and Nora said even Robert Downey, Jr."

"Shit, and us without our drug kits."

She punched him. "Stop it." She smiled. "You're gonna love it."

Seconds later they turned off the Coast Highway into the Colony. They pulled up to the guard, who frowned at the unwashed Acura. Then came the ritual giving and checking of names, the showing of the invitation.

They were validated.

A short drive down into the Malibu Colony and they were handing the dusty Acura over to a valet with surfer-blond hair wearing a red coat with gold buttons. It fit him better than Shane's blue blazer. Another valet was just driving a white Bentley away from in front of the house.

There were still a few tardy arrivals lined up at the front door. "See, we're not that late," Alexa said as she and Shane headed up the stone walkway.

Farrell Champion had built a French Provincial on two oceanfront lots. The house was grotesquely large, dwarfing its neighbors, and Shane thought it seemed pretentious and out of place, only forty yards from the crashing surf.

They got in line behind a beautiful woman who was wearing a beaded dress, very low cut, and an older gentleman with silver hair in a tuxedo with a black silk shirt — they looked like Bentley owners.

"We're underdressed," Alexa hissed in his ear as she looked at the woman's evening gown. Alexa had ended up wearing a white pantsuit with a wide belt and sandals. She looked gorgeous. Her blue eyes and sculpted face dominated a slender, athletic body.

Shane whispered back, "How can you underdress for a beach barbecue?"

The couple in front stepped over the threshold and Shane could hear a booming voice he guessed was Farrell Champion's, followed by Nora Bishop's tinkling laugh.

"Boris." Farrell's baritone. "Great opening weekend grosses on *Horizon of the Damned.*

11

You're up five percent prorated from holiday weekend totals last year."

"But the P and A sure set us back a bundle," the tuxedoed man replied. "It's a step release. We're going wide next week . . . twenty-six hundred screens."

"Thelma, you look devastating, as always. . . ." Farrell again.

"Sorry about being so overdressed, Farrell. We're leaving here for Calvin's opening at the Taper."

Shane heard Alexa let out a sigh.

After a few air kisses, Thelma and Boris moved on.

Alexa was holding Shane's hand and she gave it a little hopeful squeeze. It was their turn. Show time.

They stepped into the magnificent, antiques-laden entry hall and Shane hugged Nora. She was a beautiful, dark-haired, forty-five-year-old woman with a sweet, tender quality that always made him want to protect her. She was also one of L.A.'s premiere interior decorators. In the last few years, Bishop Interiors had done a lot of the big homes in Beverly Hills, Malibu, and the Palisades. And despite her exposure to some of L.A.'s most demanding A-type personalities, Nora never provoked any discontent. She had a way of getting you to behave by making you feel good about yourself. She was ten years older than Alexa, and had been Alexa's baby-sitter back in Michigan when she was twelve. That was the year after Alexa's mother had died. Shane had always wondered if Nora's move to L.A. foreshadowed his wife's decision to come West as well, as if she needed to be close to Nora, who was like a big sister or maybe even a surrogate mother.

Alexa usually projected strength and determination, but around Nora she became strangely girlish. With Nora, she giggled. Sometimes, as Shane watched them together, he would get a glimpse of what his wife must have been like as a child.

"Shane, Alexa, thank you guys for coming. You're the best." Nora flashed her irresistible smile, then hugged Alexa. "I love that outfit, where did you get it?"

"This? It was on sale at May Company." Alexa wrinkled her nose in apology. "It's just an Adrienne Vittadini copy."

"On you it looks like a Dior original." Nora turned to the handsome fifty-five-year-old man beside her. "You guys haven't met Farrell. Farrell, these are my dearest friends in L.A., the Scullys."

Farrell grinned, and they shook hands and all started frantically searching for common ground.

"Nora, you didn't tell me Alexa would be so sexy. This is no meter maid you've got here, Shane."

Nine out of ten guys who said something like that would have pissed Shane off. Not that he

13

was overly jealous, but there was some primal piece of him that didn't like handsome guys fawning over his wife or calling her sexy. But Farrell got away with it. Something in Farrell's demeanor said "Just kidding, don't take this the wrong way." He had a personality . . . Shane hated the word, but okay, a *vibe* that was warm, engaging, and funny. In seconds, Shane could feel himself being won over.

Furthermore, Farrell Champion was extremely attractive and his looks drew you to him. He was fit, but not musclebound, not a fanatic. His silver-gray hair was swept back off his tanned forehead and his dark eyes looked right at you, focusing, making you feel important.

"What a beautiful house. . . . It's refreshing to see this kind of architecture on the beach." Shane couldn't believe such an egregiously phony sentence had come gushing out of him.

"Making movies isn't brain surgery, Shane. You gotta take all of this with a grain of salt," Farrell whispered with a wink. "No matter what anybody tells you, show business isn't creative art, it's a racket."

"Did you see the engagement ring?" Nora said, throwing her hand out for Alexa's examination. The diamond was huge — over six carats.

"My God, Nora, you must need someone to carry your hand around for you."

Farrell grinned. "Listen, you guys, I think everyone's here now, so I can stop standing in the

14

entry like a nervous doorman. Come on in. Shane, can I get you and Alexa something? How about some white wine, or I have mixed drinks."

"Alexa likes chardonnay, I'll take scotch," Shane said.

Farrell steered Nora and Alexa into the plush living room full of beautiful people, then left them staring at the high-profile crowd while he headed toward the bar. Alexa grabbed Nora's hand and squeezed it.

"My God, Nora . . . he's gorgeous."

"Not bad, huh?" Nora grinned back. "After all those foul tips, I finally got some wood on the ball."

Shane nodded and smiled broadly, the kind of smile you wear when you can't think of a damn thing to say. He had come here fully prepared to hate Farrell Champion . . . hate him for his fame and success, his wealth and connections; hate him just for having a name like Farrell Champion. But in forty-five seconds or less, while standing in the doorway, Farrell had completely rewired all those feelings, leaving Shane groping for a new take.

Shane's eyes were sweeping the party. Everybody who was anybody in L.A. was there. He spotted faces he had only seen in *People* magazine.

"There's Kobe Bryant," he whispered, seeing the Lakers' great only a few feet away talking to ex-Mayor Riordan. Then Farrell was back, handing out drinks.

"Alexa, you had chardonnay . . . Shane, scotch rocks — that's Dewar's, hope you like it . . . Nora, here's your Campari and soda." Then Farrell took them both by the arm and steered them through the room. "Come on, let me introduce you to some friends." So off they went, on a celebrity tour of L.A.

"Nicole Kidman, this is Nora's dear friend Alexa Scully and her husband, Shane." The beautiful Australian actress smiled warmly, shook their hands, and they exchanged a few remarks. Then Farrell moved them on. "And this is L.A.'s resident bad boy, Jack the Mack . . . Jacko, want you to meet some friends of Nora's . . ." *Jack fucking Nicholson,* Shane thought, feeling starstruck as he shook the famous actor's hand.

More small talk until Farrell carried them along. . . . "Barbra and Jim live just down the street. Meet Nora's dear friends, Shane and Alexa." *It was Streisand and Brolin.*

It went on like that until finally Alexa got pulled away by Nora to meet some of the other bridesmaids, and Shane had to go to the bathroom. He used the one in the hall, thinking he was having a great time in spite of himself. *This was one pretty amazing party.*

When Shane came out of the bathroom he ran into the last person he would have ever expected to find at Farrell Champion's house.

2

THE BAD JOKE

Nicky Marcella was waiting to get into the guest john as Shane exited. They looked at each other like competing art thieves casing a Sotheby's auction.

"My God, Shane Scully," Nicky said. He was wearing a beautifully tailored, if somewhat gaudy, orangish-brown suit — or was it brownish-orange? — hard to tell because the colors strobed when he moved. Either way, it took some doing to pull off. Maybe the suit was helped by the fact that there wasn't all that much of it — Nicky being only five-foot-five, top to bottom, including his stacked Cuban heels. He was also rail thin — Mick Jagger thin. He had black hair, close-cut on the sides and slightly longer on the top. He was wearing an open-collared silk shirt with a few too many gold chains. His smile was warm, but he was narrow-faced and strangely ferretlike.

"Nicky, how you been?"

"Staying outta jail, I'll tell you that much."

"Glad to hear it," Shane said, and he was. He hadn't seen Marcella in four years. Nicky was a Hollywood character. When Shane met him he was doing street-corner cons — green-goods hustles and pigeon drops. Shane had first busted him when he was still a rookie working vice in Hollywood. He'd rolled him up twice more in the Valley when he was riding around in a plain Jane doing a straight eight in uniform. Sometime in the mid-nineties Nicky had switched from short cons to running bets for bookmakers, then had taken a short fall and ended up doing a bullet in County. When he got out, he moved on to straight-up bookmaking, writing betting slips out of a porn shop on Little Melrose. Nicky Marcella had dabbled in the criminal arts for almost the whole fifteen years Shane had known him, and now here he was, in Farrell Champion's house, rubbing shoulders with Hollywood's elite.

"Whatta you up to? Or should I just count the silver?" Shane smiled.

"Can't blame you for that, Shane. But I'm clean as the Board of Health these days. Just a minute, don't go away, gotta tap a kidney."

Nicky pushed past him into the bathroom while Shane stood outside wondering what on earth Nicky Marcella was doing at this party full of heavy-lifters. Even so, Shane had to admit that, over the years, he'd come to enjoy the guy. Nicky had an infectious personality and never took himself too seriously. Of course, he was shamefully easy to arrest, a wonderful quality in a criminal. No toe-to-toe scuffling or bruised ribs with Nicky. At five-foot-five, he was not the kind of perp who fried your nerves with adrenal overload. Nicky was also a fountain of gossip. Shane would sometimes put the word out on the street, with his C.I.'s and snitches, that he needed some particular piece of intelligence, and more times than he could remember, Nicky Marcella would be the one to call in and drop the science on him.

Another strange thing was that Nicky never wanted anything in return. It was almost as if he were trying to buy Shane's friendship, not his gratitude. And slowly, over the years, Nicky had managed to do it. Shane had really come to like the little grifter in that strange way that cops can like criminals but still not respect them.

The door opened and Nicky walked out smiling. "Man, you look great. You got a trainer?"

"Yeah, the P.T. instructor at the Academy."

Nicky nodded and shifted his weight. "Don't tell that to any of those silks out there," he said, pointing toward the room full of celebrities. "In this crowd, you gotta have a personal trainer and he's gotta have a shtick like the Tae Bo guy.

Trainers around here interview the celebs, not the other way around."

There was a pause while both of them pondered the same question: What the hell are you doing here?

"Okay, you first," Shane finally said.

"I'm in showbiz now." Nicky smiled. "I guess I always was in the business of show. Hey, what's a street-corner hustle if it's not a good performance? I'm not selling bets on the nags anymore either. . . . My bets are all at the box office — on movies, which we bullshitters in the cinematic arts always refer to as 'film.' "

"You're in the movie business?" Shane said, finding that hard to believe.

"Yep, producer. Got my own company, Cine-Roma Productions. We're in preproduction on a film right now. I've also got a big development deal with Farrell over at Paramount, on a novel I bought called *Savages in the Midst*."

"The sequel to *Gorillas in the Mist*?"

"Midst . . . Midst, with a *d*, Shane. Like in our midst . . . like that. It's about the meat-eaters in showbiz, and a girl from Illinois who's looking to be a star, and about savages in suits who ravage her body and, eventually, her soul. We could cast the fucking thing off this party's guest list. Farrell is talking Gwyneth, but I'm not so sure. I'm thinking more like J-Lo. Do it a little harder edged. Make the statement seem integral . . . amp up the verisimilitude."

"The what?"

20

"Verisimilitude — means the appearance of truth. You have to learn these words, and some Yiddish, if you wanna be a player." He put his hands in the pockets of his ridiculous multi-colored suit, rocked back on his Cuban heels, and regarded Shane. "Now you."

"Huh? Oh . . . Just Alexa and Farrell's fiancée, Nora Bishop, are old friends. Nora used to be Alexa's baby-sitter when she was a kid."

"I like mine better." Nicky smiled.

"Me too," Shane admitted.

"Listen, bubee, seeing you here might be for-tuitous."

"Yeah?" Shane looked puzzled. "How's that?"

"I was thinking of calling you last week. Isn't that a *mitzva?* Haven't seen you in four years, thinking about calling you . . . kaboom, here you are. That's what we in the biz call —"

"Verisimilitude?"

"With a dose of righteous karma." He smiled. "Shane, I'm looking for a girl who's dropped out of sight. This is silly really, but I bet you could pull this off for me. Her name is Carol White. She's perfect for a part in this movie I'm casting."

"*Savages in the Midst.*"

"No, the other one, the one I'm doing at my shop . . . at Cine-Roma. This film I'm talking about already has a green light — what we call a firm go. The girl I'm looking for, Carol

White, is perfect for the part of Cherri, which is a showy little role . . . the lead character's best friend. Carol has this ethereal quality, which is a word we use in film meaning translucent, delicate, refined . . . very hard to find these qualities in a young actress. Okay, so here's my problem. She used to do some low-budget stuff around town and some TV, shit like that, and then she kinda disappeared. I checked with SAG, and they got no current address on her. I think she may have even dropped out of the business altogether. I don't know who her current agent is."

"I can promise you, I'm not representing her," Shane said.

"I was thinking you could maybe go into the police computer. Carol White . . . ten little keys that spell 'Big Break.' If she's had a traffic ticket or owns a car, you could get her address, then I give her the part that kick-starts and totally redefines a career. When they do the 'E' Celebrity Profile on her five years from now, she's gonna be up there saying, 'I owe it all to an L.A. cop, and a helluva guy, Shane Scully.' "

"Listen, Nicky. You probably haven't heard, but I've been on a medical leave of absence for almost a year. I don't go back on the job until next week. So I don't really have any way into the police computer right now. They change the access codes all the time. So mine's not even current anymore. I mean, as much as I'd like to help and all that . . ."

"Right." Nicky smiled but stopped tipping back on his stacked heels. "Hey, listen, I was probably way outta line there anyway. I mean, the police computer isn't exactly dial-a-job."

"Right."

"Hey, well, it was just a thought. You're looking good, man. Stay healthy and God bless. You're on my prayer list."

"Your what?"

"Found Jesus. A lot happens in four years. Go figure. Spent twenty years living a bullshit life before I discover the Big Guy is my savior. Now I got Jesus and Louie."

"And just who the hell is Louie?" Shane was grinning.

"Louie is the god of all moviemaking. If Louie smiles on you, you get big stars, big grosses, and it never rains on your beach shoot. In the film business we learn these things. Take care, Shane."

Nicky turned to walk down the corridor, and Shane felt instantly bad about brushing off the favor. How hard would it be to help little Nicky? Nicky, who had helped Shane with dozens of useful tips and never asked for anything in return.

"Hey, hold on," Shane called out, and Nicky turned to look back. "I changed my mind. I gotta go down to my old homicide table tomorrow to pick up my duty jacket anyway. I'll get somebody to run her. Gimme your card."

"You always were my favorite copper, even

when you had the cuffs on too tight." Nicky grinned and pulled out an alligator wallet, removed some expensive-looking cards, then handed one to Shane. There was a logo of the Roman Coliseum embossed in gold. Under that it said:

CINE-ROMA —
NICHOLAS MARCELLA, C.E.O.

"Carol White," Nicky said, "spelled just like it sounds."

"Okay. I'll call you tomorrow if I get anything."

They separated and Shane prowled around. He was really having a good time now. He had a second scotch on the rocks, spent some time talking to Catherine Zeta-Jones, and then later, Alexa was back at his side.

"Hi. Where'd you go off to?" Shane asked.

"Just meeting the other bridesmaids and looking at pictures of the dresses Nora ordered for us. I can't believe they're getting married in ten days."

"Right, right . . . I was just saying the same thing to Catherine Zeta-Jones," Shane said, a smile twitching the corner of his mouth.

"Get outta town. . . . Where?"

Shane pointed to the beautiful actress, who was wearing capri pants and a crop-top. She caught Shane's eye as he pointed her out to Alexa and waved at him.

"Down, girl," Alexa growled, then her expression changed. Now it was her no-nonsense look, the one she wore downtown at Parker Center.

"I've gotta go. We got a one eighty-seven out in Sunland that the CRASH unit is worried about. They want me to roll on it." She held up her cell phone. "Just got the call."

"Really? Who died?"

"They think it's Kevin Cordell, but the D.B. took so much lead that they're gonna have to do the I.D. with dentistry."

"Sometimes good old street justice works," Shane said, thinking it was about time somebody put Kevin Cordell on the ark. Kevin's street name was Stone, and he'd been a Crip O.G. for over twenty-five years. Stone ran the Front Street Crips, who pretty much controlled the major drug action throughout South Central L.A. Except for a nickel jolt at Soledad for accessory to second-degree murder, up to now he'd largely escaped justice.

"If it's really Stone, it could create a power vacuum and we could end up with Crips and Bloods shooting each other and anybody else who gets in the way," Alexa said.

"You need the car. . . . I can drive you."

"No. Nora will be really upset if we both leave early. The Sheriff's Department is doing us a favor and sending a unit over from the substation here. They'll taxi me over the hill."

"You really think they need the head of the

25

entire Detective Services Group standing at a crime scene, looking down at the vic while a bunch of lab techs roll the body?"

"Hey, they're my detectives. I go whenever I'm asked. Besides, I'm only the *acting* head of DSG, so I try harder. I'm just holding that post till the chief appoints a captain to the job."

"Honey, Filosiani isn't going to replace you. You're acting head only because you're still a lieutenant and, technically, they can't put a lou in that slot. But I can read that guy — you got the job." He grinned. "You is da man, woman."

"Well, de man-woman gotta take her sorry ass to work."

"I'll stick around here for another hour until they do the steak fry, then drive over the hill and pick you up. You got an address?"

She handed him a slip of paper, then kissed him on the lips. "Only one more thing before I leave . . ."

"Say good-bye to Nora?"

"No, that's done. I gotta run this bitch in the pedal-pushers off my guy."

"Come on . . . she's happily married."

"Maybe, but in Hollywood, marriage is an eight-letter condition with the half-life of a chocolate-chip cookie."

Alexa moved off, stopped next to Catherine Zeta-Jones and said something to her. The two stood there for another moment before the actress threw back her head and roared with laughter.

Alexa turned and smiled at Shane, then went out the front door to the entry hall to wait for the sheriff's car.

That would have been all that was noteworthy, except for one last thing that happened just before he left the party.

He said good-bye to Nora and was heading up from the beach, when he decided to cut through the pool house to save the longer walk around the side of the estate. He went in the beach entrance and was immediately greeted by a heavy cloud of cigar smoke and male laughter coming from the front room. Shane walked down the hallway toward the sound, listening to Farrell's voice. He was telling some kind of story when Shane reached the back of the main room.

The pool house was large — about the size of Shane's entire house in Venice. It had windows on the west that overlooked the ocean. The windows on the other side fronted Farrell's Olympic-size pool. Nora had decorated the pool house in a quasi-African theme: lots of bamboo, grass rugs, and native art. There were ten or twelve men in the room with Farrell, all smoking Cuban Cohibas. Nobody was paying any attention to Shane.

"So, Farrell, you get Kenny to draw you up a prenup like I advised?" one of the guests asked.

Farrell lit the man's cigar with a large gold lighter. "Listen, that kinda shit's good for you guys who can't take care of business, but I don't need no stinking prenup." He did that last part like the Mexican bandit in *Treasure of the Sierra Madre*.

"Everybody needs a prenup. Ask Johnny Carson or Burt Reynolds. It's the law west of Sunset," the man persisted.

"Not me." Farrell seemed a little loaded. "Didn't need one with my last two wives. When I got tired of those ladies, they both got some bad shellfish and died of food poisoning." There was some nervous laughter, not much but some. Then Farrell swung his eyes around the room until his gaze ended up on Shane.

It's hard to explain to a civilian how a cop's hunches work, because they live in some intellectual and emotional no-man's-land somewhere between a guess and a feeling. In the end, they're not really hunches at all. They're based on keen instinct mixed with physical and emotional observations. In this case, the physical part was in Farrell Champion's dark eyes when they found Shane in the back of the room. They hardened momentarily. Even from twenty feet away Shane could see it: a tightening of the skin around the sockets, a shadow on the cornea that came and went so quickly it would have been easy to miss if you weren't trained to spot it. Suddenly the look was gone and the smiling Farrell was back.

"Hey, Shane, that was just a bad joke. Don't get the handcuffs out."

"No sweat." Shane smiled. "Why pay for a

28

divorce if you can knock 'em off with bad shrimp?"

Farrell laughed. "Exactly."

Now Shane was feeling awkward, sort of on the spot, as everyone in the room had turned to stare at him. "Thanks for the great time. Thanks for having us."

"You bet. Good you could come."

As Shane left, he could feel Farrell's eyes on him, tracking his exit across the pool deck and into the house.

The valet delivered the dusty Acura. He pulled out of the Colony wondering what he should do about Farrell's bad joke.

Hey, Shane, don't go over the falls in a barrel here, he lectured himself. *It was just a joke.* But he had seen the look in Farrell's eyes, the shadow. He'd caught a partial glimpse into Farrell Champion's soul.

It could have been embarrassment at making a morbid joke, but something told Shane that there really were two women in Farrell's past who died of food poisoning.

It was a terrible dilemma because if he did anything to screw up this wedding, he had a hunch his beautiful wife would kill him.

3

THE PROMISE

The crime scene was on Oro Vista Boulevard. Shane's badge was still in Captain Haley's safe, but he knew one of the blues guarding the chain-link gate that fronted an avocado orchard. It displayed a sign identifying it as Rancho Fuente del Sol.

He drove up the lane to a spot where the police crime-scene vehicles were parked. The makeshift dirt parking lot was within sight of Tujunga Canyon Road, which ran just north of Oro Vista in Sunland. Shane got out and locked the Acura. He walked around the front of the crime tech's van and coroner's wagon, past the three slick-backs — black-and-white detective cars without roof lights. As he glanced across Tujunga, a carload of black teenagers wearing blue headbands drove by. The car was a BMW four-door full of gangsters who stared across the street at the avocado grove, creeping along in the right lane for a block before speeding up. The car looked to Shane like a Crip mothership — a gang leader with his bodyguards. Shane waited. A few moments later, he saw another car, a primered Ford Fairlane work car with two bangers in the front seat, both heavily federated, wearing their colors — blood red. They also slowed and looked the crime scene over before speeding up and passing on. Shane watched for five more minutes as two more motherships and half a dozen work cars drove by.

These were not curious African Americans from Sunland High. They were Crips and Bloods from South Central who had heard about Stone's death, and were out there cruising the crime scene. Shane didn't like the feel of it. Any moment, these rival sets could open up on each other. It seemed strange they hadn't done it already.

As Shane watched, a car full of Crip bangers parked across the street. One of the teenagers got out wearing a blue-hooded sweatshirt with the sleeves ripped off. His muscles glistened in the overhead xenon street lighting. Even at this distance, Shane could read the angry scowl.

Shane made his way down a marked trail between a row of trees, and finally came to an opening where the lab techs were still working. It was a dirty, disorganized crime scene. Not so much because of Stone's blood, which had dried and looked black in the moonlight, but because the shooters hadn't bothered to "police" their brass, or scuff out their footprints. The forensics team was marking, bagging, and photographing the hundred or more shell casings, then logging them into evidence. The hope was that there would be a fingerprint on one of the casings. Of course, the chance of this happening was less than one percent, because the rule was that anybody who didn't pick up their brass had probably worn gloves when loading clips. The shooters were teenagers, but they were very savvy in the art of murder.

The lab would also study the casings for tool marks — the tiny scratches and indentations left by the breech as it fired and ejected the casings. Tool marks were specific to each weapon and could be used to identify the firearm if it was ever recovered. They were also pouring plaster of paris into the footprints, making molds and marking each one.

Alexa was near the body as the coroner's assistant started to roll him. Shane approached and stood silently behind her, looking down at the dead African-American gang leader as he was flopped over. His face and chest looked like meat salad, shredded and destroyed by the high-powered ordnance that had poured into him at close range. Stone had been a big man, six-five and over three hundred pounds. He had made a large target and most of the hits were above the waist. The body's surface blood was dried and the limbs flopped lifelessly, indicating that rigor mortis had already come and gone — something that takes at least six hours. Second-generation maggots were nesting on and under the body. A maggot generation was usually around eight hours. Because of these two factors, Shane judged the murder to be between six and sixteen hours old. Despite his size, the vic had been blown right out of his expensive yellow crocs . . . crocodile shoes were a gang status symbol in the 'hood.

Near the body was a cardboard sign, the message written in large block letters. It was just being bagged by the CSIs.

"Snitches get stitches and end up in ditches," Shane read the sign softly, and Alexa, who had not heard him come up behind her, turned and saw him.

"Hi," she said.

"They weren't kidding around, were they?" he said, still looking at the mutilated body. "Put enough lead in him to open a strip mine."

"So far, over a hundred rounds counted — that's five banana clips, at least."

"If you try to shoot at the king, it's imperative you don't miss," Shane observed, then added, "You got a buncha 'hood-rats cruising by on Tujunga. I spotted a lotta work cars and a few motherships."

"Yeah, it's been like that since I got here. If this is Stone, it's a big one. It's gonna change everything in South Central."

Then one of the lab techs came up and stood beside Alexa. He was a Japanese guy named Daniel Katsumota. Shane had dealt with him a few times over the years — a good scientist.

"We're gonna pull him outta here, Lou, unless your people want to take any last pictures."

"Check with Ben and Al first, but I think we're finished. Thanks," Alexa said, and they started to load the body onto the gurney.

"I can get out of here now," she said to Shane.

He waited while she went to talk to the two homicide dicks who had caught the squeal and were now the primaries on Stone's murder. Then Shane and Alexa walked back down the row of trees to the makeshift police parking area. Across the street was another mothership — a Lincoln Town Car with at least five guys inside.

"Doesn't look good," he said.

They got into the Acura and pulled out of the grove heading back to the 210. It would be a long ride, picking their way from freeway to freeway, all the way to Venice Beach.

"That guy sure looked like Stone. He's the right size," Shane said to break the tension in the car. Alexa seemed worried, and had fallen into a thoughtful silence.

"We can't make a final I.D. until we get his dental records," she said. "But his wallet was in his pocket and the CRASH unit had pictures of him from an old arrest . . . same death's-head ring, same neck jewelry, same tatts. It's Stone."

"Wonder who got him?"

"Bloods . . . had to be. But somebody close to him probably set him up. He was too careful to get ambushed. That's why he lasted so long."

"Right," Shane said, "so that means a full gang war between the Crips and the Bloods to control his drug turf."

"I've got the CRASH unit on a twenty-four, twenty-four," she said. That was twenty-four hours on, twenty-four hours off. It basically added a third more manpower to the street without increasing personnel, but it burned out the troops, so it was only stopgap at best. "I'm upping patrol units in the heavy Crip and Blood territories, the Sixties and One Twenty-nine South, where Stone's Front Street Crips hang. I've got the Hoover Street brands covered, but it's such a large area, it's almost hopeless."

"Yeah . . ."

More silence. Then like a beautiful setter coming out of a deep lake, Alexa pulled herself up from her funk, shook the water off, and fixed a smile on her face.

"So how was the rest of the party?"

"Good," Shane said, keeping his eyes on the road.

"Were Nora and Farrell upset I left early?"

"Uh-oh, gee, I don't think so. . . ."

" 'Gee, you don't think so'?" She was looking at him now, scrutinizing, already smelling a rat.

"What I mean is, they were so busy with their Hollywood friends, it was hard to tell."

"Shane, what happened? Did you do something?"

"Did I do something? Not much, really, unless you count knocking Michael Douglas into the pool and grabbing Catherine Zeta-Jones, tying her to the pool chair with my belt, and taking my pleasure with her. Everybody seemed to think it was good fun," he joked.

"Don't dodge. What happened? Something happened."

How she could do that still mystified him. What on earth had he said that had tipped her? He hadn't even been looking at her. She'd done it off one sentence and some body language. No wonder she'd been such a great detective.

"Well, something sorta happened at the end, while I was getting out of there."

"What?" She had turned to face him now, staring at him in the driver's seat of the Acura, face lit only by passing freeway signs.

"I want to know. Please, Shane, Nora is very important to me."

"Well, on my way out, I was going through the pool house and some guests were in there smoking Cohibas."

"Oh, my God. You didn't bust them for having contraband cigars?"

"Do I look like a drooling idiot?"

"Okay, go on."

"They didn't know I was there, then some

36

guy asked Farrell if he was getting Nora to sign a prenup. And Farrell said he didn't have to . . . that he'd had two wives already, and when he got tired of them, they both conveniently died of food poisoning."

She sat there and looked at him. He didn't have the nerve to return her gaze, so he kept his eyes front and center, carefully navigating the transition onto the 110.

"That's it?" Alexa asked.

"Yep. That's it. Except when he saw me standing in the back of the room, he got all froggy. Told me it was just a joke, not to get my handcuffs out."

"That's what it was, a joke. He hasn't had any ex-wives. He's never been married before."

"You sure?"

"That's what Nora said."

"Well, then we've got nothing to worry about."

"Honey, it was just a joke."

"A bad joke. It didn't go over too well, even with his Cohiba-smoking buddies."

"Shane, don't mess around and start looking into this. . . ."

"Think I got too much spare time on my hands?"

She didn't answer, but she was scowling.

"No. Come on . . . It just hit me kinda funny is all. But I'm going back on duty in two days and I've put in for Special Crimes, so if I get it,

I'm gonna be real busy. No time to go digging up bodies in Farrell's backyard."

"It was just a joke. Say it. Say: Alexa, it was just a joke."

"I thought it was a murder confession, but I get easily confused . . . so you're probably right."

"Say it."

" 'Alexa, it was just a joke.' "

"And you'll forget it?" she asked. "Promise."

"Already forgotten," he answered.

When they got home, Chooch was in his room. He heard the garage door close and came out carrying a sheaf of papers with a pencil between his teeth.

"Geez, I'm glad you guys are back. I gotta get this essay out by Friday. It's a first draft for my college application essay, and I need a copy editor."

Looking at Chooch standing in the living room of their little Venice canal house, Shane couldn't help but feel a flash of extreme parental pride. The boy had been a surprise, coming along late in his life. The fifteen-year-old arrived as a houseguest two years ago, sent by an old lover and police informant named Sandy Sandoval. Sandy had told Shane that her Hispanic son was getting into trouble, and had been hanging with some EME gangbangers in the Valley. She said the teenager needed a male role model and she had picked Shane for the job. But Sandy was killed during the Molar case — died in Shane's arms — and her last sentence revealed to Shane that Chooch was his son. A love child he'd never known he'd had. The Molar case turned into a huge police corruption scandal involving Shane's old partner. Alexa had been part of the case, which ended in a gunfight up in Lake Arrowhead.

After Shane and Alexa had healed from the wounds inflicted during that shootout, they took Chooch in. A blood test confirmed that Sandy was telling the truth. Shane was Chooch's father. A relationship that had started out as troubled had blossomed into one that Shane treasured as much as the one he now shared with Alexa. He looked at his son, who was six feet three, with Sandy's Hispanic good looks and Shane's deep sense of honor and thought: a handsome, athletic specimen with the heart and head of a champion.

Chooch was a junior at Harvard Westlake prep school in the Valley and he'd already been contacted by Joe Paterno, with the offer of a football scholarship to Penn State. They wanted to switch him from quarterback to strong safety, but Chooch wanted to keep his old position, so he was still talking to coaches at three other universities.

"Listen, Alexa, could you take a look at this college essay and tell me what you think?" Chooch asked. Harvard Westlake had students do a first draft in their junior year. These all-important essays had to be completed and sent

39

by Christmas of their senior year.

"I'll do it," Shane volunteered. But when Chooch looked over at him, he seemed puzzled, and hesitant.

"Alexa's a better speller," he hedged.

"Don't you want me to read it?" Shane asked, feeling hurt.

"Maybe later," he said, and handed the paper to Alexa.

Shane was not going to beg. He got a beer, then went out back to sit on one of the metal lawn chairs and look at the windblown waters of the Venice canal. The moon was hanging low on the horizon. The water rippled in its silver glow. He never tired of the view.

Venice, California, had been plopped down one block from the ocean in 1928, designed by an architectural dreamer named Abbott Kinney, and fashioned after a scaled-down version of Venice, Italy. The canal blocks had fallen into a state of disrepair in the seventies, but there was an old-world charm to them, as if a dreamer's vision might still be able to catch hold in this high-tech microchip world and cling to life, refusing to be banished, no matter how out of place and ill conceived. The four canal blocks of Venice, where Shane lived, were the remnants of that kind of stubborn dream. Corny plastic gondolas growing moss at the waterlines floated at docks; Old World bridges arched over narrow seawater channels only three feet deep.

The Venice canals squatted in defiance, just a stone's throw away from strip malls and steel-and-glass medical buildings. It took a stubborn heart to be so different and unrepentant.

Shane was sitting there, pondering Venice and his day — the death of Kevin Cordell and the rediscovery of Nicky Marcella. He was also trying with all his heart to live up to his promise to Alexa and not think about Farrell's bad joke.

Then she came out and sat on the chair next to him. She seemed pensive.

"What's wrong? You okay?"

"Yeah . . . It's just Chooch's essay," she said.

"Really? What's it about?"

"You'll have to get him to tell you."

Now Shane was a little angry. Why were they hiding it from him? But he was determined not to pester her or Chooch about it. If they didn't want to share it with him, so be it. He was still staring out at the rippling water when she spoke.

"Listen, baby, I was a little taken aback when you said you were putting in for Special Crimes."

"Really?"

"Yeah. That unit reports to me, and it gets some pretty hairy assignments. I was sort of hoping to make a case for your going to Internal Affairs. You know, the sixth floor at Parker Center has a thing for ex-IAD advocates. It's the fast track to the top of the department. I could get you a shot down there."

Shane kept his eyes fixed on the canal, watching a mallard duck glide across the surface, thinking, right now, that he was just like that duck: his emotions paddling like crazy beneath the water, but on the surface, calm, showing nothing. He didn't want Internal Affairs, even though he knew Alexa was right about it being the quick way into administration, but he didn't want that either. He wasn't cut out to be a manager. He was a street cop, a field man.

"I . . . I think my cowboy days aren't quite behind me yet," he finally said.

"I know . . ." She leaned over, took his hand and squeezed it. "That's what I'm so worried about. It's your decision, of course, but maybe the time has come to stop playing cops and robbers."

He looked over at her and smiled. "Is that what I'm doing? Playing cops and robbers? I thought I was policing the city, defending the innocent, protecting and serving."

"Okay. You want the real reason?"

"Might help."

"I'm worried about your safety. When you get into the field, you take too many chances. You expose yourself. You're not too risk-adverse. You've already got more holes in you than a shooting range cutout. I couldn't stand to lose you."

He didn't answer her, but her concern

touched him. He took her hand and led her into their bedroom. They could hear Chooch's radio playing rap. Shane took Alexa into his arms and they embraced at the foot of the bed. As he kissed his beautiful wife, Shane felt a longing surge over him. They pulled their clothes off and found each other under the cool sheets. The air conditioner in the window clattered, spilling cold air across them. Some ducks started quacking in the canal outside as Shane and his wife wrapped themselves around each other.

"Forget what I just said," she whispered. "I was being selfish. You go to Special Crimes if that's what you want."

"Honey, I won't let anything happen to this family. I promise."

They made love. He entered her and slowly they both came to climax, clutching each other, moaning in ecstasy until finally, in love and passion, they achieved total unity. In the midst of sexual climax, they completely lost their sense of self and merged into one.

When it was over and they were lying in each other's arms, Shane could feel her steady breathing, feel the warmth, the softened curves of her.

She suddenly separated and faced him. "You *promise?*" she said.

He didn't know for a minute what she was talking about. Then he realized they were back on Farrell. "Oh, that? Yeah, sure," he said, and kissed her. They lay facing each other, smiling in each other's arms.

But dammit, he thought, *she hadn't seen the look in Farrell Champion's eyes.*

4

PLAY BALL

Sometimes Shane didn't realize how much he missed police work until he got back inside a station house. There was something mesmerizing about it — a heartbeat . . . a sense of teamwork . . . a frenzy of activity. Even the smell. Loser sweat and Lysol. Around it all, wrapping it like sandwich paper, was the knowledge that it was also inevitable. Police work, like humanity, kept marching on, day in and day out. Good guys, bad guys; crime, punishment; life, death — all of it playing against the clock and refereed by stern-faced jurists in black robes. At the beginning of each watch, the shift commander yelled "Play ball."

Cops and criminals were locked in a deadly game together. There was a strange sort of camaraderie that came from the fact that they all knew the rules and sometimes paid the ultimate price. It was a big rough game of shirts and skins. They would hit low, bust teeth, even kill each other, but after the game, sitting in the station house, booking the losers and bandaging up their wounds, there was still that strong sense of being in it together. It was roller-ball with guns. The winners on both sides became legends. The losers populated boot hill or the penal system. Everybody talked the talk.

As Shane walked through the double doors of the Hollywood Division station house, he was suddenly reintroduced to all of this. He could feel the beat almost as if it were coming from the linoleum, shooting through the soles of his shoes, heating the nerve endings in his feet, surging up through him, lighting his eyes and putting a new spring in his step. He was back on the field running toward the bench, the cheers raining down from the stands.

He continued into the Homicide Division and heard half a dozen shouted "Hi ya, Shane" greetings. He headed down the familiar line of desks, slapping backs and trading insults with his old homicide team.

"Did you get hemorrhoids, Scully, or is that just Chief Filosiani's head sticking outta your ass?" Sergeant "Swede" Peterson joked. It was no secret that the new chief, Tony Filosiani, known on the job as the Day-Glo Dago, had taken a real liking to Shane since the Viking case.

46

Captain Haley came out of his office and the two of them smiled at each other.

"Shane, don't talk to these morons. I don't want your newly enhanced status in police work to be tarnished by proximity to lazy dirtbags."

Catcalls and hoots . . . Grinning, Shane followed Haley into his office and sat opposite his desk while the captain worked the dial on his safe, opened it, then plucked out Scully's badge case.

"I understand you're going back on the job on Monday, so I might as well give you this stuff now." He put Shane's badge and I.D. on the desk, then unlocked his drawer, took out Shane's service revolver, and laid it next to his shield.

"I'm glad you healed up good, repassed the physical, and the head check," Haley said. "Congratulations on the Medal of Valor."

"Yeah, that's why I'm here. Gotta win medals."

"I know it's bullshit, but it's good bullshit. Enjoy it."

"Some good people died during the Viking case," Shane said sadly. "Tremaine Lane had his skin peeled off, tied to a fence in Colombia. Where's his medal?"

"He was a sheriff's deputy, ask them."

They sat there looking at each other, then Haley grunted. "You're right," he finally acknowledged. "Good point."

Another pause, then Haley stood. "I already sent your jacket to the Personnel Division, including my last fitness report, which was a rave by the way."

"Thanks, Skipper," Shane said.

"Good to have you back on the team. Anything else I can do for you?"

Then Shane remembered Nicky Marcella's request. "Yeah, Cap . . . one thing. It's a favor for an old C.I. of mine. Guy used to give me some good felony bait."

"Yeah?" There was a warning in the way Haley said that one word. Cops didn't like doing favors for civilians, even confidential informants.

He told the captain what Nicky wanted — how he had a star-maker part for Carol White, but couldn't find her.

"Movies?" Haley said. "We gonna give this girl her big break?"

"Something like that. Only you're not supposed to say 'movies,' you're supposed to say 'film.' "

"How 'bout we say 'bullshit'?"

"Really." Shane grinned as Haley sat back down, turned to his computer, and started pushing keys.

Haley finished inputting her name, keyed it to the Traffic Division, and waited while the computer searched.

"Nothing in DMV registrations or traffic," he said. "Maybe she doesn't have a car."

"Well, while we're at it, try the main arrest computer downtown. If she's a friend of my old C.I., she might have something pending in the courts."

Haley raised an eyebrow but turned back to the computer.

Shane was looking at Bud Haley's back. The captain was a fit, gray-haired man, probably in his late fifties, but he looked much younger. He had smile lines around his eyes and mouth, reminding Shane more of a friendly scoutmaster than a cop. All of a sudden, the screen lit up. There were at least twenty entries on the arrest log.

"Hello, hello," Haley said. "Carol White's been busy."

Shane came around the desk and looked over his shoulder.

"Pavement princess," Haley said. "She's been down six times for prostitution in the last six months . . . two stretches in Sybil Brand — short jolts — first a month, then eighteen weeks. Let's see . . . We also have a pandering on film beef from two years back, so she was doing some porno loops for somebody. This your actress?"

"I don't know, maybe it's another girl."

"Carolyn White. She hooks under the name Crystal Glass." He leaned back reflectively. "Pretty good street name, but my favorite's still a girl we kept busting in North Hollywood, named Lotta Pussy." Haley hit a button and

Carol's yellow sheet started printing out on the laser jet across the office. Then the captain went to the last arrest report and pulled it up on his screen. "Last place of business is a motel down in Rampart called the Ho-Tell Motel. Her pimp's named Paul 'Black' Mills. His arrest record is probably a list of female assault charges that got dropped before court." As he spoke, he was punching up Paul Mills on the computer, and soon, two pages of withdrawn complaints popped up on the screen. "And the beat goes on," Haley sighed. "Carol White tested positive for drugs, six out of six arrests, so this girl's probably not gonna be at next year's Academy Awards. She's headed for a viewing room at Forest Lawn instead."

Shane walked across the office, picked up the yellow sheet, folded it, and put it in his pocket.

"Anything else?" Haley asked.

"Yeah, can you punch up Farrell Champion?" Shane asked. His heart was beating hard in his chest. It surprised him that he would fire all of his own adrenal jets at the idea of a computer run on Farrell Champion. He immediately knew that it was because he was breaking his promise to Alexa, but his gut told him there was something wrong there.

"The movie guy?" Haley was saying. "The big-time Oscar-winning producer?"

"He hasn't won an Oscar, just been nominated."

"Right . . . and he's the one who wants to hire

50

this strawberry, this Carol White person, and make her a star?"

"No, it's an unrelated matter."

"Jesus, Shane . . ." But for some reason Haley spun his chair around and started punching in Farrell Champion's name, probably because he was just as interested as Shane in knowing what kind of trouble the famous celebrity producer might have gotten himself into.

The screen came back empty.

"Clean as Crisco," Haley said, and swiveled around to look up at Shane. "Anybody else? How 'bout Tiger Woods or Minnie Mouse?"

Shane had been thinking about asking for a run on Nicky Marcella, but decided he'd worn out his welcome. He'd do it himself Monday after he went back on duty. He smiled, then picked up his gun and badge.

"Thanks for the good fitness rep, Skipper."

"You earned it," Haley said.

Shane was quickly out the door of the captain's office. He stopped at an empty homicide desk, picked up a phone, and dialed an LAPD extension. A woman's voice answered the phone. "Records and Identification Division."

"Is Lee Fineburg around?" Shane asked.

"Fineburg . . . That's Records Services Section, Special Duties. One moment please. I'll switch you."

In a few seconds he heard Lee Fineburg's voice.

"Lee? It's Shane Scully."

51

"Shane, you is da man." Fineburg's voice grinned over the line. Shane pictured the skinny geek who was also the LAPD racquetball champion. "I need a quick favor, and it has to stay covered."

"Covert ops. Love it."

"I just ran a guy named Farrell Champion through the regular mainframe downtown and he came back empty."

"No criminal beefs . . . okay."

"No. Not just no criminal beefs, no nothing. No parking tickets, no fender benders, nothing. A blank screen."

"Kinda unusual," Lee said. "Most people at least have a loud party once in a while."

"Would you do me a favor and run a deep background on this guy? Start five years ago. He sort of appeared out of nowhere in the late nineties, and there are all of these romantic stories about where he came from and what he did before Hollywood. Gunrunner in Libya is one I remember reading, and a diamond hunter in South Africa, bullshit stuff, probably planted by studio flacks, but it keeps showing up in magazines."

"We're talking about the movie guy, right?"

"Right. And maybe you could run him through NCIC in Washington. . . ."

"Sounds juicy."

"Just a precaution. I'm sure it's nothing."

"Okay, I'll call when I get something. Your Venice number still good?"

"Yep. Same cell, too."

"Got it all on my Palm Pilot so I gotcha covered."

Shane got into his car and drove down to Rampart looking for the Ho-Tell Motel on Adams.

He found it on the corner of Adams and Gilbert. It was one of those uninteresting boxlike structures that went up all over L.A. in the fifties, under the name of "clean-line" architecture. It had a sloping roof, stucco walls, and a big faded sign out front that read: HO-TELL MOTEL, and under that FREE CHEWING GUM. The chewing gum was for hookers after oral sex. "Free chewing gum" was street code for a hot-cot motel. The sign also meant you could rent rooms by the hour.

Shane pulled into the motel parking lot and got out. The lot was half-empty, but it was only eleven a.m. He walked toward the office's large plate-glass window, which was protected by steel bars and had burglar alarm tape across the bottom. Shane looked inside. The office was deserted, so he opened the door and entered. The room had one vinyl couch and an end table with a pottery lamp that was pushed against the wall. The lampshade was broken and sat at a jaunty angle, like a drunk sleeping it off in the corner.

Shane rang the little bell. A man with an Arabic-looking face and skeletal demeanor came out of the back room to stare at him. He was smoking a Turkish cigarette.

"You want room? Come by hour, day, or week," the man said in broken English.

"I'm looking for Carol White. She sometimes uses the name Crystal Glass. I understand she frequents this motel for business."

"Carol White . . . No . . . no . . . not got a Carol White." He didn't check the register book, so he knew her.

Now Shane had the big cop decision. What wallet do I go for? The badge or the billfold? The badge could clam this guy up because he was renting rooms to whores. The billfold would probably produce a better result but cost Shane money; money he wasn't sure he could get back from Nicky. Finally, he reached for his billfold, pulled out a twenty, and laid it on the counter.

The Arab looked down at the Jackson as if it were a dead cockroach the maids had missed.

Shane added another twenty and then a third. Sixty bucks was his limit. There was a market for information in L.A.

"Hey, Abdul," Shane said, leaning in and making his voice hard, "are you trying to piss me off and destroy my cooperative spirit?"

"No sir. Crystal, she a friend?"

"Right. She performs services on me." The man stared at Shane deadpan. "Do I have to spell it out?"

"Maybe across street on corner. She got corner there, she not there, you try Snake

54

Charmers Bar next door. Sometimes she go rest it there."

"Thank you."

Then the Arab did a David Copperfield on the three twenties; they disappeared before Shane's very eyes.

She wasn't on her corner, but Shane found Crystal Glass in the Snake Charmers Bar next door.

5

CRYSTAL GLASS

The Snake Charmers had wood floors, a small stage painted black, and a bar on the far side of the room. When Shane came through the door, an African-American dancer with a pock-marked complexion was standing in the center of the stage doing a slow coffee grind, while Tina Turner sang "Tiny Dancer" from the old-fashioned Wurlitzer. An overweight blond stripper sat in a metal chair with a towel tucked under her armpits, watching her colleague with listless, dead-eyed indifference. Morning dancers in nude clubs were on the bottom rung in show business, just one step from unemployment. There was a glass full of quarters on top of the jukebox; each dancer would put several in and pick her songs, then do her set and sit down. Shane looked around, and as his eyes adjusted to the light, he could see a few people sitting in the imitation leather booths that lined the walls. The windows had been boarded up and painted over to keep it dark inside. Shane walked up to the bartender, who had burly shoulders, a shaved head, and was watching a baseball game with the volume turned off on a small black-and-white TV set that was just below the bar top.

"Is Carol White around?" he asked the man, who looked up, immediately making Shane as a cop. The bartender was in his mid-forties and bald. He had green tattoos on his arms — the kind you get in prison because the only color available in the joint was the green institutional ink supplied by the government to the penal system. The man didn't answer Shane, but looked back down at the TV.

"How about Crystal Glass?" Shane persisted. "Sometimes she uses that name."

The bartender kept ignoring him, so Shane reached out and slapped the ex-con hard across the side of the head. That brought him up fast.

"What the fuck?!" the man snarled.

"Sorry," Shane said. "You had a big yellow wasp about to land on your bald head there."

"Hey, this ain't the fuckin' police department, and I ain't four-one-one."

"This bar ain't gonna be open much longer either, unless you give me a little respect."

The ex-con glowered at him, flexing his right hand, which had the word *fuck* tattooed across the first four knuckles. Classy guy.

"Eat me, cop."

Shane reached out and again slapped him hard across the side of his head. It was an open-handed slap that made more noise than damage. Suddenly everybody in the bar stopped talking and was watching. The stripper had stopped in the middle of her grind and stood in the center of the stage, her breasts sagging, hands on chunky hips. Everybody, including Shane, wondered what would happen next.

"Lemme ask you one more time before I go through this place and confiscate everybody's bag of sparkle," Shane said. "Is Crystal Glass in here?"

It was a hard moment for the bartender. He didn't like getting punk-slapped in front of his dancers, but he knew that if Shane wanted, he could make a mess of the morning business. Finally he nodded at the far booth on the right, and Shane smiled and put down a twenty.

"For your trouble."

He turned and walked up to the booth the bartender had indicated. The girl sitting there was hard to evaluate at first. From a distance, in the low light, she seemed quite beautiful. Long blond hair and a luscious body. She was dressed in a low-cut minidress, no jewelry, and some eye glitter. But the closer he got to her, the more this changed. It was as if someone was turning a time-distance dial on his first-impression meter, until as he was sliding into the booth, she looked old and used up. He could see the tangles in her hair, the droopy eyes, and the extra weight that was hanging from under her arms. Grime caked her wrists, while unhealthy skin and this morning's oozing track mark completed the depressing picture. Up close, Carol White was tarnished, dirty, and aging fast. She projected carnal desperation. But the remnants of her looks were still there. Like a child peeking around a curtain, he could still see the residue of teenage beauty.

"You shouldn't fuck with Leo," she said. "Leo shot some people and went to prison for it."

"Yeah? Well, Leo and I have an understanding. He's not gonna shoot me."

"You look like a cop, so probably you ain't here for a forty and five, right?" Talking about the hooker's forty-dollar charge with the five-dollar room fee; most likely for an hour at the Ho-Tell Motel.

"Are you Carol White?" Shane asked, jumping right into it.

"I'm Crystal Glass."

"But before that?"

"Before that?" Her eyes clouded up as if she were trying to remember.

The way she said it was sort of lost and sad, as if she could barely conjure up what her life had been like before she'd started hooking on Adams.

"Carol, I'm not here to bust you, okay? I'm here because a mutual friend of ours, Nicky Marcella, sent me."

A smile suddenly appeared in her sad eyes, then slipped slowly down her face, until it finally managed to turn up the corners of her mouth.

"Nicky the Pooh?" she asked softly.

"The what?"

"Nicky Marcella . . . That's what everybody in our high school called him, Nicky the Pooh. That was his nickname."

"You went to high school with Nicky Marcella?"

"Teaneck High. Course I didn't finish, 'cause I won Miss Solar Energy and then Miss Teen New Jersey, so I decided to take my shot, y'know?"

"Hollywood."

"Yep. The prettiest girl in Teaneck, ask anybody. Gonna be a motherfuckin' movie star. Didn't quite make it, did I?"

"It's a tough business. Only one out of a million, they say."

Carol leaned forward and now there was actually some light in her tired blue eyes. "You know how close I came?" Shane shook his head. "That close." She held up her thumb and forefinger about a quarter of an inch apart. "That close. I was up for the Zeffirelli film *Endless Love*. It was a great part . . . a film about teenage passion, y'know? It was down to just

60

me and Brooke Shields. Y'know . . . ? Brooke Shields?"

"Yeah, good actress." Shane nodded.

"Right . . . I'd been reading for Mr. Zeffirelli's West Coast casting director. She was this really nice motherly kind of lady who said I had unique qualities. That's what she said, 'unique qualities,' and after three reads, she gave me a callback to read for Franco Zeffirelli. *The* Franco Zeffirelli, can you believe that?" Shane shook his head in wonder. "I named my cat Franco because of that — I went out and bought him so I'd have somebody to celebrate with. I named him Franco, after Mr. Zeffirelli. I was so excited." He watched this memory play across her face like a faded dream. She seemed anxious to tell the story.

"Okay, so the callback was at Metro — that's MGM." She was leaning farther forward, her breasts bulging out of her low-cut dress.

"Right," Shane said, "Metro-Goldwyn-Mayer."

"Exactly . . . and he wanted us to do the original balcony scene from *Romeo and Juliet*, 'cause *Endless Love* was kind of a rip on that play. So I'd been practicing with my acting teacher all night, and I've got the scene down pat, y'know?"

"Tough scene."

"Tell me about it." Her eyes were almost sparkling now. "You gotta plead and cry, and you gotta not understand what Romeo's saying

in that scene. It's all about misunderstanding
— lotta different emotional values you gotta
play. That's why Franco had us doing it, me
an' Brooke. So I show up for the audition and I
see Brooke sitting in the other chair and she
was so beautiful . . . so composed . . . and I
sorta started to choke. I thought, how is he ever
gonna choose me over her, y'know? But I was
there, so I thought what the hell, y'know?"

Shane nodded. "What the hell."

"So I went in first and I started to do the
scene, but Mr. Zeffirelli stopped me and said,
'Do it inna da chair.' And I said, 'Mr. Zeffirelli,
I need to move around,' 'cause, see, that's the
way I practiced it. But he was walkin' around in
front of the lights waving a cigarette, sayin',
'I'm a shoot dis test widda bery tight lens ana
donta wanta no movement.' Like that, with his
Italian accent and all, and it was sorta hard for
me to understand him, and I had to get him to
say it twice. I could tell he was getting frustrated, but I asked him again, 'Can't I do the
audition standing?' And he sort of started to
raise his voice and shout. So I sat down and
tried to do it the way he wanted, but I kept
seeing my own face off to the side of the room
on the monitors, and I looked so different,
kinda pasty and white. It just kinda threw me,
y'know? I couldn't remember the words and I
froze."

She sat there, her face now in a slight scowl,
her eyes down on the chipped linoleum ta-

bletop. Then she slowly brought them up, dragged them, as if she were pulling weights. "So that was it. Brooke got the part . . . but it was close. If I hadn't had to sit in that damn chair, I bet I woulda got it. It was down to her and me — that close."

This time she put her two fingers together and smiled at him. Shane felt his heart go out to her. She was so vulnerable, so fragile, that he thought if he said the wrong thing she might break into pieces right before him. She smiled a sad smile of apology. That smile seemed to be saying: "I know I look like a cheap forty-dollar whore, but I used to be the prettiest girl in Teaneck, and I was almost in a Zeffirelli movie . . . almost. It was that close."

Shane returned her smile, but she didn't see it. She was looking at him, but her mind was somewhere else. He looked down at the twenty or more old track marks on her arms, the open one still glistening from that morning's fix. Heroin — the gift that keeps on giving.

"Listen, Carol, Nicky Marcella sent me here because he has a part for you. He's producing a film and he asked me to look you up. He said the part was very unique, that you have the exact quality needed to pull it off."

"Nicky said that?" She was smiling again. "Nicky the Pooh is such a sweet guy. He almost put me in another movie two years ago. I met his investors. Even went out with one and we partied, 'cause Nicky said the guy was about to put up more pre-production money. But I had to do a reading in front of the director. By then I'd lost my confidence. I froze there, too."

"I think he's planning on just putting you in this. He said you were the one he wanted."

She was wringing her hands on the table, over and over again in a desperate motion, as if she couldn't get them clean — the Lady Macbeth of the Snake Charmers Bar.

"Wouldn't that be something?" she finally said. "Course, I'd have to get straight. . . ."

"Right. Gotta stop shootin' slat."

"Yeah . . . yeah. Wouldn't that be somethin'? Me back in the movies . . ."

Then a shadow fell over them and Shane looked up. A skinny, ebony-black man, wearing a pinstriped suit and carrying an umbrella, was glaring at them. The man had no tie, but wore a pound of jewelry under his silk shirt — a Mr. T starter set.

"You better be pitchin' your ass, or makin' a pass, girl. 'Cause, if he ain't buyin', you be dyin'," rhyming his sentences like a Baptist preacher.

"Sorry, Black . . . I'm sorry." Carol was grabbing for her purse and starting to scramble out of the booth.

Shane reached out and grabbed her arm. "Hold it. Hold it . . . Who is this?"

"Ain't talkin' t'you, Chuck," the black man said. "I been watchin'. You ain't nothin' but a tire-kickin' Gumby motherfucker. Jus' sittin', jaw-jackin', takin' up the ho's time."

"Black, please . . . I'm going back out. No need for trouble."

"You must'a forgot you ain't Black's bottom girl no more," the pimp growled. "So you can't be settin' in d'shade, drinkin' d'Kool-Aid and not gettin' laid. You nothin' but street merchandise now — a three-way girl who don't got no bidness sittin' in the air-conditioning when Black need his stack money. So you best be puttin' it on d'street, woman, or you gonna be tastin' a wastin'."

Shane got out of the booth. This skinny asshole had to be Paul "Black" Mills. When Shane stood, he was two inches taller than the pimp, who seemed to be the only one in the place who hadn't made Shane as a cop yet. If Shane badged him, Carol White would probably end up getting beaten. So instead, he smiled at Mills. "Listen, I assume you're Crystal's business representative. I really am a paying customer. We were just coming to terms."

"Don't be fuckin' wid my shit, Chuck."

"Go back to your house next door," Carol pleaded. "He's a client, Black. We was just talkin' cash. Honest, we was."

Shane reached into his pocket, took out his wallet and handed forty dollars to Mills, thinking this "favor" had already cost him a hundred, but there was no turning back now.

"Forty and five," Shane said. "I'll give the five to the Arab over at the motel."

"This fuckin' bitch don't do 'nuf business." Black was glaring at Carol. "Yo' ass best be movin' on some heavy cruisin', or you gonna get a bruisin'." Then he turned and did some kind of gangsta-limp out of the bar, tap, tap, tapping with the umbrella.

"Thank you," she whispered to Shane. "He would have beat the shit out of me if you'd shown him your badge."

Shane nodded. "Does he sit at home thinking that stuff up?" Shane asked as he wrote Nicky's number on a cocktail napkin, copying it off the business card in his wallet, then slid it across the table.

She looked at it, afraid to even pick it up. "Thanks, but my movie days are over," she said. "Black will beat me like a Texas mule I even think about trying that again."

Then Shane handed her one of his police business cards. "You ever want me to come back down here and run that rhyming asshole off, call."

She got up, grabbed her beaded bag off the vinyl seat of the booth, hesitated, then snatched up the cocktail napkin, put it inside her purse, and snapped it shut. She gave Shane a timid smile, then hurried out the door.

How did the prettiest girl in Teaneck, New Jersey, end up selling her body to strangers on Adams Avenue? Some things, while on the one hand were easy to understand, at the same time defied all human logic.

66

6

BOOTS AND BIKINIS

When Shane left the Snake Charmers Bar, a cold breeze had just started blowing out of the north. The stiff winter wind took the new spring leaves off the trees, then swept them along until they collected against the curbs and the sides of houses, where they fluttered in the cracks and crevices like tiny green-winged butterflies.

Shane was making the drive from Adams to Hollywood General Studios, where Nicky Marcella's office was located. The afternoon sky was cloud-blown and cobalt blue. The air sparkled with a heart-quickening freshness.

Despite all these natural splendors, Shane's mind was still back inside the grimy Snake Charmers Bar. He couldn't get the picture of Carol White out of his mind — a picture of desolate remorse. Shane's friend and ex-partner Jack Wirta used to say that God gave with one hand but took away with the other. And it was often true. God had given Carol a beautiful body and the face to go with it, but had taken away the toughness she needed to survive in the glitzy world that would ultimately beckon, creating a circle of preordained failure.

Franco Zeffirelli hadn't let her move during the audition, made her sit in a chair, and, according to Carol, that one moment had changed her entire life. Her dreams of stardom were now reduced to that one pathetic memory. "I came this close."

Shane shook his head as he drove north on Highland Avenue. She probably hadn't been close at all. From the day she arrived in Hollywood, she had been low-end fuel for the system. Hollywood needed its losers, its fallen dreamers. Without the Carol Whites, what does it count to be Julia Roberts? There had to be profound tragedy to define overwhelming success.

So Carol was in the Snake Charmers Bar with her pincushion arms still oozing from the morning's jab-job, telling Shane about her brush with stardom. It almost made him want to cry.

Why were the losers affecting him so much lately? A few years ago he could have looked at Carol White, put the cuffs on her, and never looked back. But now it was almost as if he felt responsible for her plight, as if she existed in her current wretched state because Shane Scully had not done his job correctly, had somehow failed her personally. He knew that cops usually couldn't change the way things were, but since the Viking case, he had started to see the remnants of humanity inside all of these human flameouts.

He had looked past the surface of Carol White. Behind her red-rimmed eyes he could see the beautiful girl from Teaneck, New Jersey, still alive inside looking out at him, bewildered at how she'd ended up this way.

And that's what haunted him. That's what was ruining this beautiful windswept day.

Hollywood General Studios was on Seward, just five blocks east of Highland. The studio was one of the oldest in Hollywood and had always been a rental lot. Shane thought he remembered hearing that *Ozzie and Harriet* had been shot there.

He pulled up to the main gate and stopped as a uniformed guard with a clipboard came over. "Shane Scully to see Nicky Marcella."

"He's casting today. Is Mr. Marcella expecting you?"

"No, sir, you'll have to call."

The guard went into his wooden shack and picked up the phone. Shane could see past the gate into the studio lot. Hollywood General occupied one large city block and had five or six soundstages. There was also a construction mill and some postproduction facilities. The guard came back and nodded, leaning toward Shane. "You know where Building Six is?"

"No, sir."

"Go through the gate, turn left, and find a visitor space along the front of the administration building. Then walk north toward the low one-story building at the end of the lot. Mr. Marcella's office is number six forty-five, end of the hall."

"Thank you."

Shane did as instructed and found a parking place in front of the ranch-style administration building. He got out and locked his car, then looked around. The studio buildings were mostly one-story stucco, with slanted slate roofs. The warehouse-size soundstages loomed above them. Everything was painted a strange reddish-brown color, and the little patches of grass that were part of the meager landscape plan were now engaged in a desperate struggle for dirt with some kind of wiry, weedlike growth.

As he walked toward Building Six, he passed a new maroon Bentley convertible parked across two stalls. One of the blocked stalls read: *Nicholas Marcella*.

As soon as Shane entered the corridor, he could see perhaps twenty beautiful young girls sitting in metal chairs that had been placed along the walls. They were all dressed in short-shorts, heels, and halter tops despite the cold

70

wind whipping around outside.

As he moved down the hall, he could see that most of them were studying their audition scenes from miniaturized Xeroxed script pages, which he remembered a casting director once had told him were referred to as "sides."

Shane walked past the line of actresses who were sitting outside Nicky's production company, identified by a gold relief of a coliseum bolted to the door — and under that a gold sign:

CINE-ROMA PRODUCTIONS
NICHOLAS MARCELLA, CEO

Shane continued through the door and found himself in a very commodious reception area. Several huge posters of hit movies that Shane knew Nicky had nothing to do with hung on the walls. A very pretty young girl with coal-black hair was typing with two fingers on a computer keyboard. She glanced up in frustration as he approached her desk.

"I'm Shane Scully, here to see Nicky Marcella."

"Mr. Marcella is in a reading right now. I'll tell him you're here once the actress is finished with her audition. We never interrupt a reading."

"Right," Shane said, "wouldn't want to do that," and he sat on the beige leather sofa.

One of the short-shorts and halter tops came

in and hovered next to the receptionist's desk. "Excuse me, I'm Donna Daring and I have another appointment across town at three. Is it going to be much longer, or would it be possible for me to read next?"

The receptionist looked up at her and scowled, then picked up a casting sheet. "Your time was two-forty, Ms. Daring. We're running about fifty minutes behind. That's all I can tell you," she said, clipping her words, pissed off at the request.

"Okay," the girl said. "Can I use your phone to call my agent?"

"Sorry, I have to keep these lines open. You should carry a cell."

The actress scowled, then teetered out of the office, her long dancer's legs tapering down into five-inch fuck-me pumps that forced her to stumble along, leaning slightly forward.

A few minutes later the door to Nicky's office opened and Shane could hear men laughing at something a girl said, then a particularly beautiful blond actress teetered out in stiletto heels and butt-clinging booty shorts. She had tears running down her face but a smile on her lips. She gave the receptionist a thumbs-up, then handed her a slip of paper.

"Mr. Marcella wants me to get some new head shots and suggested I should use this photographer. He said you could set it up for me?"

"Sure, glad to. Congrats." Then the receptionist leaned forward and whispered, "He usually only does this for the actresses he's thinking of casting."

Shane got up and, without waiting to be invited, stuck his head into the office. "Nicky . . . Got a minute?"

The receptionist exploded out of her chair and dove through the door in a failed attempt to stop him. "I'm sorry, Mr. Marcella, I know you said you'd see him, but he doesn't have an appointment and we're running late."

"No problem, Daphne. Come on in, Shane. I want you to meet some people."

Shane entered a large paneled office. On the shelves were all kinds of knickknacks and awards. The desk was the approximate size and shape of an Egyptian sarcophagus. There were two large leather couches, some pull-up chairs, and five seedy-looking men in short-sleeved polo shirts and pleated pants. They were all fat, and three looked like they were hiding watermelons under their shirts.

"Shane, I'd like you to meet the investors," Nicky enthused. A round of names was exchanged, which Shane made no effort to remember.

A toilet flushed and a door in the back of the room opened. A sixth man came out of Nicky's private executive bathroom. He was in his middle to late fifties, with a sallow complexion, and was wearing a baseball cap backward. A dangling cross hung from his left ear. Had to be the director.

"My God, that girl is the one," the man said. "What acting chops. New York–trained. I saw some Stella Adler in that read. When she found the baby in the Dumpster and did the dead Marine soliloquy seriously, I like fucking almost lost it myself."

"We've got our Marsha," Nicky exclaimed. "My God, that really takes the pressure off. Who's her agent?"

"Inter-Talent," the sallow-faced man said, looking at the casting sheet. "Whatever you do, don't tell that shmuck Marty Kittlebaum that she's got the part. Just say you hated her read but I begged you to keep her on the list. We gotta keep her price down if we can."

Nicky grinned and nodded, then made an expansive introduction. "Shane Scully, this is our director, Milos DeAngelo. You probably remember his simply brilliant, award-winning film *Intermezzo*."

"I musta been outta town that weekend," Shane said.

"He also did *Mandalay Music* and *The Grasshopper Factory*."

"Missed those as well."

The director glowered. Shane hadn't seen his work. Milos angrily turned away, snapping up the casting sheet instead, checking to see who was next.

"Nicky, I need to talk to you," Shane said.

"Did you find Carol White?"

"Yes."

"He found our Cherise," Nicky proclaimed to the investors and Milos, clapping his hands with glee. "Wait'll you see this girl, she's perfect. This is some lucky day. First our Marsha, now Cherise. Awesome, awesome news, Shane."

"Can I talk to you alone for a minute?"

"Yeah, sure." He turned to Milos. "Why don't you guys read the next girl? I'll be right back."

He led Shane out of his suite, across the hall, past the lineup of girls in the chairs, and into an adjoining office. They entered and he closed the door. "Are these girls gorgeous?!" Nicky beamed. "You wonder why they all came dressed in heels and booty shorts?"

"No."

"I put it in the damn script . . ." He grinned, then he pulled a set of sides out of his pocket and pointed to a shot description and read it for Shane aloud: "Marsha is a beautiful girl, wearing extremely tight short-shorts, four-inch stiletto heels, and a revealing top." He grinned at Shane. "These are the little casting tricks you learn when you're a player," he bragged, "otherwise casting days can get long and boring."

"Nicky . . . please, can we talk about Carol?" Shane said, not in the mood for any of this.

"Right. So you found Carol . . . this is awesome news, Shane. Go on, tell me. Where is she?"

"She's a junkie, Nick. Heroin or eight-balls. She's shooting something hard and turning tricks down on Adams Avenue. Got a pimp named Paul Mills, a real dink — carries an umbrella. She's got ten current unadjudicated 167-Bs."

Nicky looked puzzled.

"That's straight street hooking. You didn't know any of this?"

Nicky shook his head.

"She also told me you two went to high school together, something else you forgot to mention."

"Yeah, Teaneck High School. New Jersey. We met in ninth grade." He seemed saddened by this news about Carol.

"She's not gonna be acting in your movie."

"Film."

"Right. But if she's your friend from high school, you'd better call her folks or, better still, go and get your hands on her yourself. She's in bad shape."

"Jeez . . . holy-moley . . . a prostitute . . . and you say she's on heroin . . ."

"She's got more tracks than the Southern Pacific. You really didn't know?"

"No. A while back I had her in here to read. She kinda froze during the audition, but it wasn't like she was strung out on bang, or anything."

"If you're her friend, just go down there and get her. Here's the address." He handed Nicky a slip of paper with the location of the Snake Charmers Bar on Adams.

"Absolutely . . . absolutely. My God, anything else you can tell me?"

Shane was already at the door, but he turned back. "Yeah, some asshole parked his Bentley in your space."

"It's mine, Shane. My Bentley." Then he grinned. "Like I said, things have really turned around for me."

"Nicky, go get her," Shane repeated. "Go get Carol before she dies down there with a spike in her arm."

"I will, Shane. I promise."

Shane walked out of the office and back into the hall. One of the sides was lying on the seat of an empty chair. He picked it up. The name of the movie they were casting was *Boots and Bikinis*. Shane had just started to read the scene when one of the actresses interrupted him.

"It's about post-traumatic stress syndrome in Gulf War nurses, only we all live in Huntington Beach now and we're dancers in a club called Boots and Bikinis. We dress like hookers and screw like bunnies. The script blows. I'm outta here." She turned and walked down the hallway while the other actresses watched her go.

Shane put the sides back on the chair and followed the beautiful actress out into the cold April day.

7

LA EME

"You think you could get in touch with American Macado?" Alexa asked Shane after dinner. They were standing in their little kitchen in Venice. He was rinsing dishes while Alexa put leftovers away.

"I don't know," he hedged. "Amac isn't exactly what I'd call a friend." Shane was looking into the sink, watching the residue of dinner swirl off the plate and disappear down the garbage disposal. American Macado was a Mexican gangbanger with whom Shane had a very unusual relationship.

Before he learned that Chooch was his illegitimate son, Shane had discovered that the boy was hanging out in the Valley with a bunch of La Eme. *Eme* is Spanish for the letter M — Mexican Mafia.

After the Molar case Shane needed to put

some closure on Chooch's gang affiliation. The set Chooch had been running with was the 18th Street Sureños, a Southern California branch of La Eme.

Shane found out from Chooch that he had not yet been officially "jumped" into the 18th Street gang, and was still considered a peewee gangster or a "P.G.," a preinitiate who did errands and drug lookouts.

The blood-in, blood-out oath of La Eme stated that the only way into the gang was to shed blood at the hands of the set, and the only way out was in a casket. Shane wasn't sure how this applied to Chooch. As a P.G., was he subject to some form of retribution if he tried to "drop the flag" — the gang expression for leaving the set?

Like all P.G.'s, Chooch had a *carnal grande*, big brother, in the Sureños. He was a hardened, nineteen-year-old Hispanic street soldier with the unlikely name of American Macado, known by his *carnales* as Amac. His parents were both illegal, but American had been born in the United States so he had an American passport. His father, Juan, was killed in a bar fight when Amac was only nine. Back then Shane had read the CRASH gang report that said that American was living temporarily with his *tía*, who was sick, so Shane had decided to pay the *soldado* a visit. The house was in the foothills of East L.A., just twenty minutes from downtown in an unincorporated area known as Las

Lomas, The Hills. The narrow streets meandered aimlessly and the houses were all old, mostly made of unpainted, weathered wood. Chicken-wire fences transected everything, the cadaverous remains of rusting trucks hosted flocks of skinny roosters and wandering goats. The many vacant lots were trash heaps, littered with broken lamps and unwanted household garbage. The predominate language in Las Lomas was Spanish.

Shane arrived at the aunt's house uninvited, and was met at the door by a beautiful teenage girl who introduced herself as Delfina. She had long coal-black hair and warm eyes that seemed to look right through you. She was around Chooch's age, or maybe a year younger, perhaps fourteen.

"*Mi tío* is out back," she said, and led Shane to a precarious, broken-down structure that was once a garage. American Macado was working on his cut-down '78 Charger low-rider, which was painted blue, the gang color of the 18th Street Eme. Delfina left and Shane began a tense negotiation. He tried to convince American that Chooch had a chance for a better life. Slowly, Shane was able to see past Amac's street-hardened exterior. What he saw was a huge personal charisma. American Macado was an exceptional youth caught in a violent world he had adapted to and was learning to master. There was no doubt in Shane's mind that if he lived, Amac would become a force in the 'hood.

After two meetings at the house in Las Lomas, Shane had finally convinced the battle-hardened street soldier to let him present Chooch's case to the gang council. This meet was held once a week in a park off Francis Street in East L.A., where the 18th Street Sureños got together and "kicked down" their street taxes to *veteranos*.

Shane had been told to stand alone and un-armed on a street corner in the Valley, two blocks from the police station. He did as Amac had instructed. At ten p.m. he was picked up by four Sureños, including American Macado, in a low-rider. The muscular teenager said nothing as Shane was shaken down for guns and a wire, then blindfolded and taken to the sit-down.

When he arrived, he found four *veteranos* seated at a park picnic table. *Veteranos* were the Latin-American equivalent of a Crip or Blood Original Gangster. Over thirty, they had sur-vived against the odds to become set leaders. Shane could see carloads of young *vatos* in trademark blue headbands patrolling the park's perimeter streets in slow-cruising low-riders.

At the meeting, Shane made the case that Chooch should be allowed out of the gang without a penalty due to his youth and because he now had a father to look after him. He ex-plained that his son lived in two worlds. He was not a full-blooded Mexican, because half his heritage was Anglo, from Shane. He talked about Chooch's chance for an education and one day, even the dream of college. The set leaders listened as Shane made his pitch. Then an 18th Street *veterano* named Raul Cantaras asked, "Dis P.G. took de pledge, *es verdad?*"

"But he was very young. . . . He didn't realize that he was signing up for life," Shane said.

"He is a man now, he is ready to wear the thirteen," Cantaras persisted. The thirteen was a tattoo that stood for the thirteenth letter of the alphabet, M — *Eme*. You only got to wear the thirteen after you were jumped in.

"If he is ready for 'courting in,' then it is too late," another *veterano* said.

Then the oldest *veterano* spoke. Shane knew him from the gang briefings. Carlos Martinez was an East Valley Inca. Incas were supreme leaders.

"In this situation, the *vatito* cannot go unless you could make an agreement," the man said. He looked right at Shane and added, "You are *chota*. What promises can *la policía* make to us? What favors do you offer?"

"I can make no promises and grant no favors. I am a man of honor," Shane said softly.

The *veteranos* all frowned. Then American, who had said nothing up to this point, stood. He was only nineteen, but these older men were prepared to listen respectfully. He was already known on the street as one hundred proof, having earned the three *R* tattoo: Respect, Reputation, and Revenge. They all paid close attention as Amac spoke. He told them Chooch was his *carnalito*, his little brother . . . that Amac had promised the peewee he would hold his back, look out for his best interests. He said he wanted this chance for Chooch . . . that the feeling was *de corazón*, from his heart. He promised the *veteranos* that in return for letting Chooch out, he would kick down double his normal street taxes for the next year.

An hour later the meeting was over and Chooch had been released from the 18th Street Sureños without condition. It had been Amac who made it happen.

On the slow drive back to where Shane had been picked up, the Emes in the low-rider said nothing, but as Shane got out of the car American Macado stopped him. "Hey, *gabacho*, promise me you'll make this chance count."

In that instant, Shane saw in Amac's face a desperate longing, as if he were looking over a fence as his little brother Chooch achieved something he would never have — freedom from the gang life. But there was no turning back for Amac, and they both knew it.

"I promise," Shane said. Then he walked away. He and Chooch had seen American a year and a half later at Magic Mountain amusement park. Shane looked over and saw the twenty-year-old Eme with half a dozen G'sters standing in the Batman roller-coaster line. Amac walked away from his *vatos* and approached Shane and Chooch. He had shaved his head since that night in the park, and was heavily sleeved with new tattoos. Shane saw a new T4L inked on Amac's right shoulder, which meant "Thug for Life." By now, it was certainly true.

"*Qué pasa, carnalito?*" Amac asked Chooch.

"I'm good. I was hopin' you'd come to one of my football games. I was starting as quarterback at Harvard Westlake this year."

Amac smiled. "A quarterback is just change on a candy bar, dude."

Chooch smiled but didn't say anything, so Amac continued.

"Glad to see you takin' good care of yourself since droppin' the flag. I'm countin' on you to not get off the gate. *Tú no quieres mi vida loca.*"

Chooch nodded.

"*Que viva la raza,*" Amac said. Long live the race. Then he turned and walked away to rejoin his group.

Shane had heard during various LAPD gang briefings that Amac had been bumped up to "big boy," which was a set leader. Now, at the unheard-of age of twenty-one, he had replaced Martinez as the Inca for the East Valley. Shane was not surprised because he'd seen Amac's power and leadership that night two years ago when four thirty-year-old *veteranos* had listened respectfully while the then-nineteen-year-old helped Shane.

Shane turned off the water in the sink and

folded the dishrag over the gooseneck spout. "I'm not sure it's good for me to be talking to him," he told Alexa softly. "He's not just a street soldier anymore; he's the Valley Inca."

"I know what he is. I read CRASH briefings. But we've had two more assassinations. This time both were Blood O.G.'s. I think this city is about to erupt in interracial gang war. At first I just thought it would be Crips and Bloods, but the kicker here is that the wit who saw the last two killings says that the shooters were Mexicans, not blacks."

"You said there was going to be a power vacuum. Maybe with Stone down, the Mexican Mafia is going for their share of this," Shane said.

"We need to pick up some street intel. I've got a feeling there's a big piece missing. We don't have the whole picture and right now we're getting zip from our regular snitches."

"And you think I can just go to the head of the local Emes and get him to tell me?"

"I thought he was your friend. It was just a thought."

"Well, it's a shitty thought," Shane said angrily, and walked out of the kitchen into the living room. Although he felt a strong sense of gratitude toward American Macado, Shane was also afraid of him. Not in the way men on opposite sides of the law usually fear one another, but in a more personal way. He'd always suspected that there was still a deep bond between

Chooch and Amac, which was stronger than Chooch had let on. Shane feared that if Amac ever called out to Chooch for help, his son would drop everything and respond, that his son, out of some sense of brotherhood or Hispanic loyalty, might be drawn back into that dangerous world. Even with Chooch on the verge of going to college, Shane still feared it.

But at Magic Mountain, Amac had looked at Chooch and warned him, *Don't get off the gate.* Don't come back into this. Then he had said, *"Tú no quieres mi vida loca."* You don't want my crazy life. So maybe Shane *could* kick a sleeping dog, just this once, and get away with it. He was a cop; people were dying. He had a duty to try and find out what was going on.

Shane turned and walked slowly to Chooch's room. He hesitated for a moment before he knocked.

"Yeah," he heard his son call out.

"Got a minute?" Shane asked as he pushed the door open. This had once been a guest room; now it was Chooch's territory: floor-to-ceiling pictures of him playing football, school artwork — freehand sketches of huge, doomlike monsters, dragons with bat wings — good drawings but a little off-putting. Over his dresser were the required posters of Shakira and Jennifer Lopez along with a collection of Harvard Westlake prom night photos.

As Shane crossed the room and sat on the bed, Chooch quickly turned over his essay and laid it facedown on the desk. Shane experienced another moment of annoyance, but pushed past it.

"What is it, Dad?"

"Do you ever hear from Amac?" Shane asked.

"American?" Chooch's eyes went a little shady and he glanced away.

"Yeah, American. You ever hear from him? He ever call you or anything?"

"Gee . . . uh . . . I don't think so . . ."

"Gee, uh, you don't think so?" *The males in this family are shitty liars,* he thought. "Here's the reason, okay?"

"Sure."

"You know your mom's handling all this gang violence that just started, the killings they're talking about on TV."

Chooch nodded.

"At first she thought it was going to be a shootout between the Bloods and Crips, but now it looks like La Eme is in the mix."

"Really?"

"Yeah. And I was thinking if you had Amac's number or some way to contact him, maybe I could try and get in touch. I need to talk to him. He might be getting into something dangerous."

"You told me not to have anything more to do with Amac."

"Yeah, I know. I just thought —"

"That I'd disobey you?"

"Well, not disobey, exactly . . . I thought on his birthday, or yours, maybe you guys still got in touch."

There was a long silence. This time Chooch held Shane's eyes, but said nothing.

"Okay . . . How's that essay coming?"

"It's . . . I'm still working on it."

"Am I ever gonna get a chance to read it?"

"Well, thing is, I . . ." and he stopped.

"Forget it . . . talk to you later."

Shane left the room. Whether it was the conversation about Amac, or because his feelings were hurt over that damned essay, Shane was definitely off balance. He almost turned around and went back in to talk with his son again, but then at the last moment decided not to. He pulled himself away from Chooch's door and moved down the hall and out into the backyard.

Alexa was sitting there, looking at the canal. She had two beers and gave Shane an Amstel Light as he sat down next to her.

Shane reached into his pocket, took out his shield, and handed it to her. "Forgot to tell you, Captain Haley returned this to me today."

She took it, rubbed her thumb over the badge, and smiled. "Y'know, I never would have thought I was going to marry a cop. On balance, cops are such cynics. But you taught me it doesn't have to be that way. You taught me that cops can even be great lovers. I don't know if I ever thanked you for that."

Shane thought she was really trying to tell him she was sorry about asking him to invite a dangerous gang leader back into their lives. He smiled and squeezed her hand, but didn't answer.

The phone started ringing, so Shane got up and walked into the living room, where he picked it up. "Yeah."

"Shane, it's Lee Fineburg. I got something on this Farrell character you asked me to run."

"Really?" With a sudden pang of guilt, Shane looked over his shoulder at Alexa, who was still sitting on the back lawn out of earshot. "What is it?"

"When I first started, it was more what it's *not*, if you know what I mean." He paused, then continued. "There was nothing anywhere on this guy. It's like three years ago he parachuted in here from Pluto. My brother's looked everywhere: the Justice Department computer, the IRS, even VICAP. You'll never guess where he finally turned up."

"Where?"

"WITSEC over in the U.S. Marshal's office. He's in their computer, and nowhere else. The marshals must have erased everything."

"Witness Protection?"

"Only now they call it Witness Security. My brother couldn't break the nine-digit spaghetti code to get the actual file, but Farrell Champion is definitely on an asset list in their mainframe."

89

"Wait a minute . . . hold on. That doesn't make sense. WITSEC isn't going to give a new identity and protection to a high-profile guy like Farrell Champion. Everybody knows who he is. He's in half of last year's *People* magazines, for Chrissake."

"Shane, if you wanna argue with me about it, help yourself. I'm just telling you what my brother found. This guy looks like he's a protected witness. That's gotta be why there're no IRS or LAPD records. Because the Justice Department keeps him scrubbed clean — no back story, no records, nothing that can be used to trace him."

"Then why would WITSEC let him be so high profile?"

"I don't know, I agree it's weird. But unless we got two Farrell Champions, which seems highly unlikely given the unusual name and the circumstances, your boy is in the program."

Shane knew that a lot of the clients of WITSEC were violent criminals who turned State's evidence to keep from going to jail. Sammy "The Bull" Gravano, who killed nineteen people for John Gotti, was the poster boy for that fact.

"How do we find out for sure?" Shane asked.

"My brother Doug said if you can get a set of his prints, he can keep going, try to find out his real name. To make it quick, he needs a thumb, index, and at least one digit. Doug says that somewhere there's a record. Those prints are gonna go back to some original piece of I.D., like an old state driver's registration or hospital birth records — something sitting in somebody's computer. You can't erase everything. Get me those prints and we'll give it a go."

"Okay . . . okay, I'll try." Shane looked over again at Alexa, who still had her back to him, sitting in the metal chair, staring out at the still canal. "Thanks, Lee. I owe ya. Talk to ya tomorrow."

He walked back outside and sat down again. "Who was that?"

"Captain Haley. He left something out of my package. I gotta swing by tomorrow and pick it up." A little lie, but a lie nonetheless, and Shane felt shitty about it.

"Honey, Nora called today," Alexa suddenly said. "Farrell's having a bachelor party and he wonders if you'd like to come. It's this Friday night at the Jonathan Club, on the beach."

"Sounds like fun . . ." Another alarm bell went off in his head. Shane wondered why Farrell Champion, a man he'd only met once, would want him at his bachelor party?

"Should I tell her yes?"

"Uh, well, maybe we should wait and see what happens when I get back on duty. See what my hours are, what kinda caseload I've got."

"Oh, sure, if you think." She fell silent. "I also told Nora I'm giving her a bridal shower. I'll have to throw it together quick, because we're running out of time. The wedding is in less than two weeks."

"Gee . . . yeah." He glanced over at her, hoping she wasn't going to bust him for that bullshit sentence. But she was still looking out at the calm waters of the canal. "Anyway, I was thinking of doing it this Thursday at our house. These streets are so damned narrow out front, parking will be a bitch, but maybe if it's in the afternoon while they're all at work, the neighbors won't complain."

"You want, I'll go door to door and tell them," Shane offered, still feeling guilty.

"Would you?" She reached out and took his hand. "I'm so happy for Nora. She's finally found someone who can take care of her, someone special who won't break her heart."

"Mummmmph," Shane replied softly.

Later that evening, when they were going to bed, Shane found a slip of paper on his pillow with a phone number, and a note written in Chooch's hand that read:

Amac says you can reach him at this number first thing tomorrow.

8

AMERICAN MACADO

Shane couldn't sleep. After almost an hour of tossing and turning, and one or two warnings from Alexa to stop moving, he got out of bed, grabbed his jeans, sweatshirt, and Chooch's note, then got another beer and went outside to sit again on one of the metal chairs in his tiny backyard. A half-moon shone through his large eucalyptus tree and lunar shadows from the fingerlike leaves danced in fan-shaped patterns on the grass around him. He inhaled the tree's pleasant, peppery scent. He couldn't do anything about Farrell until tomorrow, so he walked inside, picked up his cell phone in the living room, and dialed Amac, reading the number from Chooch's note. After two rings, a Hispanic voice was in his ear.

"*Quién habla?*"

"Is Amac around?" Shane asked.

"Who d'fuck is dis?"

"Tell him it's Shane Scully and I need to talk to him."

"Momento," the man said, then put him on hold while Shane went into the kitchen, took another Amstel out of the fridge, opened it, then walked back outside and stood in his yard looking at the canal.

"Scully, *qué traes tú?"* Amac's voice came over the phone after almost five minutes.

"I'm fine, but I need to talk to you."

"I got my hands full, *ese* . . . got my sevens around me now, tellin' me how I gotta do things."

"Sevens" were gangsters, *G* being the seventh letter of the alphabet.

"I need to talk. I'll do it any way you want. I'll go stand on a street corner like last time. You can blindfold me . . . however you want to do it."

"Only way that's gonna happen is if you got some four-one-one to sell."

"I'm not selling, I'm trading. It's gotta go both ways," Shane replied, angry because now he'd have to wake up Alexa and talk her out of some street intel he could trade with Amac. He knew the CRASH unit probably had picked up something Alexa could share with him.

There was a pause, then American said, *"Momentito,"* and Shane was on hold again. He stood looking at the canal until Amac came back on. "Okay, go out of your house and stand on the corner of Largo and Abbott Kinney. I'll pick you up."

"When?" Shane asked.

"An hour."

"I'll be there." And then he was listening to a dial tone. Shane got his ankle gun out of the locked desk drawer in the living room and strapped it on. He was pretty sure it wouldn't make it past the "*cuete* inspection," but it was worth a try.

He went into the kitchen and fixed something to eat, dreading having to wake Alexa and fill her in; knowing she would be pissed when she found out what he was planning to do. He finished off a piece of leftover steak, drained his beer, and was just putting the bottle into the trash when he became aware that someone else was in the kitchen. He spun around and caught Alexa standing in the doorway. She had put on her robe and had her arms wrapped tightly around her.

"I woke up. You weren't in bed," she said.

"Couldn't sleep."

"What're you doing?"

"Gonna go see American. I just talked to him."

"Alone?" She seemed appalled. "You can't go see him alone. What the hell's going through your head, Shane?"

"Hold it. Didn't you just ask me to get in touch with him?"

"Yes. In touch . . . call him . . . talk on the phone."

"Alexa, he's the Inca. He's not gonna have an important conversation with me on the phone. This guy is too careful. He'll think he's being bugged. Besides, he'll want to be looking into my eyes when he talks, and I want to look into his. Eyes are the best lie detectors."

"He's a killer, Shane. His yellow sheet is a bible of street violence."

"Jesus, be fair. You asked me to get in touch with him. I got in touch. This is the only way he'll do it, and you damn well know it."

"How?" she asked.

"How'm I meeting him?"

She nodded.

"I'm . . ." He started to say it, then stopped. "You don't want to know."

"The hell I don't. Spit it out, buddy."

"Okay. I'm going to the corner of Largo and Abbott Kinney. I'm gonna stand there alone, until they send a war wagon down to pick me up. Amac might be in the car or it might just be a buncha *califas* who'll escort me to him."

"Over my dead body. You need a tail, some backup."

"Alexa, I have to go alone. He'll spot a tail. I called *him*. I can't back out. If I'm not on that street corner he's gonna think I was setting him up. It'll piss him off and he'll never trust me again. This is the only way."

She changed her posture and was now

standing defiantly in the kitchen doorway, her legs apart, hands on her hips, trying to figure a way to stop him.

"Amac may be violent, but he's a man of honor — a *mara salvatrucha*. Three Rs — womb to tomb."

"Don't pitch that gang tripe at me. I ran the CRASH unit. I busted a kid once in a Catholic church. He'd just done a triple drive-by. We caught this *vato* on his knees, lighting candles, thanking God for assisting with the killings. They're twisted. Amac especially."

"Amac is different. He'll guarantee this one free trip. In and out. If he doesn't like what I've got to tell him, that will end it."

"And what *are* you going to tell him?"

"I was just about to wake you, because I need something to trade."

"Now we're giving *him* intel," she said. "It was supposed to work the other way."

"Honey, it's a negotiation. He's not gonna let it be a one-way street."

She sat down at the kitchen table and rubbed her right forearm. Shane knew it still went numb at times from the shot she took in the shoulder at Lake Arrowhead, when she saved his life at the end of the Molar case. "You're nuts, you know that?"

"I know. It's why I'm seriously considering a posting at Internal Affairs. I should fit right in with that bowl of fruits and nuts."

Then, slowly, a smile twitched at the corner

of her mouth and he knew he had her. "Okay. I don't have much, but we did pick up one piece of interesting street info. There's some new heroin that's supposed to hit the street soon. It's called White Dragon, and according to our source, there's a huge shipment coming in from Mexico. I think the Crips are moving it. We don't know who's sending it in, but we've had the product line described to us. It's snow-white heroin, probably China White, wrapped in cellophane with a white dragon outlined in red on the bag. Also, there may be some kind of Arizona connection. The Crip banger we got this from had a stolen credit card. For the last two months this guy, who's never been outside South Central since he was born, has been making more trips to Arizona than the Monsanto regional sales rep. We've traced him through the card charges: motel rooms, gas, restaurants, like that. The Arizona cops also picked up a rumble that Arizona is the new point of entry for this White Dragon line, probably the general distribution site as well. But most of this is more gossip and guesswork than fact."

"It'll have to do."

She followed him to the front door. "I really hate this," she said. "I'm just supposed to wait here and pray for your safety?"

"Honey, no prayers necessary. Amac is guaranteeing my safety. That's the way it works." He turned and smiled at her. "Didn't you ever see that 1950s classic Western *Broken Arrow?* Cochise guarantees Tom Jeffords that he can ride safely into the Apache camp and trade wampum. The next thing you know, they're best buds, and there's peace in the Valley. Simple as that."

"Get the fuck out of my house," she said in mock anger. But as he turned to leave, she grabbed him and hugged him. "Shane, you see? This is exactly what I meant about not being risk-adverse."

"Yeah, maybe, but let's not forget whose idea it was."

He left the house and walked toward Abbott Kinney. He knew without looking back that she was still on the porch, still had her eyes on him until he turned the corner at the end of the street.

9

PARADISE SQUARE

The Impala low-rider with a yellow-and-green glitter paint job made one slow pass down Abbott Kinney Boulevard without stopping. It was a show car, a lowered '63. It finally came around again, then stopped half a block away. Two *vatos* got out dressed in baggy jeans and barrio coats buttoned at the top gang-style; a fashion that allowed easy access to belt-holstered weapons. They walked toward Shane, moving deliberately. As they drew closer, he could see they were both in their middle teens. One was dark-skinned, almost black; the other had Inca-Indio features, common to Central Mexico.

"*Hola,*" Shane said as they approached.

"*Chúpame,* motherfucker," the darker one replied.

"Not unless I get a ring first," Shane quipped.

The Indio pushed Shane toward the building. "Turn around. Hands on the wall."

Shane did as instructed. They quickly found the ankle holster and stripped it off.

"*No cuetes,* asshole."

"I'm a cop. We're required to pack," Shane said, cursing the decision because he had just lost a four-hundred-dollar Beretta Mini with a custom grip and laser sight.

They waved at the Impala, which made a U-turn, then came back. There were two more Mexicans in the low-rider, both heavily sleeved with interlocking *M* and *13* gang tatts. Amac was not in the car. Shane was pushed into the back and a black pillowcase put over his head, then he was shoved down onto the floor between the seats.

The next half hour was an uncomfortable ride across town. Then they were leaving the freeway, moving slower as they headed down bumpy-surface streets. He heard the distant wail of a siren and laughter from a passing bar. Then the car finally slowed and came to a stop.

"*Manolo, tu ranfla adentro,*" a new voice said through the window, instructing the driver to move the car inside. A *ranfla* was a cherried-out low-rider.

The Impala started again, drove about twenty feet before the engine was shut off. Shane heard metal hinges squeaking and a heavy wooden gate close. Then he was yanked into a sitting position; the pillowcase was snapped off his head, and he was being pulled out of the low-rider, pushed up against the passenger door.

"Stand there, *gabacho*," one of the *vatos* ordered.

He was in a Spanish-style courtyard reminiscent of a fortress that looked as if it took up the better part of a city block. There was an old three-tiered stone fountain dripping water in the center of a tiled patio. The building that surrounded the courtyard on all four sides was three stories high and constructed of tan California adobe. Tile roofs sloped down toward the patio. Shane could see several Emes lying prone up there, armed, their muzzles pointing down into the street outside. Shane guessed by the architecture that he was in the heart of L.A., probably somewhere down by Alvarado Street, one of the few places where these two-hundred-year-old Mexican buildings still existed. He saw a brass plaque on the wall identifying this landmark as *Plaza Paraíso* — Paradise Square.

A large wooden door opened behind Shane, and Amac stood on the threshold, flanked on two sides by Eme guards. He wore baggy jeans and a gang-tank jacket with "18th Street Sureños" on the back. As he walked across the tiled courtyard, his booted footsteps echoed against the adobe walls. Shane pushed away from the fancy low-rider and crossed to meet him at the fountain. Finally, they were face-to-face.

"Qué pasa, hombre?" Shane said softly.

Amac shrugged. *"Así es, así será."* This is how it is and how it's gonna be.

"You got that right," Shane answered.

"Like I said on the phone, *ese,* I got my hands full right now. We're down with this shit, so you got something to tell me? Let's hear it."

"I need some insight, Amac."

" 'At's why they got churches, Scully."

"Somebody killed Kevin Cordell; lured Stone into an avocado orchard and assassinated him. Now O.G.'s from both the Crip and Blood sets are starting to get shot. At first we thought Stone's death had created a power vacuum between those two sets, but yesterday somebody witnessed a drive-by. Two Crips went down. They said the shooters were La Eme. Alexa thinks this might be turning into some kinda intercity drug free-for-all. That's not gonna be good, man. Innocent people start dying and the governor could call out the Guard. There could be some serious shit to pay. I want to stop it before that happens. To do that, we need to know what's going on and why."

Amac looked at him for a long moment. *"Qué jodido!"* he blurted. "So you come down, pull on my coat."

"Yeah, that was my plan."

"Maybe while I'm at it, I should grab the *vatos* who did that piece a work, turn them over to you?"

"I got some useful stuff to trade."

"You got shit. You're so far behind the curve, you ain't approved to do business."

"Who shot Kevin Cordell? At least gimme the spill on that."

"Kevin Cordell . . ." He spit the name out like a fruit seed. "That transforming piece a shit sure deserved to die, but now I'm beginning to think we was all better off when he was alive. At least he kept them *dedos locos* a his from goin' off the reservation. Now we got a fucking street war with *mayates* rollin' around in work cars, shootin' anything that moves."

Shane stood still and waited.

"Okay, Scully, you wanna know who dropped Cordell? It was his own people — his own 'big boy.' Least ways that's the way we hear it."

"His big boy — his right-hand man?" Shane asked.

"Yeah. An O.G. from the Front Street Crips. His name's Russell Hayes — they call him Hardcore way we heard it, him and his cousin, some crazy coffee-colored *maldito* with a *trenza* braid halfway down his back did the hit."

"Why would they kill Stone?"

"They're *mayates,* man. Fuckin' jungle bunnies."

"You're smarter than that. Help me, Amac."

American seemed to consider this, then nodded. "Stone was the one who kept the war between the Crips and Bloods hot. That was his thing. The way he kept control . . . and it was good for us, too, y'know? With them always fighting, we took over half the city. His people finally wised up, but Stone had too many enemies. In order to unite the Crips and Bloods, he had to go." Then Amac stopped. "I'm doin' all the talking here, *ese*. You said you had something for me?"

"You know about this new White Dragon?" Shane asked softly. "It's Chinese heroin and it's hitting the streets soon. Supposed to be a big supply coming up from Mexico."

"So what? Drugs is always comin' up. Tell me somethin' I can use."

"This stuff looks like it's heading to Arizona. It's a new distribution system that's gonna be warehoused out there and then, most likely, moved from Arizona back to L.A."

Amac shrugged and glanced at his watch.

"We're pretty sure somebody's setting up to make a big score," Shane continued, trying to shine this one meager fact up so it would seem worth trading. "It looks now like the black gangs are the ones moving it. At first we thought Crips, but now with what you said, it could be both sets. This much I can tell you: It'll have big value . . . lotta money on the street. It's high quality; it's gonna blow the market out."

Amac pulled a quarter out of his pocket and held it up for Shane to see. "You know what it says on this U S of A coin?" Shane waited. "It says 'Liberty' right there under George Washington's double chin. 'Cording to this U S of A quarter, money supposta buy us liberty. But you know something strange, Scully? Liberty ain't freedom. Not even close. The dictionary says freedom is liberation from the power of another. I don't have that. Yet. Money can't never buy us freedom We don't have control over the way Anglos deal with us. In this country I can have liberty, which is the power to enjoy *various* social and economic rights. I can move around and buy stuff, but my nature and my heritage and my Indio skin prohibit my freedom, *comprende?*"

Shane held his gaze but didn't respond.

"This country won't accommodate us, so they criminalize us instead."

"Come on, the laws prosecute criminals, not ethnic groups," Shane argued.

"In school, they tell me, Hey, Amac, stop bitchin'. It's about the USA, it's not about U, *ese*. But that was all bullshit, man. When I was a boy, only ten or eleven, I once tried to sell lemonade on the street corner. The police saw me and *la chota* arrest me for selling without a peddler's license. I wasn't breakin' no law. White kids do that in Beverly Hills with no hassle every day. But they was fuckin' with me 'cause I was a Mexican, and they don't want me to have no freedom. People in this country can't consume unless they can sell, *ese*. If they can't start a legal business, then they'll run an illegal one. Sell dope, stolen cars, radios — anything to feed their families. Some *chavalas* even sell their bodies. If a Chicano tries to challenge the power structure in America, he'll get beaten or jailed for his trouble."

Finally Amac tossed the quarter into the fountain. "So I make a wish. My wish isn't on that coin. I want freedom — freedom from poverty, from my own ignorance and self-hatred, from Anglo prejudice. There is more at stake here than who gets rich or who dies. There is a small but dangerous fire burning, *hombre* . . . and nobody is even watching."

Shane looked down at the quarter wavering in the pool of water. "Amac . . . don't start a race war."

Amac looked toward the car where his *vatos* stood. The young one with the black complexion had never stopped glaring at Shane.

"You see that dark one?" Amac asked. *"El prieto?"*

Shane nodded.

"His street name is Midnight. He's mostly black, maybe all black. Nobody knows. He don't even know 'cause he never met his parents. He was homeless. When he was five, I found this little *flaquillo* eating outta trash cans. I gave him a place to stay, gave him food. Now he's not a *mayate* no more. Now he's a *vato* — my *carnal*. So don't talk to me about race wars. This ain't about race, it's about respect."

Amac walked away from the fountain, but then, halfway to the door, he turned and looked back. "Listen, Scully, you always treated me like a man. You gave me respect. You also got *ganas*. You came to the park two years ago, not knowing what would happen to you; you came here alone tonight. I respect that."

Shane waited.

"But I ain't in the same place no more. I got my people lookin' to me. So we can't be doin' this. Next time you see me, figure I'll be tryin' to take you out."

"If we have respect for one another, we can work together . . . help each other."

"You got freedom, *ese*. I only got liberty."

Forty-five minutes later, Shane was standing back on Abbott Kinney Boulevard with his empty ankle holster in his hand. He walked the four blocks to his house. When he entered, he found Alexa sitting in the club chair in the living room, waiting.

"Thank God." She let her breath out and stood. "What'd he tell you?"

"The Bloods and the Crips have united and are at war against the Emes."

"I was afraid of that. Does he know who killed Stone?"

"He thinks it was Russ Hayes and some cousin of his with light skin and a braid."

"Russell 'Hardcore' Hayes?" Alexa said. "It's hard to believe. . . . He and Stone grew up together. According to the gang book, they were like brothers."

"This isn't about brotherhood, it's about cash. They had to clear him out to pull the drug gangs together. You can pick up Hardcore and his cousin for Stone's murder, but without witnesses willing to testify, it's just street rumor, and your bust won't stick."

She nodded.

"Amac thinks Stone died so the Crips and Bloods could unite, but I think something else is going on, something bigger."

"What?" Alexa was studying him closely in the darkened living room.

"I don't know, but when I told him about the China White and the Arizona connection, it didn't seem to surprise him. I think he already knew. I also think there are some other big players in this, Mexicans or Colombians, and Amac knows who they are. Somebody's setting up the supply for Russ Hayes. Somebody big is pulling the strings."

Alexa started frowning, then shook her head. "We're working closely with the feds. They're all over the Mexican and Colombian suppliers. If it was a regular source, DEA or Customs would have picked up on it."

"It was just a hunch. I felt like I didn't tell him anything he didn't already know."

Alexa was still deep in thought.

"One other thing . . ." Shane added. "Amac may be an Eme drug dealer, fighting the black gangs for his share of the market, but he's also turned into something else."

"What's that?" Alexa asked.

"A revolutionary."

10

THE LAST LIVING PRINCE
IN AMERICA

"I'm gonna spend the night over at Billy Rano's," Chooch said as Shane put breakfast down in front of him. Billy Rano was a classmate who had also been Chooch's favorite target at wide receiver last year.

"His mom and dad know you're coming?"

"Yeah, it's all set."

Shane carried his own breakfast to the table and sat down. He could tell the boy was uncomfortable, and when Chooch finally spoke, the reason became clear.

"You really gonna try and get in touch with Amac?" Chooch was looking at his plate.

Shane laid down his fork and tried to engage his son's eyes across the small table. "I already called. Talked to him last night." He didn't think it was smart to tell Chooch he'd also gone to see him.

"How is he?" Chooch looked up.

Shane took a minute to decide how much he wanted to say. Chooch was seventeen, striving for adulthood. Shane had always preached that adults get to make their own choices, but must also take full responsibility for the consequences of their actions. However, in this case, Shane worried that Chooch's sense of loyalty might overcome his good judgment. "He's not the same guy he used to be."

"Yeah? How so?" There was a hint of a challenge now.

"Amac did us a big favor two years ago. He was the right guy at the right time, but nothing stays the same. You know that, everybody moves on."

"What's that suppose to mean?"

"Amac is running all La Eme sets in East L.A. He's an Inca now. I think he's at war with the black gangs in South Central — both Crips and Bloods. It's a free-for-all. A lot of guys are going to die. . . . Amac may be one of them."

"That pretty much sucks," Chooch said.

"Right, I know it does, but that's the way it is. There's nothing I can do about it."

"Dad, you're a cop. You could do something if you wanted. You could protect him. You could even arrest him if you had to . . . find a way to get him out of it somehow, so he doesn't lose his honor."

"If I could catch him, and I had a charge that would stick, maybe. But he's gone to ground. He's got his Sevens guarding him. He's not gonna be easy to find." Shane knew Amac wouldn't stay at Paradise Square. In a war, he'd keep moving.

Chooch sat in silence, then put down his fork and stopped eating his eggs. "Y'know, Dad, when I was with him before, back when Sandy was still alive, Amac and I got really close." Chooch always referred to his mother as Sandy. Her death came in a heroic bid that saved his life but had not erased the pain of that long, failed relationship. "Back when I was still gaffeling on the street, Amac came to me and said, '*Vatito*, I need you to do something.'" Chooch stopped, searching for the right words. "Back then he was the only person in my life who cared what happened to me. Anything he wanted, I would do."

Shane nodded.

"So I got in his car and we drove to Chavez Boulevard, out past Francis Park, and I asked him, 'Where are we going?' He said it was *a la brava*. You know what that is?"

Shane shook his head.

"It's like something you do, whether you want to or not. Kinda like a duty, but with a sort of upside, too. Y'know?"

Shane nodded.

"He takes me to the New Calvary Cemetery out on Third, and there's like ten other peewee

113

vatitos, all from different sets of the Sureños. They were waiting there for Amac; all of them between twelve and fifteen, standing in the parking lot dressed in our gang blue. Even though I never met these *vatos* before, we were *carnales,* you know, brothers. Anyway, we all go upstairs in the mortuary there, to this room where they have the caskets on display. Then all the peewees, they start moving around, while this old man in a black suit is watching us like we're about to steal something. I'm standing there thinking, what is this? Did someone die and we gotta pick out his casket? Then I finally begin to realize that all these guys are selecting their own coffins. They're running their hands over the polished mahogany, saying, 'Hey, *ese,* lookit dis one.' " Chooch, now imitating a *cholo* accent. " '*Qué maravilla.* Gotta fine satin pillow. You gonna be *con safos* in dis one, homes.'

"So I asked Amac, why are they doing this? It seemed so sad to me, but they were all smiling. Amac said they were happy because their funerals would be huge celebrations . . . tributes to their *ganas.* They would be laid out in their expensive new mahogany coffins, and all of the Sureños would come to celebrate their lives and their bravery. The Emes would be at the funeral all fronted out. They would look down at the beautiful casket and say, 'This *ese* was *rifa,* the best.' And then Amac said to me what he always says: '*Así es, así será.*' "

There was a long silence while they sat across from each other, both thinking about the P.G.'s buying caskets at the New Calvary Cemetery.

"Then Amac asked me to pick out a coffin. He said he was prepaying for them and the grave sites out of the Eighteenth Street Sureños's war chest. I told him I didn't want to buy a casket, that I didn't want to die. And you know what he said?"

"No."

He said, "You're already dead, homes. You were dead the day you were born. We just been waiting for the right day to bury you."

"So what happened?" Shane asked.

"I picked out a casket and a grave site. Amac paid for it. My casket is a big mahogany job with chrome rails, called a Heaven Rider. Don't ya love it? A Heaven Rider . . . like it's a damn chariot gonna take me to the Promised Land. They're holding it at New Calvary Cemetery until my blessed day."

"Why're you telling me this?" Shane asked.

"Because Amac thinks he's a dead man, too, Dad. He always has. So do all the others. They all have their caskets, their burial plots — everything prepaid. Now all they got left to do is fill the hole in the ground. They're all dreaming about their funerals with *veteranos* praising their bravery in death. It's like the most hopeless thing I ever saw."

"And how do I change that?" Shane asked,

marveling at the depth of Chooch's realizations.

"You gotta stop this war from happening, Dad. You gotta save him, 'cause he can't save himself."

They sat there for a long moment while that impossible mission hung before Shane.

Suddenly, Chooch got up and grabbed his book bag. "Gotta go or I'm gonna get a late slip." He walked out of the kitchen, pausing at the door and turning back. "I love you, Dad."

"I love you, too," Shane answered.

When his son was gone, Shane felt strange. It was almost as if Chooch had been saying good-bye. Then he heard his son's Jeep Cherokee start up, pull out of the drive, and power away.

Shane washed off their breakfast plates, then got Alexa's backup gun and holster, a Smith & Wesson .38 round wheel. He locked the back door, climbed into the Acura, and pulled out of the garage onto the 405 Freeway North. He transitioned to the Santa Monica Freeway, then headed toward Malibu.

He was still bummed by his breakfast conversation. It carried a sense of impending disaster. As he drove, he told himself to calm down. He was no psychic; he was overdramatizing.

It was another crisp day, with cold northern winds blowing the smog out to sea, freshening the air. But as he wound his way up the coast, Shane kept picturing the roomful of teenagers selecting caskets. He knew that the gang experience in L.A. was a death sentence, and that all the young men who wore La Eme colors knew they were probably signing up for a short, violent ride. And now Chooch had his own mahogany Heaven Rider in storage, waiting for that day when he would fill it — a frightening thought.

Then he was in Malibu pulling up to the Colony guard gate. This time he had his police creds, so he didn't intend to take any guff from the old man who demanded his name and the name of the resident he was there to visit.

"This is a police matter," Shane said crisply as he flashed his badge. "Open the gate, please."

The guard complied and Shane pulled through, thinking it was great to have his tin back. He drove up to Farrell Champion's French Tudor and parked so that he was within sight of the garage. Then he waited.

At a little past ten, Farrell Champion pulled his black Testarossa out. He gunned the quarter-of-a-million-dollar Ferrari once, then zoomed off without a look back in Shane's direction.

Shane got out of the Acura, walked across the street, and rang Farrell's bell. A few minutes later, the door was opened by Nora Bishop, wearing a robe and carrying a cup of coffee. Her dark hair was still wet, but she looked happy to see him.

"My God, Shane, I just got through doing

my laps. You missed Farrell, he left a minute ago."

"What a shame. I would've loved to have some more time with him. Great guy," he lied.

Nora smiled at him, cocking her head. "He sure is. Y'know, Shane, except for you and Alexa, I don't have that many good friends here in L.A. It seems everyone in this town lives right on the damn surface. I don't have to tell you, some of the guys I was going out with were pretty sleazy." She smiled. "And then, along comes the last living prince in America. And not only does this incredibly funny, sexy guy think I'm interesting and entertaining, but by God he even wants to *marry* me. Sometimes I feel like I'm walking around in a dream."

Shane felt his ears turning red as he grinned and nodded, muttering things like: "Yep, yep . . . Farrell Champion . . . Sure got one there, honey."

Then she led him into the foyer. "What can I do for you?" she asked.

"Well, it's kind of a long shot, really. But I lost my wallet somewhere a day ago. All my credit cards, my license, social security . . . I've checked with the card companies and nobody's using them, so it's probably under a sofa somewhere. I've checked everywhere else and the only place I can think I haven't looked is here."

"You think you might have lost it at the party?"

"I don't know, possibly."

"Well, I haven't seen it, but come on. Let's see what we can find." She led him into the living room, which had been dusted and vacuumed back to its pre-party elegance. Nora really was a superb decorator. Cinnamon walls, with fresh white trim, beautiful paintings, and matching floral fabrics . . . just enough flash, but not too much glitter.

"Any ideas where to start?" she asked.

"Well, I know I didn't sit down in here, but the pool house . . . I sat on the couch out there."

"Let's go," she said, leading the way.

They walked across the deck, and as soon as they were outside, Shane could again smell the cool, damp scent of the Pacific Ocean. He followed Nora down into the large pool house. Shane already knew what he wanted to steal, but he was going to have to distract Nora. She was dogging him, chattering excitedly about her wedding. "Farrell wanted to do the ceremony in Monaco, can you believe that? What a romantic that man is. He wanted to fly all of our friends there on the BBJ."

"The what?"

"It's a huge Warner Brothers plane he gets to use. It's called a Boeing Business Jet — a BBJ. He was going to put everybody up at the Hotel de Paris, do the reception at Jimmy's. But in the end, I just wanted it to be more normal, y'know? More spiritual."

"Absolutely," Shane said. "A Monaco wedding does seem to lack a certain sense of spiri-tuality."

"So as you know, we decided to use that wonderful chapel up in the hills above Pepperdine University. You know . . . the one with the glass atrium. I've always loved that setting. You can see all the flowers and the trees outside, the spectacular views of the Pa-cific. . . ."

They were in the main room of the pool house now, and Shane was down on his knees, reaching around under the sofa cushions, looking for his "lost" wallet, which was, of course, safely tucked in his back pocket.

"Nope, not here," he said after retrieving a few quarters. Then he spotted what he'd been looking for: the large gold lighter that Farrell had used to light everyone's Cuban cigars. It was resting on an antique sideboard. It had a broad, flat surface, which should have retained Farrell's thumbprint along with an index and at least one digit. "Nora, would you mind checking the bathroom?" Shane smiled. "Look behind the toilet? The wallet's a worn brown leather job. Nothing too special."

"Sure," she said, heading off to the guest bath while Shane slipped quickly across the room and stole the large lighter. Using only his fingertips, he dropped it into an evidence bag, which he then sequestered in his side jacket pocket. Next he took out his wallet and laid it on the top of the bar, in plain sight. When Nora returned, Shane was on the far side of the room by the window, down on his knees, searching under a club chair.

"Not in the bathroom," she announced as she moved toward the bar. "Is this it?" Nora suddenly asked, and when Shane turned, she was holding up his wallet, smiling triumphantly.

"That's it!" He grinned. "Where'd you find it?"

"Right on the bar. The maids must've picked it up and set it there." She handed it to him.

"Man, I'm glad I don't have to cancel all these," he said, flipping it open and looking at his two minimum-limit Visa cards. Then he put his wallet away and Nora led him out of the pool house.

"Can you stay for a cup of coffee?" she asked hopefully.

Shane sure as hell didn't want to stay. He already felt like a big enough asshole and traitor, but he was trapped. "Coffee sounds great," he said.

They each had a cup of fresh-ground Colombian. Nora told Shane how hard it had been for Alexa after her mother died, and how vulnerable she was during that first year.

"Underneath that tough cop exterior is one of the sweetest people we'll ever know," she told him.

An hour later he was back in his car, feeling like Judas. He dropped the lighter off at SID in

Parker Center, with instructions to send any latent prints up to Lee Fineburg in Records Services.

All in all, it had been a grimy little mission, but he was pretty sure that Farrell Champion was another in a long line of Nora Bishop's romantic mistakes, so what choice did he have? Was he just supposed to accept this handsome Hollywood phony at face value?

The last living prince in America, my ass, he thought.

11

THE PHONE CALL

Later that afternoon Shane returned to his canal house in Venice. He called out, but immediately knew that the place was empty. The house had that strange stillness that told him nobody was home.

It was five-thirty, so he took a beer out of the fridge, and again took his place in his chair on the back lawn. He was beginning to feel like a terrible creature of habit. Like one of those tired, dusty wharf pelicans who had finally given up foraging for food and sat on a concrete piling, taking french fries from tourists, never moving until, with clogged intestines, it finally toppled off the pier into the water. Shane sat on this damn chair way too much, looking at these same unaltered vistas. His view of this canal never changed, but in his mind, somehow it always looked slightly different.

Maybe it was a new shadow on the water, or a shaft of sunlight through a cloud, or maybe he was just sliding into some early form of geriatric senility. He pulled out his phone and called Alexa, but only got as far as the X.O. at Detective Services Group, who told him that his wife could not be disturbed. She was in a briefing with the chief.

"Tell her that her husband called and —"

"Right," the sarge said, and was gone before Shane could continue his message. Obviously they had very little patience for the spouses of commanding officers right now. There was a clipped irritation in the man's voice, which told Shane that all was not well on the sixth floor at Parker Center.

He spent the early evening going through the bills on his desk, trying to clear the decks for tomorrow's return to duty. His meager bank balance was $437.86. Depressing. Two hours later he put everything away in the desk drawer and locked it. It was after nine. He was looking at the phone on his desk, thinking he shouldn't make this next call, but already knew he was going to. A valiant little internal struggle ensued where the outcome was never really in doubt, so he finally went into Chooch's room, found his school phone directory, looked up Billy Rano's number, and dialed. Mrs. Rano picked up on the second ring.

"Yes?" Beth Rano was a professor of African Studies at Pierce College.

"Hi, Beth. This is Shane Scully. I need to talk to my son. I understand he's over there."

"Chooch isn't here, Shane."

His heart started beating faster. "He said he was spending the night with Billy."

"I'm sorry, I don't know anything about that. Billy's here, you want to talk to him?"

"Please . . ."

After a moment he heard Billy Rano's soft African-American lilt.

"Wassup, Mr. Scully?" the tall, quick wide receiver answered.

"Hi, Billy, I'm looking for Chooch."

"Uh, I left him at the library around five o'clock."

"I thought he was spending the night over there."

"He was, but he said something came up. Didn't say what."

"Okay, thanks," Shane said. "If you hear from him, tell him to call home."

"Yes, sir."

Shane hung up and his imagination immediately started to run away with him. What if Chooch went to see Amac? Of course, that was about the stupidest thing Chooch could do with the Emes in a citywide war. But the more he thought about it, the more he was sure that was exactly what his son had done.

He dialed Chooch's cell phone, and it started ringing down the hall in his bedroom. His son hadn't taken it with him.

He called Amac's cell number and got an "out of the area" recording. He called Alexa again and this time, by claiming a personal emergency, was put directly into Chief Filosiani's office.

"I'm sure he's okay," she said after listening to his concern. "He's probably studying with somebody, or maybe he's at the library. Did you try to call him?"

"He left his cell here. I think he's with Amac," Shane said. Then he heard the back door slam. "Hold it. I think he just came in. Talk to you later."

Shane hung up the phone and met his son in the kitchen.

"Where've you been, bud?" Shane asked with a little too much force, and got the teenage mantra.

"Out," Chooch stonewalled.

"Right, but out where? I called Billy. He said he left you at five. It's after nine."

"Don't you trust me, Dad?"

Shane had one of those parental moments. Did he want to make this a battleground where Chooch's word was at stake? "You know I trust you."

Chooch nodded, retrieved a soda from the fridge, then walked past him without saying anything else.

Shane wanted to be fresh for tomorrow's meeting with Chief Filosiani, so he went to bed at ten and was sound asleep by 10:02.

He had an unsettling dream.

Chooch was dragging a big mahogany coffin up the hill at the New Calvary Cemetery, tugging it up to the edge of an open grave. When he got it there, he looked at Shane and smiled.

"It's called a Heaven Rider," his son said proudly in the dream. "My *eses* will all come. *Vatos* will talk about my bravery. They will celebrate my life." Suddenly, the chapel bell started ringing, and then it sounded more and more like a telephone.

Shane opened his eyes and looked at the bedside clock. It was almost eleven. The phone kept ringing. He sat up in bed and fumbled the receiver out of the cradle, noticing that Alexa still wasn't there.

"Hello," he said.

"Is this Sergeant Shane Scully?" a woman's voice asked.

"Yes. Who is this?"

"Detective Carla DePass, Homicide."

Uh-oh, Shane thought, but said, "What can I do for you, Detective?"

"My partner, Detective Lou Ruta, and I are working a homicide at West Eleventh Street, just east of Hoover. We'd appreciate it if you could roll on this, right now."

"I'm not assigned to Homicide. In fact, I don't even go back on active duty till tomorrow."

"We don't need help investigating the murder. We need some help identifying the vic.

We're at 2635 West Eleventh, Los Angeles. How soon can you make it here?"

"That's gonna take me half an hour."

"Don't let it take any longer," she said, and was gone.

He sat up and rubbed his eyes. That address was somewhere down in the Rampart Division.

Then he had a dark premonition as to who died.

12

STAR

"Detective Ruta's in the back by the garage," a young uniformed policeman told Shane after he had identified himself. Shane hung his creds in the handkerchief pocket of his blazer and started up the narrow concrete driveway. The house was a ramshackle California Craftsman, an architectural style popular in Southern California in the thirties and forties. This one had seen better days. The low wood dormers flaked paint, and sagging drainpipes and window shutters made the once fashionable structure look forlorn. This part of Rampart was ethnically mixed; the house on West 11th was located on a street that, a few years back, had been all Hispanic, but Vietnamese and Koreans were beginning to buy up the neighborhood. Asian and Mexican families were standing in their doorways up and down the street, looking

129

at the police circus parked in the center of the block.

Shane got to the head of the drive where Detective DePass, a middle-aged blonde in plainclothes with a weight lifter's build and close-cropped white hair, stopped him. "You said half an hour. It's twice that. Ruta is chewing my ass."

"Well, let's go calm him down then," Shane said. "Which one is he?"

She pointed out Detective Ruta.

Ruta was one of those police nightmares that every cop looks at and thinks *Please dear God, don't let me end up like that.* He was at least seventy pounds overweight with a drinker's beet-red complexion and a nose like a small Idaho potato. His unkempt mustache was growing down both sides of his mouth in a modified Fu Manchu, or was it a Pancho Villa? He looked like he was just waiting for somebody to say something that would give him an excuse to kick the shit out of them.

A second Blue stopped Shane before he reached Ruta. "You have to sign the Crime Scene Attendance sheet, Sarge," the rookie said, so Shane took the man's clipboard and signed himself in at 12:07 a.m.

"Scully, you're with me," Ruta called, waving a meaty hand at him and walking toward the back porch. He had never met Ruta, but Shane had gotten so much press coverage in the last two years that most cops knew him on sight.

Shane ignored the fat sergeant and veered toward the garage. He could see crime techs working inside through the half-open door. There was a police evidence table out front and he could see the contents of a beaded purse set out on its surface: no wallet, but a few bills and several pictures of a marmalade cat. Shane headed past the table. He wanted to see the body, but Ruta moved quickly and grabbed Shane's arm, pulling him toward the back porch.

"Hey, Detective, you wanna take your hands off me?" Shane complained. Ruta looked at him for a long hard moment before finally releasing him.

"I'm working this hit and I don't need you climbing all over my crime scene, fucking up my forensics, okay?"

"If you didn't want me here, why did you call me?" Shane asked. Now he thought he could also smell booze on Ruta's breath.

"Don't be a smart aleck. I'm gonna ask ya just this once to try real hard not to go up my ass. Zat gonna be too much trouble?"

"Why am I here?"

"I need you to put the hat on this vic for me. No wallet, no I.D. It's a whodunit." In homicide, whodunits were mysteries without suspects. Until a homicide dick knew the identity of the victim, it was impossible to make up a suspect list. Every investigator called out on a murder investigation prayed he would find an enraged spouse or burglar standing over the body waving the murder weapon. This one was going to cause Ruta to burn some shoe leather, and he was already pissed about it.

"How'm I gonna I.D. the vic without a visit to the crime scene?" Shane asked.

"Don't start up with me, okay?" Ruta growled. "Way you're gonna do it is to follow me. We walk through the side door in the back of the garage, and without touching anything, you tell me who this junkie bitch is. Then we're gonna step back outside and have further discussions."

"By 'junkie bitch,' are you referring to the deceased?" Shane was already burning with anger. He didn't need to see the body to know who it was.

"Let's go," Ruta said, then led Shane off the sloping porch. Through the rear windows of the house, Shane couldn't see any furniture inside. The rooms looked vacant, the house deserted.

They walked across a weed-strewn lawn and through the rear door of the garage.

"Don't touch anything," Ruta repeated.

"You mean I can't pick any of the evidence up, put it in my mouth or play with it?"

"Just I.D. this cunt and we're outta here."

Then the big plainclothes dick stepped aside.

There were lab techs, photographers, forensic scientists, and DNA experts; maybe fifteen people busily working in the garage. Hanging from a beam in the center of all this activity was Carol White. She was naked and her hands had been lashed behind her. Somebody had done a pretty good job on her face before she died. Her eyes were swollen shut and caked with blood. Her lip was split and a peri-mortem bruise decorated the right side of her face.

In Shane's head a familiar whistle blew . . . somebody yelled, "Play ball."

"She had your business card in her purse," Ruta interrupted, "so who the fuck is she?"

"Her full name was Carolyn White but she went by Carol. She's a hooker. Her street name was Crystal Glass."

"Okay, let's go. We can do the rest outside." Ruta led him out of the garage. Once Shane was back on the lawn, the overweight detective turned and stepped forward, using his huge gut to back Shane up against the wall.

"Hey, Detective, you wanna ease off a little?"

"Let's lay some conduit, Scully. To start out, I don't like you."

"Back up or I'm gonna give you a good fucking reason," Shane hissed, and after a minute of appraisal, Ruta took a half-step back, giving Shane a little breathing room.

"Ray Molar and I were in the Academy together," the fat detective vented. "Ray was the best cop I ever knew, and you put him on the bus."

"Ray Molar was a violent, out-of-control asshole who was shooting his arrestees and holding court in the street."

"You piece of shit, there's still a lotta people on the job lookin' to close your show."

"If they're all drunk whales like you, then I'm probably not in too much danger," Shane said. Suddenly, without warning, he chucked Lou Ruta hard, with both hands to the chest, pushing him away. The heavy cop took a staggering step backward but held his ground. His rummy eyes were smoldering with hatred.

"You wanna talk about this murder, or you wanna stand out here and blubber about Ray Molar?" Shane said.

"Why'd this hooker have your card in her purse?" Ruta growled as he wiped the back of his hand across his mouth, clearing some spittle off the bottom of his Fu Manchu. "You a client? You fuckin' her?"

"I was doing a favor for a C.I. of mine. He was trying to find her. I located her in the vice computer and paid her a visit. She was in a bar called the Snake Charmers, a few miles from here."

"That junkie whore couldn't charm anybody's snake," Ruta snorted.

"Hey, Ruta, you wanna hear this or you wanna stand out here and disrespect your victim? You're supposed to be her advocate.

You're supposed to speak for the dead."

Lou Ruta didn't say anything for a minute, just kept his pig-mean eyes on Shane.

"She's got a pimp named Paul Mills," Shane continued. "His street name is Black and I think he lives near the Snake Charmers Bar. When I was there, she told him to go next door and hang. You might pick him up and see what you can get out of him. He's a skinny fuck who wears a pound of gold jewelry and carries an umbrella."

"So you found Carol White, and then what? You told your C.I. where she was?"

"Yeah."

"I want the C.I.'s name. He just went to the top of my suspect list."

"Hey, Sarge, my C.I.'s not a hitter. He didn't do this, okay? I'm not gonna roll him up for you."

"This is a murder. *My* murder. You don't tell me what you're gonna do. *I* tell *you*. I want the fuck's name."

"Well, you're not getting it. Best I can offer is, I'll go talk to him myself and then, if I think he looks good for any part of this, I'll hand him over to you."

"You don't get to make that choice, Scully."

"How many of your C.I.'s have you given up over the years? Without confidential informants, the police clearance rate in this town would be zero. I'm not giving up my guy unless I have to."

"Then you're under arrest for obstruction of justice."

"Blow me."

The two of them stood nose to nose for about a minute. Ruta was barely in control of himself. The vein in the center of his forehead was throbbing ominously. He looked to Shane like a pre-op heart case.

"I could call one of those Blues over and you'd be explaining this to my lieutenant downtown. You want that?"

"What division does your lieutenant work for?"

"DSG."

"Then I've got some bad news for you, Regis. . . . The head of DSG is my wife. So unless you're sleeping with your lieutenant, guess who's gonna win this one? We'll see who ends up with days off for calling his vic a junkie bitch and a cunt, and for drinking on the job."

Ruta's big belly was rising and falling with each angry breath.

"Gimme your card. I'll call you if my C.I. looks dirty," Shane concluded.

After a long time, Ruta pulled out his card, and in a childish moment, flipped it at him. It fluttered to the ground between them. Shane squatted to pick it up, then stood and put the card in his pocket.

As Shane walked down the drive, his stomach was turning sour, his face felt flush, and it wasn't Lou Ruta who had caused it. It was Carol White hanging from that rafter, naked, with her face a bloody mess. She finally got her big part. She was starring in her own murder investigation.

13

THE INEVITABILITY OF BEING

Nicky lived in one of two older steel-and-glass high-rise towers off Sunset, built in the late sixties. The condo buildings were called, appropriately enough, Hollywood Towers. Nicky Marcella had one of the East Tower penthouses, P-4.

Shane had been there before and knew they had security elevators, so he parked out front and pulled a big empty pizza box out of his trunk, which he sometimes used on occasions like this. He climbed back into the front seat, took off his jacket, rolled up his sleeves, and waited. It was 12:50 a.m., but one of the advantages of working Hollywood was that the town never slept. They didn't roll up the streets at eleven.

Shane only had to wait about ten minutes before he saw an attractive thirty-year-old woman pull into the underground parking garage of the East Tower. She looked flashy, with blond hair and hoop earrings. He got out of the Acura, grabbed his pizza box, ran across the street into the building, and ducked under the closing garage gate. The woman was hurrying toward the tower elevator, where she used her security card. The elevator doors opened and she entered just as Shane arrived with the pizza box and caught the closing door.

"Hold it! Only three minutes till I'm over my half-hour time limit." He smiled, then crowded into the lift with her, easily bypassing the building's only general security feature. The woman seemed slightly annoyed and maybe a little frightened, so Shane tried to put her at ease. "Pizza Hut . . . I don't usually deliver, I'm the night manager, but this flu epidemic's got me down to three drivers."

She smiled, more relaxed as Shane pushed the "P" for penthouse.

The door opened on nine and she got off. Shane rode up to the penthouse on the twenty-fifth floor. When he stepped off the elevator, he was facing a smoked, marbleized mirror. Very sixties.

Nicky's apartment was at the end of the hall. Shane rang the bell. Nothing. He rang again. Still nothing. Then he reached into his back pocket and pulled out the leather case containing his lock picks. Fortunately, this door had deadbolts. There were no electronic locks when the Towers were built. Nicky had not upgraded his security — strange behavior for an ex-crook.

It took Shane four minutes to work the tumblers. First he slid in the long, flat, narrow pick, then fed in the smaller picks with hooks on the ends, jiggling each one until the pick lodged itself in a tumbler. When he had enough picks inserted into the lock so the tumblers were all engaged, he took the handful and turned them together. The lock clicked. The door opened.

The Hollywood Towers were old buildings, but they were well placed, and the views were magnificent. Nicky had furnished his penthouse lavishly: plush pile carpeting, antique wood pieces, fawn-colored tie-back drapes. A few brightly painted Chinese screens hung on the interior wall. But the dominant feature was the magnificent view. Two walls were wrapped with floor-to-ceiling glass, which showed the twinkling lights all the way to Santa Monica.

Shane went through the place, frisking it quickly. He started in the bathroom, which all cops learn is the temple of human weakness. But Nicky was playing it pretty straight — no drugs, no Viagra. He was, however, using some hair color — Just for Men, Dark Brown.

When Shane finished searching the bathroom, he moved into the bedroom. In the closet hung twenty rather garish suits, including the orange-brown number Nicky had worn at Farrell's party. There was a rack of expensive shoes. On the top shelf, in a shoe box, he found a 9mm Beretta with two clips, both loaded. He replaced it, then finished the closet, remembering to search the suit pockets, but he found nothing. Next he moved to the dresser.

The sock drawer — always a treat.

Under Nicky's argyles, Shane found a small leather book with twenty Polaroid pictures of beautiful half-clad or naked women. They were carefully mounted under plastic, each with a code number written on a slip at the bottom. Shane flipped through it twice. Carol wasn't in the book. He put it back, wondering if it was some kind of out call or trick book.

Half an hour after entering, he had done his search. He settled himself in a big overstuffed chair in the living room, where he had a commanding view of the twinkling lights of the city. Off to the east, he could see the high-rises of the financial district; off to the west, about five miles away, the lights of Century City glittered. Shane watched them shine while his own spirits darkened.

Of course, there was very little he could do to escape the fact that he had probably played a key role in Carol White's murder. He didn't think Black Mills would beat one of his own meal tickets to death. Shane had found this poor girl for Nicky, had told Nicky where she was, and now, less than ten hours later, she was dead, hanging in a garage on West 11th in Rampart.

141

Shane looked down at Sunset Boulevard below and wondered at the allure of Tinseltown, the glitzy magnet of fame and stardom. Shane did a rough chronology, playing the "Where Was I Then" game.

When Mr. and Mrs. White had conceived Carol, where was Shane? He did the math. Was he still living with foster families? When she was still in high school, he was getting ready to join the Marines. Then she won Miss Solar Energy, came to Hollywood, and was almost a star.

Almost . . . I was that close.

Yesterday their paths finally crossed. They looked at each other across the chipped linoleum-topped table in the Snake Charmers Bar. The cop and the hooker. She had told him who she was . . . not so much by what she said but with her eyes. He saw her lost dream in their sparkle as she remembered her chance at stardom. When she told that story like a zombie, she seemed to rise from the dead.

Somehow, Shane had connected with her tragedy. He had sympathized. He wished that Franco Zeffirelli had let her out of that damn chair, because then she would have known. She would have been able to leave the memory behind. This way it had only served to defeat her. And now, because of Shane, she was dead.

Shane felt his chest tighten. He tried to tell himself it was inevitable. *Hey, she was already on this trail before I met her. If it wasn't one thing that got her, it would have been another, right? The drugs or a pissed-off john. Death was the price of life. It was the inevitability of being. She was born to lose; born to die young.* But he couldn't quite get there. Despite all the rationalization, he felt guilty and sad.

Shane knew these ruminations contained nothing useful for him, but he couldn't stop. They were the kind of thoughts rookie cops get when they roll on their first homicide and see maggots and green flies crawling in the victim's mouth. Or when they catch their first blood-soaked T.A., where they have to pry some poor guy off his steering wheel and watch his guts run down onto the dash. *Where was I when he ran this stop? Where was I when the fatal shot was fired? Why couldn't I have stopped it? Am I doing anything here, or am I just a glorified janitor cleaning up the mess?*

Then he heard a key in the lock and the door to Nicky's apartment opened. Shane sat very still as the little hustler entered the room. Nicky turned and relocked the door, then started across the living room. He was moving uncertainly, or maybe he was slightly drunk. He stripped off his tie and let it fall on the carpet as he entered the bedroom, not once glancing in Shane's direction.

Shane got to his feet and followed. He heard Nicky whistling something off-key in the bathroom. Shane crept silently across the carpet and stood in the doorway. Nicky was taking out

143

his contacts. He had one finger up to his right eye, and was just about to remove a lens when he glanced in the mirror and saw Shane standing there.

"Hi," Shane said.

"*Fuuuuckkk!*" Nicky shrieked.

Shane took two steps into the bathroom, grabbed Nicky by his silk shirt, and pulled him out of the room. The little bullshitter stumbled and fell onto the bedroom carpet, then scrambled to get away. Shane reached out his foot and tripped him. Nicky sprawled.

"Stay there, Nicky," Shane ordered. But Nicky came up again and made a dash for the bedroom door. Shane grabbed him, spun him, then ran Nicky backward across the room and slammed him into the closet door.

"*Ooooohhhhf,*" Nicky gasped.

Shane jerked him around and held him by the collar of his expensive shirt, roughly yanking him close.

"Shane, what're you doing? Leggo!" the grifter croaked.

"I don't like being played, Nicky."

"I . . . I . . . I didn't. Whatta you talking about?"

"Carol White. I wanna know why you were looking for her, and if you try and tell me you wanted to put her in a movie, I'm gonna kick the shit outta you."

"Shane . . . I . . . she . . ."

"Your part called for translucent? She was

144

about as translucent as a concrete wall. I should've smelled your con when I first saw her. It was all bullshit, hadda be."

"Shane, look . . . look, will ya, for Chrissake. Let go of me. This is a custom-made raw silk shirt here. I send to Hong Kong for these. You're gonna tear the stitches."

Shane turned him loose.

"Jesus H. Christ . . ." Nicky wheezed.

"You praying now, or are you just taking your Savior's name in vain?" Shane snarled.

"Shane, will you calm down, please? What's this all about?"

"She's dead, Nicky. Somebody beat the shit out of her, hung her from a rafter in a vacant garage in Rampart."

"Dead . . . ?"

"Dead. Gone. On the ark with extreme prejudice. Somebody made it hurt, then they killed her."

"Oh, my God," the little hustler said as tears sprang into his eyes.

The tears surprised Shane, so he took a step back to reconsider.

"Oh, my God . . . Please, no. Not little Carol . . . not her . . ." Nicky wailed. "Are you sure?"

"I identified the body."

Nicky sank down on the bed and began to weep. It sort of threw Shane, who was right in the middle of one of his patented tough-guy performances. It was disconcerting to all of a sudden have the mark start crying. But Shane reminded himself that Nicky Marcella was a street hustler, a con man who could probably break down and cry at a Tupperware party.

"Cut it out," Shane finally barked.

When Nicky looked up, his lower lip was trembling. "I didn't mean for anything to happen to her. Honest, Shane, I swear."

"Who did you tell? Somebody else wanted you to find her. Who were you working for?"

"Look, Shane . . ."

"Nicky, in about five seconds I'm going to introduce you to the biggest shithead on the LAPD. His name is Lou Ruta. He's not a prince like me. He's a farting, growling nightmare with a rubber hose. He caught Carol's murder and he's gonna hang it on the first person he can find who looks half good for it. He'll lock you up in one of the iso cells they got at County, and before he's done, you'll be confessing to the Black Dahlia murder."

"Okay . . . okay . . . but this is . . . this is kind a ticklish."

"No it's not, Nicky. It's murder. A brutal first-degree homicide. And you're gonna start spitting out info or I'm takin' you downtown."

Then Nicky told Shane a story he found almost impossible to believe.

14

NICKY'S STORY

"The guy I was trying to find her for is Dennis Valentine." Nicky actually whispered when he said the name, as if Valentine was some sort of godlike eminence.

"Who the fuck is Dennis Valentine?" Shane growled.

"Well, to begin with, his real name is Dennis Valente, but he Americanized it to Valentine. He's . . . he's related to Don Carlo DeCesare, the godfather in New Jersey. You musta heard of him. They call Don DeCesare 'Little Caesar.' Dennis's mother and Don Carlo are brother and sister, so he's, how you say, like his nephew."

"A made Mafia guy, right?"

"He's . . . well, he's . . ." Nicky stopped and looked at Shane in panic. "If this gets out, that I blew him in, my life is worth *bubkes*, y'know."

147

"Who is he, Nicky?"

"I told you."

Shane grabbed his silk shirt collar again.

"Okay, okay," Nicky stammered, "Dennis Valentine is like out here from New Jersey and he's tryin' to . . . how we say in film, get hooked up with talent vendors. He's opening up a film company."

"Wise Guy Productions?" Shane sneered.

"You laugh. But yeah . . ." Nicky took a deep breath to calm himself. "He's convinced that the key to power in L.A. is showbiz. It's our state's largest industry, even bigger than citrus now. Film is the perfect state industry. It's nonpolluting, labor and cash intense. These are words we use meaning —"

"I know what they mean," Shane interrupted. "Go on."

"Dennis says the State of California needs its film business to survive. 'Control showbiz and you control the entire State of California politically and economically.' And Valentine's not altogether incorrect. You see, Shane, according to California's tax base estimates, every dollar spent here gets multiplied seven times each year."

"What?" Shane was lost. "How d'ya figure that?"

"It gets spent seven times in twelve months. I pay the dollar to you, you pay it to your grocer, and your grocer pays it to his dry cleaner . . . like that. In a year, that same buck is spent seven times, and each time it gets spent, it gets taxed. So when you add up the seven multiple, showbiz is worth fifty, sixty billion a year to the California tax base. Control that, you got one fuck of a lot of power. Dennis thinks he can control it by taking over the show business unions."

"Can he do that?"

"Yeah, maybe . . . you see, in showbiz, we got what we call your above-the-line unions and your below-the-line unions. Boiling that down, your above-the-line handles all the creative people: writers, that's the Writers Guild of America — but to be frank, nobody gives a shit about writers, so forget the WGA. You also got SAG, the Screen Actors Guild. Then there's the big kahuna of all the guilds, the DGA, which is the directors' union. Directors are the real power players in film — the auteurs."

"And Dennis Valentine thinks he can organize a bunch of actors and directors? People who live in multimillion-dollar Malibu houses? What's he smoking?"

"No, no, Shane. He doesn't want to organize the above-the-line — those guys are untouchable. He wants to organize the *below*-the-line guys — the I.A."

"The I.A.? That's like an alliance of unions, right?"

"Exactly. The full name is IATSE, stands for International Alliance of Theatrical and Stage Employees. These unions include all the dumb everyday working stiffs who actually *make* the damn films — the grips, the set decorators, costumers, hair and makeup . . . like that." He grinned. "We call hair and makeup the 'pretty departments.' I think that's cute. You learn these terms when you're a player."

"I don't need the travelogue," Shane growled.

"Dennis thinks these below-the-line unions can be taken over. I think they've already bought some guys at the top, or threatened them — something. Anyway, IATSE is onboard already. Next, Dennis is going to use his uncle's contacts with the national brotherhoods in D.C. to put pressure on all these IATSE locals to negotiate with Dennis. Eventually, Dennis thinks he can control the cost of each film made in Hollywood."

"How?" Shane asked.

"If he says to a producer, 'You shoot your film and the unions will work at a cut rate,' the producer gets a great bargain, movie gets made. If he says, 'No deal, Mr. Producer, you gotta pay full boat,' or worse still, 'I'm gonna sock you with beaucoup overtime and a lotta expensive fringe bullshit,' then the producer gets screwed and his profits are destroyed. In so doing, Dennis thinks he can leverage that power to gain a percentage of ownership in the films made here. Pretty soon, nobody can shoot a union film in California without his say-so. See, he becomes like the czar of all filmed entertainment. That means he's got his hands around the throat of this sixty-billion-dollar tax base. He could call a strike, shut down the state, and all the schools would have to close. Even your fucking LAPD check would bounce. He becomes unstoppable, economically and politically. It's brilliant."

"You're screwing with me, aren't you?" Shane said.

"I swear. He's out here with his uncle's blessing, trying to set this up. I've been working with him on some deals. He knows I got connections. He's the one who wanted me to find Carol White."

"Why? What's he care about her?"

"We all went to Teaneck High together. We were all friends in the ninth grade."

"Awww, come on, Nicky . . . a class reunion?"

"Shane, it's true. Carol and Dennis were kinda the hot couple on campus back then. He was the BMOC, 'cause he was a big athlete and his uncle was the godfather of New Jersey. Carol was head cheerleader. She won some beauty contests, then came out here to be in films. Dennis used to make trips to L.A. to visit her. He and I hooked up 'cause I'd gone to USC film school, I'd learned my Yiddish by then. I could talk the talk. It was during one of those trips that he got the idea to take over the showbiz unions."

"Where is Valentine now?" Shane asked.

151

"He was living at the Bel Air Hotel, but he just moved to Kenny Rogers's old estate up on Mandeville Canyon Road. Thing's a mausoleum, sits on five acres. Musta cost him a fortune. Everything's real classy. He's not your normal garlic breather. He calls himself Champagne Dennis Valentine — drinks nothing but Taittinger, which he calls the champagne of champagnes. He's loaded with personality tics. He's a germ nut — won't even shake hands. He's a health-food nut, a vegetarian. Eats mostly broccoli and spinach. I swear, Shane, you go to his place for dinner and it's tofu and brown rice. I'd rather eat a hairball."

"And you're working for him?"

"I've got a co-production arrangement hammered out with his company, Heart-Shaped Films. Valentine . . . heart-shaped — get it? We're going to do a film or two. I'm doing a lot for him, like arranging the party tomorrow afternoon to introduce him to the big players in Hollywood — agents, managers, and such. I'm not going to accept some snowball definition of net profits or rolling break-even. My piece on our co-productions has to kick in from first-dollar gross, after P and A, of course." Nicky talking the talk.

"I haven't heard so much sleazy bullshit since Clinton testified."

Nicky held up his hand. "You aren't a player, so naturally you don't get it."

Maybe not, but Shane had been getting one

good idea. So he sat down on the edge of the bed beside the little grifter. "Guess what, Nick? This is your lucky day."

"I don't want a lucky day."

"Well, you got one. While you were just sitting here talking about your deal with this mobster, and this great life you finally got, I had a great idea."

"*Bubee,* ain't ya heard? There's a twenty-year-old reward out for a cop with a great idea."

"You're about to get a new fifty-fifty partner at Cine-Roma, and you're looking at him."

Now Nicky actually looked frightened. "Whatta you mean, 'partner'? Do I look like I want a partner?"

"Nicky, this isn't a negotiation. It's a condition. Either I come in for half of your company, or you take the pipe for Carol's murder. Say no, and I'll sell you so fast you'll think you're a used Bentley."

"Shane, why are you doing this to me?"

"Because I want this guy, Nicky. I think he killed Carol and I want him."

"Why? Why would he kill her? It makes no sense."

"Who knows why? Because he's a *goomba,* or because he eats too much broccoli. Maybe she knew his plans to infiltrate Hollywood and when she started shooting heroin, she became a liability and had to be fixed."

"Shane, he wouldn't do that."

"Or maybe she was shaking him down for

money, to buy drugs. Who knows? Look, Nicky, I'm not arguing here. You've got no choice."

Little Nicky looked at him and actually started to weep. Tears came down his face, although for some strange reason, this time he made no crying sounds. Then he got control of himself.

"How much are you gonna pay me for your end?" he finally said, hope reappearing on his tear-stained face. " 'Cause it won't be cheap. Cine-Roma has a book value of slightly over five mil. That's not counting goodwill with agents and distributors and unearned assets like future profits on *Boots and Bikinis*."

"Five mil sounds high." Shane opened his wallet and took out one dollar and handed it over. "How 'bout one dollar and other considerations? I believe that's the legal necessity to guarantee a contract in the State of California."

"No fucking way," Nicky howled.

"Don't lose sight of the fact that the other considerations in this case include my keeping you off Lou Ruta's suspect list. I'll have somebody in the LAPD Legal Affairs Department draw up the contract."

Nicky Marcella sat there looking at Shane for a long moment, then he finally sighed and nodded. "I guess we should say a prayer or something."

"You pray over deals?"

"No. I wanta pray for Carol. We should do

that, don't you think?"

Shane sat looking at him for a long moment, trying to assess if he was serious, and for some reason, Shane knew he was. It surprised him. But that was the thing about Nicky; he wasn't just one thing. He could catch you off balance. "Yeah, sure, let's do it," Shane agreed.

So they held hands while Nicky the Pooh bowed his head and prayed for Carol White's newly departed soul.

15

PARTNERS

Even though he didn't get home until three in the morning, Shane was up at six. He left the house shortly before Alexa and Chooch and headed to the Hollywood division. Today was the day he was supposed to go back on duty, but now he wondered if that was the right move.

Once he arrived at the Hollywood division, he went directly up the stairs to the computer room on the second floor.

"Hi ya, stranger," the morning-shift computer tech called out as Shane walked up. Shane couldn't remember the guy's last name, but like a lot of computer nerds at the LAPD, his nickname was Sparks.

"Hey, Sparks, you still hooked to Lexis-Nexis?" Shane asked.

He smiled and gave a thumbs-up.

LexisNexis is a search service that transcribes

legal publications and news. It's all-inclusive and references everything from newspapers and technical journals to the typed transcript of every episode of *Larry King Live*.

"Whatta you need?" Sparks asked.

"Can you see if there's anything on a guy named Dennis Valente — a.k.a. Valentine? He calls himself 'Champagne' Dennis. My guess is anybody who has that kind of handle probably likes to read his name in the papers."

"Got it . . . Valente . . . a.k.a. Valentine, 'Champagne' Dennis." Sparks turned and logged on, accessed the welcome screen for LexisNexis, then typed in Dennis's name and hit the screen designation for "All News." A few minutes later the screen flashed: fifty-eight stories. All of them under Valente's alias, Valentine.

"CITE 'em," Shane said. Sparks clicked the CITE command and topic sentences for each story appeared on the screen, along with the date and the original source the story had appeared in.

"Which ones do you want?" he asked.

Shane started scanning them. "That one, from the *New Jersey Sentinel* in 'ninety-five, 'Mobster Gets Producing Bug,' and the one from the March five, 'ninety-nine, Trenton paper, 'Valentine Goes Hollywood.' Lemme have last year's *Union Telegraph* piece, 'Champagne Corks Pop for New Showbiz Enterprise.' "

The rest looked like stories about his uncle: Don Carlo DeCesare. Shane picked one or two of these just for background, then asked Sparks to print everything.

The pages started spitting out into the tray across the room, and when the printer stopped, Shane picked up his articles and went to get some coffee in the little snack room downstairs.

He sat at a table and went through the articles, which ranged from 1995 to the present. Even when he was still busting heads for his uncle in Jersey, it looked as if Champagne Dennis Valentine was a show business wanna-be. There were no pictures of Valentine, because LexisNexis didn't supply photos, but he was described in one article as "a handsome Sonny Corleone type."

In one 1995 article, Dennis Valentine talked about "one day investing in a film." As Shane read on, he started to pick up a thread that fascinated him. Almost all of the stories mentioned Michael Fallon, a handsome, dark-haired movie star who had appeared in dozens of gangster or action flicks. In one story, he called Fallon "one of America's enduring filmic treasures." In another: "Fallon has redefined the essence of modern filmography with his extraordinary screen presence." In a third, Dennis Valentine had gushed, "My fondest dream would be to one day do a film with the great Michael Fallon."

Nowhere was Carol White mentioned.

At nine a.m., Shane pulled up to the front gate of Hollywood General Studios.

"I'm sorry, Mr. Marcella isn't in yet," the guard said. Shane got out of the car and walked up to the old, gray-haired man in the dark blue studio-issue uniform.

"Before you started doing this, were you by any chance on the job?" Shane asked.

"Yeah, thirty years in Marys," the guard replied. The Mary unit was cop slang for motorcycles.

Shane took out his badge and showed it to the man. "I'm working a gig here, undercover. I'm gonna be getting a parking pass and an office today. If I need any backup down the line, can I count on you for help?"

"In a heartbeat, Sergeant," the guard responded. "I'm sick and tired of smelling pot in these cars and taking shit from these twits. I used ta kick ass for that shit, now I gotta call 'em sir."

"Can you give me a little background on Nick Marcella?" Shane asked.

The old motorcycle cop had plenty to say. He filled Shane's ear for almost half an hour.

Nicky didn't arrive until eleven-thirty, parking the maroon Bentley in one of his two spaces. Shane's black Acura was in the other. The guard had told Shane that Nicky usually poached that second spot to protect his side panels.

Shane was standing just inside the glass door in the entry hall of Building Six, watching as Nicky got out of his Bentley. He glared at Shane's car before kicking the side of the Acura, leaving a scuff mark. Then he grabbed his heavy briefcase and headed toward the entry. When he walked through the lobby doors and saw Shane waiting, he came to an abrupt halt.

"What the fuck are you doing here?" he blurted.

"Don't tell me you forgot about our deal already, partner."

"I've got casting. There are thirty girls coming in today and I'm already an hour late."

"No *problemo*, I let 'em all go."

Nicky glared at Shane. "I beg your pardon?"

"I let 'em go, Nicky. They're not here. *Pfft* . . . gone."

Nicky stalked toward the corridor door and went through. Twenty empty chairs were lined up along the wall with script sides on the seats.

"This fucking pisses me off. I have the investors coming in for final callbacks with Milos today. I'm looking to roll film in three weeks. Milos has another film booked. I can't push back 'cause he's scheduled to do a huge big-budget Western at Fox in three months. You don't understand this business, *boychik*. Our little whatever-it-was last night is not a legal deal, it was achieved under duress. I'm reneging."

Shane grabbed Nicky by the coat collar and yanked him down the hall toward the same empty office they had used yesterday.

"Get your hands off me. Stop pulling me around. I'm not a fucking albacore."

Shane dragged him into the office and closed the door, then pushed Nicky, hard. The little man stumbled backward and landed in the swivel chair. Shane closed in on him and leaned down into his face. "Nicky, let's you and me get something straight, okay? You are an accessory to first-degree murder. *Murder one!* So don't fuck with me. Beyond that, I've been asking around, checking out this operation of yours. Cine-Roma Productions is just another one of your storefront street hustles with better props and girls in short-shorts."

"I beg your pardon?" Nicky said, trying for some righteous indignation.

"You've been casting this same movie for three years, and from what I hear, the only thing Milos should direct is traffic. His last job was an episode of "Mr. Ed, The Talking Horse," thirty years ago. Back when I was in Hollywood Vice, I worked some of these show-biz hustles. You want my take on this one?" Nicky didn't answer, so Shane charged ahead. "You've got these poor *actresses* coming in for casting, but my source tells me they're just students enrolled in *your* acting school in San Diego."

"How did you find out about San Diego Artisans?" he sputtered indignantly.

"You get the attractive female students in your acting class up here, and also pass your cards out to every pretty girl you see, along with some tired 'You oughta be in pictures' B.S. They all come here dressed like contestants in the Miss Tropicana Contest, thinking they may actually get cast in this movie of yours. The investors, my source says, get fed up and change periodically. They're just a buncha horny dentists who you've talked into putting up small amounts of preproduction money so they can sit in on casting sessions and see pretty girls in heels and short-shorts. You get the girls who are desperate enough to sleep with the investors or party with them so they'll stick around and put more money into this turkey. But there is no preproduction and you just spend the money to live on. That's the movie part of the scam, but you're also working a photo scam. New head shots for these girls at four hundred dollars a sheet, where the sleazeball photographer kicks back half to you. Add that all up and you have a pretty good criminal picture of Cine-Roma Productions."

Nicky was sitting in the swivel chair, breathing hard and looking pale. "I resent that, Shane. You hurt me deeply."

"Really? Shall we take it downtown, then?"

Nicky looked out the window, close to tears.

"The only thing that's keeping you out of the felony lockup is your tenuous connection to Dennis Valentine, who I think killed Carol White. If I can turn that into something, then maybe . . . just maybe . . . you won't do another stretch for this horseshit."

"I don't want to run a hustle on Valentine," Nicky said. "The guy is a killer. He's a made guy, Shane. I won't work him. If he finds out I'm setting him up, he'll feed me to the fish."

"Nicky, I don't like hearing words like *don't* and *won't*. These are bad words, okay? These are words that put you straight back on the main tier at Soledad. The kind of words I wanna hear are *can do* and *will do* and *What's next, Shane?* These words keep you breathing my air. The first time you disappoint me, Nicky, I'm gonna put the bracelets on and roll you up like a Turkish rug."

"You're gonna get us both killed."

"Be brave. It hasn't happened yet."

"I've gotta tell the investors we're not gonna cast today," Nicky said, pouting.

"Done," Shane said. "They left an hour ago. See what an efficient partner I can be?"

"Why are you doing this to me?"

Shane moved around the desk, sat on the corner, and looked down at Nicky, who seemed terrified of him, or Valentine, or maybe just of life in general. "Nicky, you used me to find Carol. I found her, and I don't know how it happened, but she got to me. Some part of me, Nicky, has been sitting around lately wondering why I'm here, why I'm a cop, why I even bother anymore. But when I saw her hanging from that rafter, I promised myself somebody was gonna finally give a shit what happened to Carolyn White. If Dennis Valentine killed her, he's going down for it. And if I have to waste you to make that happen, that works, too."

Half an hour later they were in Nicky's office with the door closed. Nicky was pacing. "Michael Fallon?!" he said. "You gotta be kidding! This guy gets megabucks to star in films."

"So?" Shane answered.

"I hate to introduce you to the economic realities of film production, *bubee,* but making big-budget movies requires big bucks. We don't have big bucks. How the hell can we afford Michael Fallon, whose last quote was near twenty million, if I recall what I read in the trades? How do we get a *macher* like him to work for us?"

"Okay, all these big stars have pet projects, right?"

"Huh?"

"John Wayne had *The Alamo,* remember? Worked for next to nothing to get it made."

"Old news, bunkie. You may not have heard, but the Duke's dead. Man hit the slab more than twenty years ago."

"Okay, John Travolta, then. *Battleship Earth.*"

"Better," Nicky conceded.

"These stars are all in the script market, so all we gotta do is find out what script Michael Fallon is passionate about and wants to make, then we option it."

"You don't want to make the script that Michael wants to make," Nicky said.

"So there *is* one. . . ."

"Yeah, it's like a cocktail party joke in this town. It's radioactive. Nobody should touch it without wearing a lead vest."

"It can't be that bad," Shane said, warming to the fact that his plan might actually have some merit. "On the bright side, if nobody wants it, the price will probably be in a range we can afford."

"Oh, ye of little understanding." Nicky put his ferretlike face in his hands.

"Tell me, Nicky."

"It's called *The Neural Surfer.* Forget that it makes no sense and starts with the ending and ends with the beginning. Forget its simian logic and clunky dialogue. There's a bigger problem. It was written by a holy man, and I use the term generously. He's really more of a cultist and a con man. The author of this New Age turd is a guy named Rajindi Singh, the grand mucky ducky of the Singh Church of Meditation and Herbal Healing."

"I can live with that."

"Live with this: He's also a certifiable nut

case who thinks that his screenplay, *The Neural Surfer*, is biblical. I haven't read it, but from the coverage, the story all takes place in Singh's mind. It's about his schizophrenic battle with his changing concept of life, and the new concepts materialize as monsters called neural dragons and they fight with him. There are nightmare sequences called neural storms and corny life lessons that are two-page soliloquies that sound like old Jimmy Swaggart sermons. It's drivel. Singh has a price tag of two hundred thousand for a six-month option. Beyond that, he's insisting on no changes. It's impossible to even rewrite this turkey. And Shane, we *are* talking turkey here. This script is a Thanksgiving feast, a feather-covered gobbler."

"Then why does Michael Fallon want to make it?"

"Fallon's also some kinda Grand Pooh-bah in the Singh Church of Meditation and Herbal Healing. He's a minister and a true believer. He worships Rajindi Singh. They go on retreats together. He's as nuts as the writer. Are you getting the picture, *bubee?* This is lose-lose. The script is uglier than a hemorrhoid cluster."

"Cine-Roma is going to option it."

Nicky groaned.

"If Michael Fallon wants to make *The Neural Surfer*, he'll work for us on the cheap. Dennis Valentine worships Michael Fallon, ergo, if we control the material, we get Michael Fallon, and Michael Fallon gets us Dennis Valentine.

166

It's perfect. Valentine will come to us. *He'll* solicit *us*, not the other way around."

"Why does that matter?"

"If we solicit him, he'll be suspicious. He's gonna have his guard up. However, if it's his idea to go into business with us, we gotta new ball game. He's ours."

"How are we gonna get the two hundred K to option this thing?"

"We're gonna sell your Bentley." Shane smiled.

"Fuck you, it's rented," Nicky snarled. "Everything I have is rented, right down to this." He went to the shelves and took down a gold statuette, turned it over, and read the tag aloud. "Property of The Hand Prop Room, Hollywood, California." He glared at Shane. "See, no money."

"I'll get the money," Shane said, and got to his feet. "I want you to set up an appointment with Rajindi Singh's agent and then I want to meet Dennis Valentine, but it's gotta be casual. It can't look planned. That party you mentioned you're throwing for him sounds perfect."

"Shane, this is off my scale. I hate to admit this, but I'm something of a coward."

"Nicky, you'd better not wobble on me, guy. I'm looking for backup."

"Shane, I'll . . ."

"Do it for Carol."

Then Nicky surprised him again. He lowered his eyes and spoke softly. "You know, when we

167

were kids, when everybody picked on me, Carol always made 'em stop." He smiled at the memory. "She was such great-looking quiff, the guys at my school all wanted to please her. 'Don't tease Nicky the Pooh,' she would say. 'Nicky is my friend.' " Then he looked up and again Shane saw tears in the little grifter's eyes. "God, I'm so sad she ended up a junkie and a prostitute. I should have known. If I had, maybe I could have stopped it. I'm so sad she died that way."

Nicky Marcella was a complicated guy.

16

TOP COP

Shane was fifteen minutes late for his two o'clock meeting with Chief Filosiani because he had stopped by the LAPD computer center in the Valley to collect more research. Alexa was waiting for him on the sixth floor of Parker Center as he came off the elevator, lugging his newly filled briefcase. His wife had an armload of gang folders crammed with yellow sheets; she seemed irritated and tired. Shane couldn't ever remember her looking so stressed.

"Jesus, where've you been?" she asked.

"Alexa, I need to talk to you before I talk to the chief."

"Not now. We're already a quarter of an hour late. The chief is scheduled on half-hour intervals. He's asked me to attend the meeting."

"Okay, good. Then you can back me up."

They hurried down the hall and stopped before the large double doors that led to Filosiani's office. Alexa walked him in and Shane found himself in the chief of police's outer office.

Filosiani's secretary was a hawk-faced woman named Bea; she looked like Whistler's mother in a blue pantsuit but had a heart the size of Texas. She knew they were late and showed them right in.

Filosiani's office was huge. The Day-Glo Dago had taken the antique furniture and expensive wall art that had filled the office of ex-chief Burl Brewer and sold them at auction, using the money to buy state-of-the-art Ultima flack vests for the SWAT teams. He was a no-frills guy from Brooklyn who, in the wake of Brewer's corruption, had proven to be just what the LAPD needed. The office was now furnished like a Xerox room. A long metal table sat next to one wall under a bulletin board with pushpins holding up each division's crime stat sheets. In counterpoint to all this was a breathtaking view of the Financial District through the huge plate-glass windows. Chief Tony Filosiani was standing in the center of the room grinning as Shane and Alexa came through the door.

"How'sa guy?" he caroled. He was a shade under five-foot-five and his fat, round pie-pan of a face framed piercing blue eyes that sparkled under a pate of shiny pink skin. Chief Filosiani would have been perfectly typecast to play the butcher at your corner market, but he hardly looked like he should be running one of the largest and most complex law enforcement agencies in the world.

"We're finally getting you back on the job." Filosiani beamed. "Alexa told me you want Special Crimes, so if dat's what you want, dat's where we're gonna put ya." All of this in his trademark Brooklynese.

"It's what I want, Chief, but I have something I need to tell you and Alexa about first."

"Okay." Filosiani glanced at his watch.

"Last coupla days, I think I may have inadvertently stumbled into something, and if it's what I think it is, it could be big, and it needs to be worked immediately."

This was all news to Alexa. A frown appeared on her sculpted face. Of course, for the last two days she'd been practically living at Parker Center, so she and Shane hadn't had much chance to talk.

"Let's hear," Filosiani said.

So Shane launched into the story, first telling the chief about finding Nicky Marcella at Farrell's party. He went on to recount Nicky's criminal past, and his request that Shane find a missing actress named Carol White so Nicky could cast her in a movie he was producing. He told them how he had found Carol and that she had become a hooker, that he'd left his card with her. Then Shane told them about the call from Sergeant DePass, and the meeting with

171

Ruta at the house on 11th Street, leaving out his distressing evaluation of Ruta's demeanor and police skills. He went on to explain that he went to Nicky's apartment later that night, and how he forced the little grifter to admit that he'd been trying to find Carol for a New Jersey mobster named Dennis Valente who had changed his name to Valentine.

Here Shane opened his briefcase and pulled out the research he'd been doing on Valentine and the DeCesare family. He handed it to Tony Filosiani, who scanned it quickly.

"This guy's a made DeCesare soldier. I know him," Filosiani said. "Some of these Jersey mob guys did business on my old beat back East. I know the whole family. A buncha mouth-breathers."

"Then you know that if Don Carlo is trying to locate a branch of his crime family in L.A., we don't want to ignore him."

Filosiani nodded and handed the pages back.

Shane explained about Valentine's plan to organize the below-the-line show business unions.

By this time, the chief's next meeting was waiting in his outer office, but Filosiani was hooked. He buzzed Bea and asked her to re-schedule it, then turned back to Shane.

"Is that possible? To get entertainment unions t'kick back money?"

"I don't know," Shane admitted. "I'm just telling you what Nicky told me. It sounded plausible, but I guess all that really counts is that Valentine believes it."

Filosiani nodded and Shane continued. He explained Valentine's fascination with Michael Fallon and how Shane wanted to option a script called *The Neural Surfer* so Fallon would, hopefully, agree to star in it.

"Who's gonna pay for the script?"

"You are. At least that's what I was hoping. I thought we could run it off the Organized Crime Bureau's budget."

"How much?"

"Two hundred thousand," Shane said, and heard Alexa gasp from someplace behind him.

Now Filosiani was frowning, too.

"Okay, look, I know this is kinda unconventional, but let's look past the fact that it's a script I'm buying, and focus on what we're trying to do." Shane was now pitching like an Amway salesman. "In the past, when we've heard mob guys were heading into town, we spent heavy bread to convince 'em to go home. We had people meet 'em at the airport, followed them around in white vans, bugged 'em and ran surveillance on 'em, the whole Blue Plate Special."

"So?" Filosiani said.

"So, how much did all that cost?"

"Plenty."

Shane opened his briefcase again, took out some papers and started shuffling through them. "I dropped by the budget office this afternoon, and here's what I found. In 'ninety-six, we worked a crew of Gambino guys. They were planning on setting up a sports-betting franchise in L.A. Cost us three hundred grand for wiretaps and round-the-clock surveillance. It went on for two months before they got tired of us and went home. In 'ninety-nine, we worked a crew of Arcado guys from Chicago. Same drill, little less — cost one-fifty."

"Okay, okay . . . I admit we spent some OCB money to keep these guys at bay," Filosiani said, "but we weren't buying movie scripts."

"All I'm doing is spending money to lock this guy up. This script will bring us Fallon. Fallon will bring us Valentine. I wanna work Valentine from the inside, be right next to him. I wanna set up a RICO case for union fixing and I want to see if the SOB killed Carol White."

There was a heavy silence. Shane heard a clock ticking somewhere but couldn't spot it.

"How you gonna work from the inside?" Alexa finally asked. "Everybody knows you're a cop. He's not gonna let you get very close."

"I'm not gonna hide it. In fact, I'm gonna talk about it. We put on a show. Instead of putting me back on the job, the chief knocks me down in grade because of stuff he discovered in this yearlong review I've been under. I get pissed off and quit. We get Press Relations to plant a big story about it tomorrow in the *L.A. Times*. Call it trouble in the ranks or some-

174

thing. That's where you come in, Alexa."

"Me?"

"The mob has never had a foothold in L.A. because L.A. cops have never been for sale. You're gonna change that. I want to set you up for Dennis Valentine so he'll try and buy you."

"The head of DSG?" She sighed.

"Yeah, he'll go for it 'cause in that newspaper story, after I get trashed, it's going to mention how angry you are that your husband got screwed. Maybe a few guarded quotes about the LAPD's lack of support, given the fact I just won the Medal of Valor. Then the chief's comments follow. He says I'm off the page and untrustworthy. Maybe kicks some mud on your reputation, expresses some doubt about the open gang war that's breaking out and the way the Kevin Cordell investigation is being handled."

Alexa was tired, her nerves were frayed, and she sort of lost her temper at that. "Can't I just do my job without all this? Besides, we just got that case. It's not even fifty hours old."

"Don't lose your temper, honey," Shane said.

Alexa stiffened slightly. This was a police meeting. She was Shane's boss as well as the head of DSG. He instantly knew he shouldn't have called her "honey."

He pushed on. "I'll tell you why. Once I get close to him, I'm gonna set you up to be his inside person, his Judas on the department. You're the acting head of DSG, so you're the perfect choice. You could control any investigation we started up against him."

"He's not gonna believe that."

"Yes he is, because he *wants* to believe it. If we do it right, he'll jump at it. We're also gonna be living way over our heads. We're gonna look like we have big money problems."

"We live in Venice, Shane. You can't live any more economically than we do."

"I wanna move out of there for this case. I've got the perfect place staked out and it won't cost the department a thing. Tony, you remember that house on North Chalon Road in Beverly Hills? The one our drug team took down six months ago, belonged to some Guatemalan heroin dealers?"

"Yeah."

"It's an asset seizure, we own it. Furniture's still in there. All we gotta do is cut the lawn and we're ready for business."

"You got this all worked out, don't you?" Filosiani said, trying not to smile.

"Yep. All I need is a measly two hundred large."

Now the chief paced in his nearly empty office. He stopped in front of the huge plate-glass window and stared out, looking small and round-shouldered against that huge expanse of glass. "I can't give you two hundred thousand for a screenplay, Shane. I'll get laughed out of my budget review."

"Gimme half, then. Gimme a hundred."

"Can you do it for a hundred?"

"I don't know. I can try."

Finally, Filosiani turned, and now his round face was beaming. "Okay, you got it — plus the house on North Chalon. But Shane, you should sweep it daily. Go to the Electronic Surveillance Division and check out one a them new twenty-three-hundred Frequency Finders we got from the feds last June. Little unit will pick up anything, even low-voltage VHF stuff." He grabbed his phone and instructed Bea to call ESD and make one available. When he hung up, he said, "I know these mob smart-heads, they're all paranoid. Even though Valentine's gonna be coming to you, he's still gonna wanna know what you're saying when he's not around. If he puts a bug in that house and we can find it, we can use it against him."

"Good thinking," Shane agreed.

"Okay, get the hell outta here. You're officially back on duty. You're gonna be working U.C. but you don't report to Organized Crime. You report directly to Lieutenant 'Honey' here." He grinned and Alexa sighed.

"That's gonna make it easy, 'cause she's gonna be living with me in that house on North Chalon Road."

"Nice of you to ask," Alexa quipped.

Filosiani tore off a slip of paper and handed it to Alexa. "Give this to the budget office down the hall. They'll set up a blind account for Sergeant Scully so he can write checks on the hundred grand. Then get together with Press Relations and draft the story. I want to see it by five tonight. Tell Captain Cook I want it in tomorrow's paper." Filosiani grinned. "Welcome back, Shane. I miss this kinda stuff. You come up with great ideas."

Shane and Alexa left the chief's office and headed down the hall. She was strangely quiet.

"Let's get something to eat," she finally said. "I've been inside this damn building since seven this morning, I need to get outta here for a minute."

The Peking Duck was a cop restaurant one block from Parker Center. It was almost three in the afternoon. The late-lunch crowd had already left so the place was unusually quiet. Shane and Alexa ordered two beers at the bar, then carried them to a booth by the wall. When the Chinese waiter arrived they ordered dim sum and egg rolls.

"You're kinda quiet, whatta ya think?" Shane said.

"I think you're out of your mind," Alexa answered. "You and Tony . . . it was like the Bowery Boys in there. 'You're my favorite guy. I miss dis kinda stuff. You always come up widda best ideas.'" She was doing a reasonably good Day-Glo Dago impression, but at least when she was through, she was more or less smiling. She reached out and took his hand.

"You think you fool everybody, Shane, but I

read you like the morning paper."

"That badly written?"

"That transparent. I watched you when you told him about that dead prostitute, Carol White. He didn't see what I saw. He didn't see the sadness and the guilt." She was squeezing his hand across the table.

The waiter returned and put their food down, then handed them chopsticks and left.

"You don't owe her anything, honey," she said.

"Yeah . . . ?"

"You don't. I mean, it's fine you want to run Valentine off. I agree with you there. If he gets a foothold in L.A. we'll end up spending millions trying to police him. So tie him up on a RICO prosecution, but leave Carol White's murder to homicide."

"Yeah, good thinking." For some reason this was making him angry.

"If Valentine had her killed, it was a professional hit," she continued. "The guys who did the work are already back in Jersey."

He didn't answer, so she went on. "I'm just saying, let homicide do the Carol White investigation. I've got good people on that."

"You got a drunk, overweight dirtbag on it. Lou Ruta is the primary. He's gonna work it for the minimum forty-eight hours required on an active homicide, then it's gonna go in the cold case file because he thinks she was just a junkie whore and he doesn't want to waste his precious time on her."

"I'll make a reassignment. I'll give it to Sergeant Peterson. You know Swede; you like him. He's a hard worker."

"He's in Hollywood, not Rampart."

"You're quibbling. I'll talk to both division commanders and set it up."

"Okay," he said, and took a swig of beer. It tasted flat.

"You know, I do love you for caring."

"Yeah."

"No, really."

"Look, Alexa, I know you mean well here and I know you're trying to make me feel better. But do me a favor: Let's save this for later, okay?"

"Done," she agreed. "So how 'bout them Dodgers, huh?" She was bone-tired but suddenly smiling, trying to help him get past it.

His wife was beautiful. She could take his breath away. She was funny, tough, smart, loyal, and she was his. So why couldn't he forget about Carol White? *Why am I acting like such a rookie over this?*

"Wait'll you see our new house on North Chalon. You're gonna love it," he said.

"*It was down to just me and Brooke . . .*" Carol whispered in his memory.

"Another beer?" the Chinese waiter asked.

17

THE ART OF THE DEAL

"These guys are soulless killers," Nicky was saying. Despite the frigid air-conditioning, he had started sweating; the collar and front of his silk shirt were drenched. They were sitting in the magnificent lobby at CAA, one of the most powerful and respected talent agencies in show business.

"You gotta let me do all the talking, *bubeleh*," Nicky instructed. "I know how these deals are made. Singh's agent, Jerry Wireman, is a fire-breathing serpent, a *gontser macher*. He's gonna want his pound of flesh."

"How can it be that tough? We've got a hundred thousand dollars. They've got a script that's collecting dust. We trade."

"The hundred large is *bubkes* . . . parking meter cash. You gotta readjust your thinking, babe."

"What time is Dennis Valentine's party?" Shane asked, trying to change the subject.

"It's at six this evening in the garden patio of the Beverly Hills Hotel. The guy loves that hotel; drives all the way from Mandeville Canyon in the Palisades to have what he calls his power breakfasts in the Polo Lounge every morning at ten. Only he eats alone or with one a his apes, so it's more like breakfast at the zoo." Nicky's gaze shifted down to Shane's blazer. "Where'd you get that thing?" He scowled. "The Navy Surplus store?"

"What thing?" Shane looked down at his jacket.

"If you're gonna be my partner, we gotta do something about your threads. You dress like an NBC page. 'Zat tie left over from when you were in the Boy Scouts?"

Shane glanced down at his plain blue tie. When he'd picked it out this morning he thought it looked nice with his dark blue blazer. Now, in the harsh sunlight streaming through the glass lobby of CAA, he had to admit it was pretty cheesy.

"Mr. Wireman is ready to see you," a very attractive black woman said from behind her two-ton semicircular, granite reception desk. Roman legions had held passes in the Alps with smaller fortifications. Shane and Nicky stood.

"Sixth floor, end of the hall," the receptionist said. "His secretary, Barbara, is waiting for you."

Barbara was pretty enough to be an actress herself. She led them down a very busy corridor where hyperfocused secretaries of both sexes were hammering out deal memos and contracts on computer keyboards. She showed them into Jerry Wireman's office.

The agent was aptly named: wiry body, wiry hair, wire glasses, wire-gray eyes . . . Wireman. He exuded all the personal warmth of marble statuary.

"Sit. What's up?" That was all he said. He made it clear by his elimination of all superfluous words that he had a minimal amount of time for them.

They sat.

"Go."

This guy is going to be a treat, Shane thought.

He waited for Nicky, who was their predesignated talker, but Nicky didn't say anything. Shane looked over and saw that his new partner had frozen. He was just sitting there, his hands clasped together, breathing through his mouth, jaw clenched. Sofa art.

"Go," Jerry Wireman repeated impatiently, frowning at his Cartier timepiece as if the watch dial contained distressing results from his last cholesterol test.

"Mr. Wireman, Mr. Marcella and I are partners in Cine-Roma Productions," Shane started.

"Never heard of it."

"Yes, well, we have become extremely interested in a script I believe you represent, called *The Neural Surfer*, by Rajindi Singh."

"Great merchandise. *Ferae naturae* — a term we use, meaning full of untamed nature. That product has endless shelf life. It's why we've been in no hurry to accept an offer. *The Neural Surfer* demands concept-friendly execution."

Shane looked over at Nicky, who was now sweating big drops. They were dampening and curling his hairline. He seemed to have gone into some kind of semiconscious trance. "Jerry, we share your enthusiasm for the material," Shane finally said.

"Hard not to," Wireman said. "Piece is transitional .. . . transcendental. It blends neo-impressionist heroism with gut-wrenching social commentary."

"Exactly." Shane didn't have a clue what he had just agreed with.

"Okay, good deal." Wireman glared at his watch again and frowned. He looked as if he were about to start tapping the dial.

"So gimme the drill," he suddenly said. "Does Cine-Nova want to buy it?"

"Cine-Roma," Shane corrected him. "Not buy it just yet. What we'd like is to get an option."

"A priori of that, we have an existing quote sheet on this material, and I'm afraid our price is solid. We're not negotiating."

"Apre-what?" Shane asked, bewildered.

"A priori," Wireman responded, "means conceived beforehand." He looked at them askance. They didn't understand Latin. They had just lost important player points.

"Oh, I see," Shane said. "So what *is* the price?"

"The cheapest, front-end-friendly option I can offer is two hundred thousand for six months. The important non-negotiable soft clauses include no rewriting or line changes without Mr. Singh's written approval, and all rights revert back to Mr. Singh in six months. Absolutely no extensions — *hoc tempore.*"

Shane wanted to hit him, but said instead, "That sounds like a pretty tough deal."

"We're talking filmatic breakthrough here. This isn't *Charlie's Angels* where you got three gorgeous chicks running around in see-through dresses. This is a work of inestimable depth — *fac et excusa.*"

"Huh?" Nicky grunted from the sofa, finally reentering Earth's atmosphere.

"Means make your move. This is a straight yes-or-no proposition."

Shane was close to feeding this asshole his wire-rimmed glasses. He looked over at Nicky, who was still leaking water like a Mexican fishing boat.

"We don't have two hundred thousand to pay for an option," Shane said.

"*Tempus omnia revelat.*" Wireman sneered. "Time reveals everything. . . . Catch ya on the flip-flop." He stood, shot his cuffs, and motioned toward the door.

"Excuse me, we have a counterproposal," Shane interjected.

Jerry Wireman wrinkled his nose as if the strange smell of decaying flesh had just wafted into his office through the air vent. "Go." They no longer merited even a short Latin phrase.

Nicky looked like he was about to start convulsing.

"We'll pay you one hundred thousand for a one-month option," Shane continued. "All rights revert back to Mr. Singh at that time. If we have not set the script up at a studio or obtained our financing within a month, we may need another month extension. I'm willing to pay you an additional one hundred thousand for that second month."

Jerry sat back down behind his desk, grabbed a yellow pad and made some notes. "Interesting." He leered. "So restating it *per gradus*, what you want, in essence, is a step-deal on a short clock for the same two hundred. I like that. We come off our stated front-end price, and you tighten up the timetable with two option bumps . . . that could fly. Of course, we're gonna need ten back-end points calculated from first-dollar gross, against a purchase price of two million, or ten percent of the budget, whichever is higher."

"No problem."

"And there are some boilerplate creative and approval issues. Nothing too onerous."

"Let's draw it up," Shane said.

"What was that name again?"

"Shane Scully."

"The Big Double S." Wireman smiled warmly. In seconds, Shane had gone from an extreme annoyance to the Big Double S. Showbiz. "I like the way you do business, guy," Wireman enthused. "Let's get this into memo form and you can write the agency the first check to hold the deal in place."

"Sounds good," Shane said.

Then everybody was smiling except for Nicky, who seemed to have turned into stone — *hoc tempore*.

An hour later Shane had written the check for one hundred thousand, draining the bank account Alexa had just set up. He learned that Michael Fallon was also a CAA client. In fact, Wireman informed them that it was Fallon who had arranged for Rajindi Singh's representation at the agency. Jerry Wireman agreed to arrange a breakfast meeting with Fallon for ten the next morning at the Polo Lounge. Then Shane and Nicky signed the deal memo.

An hour and a half after arriving at CAA, they were walking out of the air-conditioned lion's den, back into the late afternoon L.A. heat, heading toward Nicky's maroon Bentley.

"You have just made the shittiest script deal in the entire one-hundred-year history of moviemaking," Nicky groused. He was out of his trance, and angry.

"Filmmaking," Shane corrected. "And what the hell happened to you? I've seen lawn jockeys with more on their minds."

"Whatever. One month for a hundred grand, ten gross points against ten percent of the budget for a screenplay that was written by a drooling idiot? We should be put in Bellevue for this deal."

"Nicky, we're not gonna make the film. It's not ever going to get shot. Got that through your fuzzy head? The hundred grand just ties up the script for a month. After that, I've either got Valentine in jail, or it's over. This is a sting, not a film deal."

"This is *farchadat,* is what it is — crazy. When this gets out, my reputation is in the shitter."

They got into the Bentley and Nicky put it in gear. He looked tiny, peeking over the wheel of the mammoth car. But Shane had to admit he loved the smell of the English leather interior, and made a resolution that, whenever possible from this point forward, he would ride with Nicky.

Then they headed across town to pick up Shane's car at the studio, before going on to the six o'clock A-list party for the New Jersey mobster at the Beverly Hills Hotel.

18

CHAMPAGNE DENNIS VALENTINE

Nicky steered Shane through the double doors onto the hotel patio, near a small grassy courtyard. Shafting late-afternoon sunlight cut through the landscaped date palms and splashed the small patio, painting it orange. Waiters in red coats served champagne in fluted glasses and hors d'oeuvres with caviar centers.

Everybody at the party looked as if they were just out of college. Shane guessed the average age to be around twenty-two. Across the patio, Dennis Valentine was working the meager crowd. He seemed angry; his jaw kept clenching.

Shane stood with Nicky, off toward the back of the party near the patio door, observing the New Jersey mobster. He was about Shane's age and had a shock of curly black hair that hung down loosely on his forehead, a bad-boy haircut that Shane was sure Valentine thought the girls adored. He was dressed in a beautiful dove-gray suit, open at the collar. There were plenty of glittering accessories twinkling at his cuffs and on his fingers. He wore gold chains instead of a tie, and his teeth lined up like polished rows of tombstones. He had full, sensuous lips . . . the guy was a fox . . . at least a nine.

"Good-looking," Shane observed.

Nicky scowled. "He gets more ass than a redneck at a family reunion. Be sure and try the champagne. It's Taittinger."

"Who are these people?"

"Players . . . heavy hitters."

"Do any of them have their driver's licenses yet?"

"It's a young business, *bubee*. You hit thirty, you're as good as dead at the studios. We make films for preteen puberty cases. That's your audience today, everybody else is just theater-seat garbage. That teen audience skew gives younger executives positions of power."

After ten minutes, Dennis Valentine was closing in on them. He saw Nicky and a scowl cut deep lines in his handsome tanned face. He excused himself from the group he was talking to and came over.

"What the fuck happened?" he said to Nicky without preamble.

"Whatta you talking about?" Nicky turned

190

pale. Shane thought he might have even flinched when Valentine spoke.

"These people are a buncha secretaries and assistants. Where're the players? It's like every heavy hitter we invited gave their fucking invitation to some flunky."

"They wouldn't do that," Nicky hedged.

"That one over there." He pointed to a pretty dark-haired girl with curly hair and jutting breasts. "She's a Xerox operator at the William Morris office. She copies scripts to go out to actors. Her boss gave her his invite."

"Oh, well, I'm sure —"

"And that guy with the eyebrow pierce. He's some agency guy's driver."

"Look, Dennis, one of the things you're gonna come to learn is that in the biz, these younger assistant-type people will shortly end up in positions of extreme power, and it never hurts to cultivate relationships with up-and-coming —"

"This fucking party is costing me a fortune!" Valentine interrupted. "I didn't throw it so I could get to know a buncha elevator operators and parking lot attendants."

"Yes . . . yes . . . well, let me get into this, Dennis."

"I'm gonna beat the cost a this bash outta you, a dollar at a time," Valentine fumed.

Nicky Marcella had turned the exact same shade of white as the lace cloth decorating the silver hors d'oeuvre tray that was just being thrust in front of them.

Dennis Valentine turned and looked at Shane. "Jesus. How'd you get in? You already grew up."

"Dennis, this is my new partner at Cine-Roma, Shane Scully." Nicky was trembling as Shane stuck out his hand.

"I don't shake hands. Germs. It's a thing with me," Dennis said.

"Right. How ya doing?" Shane asked.

"Not so hot."

"I can see."

"Well, gotta go," Shane said to Nicky. "I'm meeting Mike Fallon tomorrow at the Polo Lounge for breakfast. Ten o'clock. Why don't you join us?"

"Okay," the little grifter agreed. Then Shane started to shake hands again with Dennis Valentine but caught himself, pulled back and smiled.

"Sorry. Forgot. Nice to meet you." Shane turned and left Nicky Marcella to tell Dennis Valentine the tale.

Once he was off the patio and into the adjoining restaurant, Shane stopped and looked back through the tinted-glass window. He could see Nicky talking. Dennis Valentine was leaning forward, listening intently. At least the little grifter hadn't frozen this time. Shane didn't have to be there to read the result. Valentine had a hungry shark look on his heavy, masculine face. He was nodding and looking toward the door Shane had just disappeared through.

It was six-fifteen p.m. when Shane left the hotel, so he stayed off the freeway to avoid traffic and used surface streets to get to the office of Drug Enforcement on the fourth floor of Parker Center, downtown. He picked up the keys to the asset seizure house on North Chalon Road, then called Alexa and Chooch on their cell phones and made an appointment to meet them there at eight, suggesting they stop by the Venice house to pack overnight bags. After hanging up, he still had well over an hour, and there was something else he'd been meaning to do.

He called Alexa's office, got the new LAPD secure computer code from her adjutant, then accessed Carol White's home address from the Vice mainframe. She lived on Temple Street in Rampart, a few blocks west of Coronado.

Shane pulled up in front of a sad-looking two-story cream-and-brown apartment house. There was an old homeless woman decorating the curb out front. Parked on the grass next to her was a Vons market wire basket; a silver chariot crammed to overflowing with her priceless possessions. The woman was ageless, anywhere from thirty to sixty, dressed in fatigues and an old Army Surplus blanket cut like a poncho, with a hole in the center for her head. When Shane got out of his car and started past her, he could hear her moaning softly, so he stopped. He turned to find her rocking back and forth on her haunches, her lifeless eyes like holes cut in cardboard.

A few years back, the state mental institutions had decided to release all of their non-violent patients to cut down on costs. These poor souls were now camped out in alleys and under freeway bridges all over town. The women were particularly pitiful, becoming constant rape targets who, because of their mental illnesses, could not defend themselves. Over the past few years Shane had taken many of these dazed sexual assault victims to County Hospital. Sometimes they couldn't even remember what had happened to them. They would be treated and released. Once back on the streets, the cycle of violence and sexual assault would begin all over again. Shane opened his wallet and handed the woman a ten. She looked up at him and smiled. Through her split lip he saw broken teeth. He was in the same dimension with her, but not anywhere in her vicinity. It occurred to him that most cops didn't give handouts to homeless people. Cops were supposed to be cynics. So what the hell was he doing? Why was he turning into such a bleeding heart?

He found Carol's name on the registry board, then climbed to the second floor and walked down the narrow corridor, inhaling old urine and mildew. He stopped in front of her apartment door, which still had yellow LAPD crime tape across its threshold, took out his lock picks and, in a few minutes, let himself in.

Carol White's apartment was another surprise. The forty-dollar street whore lived in a pink-rug and white-lace wonderland. The place looked like it was decorated by a ten-year-old; cutouts of teen magazine fashion layouts were stuck on the walls, white teddy bears looked down from bookshelves. The three-room apartment was as frilly and innocent as Carol was broken down and used up. Most drug addicts stop doing housework and live in filth. It surprised him how clean everything was.

There was a bedroom and bath with a small kitchen and living room, all of it extremely neat, except for the graphite dust the Homicide print team had left behind. It darkened the doorjambs at shoulder height and was on a few kitchen and bathroom drawer handles. It didn't look like a very thorough dusting. Shane counted six general locations where the print team had smeared the hard surfaces with their number nine brushes full of dark powder.

On important murders, he had seen enough graphite to open a pencil factory. By comparison, this was pretty meager. Ruta was obviously doing a slapdash job in his effort to get done quickly and move on.

On the dresser, Shane found several old pictures of Carol in her beauty pageant days. She looked about fifteen, fresh and wholesome, standing in a white bathing suit and heels. A winner's sash was draped around her luscious body, displaying both magnificent curves and childlike innocence.

It was hard to believe that in two or three years, this beautiful child had been turned into the heroin addict he'd met a few days ago.

Shane shook out of a descending funk that was settling over him. He wasn't here to look at old pictures. He searched through the apartment but didn't find what he was looking for, so he sat in Carol's bedroom chair, across from an open window, and waited.

His mind began to wander back to Dennis Valentine. Shane had decided that a great-looking, criminally connected guy like Valentine probably wasn't used to being ignored, so that was going to be his play, but something told him to be careful. The relationship between Valentine and Nicky was complicated. Dennis had treated the little grifter like a flunky, not like the valued partner and adviser that Nicky had said he was. Shane now seriously doubted they were in a film agreement with each other.

He reached into his pocket and fingered the keys to the department's asset-seizure house, as his mind switched channels. He tried to envision living in such a magnificent home, even temporarily. Shane had been an orphan, raised by several different foster parents, all blue-collar families. But like a bony river fish, he kept being thrown back, and had ended up in a state-run group home. His idea of luxury was his small canal house in Venice; the house on North Chalon was going to be a whole new experience.

His mind flipped once more, now pondering Amac and Chooch. He found himself picking at that old scab again until it opened, oozing concern. *Was Chooch going to do something stupid? Could he trust him to stay away from American?* He had begun to sense there might be something else binding Chooch and Amac besides friendship. He wasn't sure what it was, but the more he thought about it, the more he suspected there was a hidden piece he didn't understand yet.

Then, what he had been waiting for suddenly arrived. It jumped off the tree limb outside and landed on the open windowsill, teetered there for a minute, then jumped down into the room.

Carol's marmalade cat.

"Hey, Franco," Shane said, remembering what Carol had named him. The cat froze, startled at seeing an intruder. Shane had spotted no food or water bowls in the apartment, so he got up and finally found some cat food in the kitchen, put it on a plate, then filled a bowl with water and set them both down.

Franco ran at the bowl of water, drank first, then settled on his haunches and started to devour the dry cat food.

After he finished, the cat turned and studied Shane. Cats were supposed to have only one expression, but Franco was definitely projecting sadness. Shane also saw grief and confusion in those large yellow eyes.

"She's not coming back, guy," Shane told him. "You can stay here and look for another sucker to feed you, or you can come with me."

The cat looked at him, moved his ears forward, then came over and started to wind around his feet. Shane reached down and picked Franco up, then held him and scratched behind his ears. The cat started purring loudly.

"Deal," Shane murmured.

He gathered up some cat supplies, found the litter box and emptied it into the trash, then packed everything up in the box. Balancing the supplies under one arm and Franco under the other, he left Carol's apartment.

He put Franco and the supplies into the Acura, while the old lady on the curb watched. He pulled away from the apartment with his new pet, leaving the pitiful homeless woman behind.

Only one stray at a time, he thought, then got the hell out of Rampart.

The drive from Carol's depressing, paint-peeling apartment building to the drug dealer's beautiful, two-story Colonial on North Chalon Road was a short freeway trip out of desperation into the American dream. The two neighborhoods were separated by only twenty minutes and fifteen miles, but they were light-years from one another.

19

NORTH CHALON ROAD

"I can't believe we get to live here," Chooch exclaimed. Shane and Alexa had set down their overnight bags, and were now following Chooch through the beautiful house, going door to door down the long hall, admiring the expensive artwork and plush-pile-carpeted rooms full of antiques and French twill fabrics.

Shane couldn't believe it either.

Alexa was moving slowly, walking behind them. She had a troubled look on her face. They went into the master bedroom, which had a large mirror on the ceiling over a king-size bed.

"At last, I'll be able to see what I'm doing," Shane quipped as Alexa dug him in the ribs with her elbow.

Wearing their undies, the three of them plunged into the ten-meter pool for a swim.

Shane and Chooch got into a water fight in the shallow end, and Alexa sat on the steps a few feet away, laughing at them.

She needed to laugh. The tension of the past few days had been wearing on her, and the laughter finally erased the stress lines from her face. But while they were in the pool her pager went off. She climbed out, dripping water from her soaked bra and panties, found the telephone inside the living room door and dialed the number on her beeper LED screen. A few minutes later she came back outside.

"I've gotta go."

"Oh, come on . . . Really?" Shane moaned.

"We've got three more. This time it's Emes. A massacre at one of those unincorporated nightclubs in the Las Lomas Hills."

At the mention of The Hills, Chooch waded to the shallow end. "Was it . . . is it him?"

"I don't know, honey. I just got the call. The Blues who caught the squeal said the three victims were all shotgunned."

"I wanna go with you," Chooch said.

"Not gonna happen," Shane said.

"What if it's Amac? What if it's him? I mean, wouldn't he be the number-one target?"

"It's not him, Chooch," Shane said. "He's way too careful to be hanging around in some dirt-floor nightclub in Las Lomas."

"Dad, please let me go. . . ."

"I think he should," Alexa agreed.

Without waiting for further rebuttal, Chooch

bounded out of the pool and ran inside to get his clothes.

"You can't take him to a murder scene," Shane said.

"Why not?" she shot back. "Since he's still obviously flirting with this, I think maybe he needs to see what a gang war is really all about."

"I don't want him to see it. I won't allow it."

"What about what I think, or have you forgotten I'm his adopted mother? I'll cut you some slack and put that aside because none of us are thinking too clearly right now, but I think this is exactly the right thing for us to do."

"You wanna take him to a triple shotgun murder."

"Yeah."

Shane climbed out of the pool and faced her. "Look, Alexa, I don't want him exposed to this, okay?"

"Shane, I talk to him about things he doesn't want to tell you. He's . . . he's not out of this. He's still a part of that world."

"La Eme?" Shane was stunned. "I got him out of that two years ago. Amac wouldn't take him back. He wouldn't do that to him."

"He's not an Eme. He's not in the gang, but he's still emotionally tied to it. They're his old *clica*."

Shane tried to absorb this.

"I think he needs a little shock therapy,"

Alexa continued. "Maybe this shooting in The Hills is just what we need to show him it isn't some romantic game they're playing."

Shane was stunned to learn Chooch had confided in Alexa and not him. Worse still was the idea that his son still regarded gang life as romantic. Shane thought they'd seen the end of that. "I'll go with you," he blurted.

"No, that would change it. It would force him to react differently. Let me do this."

"He can react with me there."

"Shane, he knows what you expect of him. He loves you and he wants to please you, but this is about his ethnic blood. Can't you see that? Let me take him. I'll look out for him. I won't let him out of my sight."

After a long moment, Shane concluded that, as usual, she was probably right. "How long will you be gone?"

She looked at her watch. "I'll try to be back before midnight."

"Okay," he finally relented.

They left ten minutes later. Shane was suddenly alone in the huge house with Carol's marmalade cat. Franco came over and sat right in front of him, deep hurt etched on his face. Or was Shane just projecting his own hurt into those huge yellow eyes? Then Franco started to yowl; his cries as plaintive and sad as Shane's own dark thoughts.

"Don't start up with me, man," he said. "I've got problems of my own."

Shane was asleep in the drug dealer's bed when he heard Alexa's department-issue Crown Victoria pull in. He looked at his watch: eleven-fifty. The front door opened, then he heard Alexa and Chooch talking softly. Soon she came down the hall into the bedroom.

"How'd it go?" Shane asked from his side of the king-size bed.

"I don't know. It was messy. He threw up. It wasn't Amac, of course. Three teenage kids . . . all wearing gang tatts and colors. Chooch has been very quiet since he saw the bodies."

"You think it shocked some sense into him?"

"I hope."

She undressed and climbed into bed.

They made love. It was the first time they'd had sex in three or four days. They were both tired and worried, so to be perfectly truthful, it wasn't their best effort, but afterward, they lay in each other's arms and a sweet softness descended.

"It's weird," she said.

"You mean with Chooch?"

"No," she said, and kissed him on the tip of his nose. "Screwing you in a drug dealer's bed. You've always been a unique date."

"Eat me."

"You first." Then they both started laughing softly and he took her into his arms, relishing the heat of her body and the strength of her mind.

Wrapped in the warm protection of these qualities, snuggling in her embrace, he felt the edges of his day softened, and he soon drifted into a deep sleep.

20

THE POWER BREAKFAST

It was ten-fifteen, and Michael Fallon was already a quarter of an hour late. Shane and Nicky were sitting at one of the power tables in the Polo Lounge. Nicky said it was one of five power tables located in the back of the restaurant, on a slightly raised platform, next to the wall, affording them a great view of the room. The table had cost Nicky an extra hundred bucks.

"Seating is important," the little grifter was saying to Shane. "Where they seat you in a power restaurant like the Polo Lounge speaks volumes. Like, see that guy over there, at that little postage stamp table by the window? Murray Streeterman. His last picture, *Alaskan Ice*, tanked. Look where they got him . . . *gonifs*ville."

"What bullshit." Shane glanced at his watch

and began to wonder if this movie star was going to stand them up.

"You think so?" Nicky continued. "At Universal, back in the nineties, they had this big executive dining room where the tables were lined up in rows. The head of the studio, the late, great Lew Wasserman, had his permanent booth next to the east wall. So naturally, the closer you were to the king, the more important you were. Guys under contract on that lot would fight to get their permanent tables a row closer to that wall. It was like World War Two in there — the invasion of Italy. Producers were taking tables like fucking hedge rows. If you moved one row closer to the east wall, it was like a huge career victory. Friendships were lost over it."

Just then, Michael Fallon appeared in the doorway and started talking to the maître d'.

"There he is," Shane said as Nicky let out a groan.

"What's wrong?" Shane whispered.

"He brought the fucking writer, Rajindi Singh. Nobody brings the writer to an important meeting. The writer is useless as an appendix."

"Doesn't the writer supply the material?" Shane asked. "Isn't he sort of important?"

"Writers are creative furniture. You don't like one, you get another . . . and they got no loyalty to one another either, the pricks. Don't ever share a foxhole with a fucking writer, 'cause they'll give you up in a heartbeat. Hand one a these hacks some brother writer's script, and the first thing they say is, 'Who wrote this piece a crap?' Writers are the worst."

Michael Fallon and Rajindi Singh were now headed to the table. Fallon was turning heads all over the restaurant. He was dark complexioned and implausibly handsome in a very unique way. Nothing on his face looked like it went together. His mouth was too big, his nose too long, his forehead too short. But like Sylvester Stallone, once you added it all up, it spelled movie star.

Trailing Michael like a pale orbiting moon was Rajindi Singh. Shane had been expecting an East Indian, but Singh looked more like an albino. He was so slender and washed out that Shane was surprised a team of paramedics wasn't trailing him dragging a stretcher and oxygen. He was bald, but had a few wisps of spidery white hair growing out of the top of his head.

Then they were at the table. Nicky didn't speak, so Shane stood and took the lead again.

"Hi, I'm Shane Scully. This is my partner, Nicky Marcella. We're the co-owners of Cine-Roma." He had his hand stretched out but Michael refused to shake.

"I don't shake hands," the star said. "I have a germ transfer phobia."

Is everybody in Hollywood afraid of bacteria? Shane wondered. *If they're all so scared of one-*

celled amoebas, what's gonna happen when they run into something that's got real teeth? Shane turned and shook hands with Rajindi, who had a grip like a glove full of ice water.

"Rajindi Singh," the man said in an unaccented voice as he released Shane's hand.

They all sat at the power table, looking for the right way to get started.

"Anybody left-handed?" Michael Fallon suddenly asked.

"Huh?" Nicky said. Shane was beginning to realize that Nicky wasn't much good at meetings. This surprised him, because on the street, the little con man was so full of shit, he needed constant flushing. Maybe it was the high-profile nature of these power players that froze him.

"We're not left-handed," Shane answered.

"Good," Michael said. "If you'd been left-handed, it would have changed things."

"Really?" Shane was hoping he'd explain, but the star didn't seem inclined to elaborate.

"Before we get too far ahead of ourselves, I'd like to hear how you loved my script," Rajindi said, a strand of his huge ego suddenly escaping.

"Nicky, you want to handle that one?" Shane asked, but Nicky was vapor-locked, sputtering like a jalopy with sand in the tank. Reluctantly Shane turned back to Rajindi. "We love it." He hadn't read it yet. Nobody, including Wireman, seemed to have a copy, so an in-depth discussion was going to be impossible.

"I'd like some specifics, please. There's a clause in the contract you signed that gives me approval over the producers. I need to know you grasp the global significance of the work, its Nostradamus-like projections and far-reaching social consequences."

"Oh," Shane said. "Well, Jerry Wireman didn't mention that we had to be approved."

"You sign documents you don't read?" Singh asked. One white, plucked eyebrow shot up into the middle of his forehead and arched there precariously.

Shane marveled at how he'd gotten locked up with these assholes, but he brushed the thought away and smiled. "Okay, well, I think starting at the end and ending at the beginning is brilliant."

"How so? State your rationale," Rajindi challenged.

"Time is like a man-made convenience and not too important in a conceptual sense," Shane mumbled, trying to fill dead air, but he must have guessed right because they both nodded.

"And? . . ." Rajindi said.

"The, uh . . . the whatta ya call-its? . . . The neural storms and dragons and things. Really, really inventive."

"And? . . ." Rajindi prodded.

"And . . . look, Mr. Singh, we *love* the script, okay? We both think you're a writer of indescribable talent. This is major stuff. We're talking neo-impress . . . neo . . . ."

"Neo-impressionistic heroism," Rajindi completed.

"Exactly." Shane was beginning to sweat, himself. Out of the corner of his eye, he saw Dennis Valentine walk into the restaurant accompanied by a heavyset man with extremely long arms and huge shoulders. Standard-issue mob muscle. Valentine had the Hollywood trade papers, *Variety* and the *Reporter*, in hand. He was already looking around, trying to spot his favorite actor. Then he saw Shane and Nicky at the table with Michael Fallon. Dennis Valentine and his knuckle-dragger were led to one of the postage stamp tables by the window and were seated. Valentine opened the trades, but never stopped looking over at them.

"Okay, okay, so you love the script, and you think I'm talented. So far, so good," Rajindi Singh was saying, "and I assume you know about and agree with the no-rewrite clause. I want to make sure we're not going to argue about script changes after the director is aboard."

"Absolutely. No changes," Shane said firmly.

"It'd be like stepping on a fucking Rembrandt." Nicky had regained his voice and everyone turned to look at him.

"Okay then," Fallon said, "I'm sure my agent told you that my acting price is the standard twenty mil a picture, but on *Neural Surfer*, because it's my passion project, I'll work for ten up-front and ten on the back, against twenty points from first-dollar gross."

Shane nodded.

"And of course my agent has told you about my dietary and personal needs. . . ."

"We haven't talked to him about that in detail yet," Shane said. "But I'm sure we can deal with them, whatever they are."

"I am strictly Singh Herbal Kosher. I can't eat anything that isn't prepared by the Singh Church of Herbal Healing and blessed by Rajindi personally."

"I will supply you with my catering costs," Rajindi said. "They're a bit pricey, but keeping Michael healthy and spiritually pure ought to be everybody's main goal."

"I have to eat every forty-two minutes, exactly," Fallon chimed in. "Forty-two is my genetic holistic number, perfect in its cubic dimension. Also, my personal trainer and massage therapist have to be hired at their hourly rate and housed in trailers equal to the director's accommodations. I'd be lost without them. They help me combat my panthophobia. . . ."

"Your what?" Shane interjected.

"Fear of disease. We'll supply you with a complete list of my phobias," the movie star said.

"Phobias?" Shane was getting a headache.

"That's right. Rajindi is helping me with them. We've discovered that by confronting them, and dealing with them openly, I'm much less stressed."

"It's part of a holistic herbal healing program we're administering at the Life Realization Center of my Church." Singh smiled.

"Gimme an example of what's gonna be on the list," Shane asked, fearing the worst.

"Well, obviously sinistrophobia, so we can't have any left-handed people on the cast or crew."

"Uh . . . Mr. Fallon, I'm not trying to be argumentative, but won't we be inviting a class action discrimination suit?" Shane said.

"I don't give a shit if you wanna hire *fifty* left-handed people and give them the *L.A. Times* crossword puzzle to do every day, that's up to you. I just won't have any lefties on my shooting set."

"We believe left-handed people are disciples of darkness," Rajindi Singh explained calmly. "While not satanic per se, they do attract the dark neural dragons, and quite frankly, it just isn't worth the risk."

Shane had to remind himself that none of this mattered, because they weren't going to make the damned movie anyway. *But these people were insufferable. How did movies — scratch that — films ever get made in this town?*

"Obviously, I have the germ thing, too, misophobia, and its first cousin, parasitaphobia." Michael was looking over at Singh as if to gain strength as he spoke of these fears. "I also have enosiophobia, the fear of committing an unpardonable sin. I want my soul to go to heaven."

"Very reasonable. Who can blame you for that?" Nicky brown-nosed, folding like a deck chair.

But Shane was frowning and Rajindi Singh was quick to spot it. "Dealing with our fears and weaknesses out in the open helps us adjust to them, helps us build our neural fortresses. Then, of course, we have our Three H Program that buttresses and fortifies all of that."

"You have a farm program?" Nicky asked.

"You're thinking Four H," Rajindi said. "Three H stands for Holistic Herbal Healing." Then, reading their frowns, he rushed on. "We are very set on neural healing through the practice of self-realization and dietary purity."

"Then you guys probably won't be ordering the Canadian bacon," Shane quipped.

Rajindi gave them a thin, condescending little smile. "We are quite impervious to attempts at humor at our expense," he said tightly. "Have you been thinking of a director? Michael has director approval, but we are prepared to work inside a limited A-list." Singh was not behaving like creative furniture. He was already taking over.

"I was thinking of Milos DeAngelo," Nicky blurted, referring to the sallow old director Shane had met in Nicky's office two days ago.

"Never heard of him," Fallon said.

"Extensive background . . . did some extremely creative animal films a few years back."

Animal films? Shane thought. *The Mr. Ed Episodes?*

"We like Paul Lubick," Mike Fallon offered.

"Uh, Paul Lubick . . . yes, yes . . . what an interesting idea. Very, very talented." Nicky was now in full retreat.

"Wonderful. Then we'd like you to sign him to an immediate holding deal," Fallon continued. "I happen to know he's between pictures right now and Paul and I are simpatico. We speak the same language. I have chronomentrophobia, and believe me, having a director who understands that helps me a lot on the set because we don't have a buncha A.D.'s running around yelling about the damn schedule. We work at our own pace. It's graceful, and it frees my creative spirit." Michael Fallon had a look of rapture as he spoke.

"Paul Lubick? You happen to know who his agent is?" Nicky had unholstered his gold LeBlanc and was clicking the lead down. He was poised to write the information on a piece of paper he had just pulled out of his pocket.

"He's with Talent Associates," Rajindi Singh contributed.

"Excuse me," the gray-haired, white-coated waiter said, holding a bottle of champagne. "This is a gift from the gentleman at that table." He pointed to Dennis Valentine, who gave them a little wave of his hand, flashing a couple hundred thousand worth of diamonds and sapphires on manicured fingers.

"Champagne?" Shane said, taking the bottle of Taittinger and looking at it.

"What kinda asshole sends a bottle of champagne over at ten in the morning?" Fallon asked, looking at Valentine, who was smiling like a jack-o'-lantern and waving like a starstruck tourist. Then, because Mike Fallon was still looking at him, Valentine interpreted that as an invitation, stood, and ambled over to their table.

"Nicholas, perhaps you might introduce me to Mr. Fallon," the mobster said, smiling his perfect smile. Shane had to admit that, on balance, Valentine wasn't giving away too many hottie points to the handsome movie star.

"Michael Fallon, this is Dennis Valentine," Nicky croaked. Then, simultaneously, they both pulled back and held their hands up, palms out.

"I never shake hands," Valentine said.

"Me neither," Fallon agreed.

They stood there for a second, with their palms extended, like two guys waving off a dinner check.

"I thought you might like a bottle of Taittinger," Dennis said.

"It's ten in the morning, bud." Fallon was slipping into his film gangster persona.

"It chills nicely, perhaps you could have it later."

"I don't drink anything unless Rajindi has

215

blessed it, and frankly, champagne is all sugar."

"To the contrary," Dennis said, smiling, eager to give a nutrition lesson. "Taittinger is the champagne of champagnes. It's fermented in oak casks and kept in perfect, hermetically sealed containers at predetermined temperatures. During fermentation, the champagne is constantly refreshed and at bottling has over one hundred and one vitamins and minerals, as well as an array of life-extending, body-enhancing nutrients. Health food in a bottle, I call it." His smile widened. "I'm vegetarian, so I read a lot about nutrition."

"You're a fuckin' nut," Fallon snarled. "We're having a business meeting here!"

"Sorry to intrude," Valentine said, bowing at the waist. "Before leaving, Mr. Fallon, let me just say that I have long been an admirer of your tremendous talent and magnetic film presence. I thought your performance as the taxi driver prophet in *Yellow Angel* was magic. Why you didn't get nominated an . . ."

"Get the fuck away from me," Fallon growled, not knowing he was pissing on a made guy who had killed men for much less.

But Dennis Valentine was acting like a fop prince. All that was missing was the little heel click. He backed away from the table grinning and bowing, until finally resuming his seat near the window.

"Who's that dipshit?" Fallon scowled.

"A new producer in town, quite an up-and-

216

comer," Nicky said.

"Then why they got him sitting in fucking Siberia over there, eating with all the losers?"

Nicky shot Shane a look that said "see," but Fallon was already staring at his watch.

"Okay, look. In ten minutes it's time for my next meal and neural blessing. We're on a tight clock, so we better get going." Shane thought it was a strange remark for a man with chronomentrophobia.

Nicky took out his business cards and passed them out.

"Your offices are at Hollywood General?" Fallon said suspiciously as he read it. "That's the rental lot for jerks who can't get studio deals."

"All of our money goes on the screen." Nicky was coming alive again. "We don't waste moolah on fancy overhead."

Fallon and Singh both slowly rose, then walked away from the table without even saying good-bye. Shane and Nicky were left sitting, watching them go.

"Chronomentrophobia?" Shane snorted.

"Fear of clocks," Nicky answered.

"He actually gets away with shit like that?" Shane was appalled.

"Yeah. Pretty shrewd in a totally fucked-up way. A guy with chrono-whatever doesn't ever have to deal with the film's production schedule."

Shane could see Valentine starting to get up

from behind his loser's table. "Valentine's coming. Let's get outta here."

"That's what we want, isn't it?" Nicky asked.

"I wanna troll the bait for a little longer before we hook him up."

Shane pulled the little grifter out of the booth, and they rushed to the front entrance of the Beverly Hills Hotel. He grabbed the valet ticket out of Nicky's hand and gave it to the parking attendant. The rented Bentley was parked nearby, helping to decorate the entrance.

The valet ran to get it just as Valentine's stooge arrived. Up close his shoulders were so developed, he looked like he was wearing football pads under his suit.

"I'm Gino Parelli, Mr. Valentine's assistant," the goon said in a heavy New Jersey accent. "He would like da pleasure of youse's company back in da restaurant."

"Give Mr. Valentine our regrets, but tell him we're late to a preproduction meeting," Shane said. "Have him call Cine-Roma and set up an appointment with one of our secretaries." He looked at Nicky. "Give him a card."

"Huh?" Nicky said.

"A card. A business card."

Nicky had vapor-locked again so Shane reached into the little producer's inside suit coat pocket, grabbed his billfold, extracted a card, and handed it to Parelli.

"You ain't gonna come?" the goon said, baffled. This was obviously something that rarely happened.

"Yeah, we're not coming," Shane said. "We're late. We've got a Michael Fallon film to make."

The Bentley pulled up so they walked around and got in. Nicky was moving in a frightened daze as he sat behind the wheel and drove the huge car away. The startled bodyguard was left standing there, casting a giant shadow, muttering to himself.

21

BUGS

They always left notes on the refrigerator door at the Venice house, but he was surprised to see one taped to the Sub-Zero in the huge country kitchen on North Chalon Road. It read:

> *Had to go back to the office.*
> *Chooch at Public Library till*
> *it closes, working on history paper.*
> *Chicken in the fridge.*
> *Ha, ha, ha . . . Love ya, Babe.*
> *— A*

He opened the fridge. Cold and empty as a drug dealer's heart.

The only guy eating right in the house was Franco, who was crouched over his dish of cat food, purring loudly.

Shane went back into the living room and

Franco dogged him like, well, a dog. Franco was turning out to be very uncatlike — not standoffish, like most felines; he actually liked being near you. Fido with cat whiskers.

It had been a long, hard day at Cine-Roma Productions. It turned out that Nicky had only rented the one big suite. He didn't even control the space across the hall. He'd stolen a key to get into that office. In order to keep the sting going, they would have to rent more space from Hollywood General Studios, but Shane was already out of money. He and Nicky had opened negotiations with both Paul Lubick's and Mike Fallon's agents. They were also represented by CAA, so it became something called an "Agency Package," where because they controlled three major elements, CAA also got five percent of the budget in back-end points. Once that happened, the three CAA agents started making more ugly demands than the West Hollywood House of Bondage. Shane had called Alexa at two that afternoon, pleading with her to put another fifty grand into the blind account for front-end deal money. She had reluctantly put in ten and said she would check with Filosiani on the rest. Nicky had been bustling around the office like Louis B. Mayer on speed, filing old scripts, redecorating, neatening up, polishing and moving his rented awards, getting ready for the arrival of Michael Fallon and Rajindi Singh.

Shane tried to get a copy of *The Neural Surfer*

from CAA but had been informed that Rajindi had instructed his agent that no copies be released because he wanted to do some *potch-kehing* on the script. Shane wondered if a *potchkeh* was the same as a rewrite, and if they were going to be charged for it. Several girls in booty shorts and stilettos showed up to audition for *Boots and Bikinis* but had to be turned away.

That was his day.

By the time Shane was back on North Chalon Road, he was exhausted and wished he had stopped at the market to pick up a six-pack of beer.

Then the doorbell rang.

It surprised him, because except for Shane's immediate family and Chief Filosiani, nobody else knew he was living there.

He had picked up a backup Beretta Mini Cougar from his locker downtown, and as he walked to the front door, he pulled it out of his ankle holster and relocated it in a handier spot at the small of his back, then he unlocked and opened up.

Valentine's goon was standing there, his over-developed traps still hopelessly bulging a size-fifty suit.

"Evening," the man said.

"Hi ya," Shane replied.

"I'm Parelli. Youse may remember me from this morning." In truth, Parelli was impossible to forget.

"Whatta you doing here, Gino?"

"Nice house." He was looking around, craning his neck to see more of it from the porch.

"Same question," Shane persisted.

"Mr. Valentine wanted me to give youse this." He reached into his inside pocket. Shane was poised to hit the deck and come up shooting, but instead of a gun, the gorilla removed a fat envelope and handed it over.

"What is it?"

"Open it."

Shane ripped the envelope. It was full of C-notes, at least a hundred of them.

"The price is right," Shane said, "but I should warn you, I never kiss on the first date."

Parelli didn't think Shane was funny. He just stared at him. "Mr. Valentine wants that youse keep that as his gift, and would very much like the pleasure of youse's company — no strings. The money buys a meeting. He's waiting at a restaurant not far from here, on Fairfax. Just follow my car."

"Why?"

"He don't tell me things like that." Gino gestured to the envelope. "It's ten large for an hour of youse's time."

"Which car is yours?" Shane asked.

Parelli pointed to a blue Chevy with blackwalls that was parked at the curb with a Hertz tag hanging off the mirror.

"Okay, gimme a minute," Shane said, and

went back inside. He put the money in the top desk drawer in the entry hall, reholstered the gun on his ankle, grabbed his blazer, then rejoined Parelli and locked up.

Then a strange thing happened. Parelli walked him over to the blue Hertz rental and took out a small battery-operated 2300 Frequency Finder exactly like the one Shane got from the Electronic Surveillance Division yesterday. Parelli ran the wand over Shane, checking the meter as he did.

"Sorry 'bout that. Mr. Valentine insists we scan everybody for bugs." Then he let Shane walk to the garage for his car.

It was a ten-minute drive across town before they finally parked at a valet stand in front of a newly built brick-and-stucco structure on the corner of Melrose and Fairfax. Across the front, in blue neon script, it said: Ciro's Pompadoro Ristorante.

"Best veggie lasagna in this whole fag town," Parelli said as he led Shane into the restaurant.

22

THE HOOKUP

The interior of Ciro's Pompadoro was right out of the assassination scene from *The Godfather*: wine casks hanging from nets on exposed ceiling beams, red-and-white-checkered table-cloths, straight-backed wooden chairs, and the pungent smell of garlic. The only thing out of place were the Mexican waiters, but this was true in French and Italian restaurants all over L.A. The maître d' made up for it with greased black hair, a heavy Sicilian accent, and the traditional five o'clock shadow.

"*Ah, Signor Parelli, benvenuto. Accògliere a Ciro's Pompadoro,*" he purred, then led Shane and Gino to a booth in the back. The restaurant was only half-full, but it was just slightly after seven, so it was still early.

This time, Champagne Dennis Valentine was sitting in the best booth along the back wall.

No postage-stamp loser's table for the Don's nephew at Ciro's Pompadoro. At this watering hole Mr. Valentine was a person of value, a made guy — a *caporegime*. He was wearing tan slacks, a blue cashmere blazer, and a silk shirt. Expensive getup.

Valentine was sipping from a champagne glass while an open bottle of Taittinger was icing in a bucket nearby. Shane slid into the booth as Gino went to his attack dog position at another table not far away, never taking his eyes off of them. Shane started to shake hands, but Valentine pulled away. He was going to have to break himself of that habit if he stayed in showbiz much longer.

"I'm glad you were smart and came," Valentine said, smiling.

"It was a nicely worded invitation and in my favorite color." Shane glanced around the restaurant. "This is nice. Never been here before."

"It's okay. That guy on the desk is new. He looks good but he's about as Italian as Danny Glover. He's just an actor doing the accent — you can't fool a real goomba. But it's okay. They treat me good here. Everything is prepared special for me. Great vegetarian lasagna, everything healthy."

"Do they have a good veal piccata?"

"You wanna put meat in your system, Mr. Scully, you go right ahead. With all that's been written about cholesterol and animal enzymes, it amazes me how people eat these days. Mc-

Donald's? You might as well open a vein and pour in a quart a grease."

"Right. But you gotta admit, the Beanie Babies in those Happy Meals were a classic." Shane was just fucking with him now.

Valentine didn't say anything for a second, then shook out of it, and moved on. "With me, it's healthy all the way," he said. "Taittinger has a twenty percent alcohol level, which on the surface is sorta bad, but it lowers stress and the vitamin and mineral contents are primo, so I figure, on balance, it's a big plus. I try and preserve my body; cut down on oxidants and free radicals, but I'm like almost alone in this, y'know. Everywhere people eat, I see problems. Take that guy over there with the plate a spaghetti and meatballs, the fusilli and ravioli . . ."

Shane turned to look, then nodded.

"Y'know what I see when I spot a guy eating shit like that?"

Shane shook his head.

"I see a giant digestive problem. Me? My furnace burns clean, run five miles a day, work out, take a cold swim. Back in Jersey, I'd run along the river, then when I was done, I'd dive into the water, right there by the George Washington Bridge. In the winter the water was forty fucking degrees, but after a run, you're hot, and the icy water makes your epidermis contract, forces the oil outta your pores. Real good for your skin and circulation. Healthy . . . y'know?" He smiled at Shane.

227

"What d'you do to stay in shape?"

"Well, recently I've been trying not to jack off as much as I used to. Other than that, not much."

Valentine took a sip of his champagne. "I know you're just foolin' with me, and that's okay, Mr. Scully, 'cause I gotta sense of humor. But don't waste your shots."

"Always good advice."

They sat looking at each other. Shane decided to wait him out, and finally Valentine spoke.

"I already ate, but you wanna order the veal piccata?" Shane nodded and Valentine waved the maître d' over. "Watch this guy. Lemme show you something."

"*Sì, Signor* Valentine," the maître d' said as he approached the table smiling.

"*Carlo, per favore ci serva presto, abbiamo fretta.*" Valentine rattled this in perfect Italian and Carlo blanched.

"Let me get Paolo over here to help."

Valentine smiled as the maître d' hit reverse and backed out of there.

"Fuckin' phony," Valentine said softly. "I can't stand phonies."

"Then you better get out of Hollywood," Shane deadpanned. "What'd you ask him?"

"Nothing. I just told him to serve you quickly. Guys like that ain't got it. You can't play an Italian if you haven't lived it. *Capisce?* The attitude's gotta come from the balls." Valentine reached out, grabbed the champagne bottle, and poured a glass of Taittinger for Shane.

"You probably wondered why I wanted to see you," he said as he dropped the bottle back into the bucket of ice.

"Crossed my mind," Shane answered.

"You're partners with Nicky Marcella, but I've known Nicky for a long time, so I also know he couldn't make a meatball sandwich without spilling half of it on the floor. So when I see you two guys having breakfast with Michael Fallon, I know this is not his doing."

"Don't be so sure," Shane said.

Valentine shrugged. "After this morning, I checked you out with some of my sources, even read about you in the morning paper." He reached down on the seat beside him, grabbed a copy of the *L.A. Times*, then flipped it open and dropped it on the table. Right there, above the fold in the Metro section, was the article that the LAPD Press Relations officer had planted yesterday under the headline: UNREST AT PARKER CENTER. Shane's picture was off to one side, along with Alexa's. He picked up the paper and shrugged. He'd been so busy, he hadn't seen it yet, but he knew more or less what it said, so he threw it back onto the table.

"Sounds to me like you and the little woman are getting screwed," Valentine said.

"And believe me, when the LAPD does it, it hurts," Shane grumbled.

"It surprised me, when Gino showed me this. I think you're a movie producer, next thing I read, you're a cop."

"*Was* a cop. I quit. Last few years I've been meaning to pull the pin. Been optioning properties, getting some film deals lined up. I was looking to change careers anyway."

"Cop to movie producer . . . pretty big jump."

"Mr. Valentine, not that it matters, but a lot of ex-cops have become big players in entertainment. It's hardly unique."

Valentine didn't seem too impressed with this remark, so Shane named a few: "Joe Wambaugh, Eddie Egan, Steve Downing, Dennis Farina . . . the list is endless."

"I'm not convinced."

"Don't take this the wrong way, but who gives a shit? I didn't ask to meet with you. I'm still trying to figure out what you want."

"I have plans, okay? Big plans. And I think this Michael Fallon film you and Nicky are making could fit into my program."

"Really?" Shane smiled. "Trouble with that is, you aren't gonna have one damn thing to do with it."

"But we're gonna change that."

"No, we're not."

"If I want, Nicky will hand over his whole piece; all I gotta do is ask."

"No, he won't."

"Yeah? Why not?"

" 'Cause if he does, I'll kill the little prick."

They sat there, looking at each other over sparkling glasses of Taittinger.

"I'm not used to hearing no."

"Get used to it. *No* is the principal word in entertainment commerce."

"How so?"

"Film executives are in the 'no' business. You hear a lotta no's out here 'cause a no usually doesn't hurt a studio exec, while a yes can ruin the guy's career."

"That's ridiculous," Valentine said. "How's the studios gonna ever make a film if they say no to everything? Gotta be some yesses."

"Few and far between." Shane sipped his Taittinger. "You gotta understand how it works. . . ." Shane was now recalling some of the crash course Nicky had given him yesterday. "You've got very young people of both sexes with very little experience in positions of great power at the studios. They've got money and Porsches; they get the best tables at restaurants, and the only thing that is gonna screw that up is if they say yes to a picture and the studio spends tens of millions to make and release it, and it bombs. If they say no, they won't be proved wrong, except once in a few thousand pitches, like the time some development exec at Paramount turned down *Jaws* and Universal made it and it grossed a few hundred mil. Some people lost their jobs over that, but it's a rare occurrence. The vast majority of films shot in this town tank. If you're a studio exec, your odds of not fucking up are a thousand times better if you say no rather than yes. Get it?"

Valentine nodded. The waiter came to the table to take Shane's order, but Valentine waved him off. He wanted to hear more.

"Then how *do* films get made?" he asked.

"They get green-lit when the elements are so tantalizing that only a fool would say no. For instance, let's say you have Nelson DeMille's or Michael Connelly's latest bestselling novel. You've got Spielberg to direct, Julia Roberts and Tom Cruise to star. *Now* if the film tanks, you've got a prepackaged excuse. You can tell your boss, 'How could I *not* make this picture with all these A-list people involved?' "

"I see." Valentine put down his glass and studied Shane. "You're a smart guy. Maybe you *are* a movie producer."

"I busted a buncha these A-list players for drugs when I was still in Vice. I cultivated contacts, did some favors. What goes around, comes around."

"So we work together. Your knowledge and Hollywood contacts, my East Coast relationships and ancillary toughness."

"By that, are we talking about muscle?"

"I have valuable things I can offer."

"You can't have a piece of my movie," Shane repeated. "This piece blends neo-impressionistic heroism with gut-wrenching social commentary. It's *ferae naturae,* which is a term we use, meaning full of untamed nature. Obviously I'm in no hurry to sell off pieces." Stealing the better part of Jerry Wireman's riff in these few sentences.

"I'm not used to being turned down."

"Lucky you."

"According to this news article, your wife runs the LAPD Detective Services division."

Shane nodded.

"If what I read in this paper is true, that may not last much longer."

"She's as pissed off about the way they run things down there as I am," Shane snapped.

"Maybe there's a way I can help both of you. From what I see, and from where you're living, you must be in way over your head; either that or you're already selling police favors to people with money. Maybe I can help you get more of what you want. While this is an offer, you should also think of it as a demand."

"Am I supposed to get all shook up 'cause you're a mobster?" Shane said softly. "I should agree to anything so you won't unleash Gino on me?" Shane leaned forward. "This isn't New Jersey. We aren't too scared of the mob out here. We've had a few cheeseball Mafia families over the years, but they have never been a problem for us 'cause they couldn't buy any influence. Being a mobster in L.A. is kinda like being an admiral in the Swiss navy. It's all protocol and no boats."

Valentine also leaned forward. "What if I was to tell you that's all about to change?"

"I wouldn't believe it. In order for you guys to get any foothold here, you've gotta have cops and politicians on the pad, and that's never happened in L.A."

The mobster leaned back. He seemed to change his mind, or pick a new direction. He studied Shane carefully, like he was an intricate puzzle that needed solving. "I don't wanna argue with you. You're a smart guy, but one way or another, I intend to get a piece of the Fallon movie. Gotta be a way that can happen without a lot of pain and suffering."

"It's not for sale."

"Okay. Before I give you the fist, here's the carrot. How much you figure this movie is gonna cost?"

"It's a film, and we're still budgeting it, so I don't have a clue. Michael has some very expensive codicils in his talent agreement with us, but we can get bank financing off his box-office power, so it's really a moot point."

"Okay, let's say, just for the hell of it, that it's gonna cost you fifty mil below-the-line. That sound reasonable?"

"All right, let's say." Shane tried to sound bored. He had a fair grasp of how the movie industry worked from Nicky and friends in the business, and of course, everywhere you went in L.A., people talked about film production, so you couldn't help picking some of it up. But he was far from an expert. He decided if he got in over his head with Valentine, he would just be vague.

"What if I can cut the cost of production to around half that?" Dennis was saying. "What if I can get it made for twenty-five mil instead of fifty. How many points is that worth?"

" 'Cept you can't. It's a union film. We're gonna be stuck with union rate cards, union overtime, meal penalties, force calls. No way it gets made for half-cost."

"But let's just say I can. What does that buy me?"

Shane decided on the spot that a dollar-for-dollar formula probably made sense, so he cleared his throat and said, "Okay. If you could do that, and I know you can't, but if you could, it might be worth a percentage equal to the percentage saved, less maybe, ten points."

"There, you see? We got us the start of a negotiation."

"We got shit, because nobody can cut the cost of a union shoot," Shane said. "I.A. unions don't deal on their rate cards."

"What if I put it on paper that you don't pay for it if you don't get it . . . what then?"

"I'm not negotiating with you, okay?"

The waiter returned. Valentine looked up, and the glower in his eyes was so fierce that it froze the man, who spun and left quickly.

"You ever heard of an Italian Alka-Seltzer treatment?" Valentine said softly.

"What's that, three *goombas* bubbling in a hot tub?"

"You're a funny guy, but now you're pissing me off. An Italian Alka-Seltzer is made of Semtex. It goes under your car. When it pops, you fizz. I could take you out hard, like that, or I got guys I can import who do vehicular hit-and-runs; turn you into a sack a crosswalk vegetables, separate your brain stem from your spinal column. Let you finish your tour down here sucking oxygen out of an iron lung. Or I can go easy and just put you in a body cast for half a year. These guys I got do surgical bumper and fender hits. The victims all get booked as traffic accidents. I got a guy works for me we named Thirteen Weeks. He's so good on crosswalk jobs, I once told him to put a guy in the hospital for thirteen weeks and he did it to the day."

Shane slowly stood and looked down at Valentine. "Guess I'll pass on dinner. Nice knowing ya."

"Why don't you let it percolate for twenty-four hours?" the mobster suggested. "Why don't you ask Nicky the Pooh about me. Ask him what kinda guy Dennis Valentine is. Then maybe we revisit this in a day or so." Dennis stood up and Shane rose with him.

"Anything you want. But the answer is still gonna be no."

A Mexican busboy came up to Shane. "You have telephone call," he said.

"Nobody knows I'm here," Shane said.

"You Scully?" the busboy asked.

Shane nodded, now wondering if something had happened to Chooch and they'd somehow tracked him down here. Valentine was opening his wallet.

"Let's get outta here," he said to Parelli, who had magically appeared at the table.

Shane watched Valentine throw a couple of hundreds down on the table to cover his vegetarian lasagna and the champagne. The busboy led Shane to the back of the restaurant near the kitchen, then pointed to a pay phone in the corner. The receiver was off the hook and balanced on top of the box. Shane picked it up.

"Hello?"

"Shane Scully?" a voice with a Mexican accent said.

"Yeah, who is this?"

"Momentito . . ."

Then Shane was put on hold . . . for almost a minute. As he waited, he was looking into the brightly lit kitchen when the busboy who had led him to the phone took off his white coat, revealing a wife-beater tank-T underneath. On the back of his neck Shane could see interlocking *M* and *13* tattoos. *La Eme.*

Shane held the dead receiver to his ear, still trying to make sense of it when the busboy with the gang tatts exited the kitchen through a side door.

237

The penny dropped. Shane knew what was going on.

"Shit." He dropped the phone and sprinted back through the restaurant. Valentine was not there. He had already walked out through the main entrance. Shane reached down and clawed his ankle gun from its holster as he ran, then he exploded out into the street.

A few yards away he could see Valentine's white-and-tan Rolls-Royce convertible pulling up to the curb. Valentine paid the valet and was moving around to get behind the wheel. Gino was standing nearby, waiting for his rental.

Shane heard it before he saw it. The low rumble of blown mufflers. "Get down! A hit!" he screamed at the top of his lungs. Everyone dove for cover just as an Eme work car peeled around the corner and four auto mags opened up.

Bullets ripped into the Rolls and chipped brick dust off the building behind him. Shane landed on his stomach behind the Rolls and maneuvered into a prone firing position, then started squeezing off rounds under the car in the general direction of the low-rider. He heard a taillight break as more automatic gunfire ripped the night. Somebody screamed from behind the Rolls. Then suddenly rubber squealed and the carload of Emes was gone.

As Shane stood, Valentine was just pulling himself up from the wheel-well where he had ducked. He had a little cut on his forehead

238

from a piece of windshield shrapnel. Blood was leaking down into his eye. Sprawled in a sitting position against the restaurant wall, his shirt soaked crimson, was Gino Parelli.

Valentine ran over to him. "How bad is it?!"

"How the fuck do I know?" Parelli croaked. "Fucking beaners. How'd they know where we were?"

Then they could hear the wail of a siren in the distance.

"Gimme a hand!" Valentine yelled at Shane. The two of them pulled Parelli to his feet, dragged him to the bullet-riddled Rolls, and laid him across the backseat.

Valentine got in the car and turned the ignition key. Miraculously, nothing had hit the engine and it started. Precious blood was pumping dangerously out of the bullet wound in Parelli's chest. Valentine took off his expensive cashmere coat, reached back and put it over Gino's wound. "Hold it there, tight. . . . Compress it," he ordered his gunsel. "Let's get the fuck outta here. I don't wanna try to explain this to the cops." He turned to Shane. "You saved my life. This sure as shit complicates our negotiation."

"We don't have a negotiation," Shane said.

"That's what you think. Get your car and follow me."

So Shane grabbed the keys off the valet board and sprinted into the parking lot next door. The street-savvy Mexicans had all magically disappeared.

The sirens were only a block away as Shane bounced his Acura out onto Fairfax, leaving a trail of bumper sparks on the asphalt. He hit the gas and hung a right, then followed Dennis Valentine's Rolls out of West Hollywood.

23

THE PROPOSITION

As he followed the Rolls across town, Shane tried to call the chief and Alexa on his cell, but he must have had a weak battery or something because he couldn't get a signal. They finally arrived at Valentine's rented estate on Mandeville Canyon Road, where he was greeted by state-of-the-art security: panning cameras, punch pads, motion detectors, and a sign on a not-too-friendly wrought-iron gate that announced: VICIOUS ATTACK DOGS. Shane followed Valentine's Rolls as they headed up the long designer-brick drive. Vast lawns with lit fountains decorated the landscape while they pulled up to a huge Greco-Roman house. Stone and granite pillars held up a monstrous roof with porch dormers. Motion detectors clicked on security lights, illuminating large sections of the property as they drove past.

Shane followed the Rolls around to the back, where Valentine parked and got out. No blood-thirsty dogs. Shane guessed either the sign was a fake or Dennis had phoned ahead to have them locked up. Valentine looked down at Parelli in the backseat, then waved at Shane to come over.

Shane got out of the Acura and started toward the Rolls, but Valentine was now moving away, motioning for him to follow as he headed toward the backyard. Shane didn't know why the handsome mobster was leaving Parelli, unless the bodyguard had bled out during the ride across town and was already dead. Shane veered and followed Valentine through a side gate, past an Olympic-size pool with swim lanes set in blue tile strips along the bottom.

As they walked across the deck, more lights clicked on, illuminating their way. Valentine stopped beside a lounge chair, then motioned to it.

"Wanna get Gino out of the car. We can put him on this," Valentine said, so they picked it up and carried it back to the Rolls.

"How is he?"

"Not good. The bleeding is slowing some, but I think he's going into shock. He'd be dead if those barrio rats didn't all hold their Tec-Nines sideways like a buncha rock-video gangsters. Looks cool, but nobody can hit shit that way. Musta been a lucky shot."

When they got back to the Rolls, Parelli

was trying to sit up.

"Hey, Gino, lay back. We'll do it," Valentine said, while putting on a pair of leather driving gloves to protect his skin. With a little struggling and careful tugging, they finally pulled Gino out and laid him on the lawn chair. He looked pale. A cold sweat glistened on his sallow, pasty face. With Dennis carrying the front and Shane the back, they hoisted the two-hundred-fifty-pound enforcer and lugged him back through the pool gate.

They set Gino down near the lighted Jacuzzi. Dennis told Shane to wait, then went inside the house. A minute later, he reappeared with an armload of beach towels and put one of them on Gino's bullet-shredded shoulder.

"Fucking *frijolito* dickheads," Gino grunted as he held it tightly on his wound.

"Don't talk. I called the doc from the car," Valentine ordered as he rolled up two more towels and placed them under Gino's feet, elevating them to help ward off shock. Suddenly he headed to the pool house.

"You got a doctor coming?" Shane asked, trailing after him, but by now Valentine was already inside, so Shane stood by, waiting. A minute later, he reappeared with a blood pressure cuff.

"Use this to check my pressure every day. Do it thirty minutes to the second after I swim my laps. I stay at exactly one twenty over eighty. Textbook numbers." He went back to Gino, who now looked unconscious. Dennis wrapped the gunsel's arm with the cuff, then pumped on the rubber ball.

"The fuck you doin'?" Gino opened his eyes and whined.

"Checking your pressure. Shut the fuck up and stay quiet. Now I gotta do it over." He pumped it again till he got a reading. "Eighty over sixty. Not so good. Too low. You're going into shock."

"Them fuckin' greasers," Gino growled. "Somebody in our crew musta ratted us out. How'd they know we was at Ciro's?"

"I think it was my fault. I wasn't paying much attention when I left the house. They musta tailed me," Valentine said, picking up the pool phone and hitting a buzzer.

"Lynette, you lookin' for Doctor Seligman's car?" he said, then paused. "Okay, okay, open the gate the second you see him." He hung up. Gino's teeth were starting to chatter.

"Wouldn't it be warmer in the house?" Shane suggested.

"I'll get him a blanket. Last thing I need is this guy bleedin' all over my wife's ivory carpets. I fuck up her new decorating, Lynette'll start bitching like a French whore." Valentine went into the main house and reappeared seconds later with two blankets. He draped them over Gino.

Then they heard a car pull up around the side and Valentine moved quickly to the pool gate and let in a small, balding man, carrying a doctor's bag. He rushed over to Gino and kneeled down.

Only then did Valentine turn away and walk Shane over to the outdoor pool bar. He opened the cabinet, reached for an ice bucket, filled it from the ice-maker, then grabbed a chilled bottle of Taittinger from the refrigerator. He worked off the wire that held the cork, accidentally fired it into the night, then poured himself a foaming glass, dropping the open bottle into the ice bucket. "You want a glass? Help yourself."

"You got any scotch?" Shane asked.

"Scotch? You know what you're doin' when ya drink that shit? Aside from what it does to your liver and kidneys, it's like you're eating whole wheat. It's all barley grain and rye — carbohydrates. An hour after it hits your system it turns into pure sugar. Scotch is eighty, ninety proof alcohol. Alcohol makes you retain water. You're gonna bloat."

"Gimme a fucking scotch, will ya?" Shane growled, his nerves still jangled from the gunfight.

Valentine shrugged, began hunting through his liquor supply under the bar, then finally came out with some Ballantine's. He uncapped it, smelled it, wrinkled his nose in disgust, and finally poured it into a club glass, neat. After he handed it to Shane, they clinked rims and drank.

Shane followed Valentine over to the glass-topped table near the pool house.

"Your doctor friend is going to have to report that gunshot wound," Shane said. "It's a state law."

"He's not a people doctor; he's an animal doctor, a vet. So he can report it to the SPCA."

"If Gino needs a transfusion, whatta you gonna do, give him a pint of Doberman blood?"

"Look, Scully, get outta my business, will ya? This doc used t'be a people doc, but he got busted for using drugs so now he delivers puppies and cuts off cat balls. NYU School of Medicine, so he oughta be able to handle this. If Gino don't make it, then them's the breaks, but I'm not gonna check him in at County General and have a buncha cops over there asking me why the front of Ciro's Pompadoro ate ten pounds of lead tonight."

"Why did it?"

"Business problems."

And the way Valentine set his jaw, it was pretty obvious that was all he had to say on the subject.

"Anyway, thanks. You hadn't given me that half-second warning, I'd be decorating the inside of a coroner's wagon."

Shane nodded and sipped his scotch. It occurred to him that if he'd just kept quiet, that would have been it. . . . No more Dennis Valentine. He could forget all this movie B.S., but he

246

had acted out of instinct. Besides, he was a cop. His job was to protect and serve. Even assholes like Champagne Dennis Valentine got full service.

"Now I owe you my life," Dennis was saying. "Since I can't very well turn you into fertilizer anymore, I gotta find some way to come to terms with you."

"I don't want to come to terms," Shane said. "What you're selling makes no sense to me."

Dennis sat down on one of the pool chairs, leaned back, and regarded Shane carefully. The trickle of blood from the cut on his forehead had dried. "You know what my uncle always says?"

Shane shrugged.

"He says that to know how things can be, you gotta know how they were. 'Nother words, study history and it will predict the future."

"Your uncle," Shane deadpanned. The Jersey Godfather.

Valentine pointed to the chair opposite him. Shane pulled it out, turned it around, and straddled it.

"So for that reason, I like reading history," the mobster continued. "You ever heard of the Browne-Bioff labor union scandal?"

"No," Shane said.

"Well, it happened right here, in 1933 and '34. It was a successful corruption of the be-low-the-line IATSE unions — the I.A."

"Nineteen thirty-three? Guys in snap brims

and spats? Can't you find something a little more recent?"

Dennis smiled and sipped his Taittinger. Shane noticed that there was quite a lot of Gino's blood on Valentine's tan pants.

"Back then, George Browne was just some low-level union business agent for one of the showbiz locals. I forgot which one. But with Al Capone and Frank Nitti's financial and physical help, Browne ran for the presidency of IATSE. A guy named William Bioff represented Capone and Nitti's criminal interests out here, channeling money into the right pockets and laying big hurt on anybody who talked against Browne. In 'thirty-four, they finally got Browne elected president. That meant Capone and Nitti controlled IATSE. With Capone's blessings, George Browne starts cutting new deals with producers on an ad hoc basis. If a producer was willing to send a little vig to this thing of ours back East, then he got a sweetheart deal, got to make his movie on the cheap. The scam lasted almost five years till 1940, when the Shaw brothers got thrown out of power here in L.A. and a buncha reforming assholes took over. Then the cops and the D.A. finally shut it down. So what does this tell us?"

Shane shrugged again and sipped his Ballantine's.

"It tells us that history can point us to the future. It also gives us an operational blueprint. If it could be done once, it can be done again. I bought the right people inside IATSE, and the ones who didn't want to play took unscheduled vacations they ain't comin' back from. The election for the IATSE presidency was last month. I don't have to tell you our candidate won. So now I can get you a cut rate on your movie because I'm in a position to make special deals."

Shane wasn't wearing a wire, so this heartfelt confession was lost in the wind.

"Hypothetically, even if I were to believe you, I still wouldn't want to give up a percentage greater than its dollar-for-dollar value," Shane said.

"Well, maybe to get this all started, I cut you a deal on this first film because you saved my life tonight and because I'm such a Michael Fallon fan. But you gotta look at this as more than just one movie. It's a business proposition, and if you help me with one last piece of the puzzle, I'll let you be part of it."

"What piece is that?" Shane asked.

"Once I start cutting special deals, the union hotheads are gonna start bitching. They'll go to the D.A., the D.A. goes to the cops, the cops start an investigation. That means the IATSE hard-liners will probably get a forensic audit from the city or state accounting office. Then I got a lot of troublesome legal and IRS tax bullshit. Maybe somebody I already bought down there gets jittery and decides to sell me out. Once that happens, I got the D.A. up my ass. See what I'm saying?"

"I see."

"I been lookin' for the right 'rabbi' to help me downtown." Valentine took a sip of his champagne and smiled at Shane.

"By downtown, are we talking about the police department?"

"Let's say we are. I'm thinkin' maybe you might lead me to my inside man . . . or woman."

"A cop who'll take a bribe."

"Only it needs to be someone up high enough to cut off an investigation once it starts to get troublesome."

Shane sat there and pondered it. Of course they were both thinking of Alexa, but neither said her name.

"Would have to be somebody in administration," Shane said, then took another sip of scotch. When he looked up, Valentine was staring at him.

"Let's cut the shit," the mobster said. "You willing to ask her?"

"Look, she's upset with the department right now because of what happened to me, and because of the political backlash she's getting on this gang war. I won't deny she's pissed, but taking a bribe . . . I don't know."

"You said you wanted to change careers? This could put you on top in showbiz," Valentine said. "I'm not just talking about your Mike Fallon movie. You get your wife to cooperate,

I'm talkin' about a piece of my piece of the whole scam. A small but significant piece. And your wife gets paid for her risk. Let's say we start with a hundred thousand in good-faith money just for her to say we all want to work something out. If nobody at the union squawks, and there's no investigation, she doesn't have to do anything and she still keeps the money. If there's a problem, and she has to go into action and fix something, I can pay by the job or the year. If she shuts down the right investigation, maybe there's half a mil in it for her." He sat there staring at his glass of Taittinger, then looked up suddenly. "But there's one big catch."

Shane waited.

"If you go to her and ask her, and then she gets froggy and takes what I'm telling you to the OCB, or the D.A. . . . then I'll pull out of L.A. and go back to Trenton, but I'll be pissed, 'cause a lotta time and money got wasted. This happens, you, your wife and kid — the whole Scully family — go for a deep-sea stroll on the bottom of the ocean. If you talk to your wife, you gotta control the outcome."

After delivering this bone-chilling statement, Valentine just lounged there, looking at Shane, sipping his Taittinger vitamin cocktail.

"I can control Alexa. Lemme give it a shot."

"Good."

Now the doctor was heading across the deck toward them. "The bullet went through. I've stitched him up and given him antibiotics, but I want to take him to my hospital. I can't get human plasma, of course, but I can give him intravenous saline for fluid loss. With bed rest and no complications, he should make it."

Shane and Dennis carefully carried Gino back to the doctor's car, then sat him up on the passenger side with the seat reclined. They watched as Doctor Seligman backed down the long drive on his way to an animal hospital with Valentine's pet gorilla.

24

WISEGUY THEATER

This time on his way home Shane stopped at a mini-market and bought a six-pack of Amstel Light and a bag of tortilla chips. When he got back to North Chalon Road and let himself in, he was concerned that neither Chooch nor Alexa were home yet. It was after ten p.m., so he looked up the number of the library, dialed, then heard a recorded message announcing that they opened at seven and closed at nine.

Shane glanced out toward the backyard and saw Franco outside on the pool deck, looking in through the sliding glass door. Shane and Alexa had decided to keep him inside for a few days to reacclimate him, but somehow the cat had gotten out. Shane unlocked the pool door and pushed it open. Franco rushed inside.

"Who let you out?" he asked.

Nobody should have been inside from the

time he left the house with Gino, at around seven. That only left one answer . . .

Shane went to the garage, took the LAPD 2300 Frequency Finder out of his trunk, and brought the unit inside. It had a battery pack, as well as a long, retractable cord. He inserted the plug, then began his sweep in the living room.

The first bug he found was in the phone receiver; it was the size of half an aspirin tablet. Shane found a second bug under a lampshade.

In the bedroom there were two more: one in the desk phone, another taped to the back of the headboard. A fifth bug was in the kitchen above the air vent; a sixth, hidden in the den.

Filosiani had called it right.

Shane opened a beer, then went out the front door to sit on the curb. He pulled out his phone and dialed Chooch's cell first. He got the "subscriber is outside the area" recording, then tried Alexa, who answered on the second ring.

"Where are you?" he asked.

"About a block from Chalon Road."

"Pick me up, I'm sitting out front."

He walked inside, got her a beer, then returned to the curb just as Alexa pulled up in her dark brown police-issue Crown Vic. Shane climbed in and pointed toward the end of the block.

"Where we going?" she asked.

"Tell you in a minute. You know where Chooch is?"

"Library."

"Closed an hour ago."

"Listen, Shane, he's seventeen. We lifted his curfew. He's supposed to be growing up, managing his own life. There're lots of times he gets home late. We've gotta let him have some room."

"Honey, his phone is off and I'm scared to death he's gonna get dragged into this gang case you're working." He pointed to the curb. "Here's good."

She pulled over and stopped the car. He handed her a beer.

"Why are we having happy hour in my car?"

"House got bugged."

"Really?"

"Yeah."

Then he told her what had happened, and how he had spent the evening.

She listened until he finished, then pulled the tab on her beer. It chirped loudly in the car. Alexa downed half the can at once. She drank beer like a guy. It was just one of the hundreds of little things Shane loved about his wife.

"Of course, you know if you'd let that happen, we'd all be out of the movie business by now," Alexa said. Shane nodded but said nothing.

"You report the shooting at the Pompadoro to the detectives downtown?" she asked.

"My cell isn't working too good in this weather," he hedged.

"Pretty pathetic, Shane."

"Okay, look. I've been kinda busy."

"What about Parelli, you think he's still alive, or is he L.A.'s newest one eighty-seven?"

"Far as I know, he's still breathing. But Alexa, we don't want to report it. I'm next to Valentine now. If this investigation goes wide and Dennis gets sucked in, my cover gets blown."

She nodded, then finally turned to face him. "Okay, I'll handle the chief. Don't report anything."

"Good."

"You have any idea who made that phone call at the restaurant, lured you outta the way?"

"I been trying to dope that out. Here's what I've come up with so far. . . ."

Alexa remained silent.

"Since it was Emes in that work car, it had to be Amac's hit," Shane started, "one of his *vatos* probably cased the restaurant to position Valentine for the shooters. The scout could have been at Paradise Square and saw me when they took me to meet Amac. He calls Amac, and says I'm in there. Amac calls me to the phone to get me outta the way."

Alexa looked over at him and took another long swig on the beer. "I guess it could have gone down that way," she said. "So, if Amac is trying to clip Dennis Valentine, I guess we know what that tells us."

"Tells us Valentine's probably the one organizing the Crips and Bloods, and importing the White Dragon?"

"Could these two cases really be interrelated?" she speculated, her brow furrowed in doubt. "In police work, the first rule is never trust a coincidence."

"It's not a coincidence. Valentine moves to L.A. with his uncle's blessing. But do you really think they're only gonna do this showbiz deal, or is Dennis also gonna open up all the traditional mob rackets: drugs, guns, prostitution, porno?"

"He'd try and control everything," Alexa said.

"Right. So that means we gotta figure there's a good chance Valentine is behind your drug war. The timing makes sense. He shows up, Stone dies, Crips and Bloods unite to distribute heroin, then White Dragon samples hit the street. You said the DEA would have picked up a Mexican or Colombian smuggler, but they didn't, so maybe it's the Italians. So it follows that if the Emes know Valentine's supplying the black gangs with drugs, they would want to clip him."

Alexa finished her beer in three giant swallows, then crumpled the can and dropped it on the seat between them. "Welcome to my case."

"Hey, we're a great team. Even when we

don't know what the fuck we're doing, we score."

"No shit . . . we're the best . . ." She smiled. "The rubber gun squad."

"Your call," Shane said. "I still work for you."

"I guess we go back to the house and put on a show for the bent noses."

They parked her car in the garage and went inside. Shane gave her another beer, took a second one for himself, then walked her around the house, silently pointing out the bugs. She nodded at each one, then pointed at him and mimed grinding a camera — show time.

She went to the front door, opened it, then slammed it loudly.

"Hi, honey. Where've you been?" Shane called out.

Alexa walked into the living room.

"Those pricks downtown! I swear I'd like to shoot that fucking Filosiani," she said.

They both moved over to the bugged lamp in the living room. Alexa sat near it, but Shane started moving around the room to change the sound density on the mike. He'd heard tapes on hundreds of bugs and they were never clean recordings.

"Whatta you expect?" Shane said, roaming around, picking up a magazine, then dropping it. "Y'know it's all politics down there."

"Right. I'm busting my ass and all I'm getting is grief. Did you read that horrible article in yesterday's *Times*?" she asked.

"Yeah, saw it after you left. Pathetic."

"Sometimes I just want to pull the pin. Get the hell out, like you did," Alexa fumed.

Shane crossed to her and sat. "Listen, I met a guy tonight, a guy nobody in our Organized Crime Bureau even knows is in town."

"Do we need to discuss this now?" She sounded bored. "I'm really tired."

"Yeah, we do. Our OCB spotters shoulda picked him up at LAX, but he slipped in here. Your hotshot *goomba* squad missed him completely. He's a made guy from the East Coast."

"Just what I need. Now I gotta deal with some vacationing wiseguy while I got all this other shit to contend with."

"He's not on vacation. He's in town to set up a new business."

"Who is he?"

"If I tell you, you gotta promise it stays with us. I don't want this going to OCB."

Alexa remained silent. They both waited patiently, then Alexa cleared her throat. "Just tell me; let's not play this game."

So Shane gave her a glowing account of Dennis Valentine: telling her how smart he was, how careful, and how he was intending to take over IATSE. He ran through it point by point, leaving nothing out.

When he finished, Alexa was quiet for almost a minute.

"If he tries to organize a labor union, I can

promise, we'll shoot it down — fast!" she exclaimed.

"Honey, stop thinking like a cop for a minute. This is a chance to get rich. He offered me a piece of his scam. He'll make us partners. If he pulls it off, it's worth a fortune."

"You think he can really do that? Take over IATSE? How much can that be worth?" She sounded both amazed and skeptical at the same time. Alexa, like most cops, was a superb actor.

"What if, tomorrow, I handed you a hundred thousand in cash for just having a meeting with him and saying you're willing to think about it?"

"A hundred thousand to just *think* about it? You're kidding."

"I'm telling you, this guy is for real. He's serious."

"A hundred thousand for just talking to him?"

"All he wants now is for us to agree to agree. Once he starts cutting special deals with producers and studios, he's afraid some union guy will squawk. Then it could go to the D.A. for an investigation. If it does, all he wants is for you to put the right guy on it. A guy we can control."

"You're serious?"

"Honey, this is our little winery and restaurant in Mill Valley. This is all our dreams answered; a chance at a peaceful, normal life away from all that glass-house bullshit."

She finally said, "I'm not saying I'm absolutely gonna do it, but I think we should hear him out. Why don't you call him back and set something up?"

They left the room and went out to the pool; Franco trailed along behind them. They sat on the pool deck sofa and Shane put his arm around her. She leaned her head on his shoulder, while Franco licked his paws, cleaned his face, and watched.

Shane's mind was lasering over his myriad of problems. Chooch was now exposed to Valentine as well as to Amac. Shane was worried about that and was slowly becoming very depressed over it. He wished the boy would come home so he could hold and hug him. He wished he could send his son away to protective custody until this was all over.

Alexa picked up on his thoughts like a Gypsy mind reader.

"I know," she said softly. "I'm worried about him, too."

25

OVER BUDGET

They left a new note for Chooch taped to the refrigerator, then got in the car and drove to the Valley.

Chief Filosiani's house in Studio City was a modest duplex on La Maida. Shane and Alexa pulled her Crown Vic into the driveway, exited, and found Filosiani waiting for them in the living room. He wore a red bathrobe over pajamas, and had fleece-lined slippers on his feet. He whispered that his wife, Mary, was asleep in the bedroom as he led them into the den.

The chief's den was wall-to-ceiling clutter and way too small to accommodate his vast police reference library. The Day-Glo Dago had run out of space and overflow volumes were stacked everywhere. Big, blue LAPD binders, filled with procedural manuals from other departments, were piled on the floor waiting for

262

his determination as to whether they contained anything worth implementing in L.A. He had one bookshelf packed with ten fat volumes of the *Psychological Pathology of Homicide*, another with volumes on ballistics and ESD. One entire wall was devoted to the emerging field of DNA and forensic investigations.

The chief cleared some space on the small four-foot-long sofa, and Shane and Alexa squeezed onto it together, as Filosiani lowered himself into a creaking Early American rocker. "You said on the phone it was important," he probed.

Shane and Alexa filled him in. When they got to the part about the foiled La Eme drive-by on Dennis Valentine, he furrowed his brow.

"I don't like," he said. "Means Valente's already got more traction here than we realized." He slowly leaned forward. "Do you realize how lucky we are you stumbled onto him when you did? You're on the inside now, with a real shot at busting his operation."

"That's why we came over," Alexa said. "This film scam of Shane's is good. Valentine told him tonight that he wants me to be his department mole. We've got to keep the sting operation going, but we're out of money."

"I just gave you a hundred thousand, then I get an e-mail from you this afternoon that said you put in another ten and needed forty more. I authorized it and had it transferred. What happened to all that?"

"Gone," Shane said.

"Gone?" He was furrowing his brow. "A hundred and fifty thousand in one day?"

"Well, actually, it's more like two days, but yeah. Beyond that, I've just made a verbal deal with Mike Fallon's agent. It ain't cheap, but the good news there is I don't have to pay him if the film doesn't go past the second week of preproduction. We went into preproduction today, so we've got thirteen days left. I also cut a deal with a director named Paul Lubick. Nicky and I did it over the phone with his agent this afternoon. Lubick's not cheap, either. The guy has more assistants than a NATO commander."

"Shane, need I remind you that we're not gonna ever make this movie?" Filosiani said.

"You can remind me all you want, Chief, but as long as these guys don't know it, they're gonna set up to do things the way they always do."

"How much?"

"Well, at least a hundred more to start with. I'll go back to Lubick's agent and try to cut a more front-end-friendly step-deal on a shorter clock with a trigger clause."

"What the fuck is that?" Filosiani growled, losing his impish smile.

"It's movie talk. Means we pay less now but he has a trigger date that obligates us to the whole amount in a few weeks. Normally he wouldn't get the full amount until completion

264

of the principal photography. I'm planning to set up the meeting between Alexa and Valentine tomorrow. He's talking about giving her a hundred thousand in earnest money. We might as well let Valentine finance some of this sting himself; let it go toward our overhead and expenses. That gets us up to three hundred and fifty thousand. I'll try and move this along as fast as I can, get the RICO case made before this movie breaks us. But these guys and their agents are tough. The minute I stop paying, they stop playing, and once that happens, Dennis is gonna spot this for what it is. Then everything we've spent to date gets flushed with no case getting filed."

"Okay . . . okay, I gotcha. I'll keep the money coming. But Christ on crutches, Shane, wrap it up quick, will ya?"

"I'll try."

They left Filosiani and drove back to North Chalon Road. When they arrived, it was after midnight. Chooch's Jeep was still not there. The note was still on the fridge. Shane called the boy's cell phone again, but got the same out-of-area recording.

"Maybe he left a message for us on the Venice machine," Alexa suggested.

Shane called the house and hit their retrieval code. There were two messages from Nora Bishop to Alexa, asking her to call about the bridal shower Alexa was throwing tomorrow. Alexa had changed the address to North

Chalon Road, and Nora wanted her to fax a map to all the out-of-town friends. Then, they heard Chooch's voice . . .

"Hi, Mom and Dad. Look, I won't be coming home tonight . . . maybe not for a few more days. I know you're gonna be worried and upset with me, but I gotta take care of something. I promise you I'm safe. I'll check in and leave messages every day so you'll know I'm okay. This is very important to me. Talk to ya later. I love you guys . . . Bye."

After they hung up, Shane and Alexa stood in the kitchen by the phone, staring at the floor. Both of them were flooded with emotions.

"He'll be okay," Alexa finally said. But Shane was too upset to even answer.

26

PREPRODUCTION

Shane slept badly.

Every time a car passed the house, he would wake up thinking it was Chooch's. Twice, he got up to check the garage. During one of these occasions he went outside to the pool, away from the listening devices, and attempted to reach Amac on the cell phone, calling the same number Chooch had given him, leaving a message with a Chicano who barely spoke English. He tried to go back to bed.

At two-thirty in the morning his cell phone rang. Shane snatched it up, swinging his feet out of bed, wide awake in less than two seconds. Alexa was also rolling into a sitting position.

"Yeah," Shane said.

"Scully." It was Amac.

He got out of bed and headed back out onto

the pool deck, away from Valentine's bugs. Alexa grabbed a robe and followed.

Shane could hear *folklórica* music in the background. "Chooch is missing," he said once he was away from the house.

"Just a minute," Amac said. Shane heard a door close, then the sound of the party disappeared and Amac came back on. "*Órale*. He called me."

"Where is he?"

"He wouldn't say. You remember Delfina Delgado?"

"Who?"

"You met her, homes . . . when you came to *mi tía*'s house. The beautiful *chavala* with the long black hair."

"Yeah, yeah, I remember . . . your niece."

"Well, kinda. She's in my family. *Mi tía*'s her *comadre*. It's like a godmother. Delfina is my aunt's brother's daughter, whatever that is . . . my second cousin or something."

"What about her?"

"Hey, Scully, she's Chooch's *jiana*. He's in love with her. He's been seeing Delfina for almost two years now. You ain't heard about this?"

"He never told me," Shane said softly.

"Delfina disappeared two days ago. We been looking all over for her. Don't know where she is. I can't give it much time 'cause I got this *pleito* with the *mayates* to run. When Chooch couldn't reach her, he called me. Now he's out looking for her."

That was the missing piece. "Has Delfina been kidnapped?" Shane asked.

"If the *mayates* know about her, then maybe, but you want my guess . . . I don't think so."

"Then what? Where is she?"

"I don't know, but you gotta let go of Chooch, *ese. Así es, así será.* This is how it is, how it's going to be."

"I can't just do nothing."

"What you gonna do, man? Get in your *carrucha* an' drive all around up in The Hills, looking? He'll come home."

"Have you checked your aunt's house in Lomas?"

"My aunt is back in Cuernavaca. *Estados Unidos* was not her thing. Maybe it's not for any of us. We'll have to wait and see. If I hear from Chooch, I'll call you — try and get him to go home."

"Thanks, Amac . . . and thanks for the heads-up in that restaurant."

"Don't know what you talkin' about, homes . . ." But there was a smile in his voice. Then he hung up.

"What?" Alexa said.

"Chooch has a girlfriend. I met her when I went up to talk to Amac two years ago. She's Amac's second cousin, a beautiful girl with long black hair. She's missing and it seems Chooch is out trying to find her."

Alexa reached out and took Shane's hand.

269

"You gotta admit, that's exactly what you'd be doing."

The remainder of the night was strangely more restful. Maybe it helped knowing that Chooch had not signed up to be a soldier in Amac's *pleito*.

Shane woke early, with a headache. He showered for a long time, standing in the strong, hot spray of the drug dealer's luxuriously tiled stall. The hot water relaxed his neck muscles and eased his headache. When he finished, he looked for a towel. Not finding one, he used Alexa's hair dryer instead. Then Shane slicked his hair back with his fingers, put on clean underwear with yesterday's clothes, and left. He didn't wake Alexa because it was the first time she had been able to sleep in two days.

Shane drove to Hollywood General Studios and waved as he pulled past his buddy, the retired motor cop. He had to park in a guest spot in front of the administration building because a Jag Roadster occupied his newly assigned parking space.

When he arrived at Cine-Roma Productions, he ran into a firestorm of activity. People he had never seen before were milling about in the halls, running in and out of Nicky Marcella's office, which now had a piece of paper stuck to the door that read: DIRECTOR.

Nicky was sitting on the couch and Paul Lubick was behind the desk. The director was a

270

tall, fortyish man with a beefy build and a flushed complexion. There was too much tangled yellow-blond hair matting his large head and it had been fastened into a ponytail with a thick rubber band. He was wearing a safari vest with all kinds of shit in the pockets. Lens finders and fog filters dangled from chains around his neck; on his feet, he wore an ultrahip pair of lace-up Doc Martens.

"I don't give a shit if he *thinks* he can get them or not. He's gonna come through, or he's gonna get fired." Lubick was ranting as Shane ducked into the office unnoticed. "That neural flashback is pivotal. It's tits! This whole Civil War sequence is the seminal event of the entire film — the idea of disenfranchised people, slaves to a repressive system, trapped in a world gone mad . . . the social symbolism of a nation torn in half. This is the neural manifestation of Rajindi's religious philosophy, right, Raji?"

Rajindi Singh was seated in a chair by the window, a pale ghost in a white suit. He was meditating or tripping, but either way he was in situ, eyes closed, legs crossed on the seat in the lotus position. He opened his eyes and nodded solemnly.

"It's just, where are we going to get three hundred pairs of authentic Civil War underwear?" Nicky whined. "Since it's underwear, and not being seen by the camera, it seems to me that trying to locate something that may not even exist is both time consuming and economically wasteful."

Paul Lubick got up from behind the desk and moved toward Nicholas. "You've obviously been so busy making your little skin flicks you don't understand A-list movie making. So let me lay this down for you once and for all. Reality, my little friend, comes from everywhere. It comes from the sets, the wardrobe, and from my mouth to God's ear. It isn't just some concept of acting, where you say to a performer, 'Okay, pretend you're a Civil War soldier. Pretend you're about to die from those twenty-pounders thundering on that ridge.' Sure, the performers I'll cast as principals will have some ability to conjure up these feelings, but what about the extras? Ever think about them? A bunch of nineteen-year-old California surf bums. How do I put the spirit of Gettysburg into those pot-smoking assholes? I'll tell you how. We're going to have a Civil War school. We're going to hire as many of these extras as possible, by today or tomorrow, and we're going to make them live in tents out in Reseda, at my brother Peter's farm. We'll work something out with him, pay him a few bucks — I don't know, maybe it'll have to be a lotta bucks. It's gonna be a huge imposition on Pete, but he shares the vision, thank God.

"The extras are going to wash in buckets and shit in ditches. They're gonna wear honest-to-god, lace-up, Civil War underdrawers, so every time they gotta take a piss for the next eight weeks, they gotta unlace the damn things and do it exactly the same way those poor fucks in the Georgia brigade did it a hundred and forty years ago. Only then will they begin to metamorphose from California beach boys into my Georgia rebels. When we roll, and I'm shooting in some sixteen-year-old surfer's face, he's gonna goddamn sure believe he's a fucking Confederate soldier."

After this tirade, silence fell like ash from Mount Vesuvius. Then Paul Lubick leaned down even closer, until his nose was just inches from Nicky's. "I assume you hired me because you've seen my work, and want me to bring my unique style and vision to this project. Translation: I'm gonna shoot this my way. You wanna win a real Oscar and throw all these rentals away? Then you better buy or *make* three hundred pairs of Confederate soldiers' undies, circa 1864." He grabbed a costume book and flipped it open to a picture. His face was so red he looked like he had been working out on a Stairmaster for an hour.

"Okay, got it," Nicky said. "I'll get right on it."

"And who the fuck are you?" Paul Lubick had finally spotted Shane in the office.

"Co-owner of Cine-Roma Productions. I'm also the guy who's gonna feed you every pair of those Civil War long johns if you think you're gonna waste our money on shit like that," Shane said calmly.

Paul Lubick moved toward him, but Shane took a step forward and the director saw something menacing in his eyes and stopped. The two of them stood a few feet apart, glaring at each other.

"Paul," Nicky said softly, "maybe you should tell my partner about the trees."

"That's one of my best ideas. It's tits!" Lubick picked up a drawing on the desk. "When we build the dragon's lodge, I think it's important that the ceiling beams on that set be massive. In the neural storm that follows, old Isom, the slave, says they symbolize the overbearing structure of society that hangs over us, dwarfing our freedoms, or dialogue to that effect. Excuse the paraphrase, Raji."

The writer nodded his head.

"Anyway, we'll have to find massive redwoods — I've got a guy up in Oregon looking. Once we've marked them, we'll cut the trees down and bring 'em in on double flatcars, by train. Then we'll get a construction crew into Stage Three across the lot, hoist those suckers up, and knock them into place."

"You ever hear of papier-mâché?" Shane countered. "You could make those for one-tenth the cost and no one would ever spot the difference."

"But *we'd* know the difference, wouldn't we?" Lubick cracked a tight little smile. "Any other way is simply dishonest. Translation: I'm gonna shoot this my way."

He turned away from Shane and faced Nicky. "I'm going to walk the stages, see if I want to use Stage Three or Stage Six, so we can notify the studio and tie one of them up. We need to get going on construction. He started toward the door, then stopped and looked at Shane. "For your information, Mister Whatever-your-name-is, though slightly expensive, what I'm suggesting should be of no consequence when creative gold is being mined. Let me give you a little lesson on how we do things in Hollywood. During the filming of *Bonfire of the Vanities*, Brian DePalma needed a shot of a Concorde jet landing. Of course he didn't want to buy used stock footage at five hundred dollars a shot, because it would have been film already seen in someone else's movie, and like me, Brian insists on cinematic purity. He knew it needed to be original footage because he also wanted a setting sun in the background. So he sent a second-unit film crew out to get it. He rented the entire airport and a Concorde jet. It took him three nights, three sunsets to get the shot, but in the end that Concorde landed at exactly the right second into the setting sun. That piece of film cost the studio four hundred and fifty grand, lasted ten seconds, and was worth every fucking nickel. Here's another one. Michael Cimino saw a tree growing in London that fulfilled the symbolism he envisioned for a shot in *Heaven's Gate*. He knew he would never find another tree that perfect on his location, so he had the tree uprooted. He had every leaf cataloged and preserved. Then he sent the entire thing to a courtyard at Oxford, where it was hoisted up, and the leaves were reattached to the exact same branches. Fucking brilliant, too. The tree was awesome. This is the way directors conceive. A director's dick gets hard, he ejaculates, and it becomes cinematic creation. If any of this isn't working for you, speak now, and I'll be in my Jag and gone."

Paul Lubick picked up his briefcase and turned to Rajindi Singh. "You want to walk this with me, Raji?"

Singh got up and left the office on Lubick's heels, without so much as a look at either Nicky or Shane.

"I think you ticked him off," the little grifter commented.

"Three hundred pairs of Confederate underwear? Tree trunks you've gotta ship down from Oregon on double flatbeds? This lunatic is gonna bankrupt us in two hours."

"You haven't met his staff. He brought a whole crowd of people who think just like him. Wait'll you meet Buzz, the UPM."

"The what?"

"Unit Production Manager. We also have an assistant director, a director of photography, an art director, a casting guy, and two costumers and their staffs down the hall. They're all sharing the new offices we rented, making phone calls. It's a fucking madhouse in there."

"Nicky, we've got less than a hundred grand left in the bank. That's it. After that, all our checks are coming straight from Goodyear Rubber."

"Shane, whatta you want me to do? The minute anybody criticizes Lubick, he threatens to leave and Rajindi goes with him, Fallon follows Singh, then Valentine splits and I'm back auditioning bimbos in short-shorts."

"We gotta slow him down, Nicky. We gotta find a way to build a time loop into all of this. Maybe we can put all the purchase orders on this picture through a pay office . . . hold everything, all the accounts payable, for two weeks."

"Shane, if Lubick tells these vendors to begin working, they'll start spending our money on his say-so alone. He's an A-list guy. Nobody's gonna tell him no."

"Whatta we do?" Shane was beginning to panic.

"I think we oughta consider getting the LAPD to *really* make this film. We're already in over two hundred grand on holding deals and preproduction costs. Once we factor in Fallon's step-option deal, plus Lubick's, we're gonna be pushing half a mil by Monday. The only hope we have of getting any of your money back is to shoot this thing and release it."

"Are you outta your mind?!" Shane was almost shouting.

"Shane, a strange and wonderful thing is happening." Nicky lowered his voice confidentially. "My phone hasn't stopped ringing since this morning. Thing about Hollywood is: Activity is its own endorsement. We're rolling here. We got A-list people signed. Everybody who read this script a year ago and hated it now thinks maybe they misjudged it and missed its hidden brilliance. I've got studio guys calling and offering us slots in their distribution schedule, maybe even some P and A participation." Off Shane's puzzled look he added, "That's Prints and Advertising. I think I can actually sell a piece of this film to a major studio — Warner or Universal. We got offers for housekeeping deals at two major studios. That's a deal where they give us an office and some overhead, maybe a development fund. It's like I finally broke through because of this thing, and I love you for it."

"Nicky, we are *not* gonna make this movie, okay?"

Just then, the door flew open and Champagne Dennis Valentine walked in. "Is Michael Fallon around?" he asked, smiling.

27

ZELSO

Shane found out that Paul Lubick had a few numbered copies of the script. He saw one in the director's briefcase just before lunch. He would have swiped it and made a copy, but it was printed on red paper, which defeated Xeroxes. When Shane asked for one, he was told by Lubick that he wasn't on the approved distribution list.

"I'm the producer. I'm paying your salary. How can I not be on the approved list?" Shane argued.

"Woody Allen doesn't even let the lead actors who've already been *cast* in his movies read the whole script, just the scenes they're in. You have to operate on a little faith . . . have trust in your director," Lubick said.

"But I'm the *producer*," Shane raged impotently.

"Right. And you're not on the list. I don't know you from a box a rocks. How do I know you're not gonna get it retyped on white paper? Make copies and pass 'em around town? Next thing, critics are taking shots at me before I even shoot a frame. I'm hot news in show business. When you're tits, you're prime for trashing. Right now, just the few people I need to read it will get a copy, and then only the pages they're involved with. No exceptions." He left Shane standing in the hallway.

At twelve, Shane and Dennis Valentine, who had both been more or less ignored all morning, decided to keep each other company for lunch. They walked across the lot toward the Studio Commissary, which was really only a restaurant located just off the property, across an alley in an old railroad dining car. Nicky called it the vomitorium, but the manager gave discounts to people who could show studio gate passes.

They sat in a back booth. Framed cartoon sketches of old movie actors grinned down at them from red flocked wallpaper.

"When do you suppose Michael Fallon will show up?" Valentine said.

"Don't know. You should check with Paul."

"This guy, Paul, whatta you think of him?"

"He's an asshole."

"Purebred and overfed," Valentine agreed.

They ordered. Shane asked for the twelve-ounce rib-eye. Valentine ordered steamed vegetables and Taittinger.

"We don't stock Taittinger. Got a nice Paul Masson sparkling Bordeaux," the waiter said, and got the vitamin lecture for his suggestion.

They did some showbiz small talk, and after ten minutes, Shane finally worked his way around to Alexa. "That thing we were discussing yesterday?" he began as they both picked at a lettuce and tomato salad.

"Yep," Valentine said as his order of cooked vegetables arrived, looking like a steaming plate of dinner scrapings. The rib-eye followed.

After the waiter left, Shane continued. "I talked it over with her. I think we got a player."

Valentine stopped eating his vegetables and looked up angrily. "I don't wanta discuss this here. I don't talk about business in rooms I don't trust." Valentine had undoubtedly heard the tape of Shane and Alexa from last night and was well prepared for this conversation. But just not in a room he hadn't swept.

"If not here, how about tonight?" Shane said.

"Tonight's fine." Valentine forked in some steamed cauliflower. "My house, five-thirty this afternoon."

"She's pretty busy. How's after work sound . . . around seven?"

"Sure, seven's good." Then Valentine switched subjects quickly, pointing disgustedly at Shane's plate. "Y'know how long some of that meat's gonna live in your intestines?" he said.

"Not long . . . I shit logs."

"Yeah, you laugh, but most Americans carry around ten pounds of undigested meat in their colons. You're killing yourself one bite at a time."

"I'd rather be dead than hungry," Shane said as he took another bite. "We can compare notes in hell."

Shane's afternoon was full of couldn'ts. He still couldn't get a copy of the script, because Paul and Rajindi were locked in a Concept and Tone meeting, whatever that was. He couldn't hang with Dennis, because once the mobster knew Michael Fallon wasn't going to show up, he left. Shane couldn't beat up on Nicky because he had gone with Buzz, the UPM, on a preliminary location scout out to the Disney Ranch. Shane had been fielding phone calls from vendors that Lubick had already put to work. They all wanted down payments. An extras casting company had started hiring teenage boys for the Georgia regiment, and the bank had called twice to tell Shane that they were overdrawn again.

Nicky had somehow managed to add himself to the signature card on Shane's blind account and had been writing checks. Shane had totally lost control. He felt closed in on, and impotent, so he left the studio at four-thirty and escaped to the relative safety of Parker Center.

He pulled into the vast underground garage

next to the Glass House, parked on the third level, then went to the fourth floor where the CRASH unit was located inside the Geographic Operations Bureau.

Shane found a sergeant he knew named Sylvia Hunt. Everybody in the CRASH unit looked tired and overworked.

"What d'ya need, Shane?" Sylvia said, her green eyes still on the computer screen at her desk. She was scrolling Crip gang addresses.

"With all this going on, I'm guessing you're probably working The Hills pretty hard, am I right?"

"You can't piss on a wall in Las Lomas without getting busted," she said, finally looking up.

Shane handed over the Jeep's license plate number and vehicle description, along with the photo of Chooch he always carried in his wallet. "This is my son. He's half Hispanic and has a girlfriend in The Hills who's missing, named Delfina Delgado. She's American Macado's second cousin. I'm worried my son is gonna end up in the middle of this fire zone, trying to find her."

Sylvia stopped working and focused on him. "Your son's dating Amac's cousin?" she asked.

"Yeah. Anyway, that's his picture and his plate number. He drives a 1999 black Jeep Cherokee. If anybody spots him, I'd appreciate it if you'd pick him up."

She took Chooch's picture and the paper,

and studied them. "If she's Amac's cousin, maybe she was abducted."

"Yeah, maybe. But he doesn't think so."

"Who doesn't think so?" Sylvia Hunt was now drilling him with her green eyes. "What do you know? Who have you been talking to?"

"Nothing. Nobody," he said.

"Have you been in contact with American, Shane? If you've spoken with him, the head of DSG will want to talk to you."

"Hey, Syl, I'm married to the head of DSG, remember? This is her adopted son."

"Forgot." She blushed.

Shane turned and left the bureau. On his way to the elevator, his cell phone rang.

"Yeah?"

"Shane, it's Fineburg," the little computer jock said. "I got something, but maybe we shouldn't talk on an open line. When can you come see me?"

"I'm upstairs," Shane said. "I'll be right down."

"See you when you get here."

Shane found Lee Fineburg at his console in the computer section. They headed to the coffee room at the end of the corridor. Nobody was inside, so they entered and closed the door.

"My brother finally put the hat on Farrell Champion."

"Who is he?"

"His name is Daniel Zelso, but he doesn't look anything like the picture of the guy in

People magazine. I went across the street and bought one." He opened his briefcase and pulled out a black-and-white fax photograph of a slender man with an undershot jaw, hollow cheeks, and dark hair. Then he took out the copy of *People* and opened it to a picture of Farrell at a movie premiere.

"Jesus, whoever did his face work was a magician," Shane said. "Got a new chin, different hair. Completely transformed him."

"Yep. Doesn't look anything like he does today. Back when he got busted by the feds, he was working as a money launderer for a bunch of Panamanian drug lords. The feds rolled him. The way I get it, they now fly him all over the country to testify in these complex criminal cases he woulda been a defendant in, but the feds gave him immunity. They protect his identity — he testifies behind a screen. So everything you said makes sense now. It explains how he can be so high profile and still be in WITSEC."

"How 'bout the two dead wives?"

"That's how the feds nailed him. They made him for the two wife murders — both food-poisoning cases like you said. The A.G. threatened to gas him on a double-one, and he rolled," Fineburg said, referring to a double first-degree homicide. "Under the threat of getting a cyanide pill he gave up most of his pals and Panamanian drug associates. Only he didn't roll on everyone. A few got away, most notably a Panamanian who did the Syndicate's money transfers from Hawaii. Guy is named Generalisimo Miguel Fernando Ruiz, still missing."

"So Farrell Champion is Daniel Zelso. He's testifying behind a screen in a bunch of drug cases while simultaneously producing big-budget movies and living in Malibu. The government is protecting him in WITSEC despite the fact that he killed his first two wives with poison shrimp."

"Actually, it was crab."

"I can't believe they'd shield a murderer." Shane snorted.

"Come on, lighten up. The guy only committed two murders. How many people did Sammy 'The Bull' Gravano whack and still get immunity? Nineteen or something? Two unhappy women had an unpleasant meal. We oughta be able to overlook that." Black humor.

"Thanks, Lee. And tell your brother I owe him. You happen to find out who's handling Zelso out here?"

"Can't get it. Tried. Obviously it's someone in the U.S. Marshals. They're a small unit, not more than six or seven guys in the Southwest office, so you should be able to sniff it out."

"Right," Shane agreed.

Before he left Parker Center Shane went downstairs to the Electronic Science Division and found a sergeant named Bob Alvarez. "I'm working U.C.," he told him. "My target does constant bug sweeps with a 2300 Frequency Finder. I'm working him tonight. I've got to wear a wire, and I need a way to beat that thing."

"I got just the unit, but you'll need approval from DSG to check it out 'cause I've only got two."

They called Alexa's office, but she was out, so Shane got the approval from Filosiani directly. Then Alvarez went back to his equipment room and returned a moment later with a cell phone. He placed it on the counter in front of Shane.

"This should beat the scan," he said. "It's a regular StarTAC, and if it's turned off, it doesn't transmit a signal, so the wand on the bug duster won't pick anything up. Once you've been scanned, turn it on, and lay it on the table. Cell phones are so common, these guys never seem to check 'em. The cell will record the conversation. The signal goes to a satellite and the downlink gets picked up here."

Shane thanked him, then headed home to North Chalon Road. Nora's friends' cars were parked up and down the street in front of the house. He had forgotten that Alexa was throwing Nora's shower this afternoon.

Shane was reluctant to go inside, because he knew he would eventually have to tell Alexa that Nora's fiancé wasn't just a famous producer but a drug dealer, money launderer, and wife murderer. He drove around the block once before finally getting up enough nerve to pull into the driveway.

He walked through the front door and saw them all out by the pool. Nora was sitting behind the huge glass-topped table, opening gifts and laughing while a dozen or so women clustered around, watching. Alexa was seated next to Nora, frantically writing who-gave-what-presents down in a shower book.

Shane picked up Franco and went outside to join them. Alexa spotted Shane first, came over to give him a hug, then guided him to the guest of honor.

"Oh, Shane, this new house is incredible. . . ." Nora gushed.

They descended into introductions and small talk with Nora's circle of friends and bridesmaids.

"Oh, by the way," Nora said, "Farrell's really hoping you'll be able to attend his bachelor party tomorrow night."

"I've been so busy getting back to work, I completely forgot to call him," Shane lied. "But I wouldn't miss it now, for anything."

28

BAD TIMING

They were standing outside on the front porch, away from the bugs, watching the last of the shower guests drive off. Alexa had just packed up her briefcase and was getting ready to head back to Parker Center.

"I can't do this tonight," Alexa said.

"Honey, we've gotta do it tonight. I'm running out of time."

It was already six-thirty. They were arguing about the seven o'clock meeting Shane had set up with Dennis Valentine.

"Why is it so important we do it tonight?" she persisted. "Can't we set it up for tomorrow, or on Saturday?"

"My bank account is empty. I need the hundred grand in good-faith money Valentine promised you."

"Tony just put in another hundred thousand

at two this afternoon. That means the department is out over three hundred K. There's a limit to all this insanity, Shane."

"You haven't been down there. It's a zoo. You got any idea how much it costs to FedEx a two-ton Civil War cannon from Virginia to L.A.? I've got sets being built around the clock and people up in Oregon cutting down redwoods. I'm making three hundred pairs of Civil War lace-up underwear for three hundred teenage extras who, starting tomorrow, will be on full salary out at a farm in Reseda, practicing close-order drills with muskets. If we don't get this RICO case made soon, we may have to actually shoot the damn movie to have any chance of coming out."

"You better be joking," she said, ominously.

"You haven't met Paul Lubick. When they were passing out assholes, this guy got one with fangs."

Shane pulled the StarTAC off his belt and showed it to her. "I checked this out at ESO. It has a bug inside that broadcasts to a satellite. If I can get him on tape trying to bribe you in a union-fixing scam, then I can shut this bullshit film down. I'm moving as fast as I can. I know it sounds crazy, but right now, I'm up against trigger clauses on three big talent deals. When they hit, we're fucked. We can't delay this."

"Trigger clauses. For how much, you never said."

"You don't want to know."

She glared at him, so he told her, "Seventeen million in unamortized, above-the-line costs. Ten for Michael Fallon, two for Rajindi Singh, and five for Paul Lubick."

Alexa had her hands on her hips, which he'd come to recognize during their first year of marriage as her most bellicose posture.

"But we won't have to pay it, 'cause I promise I'll close it down before that happens, but you can't build in any delays. I know it's a shitty time, but this thing sort of got away from me. I think I can hold it to under half a million if we move fast."

So ten minutes later they were in Shane's Acura, driving to Kenny Rogers's old house on Mandeville Canyon. They were both stressed, and halfway there got into another argument.

"This movie has turned into a runaway train," Alexa fumed.

"I'm doing the best I can," he flared.

"It's like everything is coming apart at once," she complained. "Chooch is missing and that's got me worried sick. This damn gang war is escalating. Now I've got this mess with Valentine, and to top it off, Nora just told me she needs more help with the wedding. One of her bridesmaids, the one from Michigan, who was handling the flower arrangements and the chapel decorations, is AWOL and won't be out here till the day before the ceremony. All that got dumped on me this afternoon."

"So tell her no."

"How can I tell her that after all she's done for me?"

Shane knew it was absolutely the wrong time to tell Alexa about Farrell Champion. So why on God's earth did he ignore his instinct? But right there, on Sunset, just as he was nearing the 405, that's exactly what he did.

"Speaking of the wedding, it's just possible that Farrell isn't all we'd hoped for." Shane had his hands at ten and two on the steering wheel, his stare locked on the street ahead, but he could feel her anger pulsing across the seat at him, heating the side of his face.

"Isn't all we'd hoped for? Just what the hell does that mean?"

"Well, remember his bad joke?"

"Oh, no. Please don't tell me you've been investigating that."

"Honey, it wasn't a joke. Farrell does have two dead ex-wives — both from food poisoning."

"You promised me." She sounded exhausted, or resigned, or maybe it was just that she was massively disappointed.

"I know I promised, but dammit, I had a strong hunch, a feeling I just couldn't ignore. I couldn't."

"Why?"

"Because this guy's not Prince Charming. He's not even a halfway decent frog. In fact, cutting to the sleazy bottom line, he's a complete shit who skagged two ex-wives, got busted for it by the A.G. in Washington, then rolled over on a drug-money laundering scam he was doing in Panama to beat the double-one." Shane pulled Fineburg's fax picture out of his pocket and handed it to Alexa, who studied it for a minute, then pitched it into the ever-increasing distance between them.

"This isn't him. It's somebody named Daniel Zelso. Doesn't even faintly resemble Farrell," she said disdainfully.

"It's him before the face job. I got prints from his house, Alexa. He's running around testifying for the feds behind a screen while they protect his identity in WITSEC."

She was staring down at the picture on the seat; then she put her hands up to her face and started to weep.

Shane had just passed over the freeway west of UCLA and was now heading west toward Pacific Palisades. As he slowed, a line of angry drivers started honking behind him, so he made a right onto Barrington. The houses here were large, the lawns well cared for, the neighborhood made famous by O.J. Shane pulled to the curb away from the streetlight and parked. In the front seat, beside him, his beautiful, strong wife was slowly coming unglued.

"Honey . . ."

"Shut up." She turned her back to him. "Just please shut up." Now facing the side window, sobbing.

Shane knew a lot of things were causing her

meltdown. Lack of sleep was probably at the center of it, plus the stress of not knowing where Chooch was. Everything seemed to be hitting them at once.

"Honey, Farrell's a bad guy. I know I made a promise. I know I broke it, and I'm really sorry. I'd do anything if it hadn't come out this way, but dammit, I love Nora, too. She's my friend as well as yours. I had a hunch Farrell was lying and now it turns out he's a money-laundering murderer."

Shane looked at the dashboard clock: 7:06. He knew they couldn't run a scam on Dennis Valentine with their personal lives falling apart like this. What was he thinking? Why the hell had he told her all this now?

Of course there were two reasons: first, Alexa was the strongest, smartest person he knew, and he needed to strategize with her; second, he simply had a horrible time lying to her.

Finally, she turned to face him. "We better get going. It's after seven," she said, opening her purse and taking out a pack of Kleenex. She blew her nose, then threw the tissues back inside the purse, snapping it shut.

"Honey, I'm sorry."

"We can't deal with it now. I've gotta get my wits about me. You said it's up on Mandeville Canyon. That's only a few minutes from here."

"Alexa . . ."

"Shane, stop it. I'll get over it. Let's go. I have to get back to Parker Center."

He put the Acura in gear, swung a U back to Sunset, then resumed his trip to Dennis Valentine's house. They turned onto Mandeville Canyon and finally pulled up to his brightly lit gatehouse. Shane looked over at Alexa. She was bathed in the glow coming through the side window. "Honey, are you sure you're up to this?"

"Just ring the fucking buzzer," she said and sighed.

29

MEET THE BOSS

They headed up the winding driveway and were met by two bodyguards in dark suits, who motioned them around to the side of the mansion. Another of Dennis Valente's long-armed, short-haired enforcers was waiting in the parking area for them. When Shane and Alexa got out of the car, the man walked over carrying the same 2300 Frequency Finder that Gino had used on him the day before.

The goon came to a stop a few feet away. "I'm Silvio Cardetti," he said respectfully. "Mr. Valentine likes to know that none of his conversations are being recorded. I'm sorry for the inconvenience, but if you could both turn around, please."

Shane and Alexa complied, then one at a time, Silvio ran the wand up and down their bodies. The little StarTAC cell phone clipped to Shane's belt was turned off so it didn't register on the meter. But Silvio did find both of their weapons.

"If it wouldn't be too much trouble, could you leave your guns in the car?"

Shane unstrapped his piece from its ankle holster; Alexa took the Spanish 9mm Astra out of her purse. They locked both weapons in the trunk of the Acura, then Silvio led them to the front door of the estate.

"How's Gino?" Shane asked to make conversation.

"Back in New Jersey, recuperating. Mr. DeCesare sent the jet to pick him up."

They walked up onto the porch and Silvio rang the doorbell, which chimed the first eight notes of Kenny Rogers's "The Gambler." The carved oak door was immediately unlatched and Dennis Valentine stood there, smiling widely. He was dressed like the Easter bunny: white shirt, white silk tie, white pleated pants, Pat Boone bucks. A three-quarter-cut white blazer with matching silk pocket square completed the ensemble. It took a very handsome, self-assured guy to pull it off. . . . Champagne Dennis was managing to stay just inside the boundaries of fashion comedy.

"They're clean," Silvio reported, holding up the state-of-the-art frequency finder.

Dennis stepped aside grandly, motioning them into the magnificent but overdecorated front room. It looked as if his interior designer had managed to sell him everything on the showroom floor. The large living space was packed like a furniture warehouse.

On the far side of the room, dressed like a Fredericks of Hollywood model, was Lynette Valentine. She was in her late twenties, with long blond hair and a centerfold's body magnificently displayed in tight, leopard-print stretch pants and a plunging black top. Decorating her dainty feet were plastic platform heels.

"I'd like you to meet my wife, Lynette," Valentine said.

She moved across the room and extended a slender arm to Alexa, while giving her a competitive once-over. It was no contest as far as Shane was concerned, but he guessed there might be some men who would prefer Lynette's neon flashiness.

"Hi, we're Shane and Alexa," he said to her.

Lynette turned to check him out before she shook hands. It was a frank, inviting appraisal.

"Can I get anybody a glass of Tat?" Dennis smiled warmly.

"Do you have white wine?" Alexa asked.

"Certainly do. And scotch for you, right, Shane?" For some reason, Valentine skipped his vitamin lecture. He crossed the room to the bar, then opened the built-in refrigerator, pulled out a bottle of chardonnay, and went to work on it with a fancy corkscrew.

"We have terrible party curfews in this neighborhood," Lynette blurted out unexpectedly.

"It's because some guy who publishes a men's magazine used to live up the street. He was trying to be Hugh Hefner or some damn thing, throwing all-nighters, cars parked everywhere. The neighbors got an ordinance passed. Denny tells me you're a policewoman."

"Yes. I'm a lieutenant in the LAPD." Alexa smiled.

"Is there any damn way to get this curfew shit eliminated?"

Dennis made a quick move back across the room with the drinks. "I'm sure they don't want to hear about that, Lynny." He handed Shane a glass of scotch, neat, and gave Alexa her wine. Nothing for Lynette. Then he picked up his flute of Taittinger.

Lynette's expression had changed to a pout, but she stood her ground. "I'm just saying, we're trying to have some charity fund-raisers, like for the Children's Hospital and the Women's Rape Center. We understand you can get a lot of important actors and showpeople to these kinds of events, but this ten-thirty curfew shit makes it fucking impossible."

"Please, Lynny, not now," Valentine ordered. The smile he was giving her would have looked good on a reef shark.

"I'm just saying, maybe they could help us get the damned curfew canned," she persisted. "My God, Dennis, it was your fucking idea to do these silly parties, not mine."

"Will ya shut up?" he snapped, then turned

to Shane and Alexa. "Why don't we go into the den?" Valentine escaped Lynette's whining by leading the way toward the back of the house.

"Nice to meet you, I guess." Lynette pouted as they left the room.

They were walking down a long corridor hung with colorful and expensive modern art. "These paintings are beautiful," Alexa said, pausing to admire one.

"You think? Personally, I don't get modern art. That's an Umberto Boccioni," Dennis said, flicking his thumb at the colorful, kaleidoscopic painting. "And that's a Gino Severini original . . . I think that's the Severini, maybe it's the Giacomo Balla, and the Severini is that one, on the other side, with all the circles and triangles." Then he stopped in front of a colorful brown and blue painting. "This is the only one I like," he said, smiling at it. "It's called *Three Bluebirds Full of Marbles*. I love that. Thing was painted by Jonathan Winters. Funny guy, but there was nothing funny about the price — and they call *me* a criminal."

He moved on, stopping at another painting. "Lookit this thing. Cost me fifty grand. It's called *Women with Flowers*. So where're the fucking flowers? Lynette and the decorator picked all this stuff out. The art in this hall cost over two mil and except for the bluebirds, there ain't one of 'em I like."

They entered his den, which was masculine to a fault, hunting trophies and gun racks. Several game heads looked down from the walls with bored, glassy stares.

Alexa sat, but Shane remained standing.

"I understand you might be interested in helping me with a little project I got going here," Dennis began. He was smiling at Alexa, leering almost. Obviously he liked what he saw and seemed a little surprised by her beauty. She was a cop, so he'd probably been expecting a weight lifter with shoulders from Gold's and legs from Steinway. Instead, Alexa was beautiful enough to model.

Shane watched uncomfortably while the handsome mobster undressed his wife with his sexy bedroom eyes.

"If you have a business proposition," Alexa said, "then maybe we should hear it."

Shane reached under his jacket, took out his StarTAC and turned it on. Dennis was watching Alexa until Shane set the phone down on the bar top between them. His eyes flicked over to it.

"I'm expecting a call from Nicky. He's supposed to phone me with the time of Paul's casting meeting for tomorrow."

Valentine nodded, turning back to Alexa. "I'm new in town," the mobster started. "I'm sure your husband has told you about my family history. . . ."

"Yes. He said you're Don Carlo DeCesare's nephew."

Dennis nodded. "I'm also a businessman

301

who occasionally takes a calculated risk with legal parameters."

"Are you trying to say you're involved in crime?"

A cold look suddenly appeared in Valentine's eyes.

"Listen, Mr. Valentine," Alexa continued, "you and I will do much better if we cut out the verbal calisthenics. Remember, cops have short attention spans and limited vocabularies. Why don't you just state what you want and we'll see where it goes from there."

Good move, Alexa, Shane thought. It would force Dennis to describe his bribe in plain terms that wouldn't be subject to legal maneuvering in court where defense attorneys could argue "That's not what he meant." It would get Valentine to make a straight pitch, thus helping to avoid an entrapment defense.

"I'm looking to do a little price-fixing in the entertainment guilds," he finally said. "This could cause some of the hard-liners to go to the D.A. to seek relief. That happens, I might need someone on the cops to work something out for me. Make it go away."

"You want me to boot the investigation?"

"However you do it, I don't want to face an indictment on a RICO statute."

"I see . . ."

"And for this service, I'm willing to pay you handsomely." He stood up and walked over to a large painting of Secretariat. It was a magnificent oil of the famous racehorse, mounted in an antique gold frame. Dennis swung the painting away from the wall and opened a concealed safe, withdrawing a small metal case. He carried it over to Alexa, set it on the bar, and popped it open. Inside the case were ten large bundles of banded hundreds. Each brick-sized stack contained a hundred bills.

"Say yes and you get to take this home with you tonight," Valentine announced. "If nothing ever happens, and I never need your services, it's yours to keep. But if I need you, then you do whatever it takes to end any investigation against me."

"I do this for a hundred thousand dollars? Pretty good deal for you, but not much of a deal for me," Alexa said.

"The hundred large is so you'll know I'm serious, and I'll know you're in the game. If I require more help, we make arrangements on a case-by-case basis. We could go as high as half a million if it keeps me from getting indicted. That's the fair market price for a police fix back East."

"Mr. Valentine, since you're new in town, maybe you don't know that the LAPD hasn't been for sale, so there is no 'fair market price' out here," Alexa said. "Beyond that, I'm not all that high on getting busted for felony bribery. If that happens, Shane and I will both end up in Soledad for the next five to ten years. Cops in prison don't do quite as well as mobsters. We don't get color TVs and yard privileges, we get the SHU," she said, referring to the Security Housing Unit where cops and high-risk prisoners were held in isolation. "If we're gonna make this deal, it's gonna have to be something that balances that risk. A hundred thousand doesn't come close, as far as I'm concerned."

"What does?"

"Half a million up front, and another half a mil at the end of the first year."

"That doesn't sound very fair to me," Dennis said softly.

Shane had to hand it to her, Alexa had upped the stakes and was trying to cover their budget overruns at Cine-Roma by getting Dennis to finance the entire sting against him. Sometimes his wife amazed him.

"Once I leave with this suitcase, I'm as guilty as if I already fixed a case," she said. "Bribery is bribery. Once we're in, we're all the way in, and you have to pay us for our risk. We'll be available to help you for a year only. No longer. After a year, it's over."

Dennis sipped his Taittinger as a small smile tugged at the corner of his mouth.

"You know, of course, what happens to you if you agree to take my money and then fail to render services as required?"

"Lemme guess. We get a nine-millimeter cancellation contract."

There was a tense silence as they eyeballed each other.

Alexa picked up the case and snapped it shut.

"Does that mean we got a deal?" Valentine said.

"Are you gonna meet my price, terms, and conditions?" Alexa asked.

"A million for a year, paid in two installments, first payment in advance?"

"That's it," Alexa said. "Five hundred thousand now gets the deal moving."

"You've got a hundred. I'll get the rest to you later." Dennis seemed irritated by her look of disapproval. "Hey, I don't keep that kinda cash on hand. It's gonna take me a day or two."

Finally Alexa nodded.

"Y'know, I wish Lynette was more like you. All she ever thinks about is shopping. She's got her fucking doctorate at Neiman Marcus."

"You wouldn't want someone like me. If you ever told me to shut up like you did with her back there, you'd get maced."

Dennis smiled. "Would you put me in handcuffs?"

Alexa picked up her case full of banded cash and stood. "I really have to get back to Parker Center," she said. "You can get the rest of the money to Shane when you get it."

"Right, right, you must be busy. According to the TV, lotta killing going on."

Shane picked up his StarTAC, clipped it onto his belt, and they headed down the hall filled with expensive modern art back into the living

305

room. Lynette was no longer there.

As they reached the front door, Dennis stopped Shane. "Gimme your cell phone number."

Shane cursed himself. He didn't even know the number of the ESD StarTAC. "This is Nicky's phone," he lied. "I don't know the number."

"Gimme it." Dennis reached and pulled it off Shane's belt. Valentine was now holding the bugged cell in his left hand, looking at it carefully. He pushed the star key, then RECALL, and the cell number appeared on the LED screen. Dennis took out a Palm Pilot and wrote it down.

Valentine looked at Alexa. "Can you give us a minute?" he said. Alexa shrugged and walked out toward the Acura. As soon as she was gone, Valentine said, "I'm going to New Jersey on Saturday. My uncle wants to meet you and talk about this whole thing. I was thinking maybe you'd come with me on our private jet. Only gonna be gone for one day. Everything works out and he gives the okay, then we got a deal and I hand over the remaining four hundred grand."

"Go to New Jersey and meet with Don Carlo DeCesare?" Shane said, still eyeing his StarTAC in the mobster's hand. Dennis nodded, so Shane said, "Sure, why not? Could I have the phone back?"

Dennis looked down at it. "Never saw a cell

like this before. Must be brand new."

Shane reached over and took it out of his hand. "I'll see ya at the studio in the morning." Then he walked back to the Acura where Alexa was waiting.

30

INVITATION TO A SIDDOWN

"I think we got him on RICO," Alexa said as soon as they left Valentine's estate. "Once we get the rest of the money, I can pay the budget office back and tomorrow you can start shutting down the movie."

"Honey, what you did back there was brilliant. That extra money buys me a few days." She turned to stare at him, so Shane rushed ahead. "Valentine wants me to go to Jersey to meet Don Carlo DeCesare. If I can get Little Caesar on tape offering us money, then we've got one of the biggest *goombas* in organized crime."

"Shane . . ." It was said as a warning.

"It'll only mean staying open till Monday, and I don't think we'll spend all that much money over the weekend. Check with Filosiani, see what he says."

"He'll say do it. He still hates the DeCesares from when he was in New York."

"Look, we've got some serious money now. Valentine's half a mil oughta see us through."

Alexa nodded but said almost nothing all the way back to North Chalon Road. Once he pulled into the driveway and parked, she finally turned in the front seat to face him. "Look, I think I need to apologize to you."

"It's okay."

"I've gotta say this." She sighed. "You did the right thing on Farrell. You read something on him at that party, you looked into it, and it turned out to be true. I was wrong to make you promise not to check him out. I mean, if I really thought Farrell was so bulletproof, what was I afraid of? I've been thinking about it since you told me. I must have sensed something wrong, too. We're cops; cops follow hunches. You did the right thing. It's just . . ."

"You want her life to be perfect."

"She's due for some happiness, Shane."

"Honey, there has to be a reason she keeps falling for these dirtbags with tans. It's like she's got some kind of tragic flaw."

"I've never seen her so in love. Now one of us has to break this to her."

"If you want, I'll do it," Shane said.

"No, I think it should be me."

"Before you do, at least let me go to his bachelor party tomorrow night."

"You don't have to do that now."

"Look, there's still an outside chance that we're wrong."

A puzzled expression crossed her face.

"I got the prints off the gold lighter he was using to light everybody's cigars in the pool house. It's possible somebody else handled it after he did."

She continued to sit very still, afraid to invest any hope in that idea. They both knew that the facts were against them. Why would he be a clean screen on everybody's computer unless WITSEC was controlling it? But for Nora's sake, they were both praying for a long shot.

"I can get a fresh set at his bachelor party. This time, I'll hand him a clean glass, make sure nobody else touches it, then we check it against the prints on the lighter. I think we should be absolutely, one hundred percent certain before we do anything."

"I guess that makes sense." She opened the door, got out of the car, and Shane followed.

Alexa took her briefcase out of the trunk, walked a few feet to the Crown Vic, then Shane opened the door for her.

"Y'know, it would be nice to have a little winery up in Napa Valley, take Chooch there. . . ." Shane said. "Live a simple life without all these hairpin turns and abrupt stops. Being in this house makes me wonder if maybe we couldn't have more in our lives." Shane hated the sentence even as it was coming out of his mouth. But then he thought, *What was wrong with trying to improve?* Shane was tired of rubbing elbows with drug dealers and gang leaders. What had once seemed a noble profession now seemed like useless calisthenics.

"You'd die of boredom," Alexa said, frowning.

"Probably right." Then, to escape her look of disapproval, he changed the subject. "I gave Chooch's plates and picture to CRASH. They're gonna look around for him up in the Hills."

"Whatta you really think he's doing?"

"Amac doesn't believe Delfina has been kidnapped, but I'm not so sure. I think there's a good chance the Crips or Bloods snatched her to slow him down. I also think Chooch is out driving around looking for her. That's what's got me frightened."

She thought about that for a few moments, nodded, then kissed him on the lips. "I'll try and get home a little earlier . . . before midnight, if I can."

Once he was back inside the house, Shane was struck by a profound sense of loneliness. He walked through the halls looking for Carol's cat and found Franco sitting on the kitchen counter. "Hope you washed your hands and feet before walking around up there." The animal cocked his head, and then, almost as if he understood, started furiously licking his paws. "Too fucking late, buddy. Damage is done."

He put Franco down, found the cat food, and

set it out. Then he grabbed the last Amstel Light out of the fridge, sat in the living room, and tried to pull his thoughts together. He had trouble simmering on all burners. It seemed a reasonable assumption that Crip and Blood gangsters would research Amac's family, his girlfriends and lovers, looking for any leverage they could use against him. His aunt had gone back to Mexico, but Delfina stayed behind, and now she was missing. Amac had told Shane he didn't think she'd been abducted, but the more he thought about it, the more he knew that was probably bullshit. The last thing Amac would want right now was police interference in his personal revolution.

Shane dreaded the idea that Chooch might be driving around South Central asking questions, searching for her. But right now, there was nothing he could do to stop it. He didn't know how to find his son, couldn't even talk to him. All he had to ease his fears were the messages on the answering machine in Venice.

Suddenly Franco jumped into Shane's lap and walked up his chest until he was standing up, nuzzling his face. Shane could smell cat food on Franco's breath. Then, with Carol's cat purring in his ear, Shane's thoughts turned once more to her tragedy. Carol had paid the ultimate price. More depressing still, nobody had claimed the earthly remains of the prettiest girl from Teaneck, New Jersey. As a teenager she'd been sought after and adored; now she was just another dead junkie whore. The cop assigned to investigate her murder regarded it as a troublesome nuisance. Nobody wanted to pay for her funeral. Her value had slipped to zero.

Suddenly the doorbell rang.

Shane didn't move; he was bone tired and didn't want to answer it. The bell rang several more times. He had a sinking feeling he knew who was out there. He put Franco down, got to his feet, and crossed the room, again re-holstering his 9mm Beretta Mini Cougar from his ankle to the handier spot at the small of his back. When Shane opened the door, Silvio Cardetti was on the porch cutting an ominous, garlic-breathing hole in the view.

"I figured it was one of you guys," Shane said.

"Mr. Valentine wants you should go to a sit-down." Only he pronounced it "siddown."

"I just saw Mr. Valentine an hour ago."

"He wants t'see you again."

"Mr. Valentine oughta start scheduling regular business appointments instead of sending you guys out to ring my bell in the middle of the night."

"Mr. Valentine don't like scheduled appointments."

"Yeah, well, I do, and right now I'm in for the night."

"Here's the deal on that," Silvio said softly. "If Mr. V sends me out to do a job and I fuck it up, then I'm in the shitter. This is not good for my career, or my health. If you cause me this embarrassment, I will be forced to hold you personally responsible, which won't be good for *your* career or *your* health."

"You threatening me, Silvio?"

"Fuckin' A. Now, come on, don't make this into something we can't get over."

Shane heaved a deep sigh. "Can I get my coat?"

"You look fine to me. Let's go."

"Do I follow you?"

"Not this time."

He led Shane over to a new blue Mercedes four-door. Two overdeveloped steroid cases in suits were standing in front; a third, even larger man was on the far side of the car. All three of these American buffaloes were on the balls of their feet, ready to rumble. Silvio opened the rear door, stepped back, then moved several feet away.

This felt bad to Shane — like a ride he wasn't coming back from. Maybe Dennis had figured him out, maybe he had someone down at Parker Center who had blown Shane's cover.

Everything told him not to get into the car. Nobody knew where he was going; he could disappear without a trace. Shane was still ten feet away from the two guys by the driver's door when Silvio made a tactical mistake. He passed between those two gorillas and Shane. In that second, he was vulnerable. Shane was tempted to push Silvio into his backup and take off, try to get away, slip between houses. But some instinct stopped him.

Then the moment of Silvio's vulnerability passed. Shane had to take the ride.

He smiled, then turned to get into the car. As he did, Silvio reached out and plucked the gun from Shane's belt, disarming him. When Shane spun back, Silvio was holding the Mini Cougar. "We're all friends. You ain't gonna need this."

Shane was pushed into the backseat of the Mercedes, crushed between Silvio and a three-hundred-pounder.

The driver of the Mercedes put it in gear. As they pulled away, Shane saw Franco watching from the windowsill in the front hall, and he wondered if he would ever see Carol's marmalade cat again.

31

RIDE TO NOWHERE

The three gunsels that Silvio brought with him all used cute nicknames. The driver was called "Cheese." Next to him, in the passenger seat, was "Terminal Tommy." The guy on Shane's right was "Little Mo." If there was a "Big Mo," Shane sure didn't want to meet him. Silvio Cardetti was "Silver." These handles would probably render the bug in his StarTAC useless, but on the hope that they might slip and use real names, Shane reached down and surreptitiously turned on the cell.

They were on the Pasadena Freeway heading east. As they drove, his abductors kept up a constant flow of complaints about L.A. They were Jersey transplants who were pissed off about being stuck in a town they thought was full of faggots and butt-boys.

Then they were off the freeway, driving in

Pasadena. In the front seat, a map-reading dilemma was unfolding. The driver was trying to
find the Devil's Gate Dam, while Silvio was
looking in the *Thomas Street Guide*. They both
frowned and scratched their heads like mon-
keys working on a puzzle.

Eventually the blue Mercedes was winding
down into the arroyo. The Rose Bowl slid past
on the right, then they were heading north toward the mountains.

"Supposed t'be up here somewhere. Supposed t'be like a little gate or something . . .
takes you up to the dam," Silvio said.

"Does Mr. Valentine always hold his business
meetings in wilderness areas?" Shane was
thinking his body wouldn't be discovered until
summer.

"Nobody's talkin' to youse, so shut the fuck
up," Silvio growled.

Climbing up out of the arroyo, they entered a
wooded area where Shane saw a sign that read
DEVIL'S GATE DAM.

"Mr. Cardetti, why are we going up here?" he
asked, identifying Silvio for the StarTAC.
Shane was beginning to panic.

"I'm tired of all the questions," Silvio
barked.

They were on graded gravel that quickly
turned into rutted dirt. The car bounced and
rocked over the uneven surface before finally
coming to a stop by a pumping station.

"Guess we're here," Silvio announced.

All the enforcers opened their doors and Shane found himself alone in the car, dreading what was about to happen.

"Get out," Silvio ordered.

Shane reached down to his belt and felt the StarTAC — it was warm and transmitting. He reluctantly got out of the car.

"That way." Silvio pointed toward a narrow walkway that led across the top of the dam.

As Shane started toward the path, he again sensed that he had a chance to take off. None of his four escorts seemed to be paying close attention, and he thought he could make it into the woods bordering the path. But for some reason, he didn't try. Some instinct held him back. It was almost as if Silvio was making it too easy. Shane climbed the few stairs, then walked out onto the lip of the dam.

His mouth had turned to paste. A light breeze ruffled his hair and cooled the sweat on his forehead. Off to his left he could see a small dammed lake. A bright three-quarter moon lit the entire basin. As he neared the center of the walkway, he could see the outlines of two men looking at the twinkling lights of Pasadena. Silvio was lumbering along behind him, again blocking any chance of escape. As he drew nearer, Shane recognized Dennis Valentine standing next to a very thin man with a long string-bean neck. As Shane got closer, the man turned and Shane saw a look of abject terror in his pale gray eyes.

"Glad you could make it," Valentine said sincerely.

"You gotta be kidding. Four guys with guns? Like I had a choice."

"Bullshit," Dennis said, then turned to Silvio. "You gave him a choice, right?"

"Yes, sir," the goon said. "He coulda split. Had two easy chances."

"What's this all about?" Shane finally asked, his heart still beating furiously.

"That was a good meeting we had earlier. Your wife is beautiful and smart, but you're the one I'm gonna be close to. I always like to invite a guy I'm thinking about doing business with on a midnight ride. He's got nothing to hide, he shows up. If he's got a hidden agenda, he's gonna take off running. You had two chances to escape, but you came through. Shit like this is ten times better than a polygraph."

Shane nodded and his heart began to slow.

"Thanks, Silvio. You can go wait in the car," Dennis said, and the bodyguard left the three of them standing on the lip of the dam.

Dennis turned back to the view. "Y'know, I almost bought a place out here. Pasadena reminds me a lot of my home in Saddleback, New Jersey. You should see some of the big houses they got down by the Ritz Carlton Hotel over there." He pointed southeast. "Lotsa trees. Not flat, like Studio City or Sherman Oaks. This Pasadena Realtor with great tits showed me around and I almost made an

319

offer on a place on Hillcrest. Same house they used in the movie *Bugsy*. The movie audience thought it was Beverly Hills, but they shot it out here. Warren Beatty goes up to the front door, rings the bell, and tells the guy, 'I'm gonna buy your house.' I loved that scene. Fuckin' thing isn't even for sale and Beatty says to the guy, 'How much? I'm gonna buy your house.' " He was smiling at Shane and suddenly Shane was smiling back.

Why he suddenly found that cinematic act of extortion funny eluded him. He was probably still so juiced on adrenaline overload that his relieved senses were experiencing a catharsis.

"Decided in the end I hadda be on the west side, in Pacific Palisades or Bel-Air," Valentine continued. "It's a profile thing. Only dentists and geeks from Cal-Tech live in Pasadena. But I'll tell ya, that was some joint. Warren says to the guy, 'How much? I'm gonna buy your house. . . .' Priceless. I love that kinda shit."

"Who is this with you?" Shane finally asked to get them off of Bugsy, or real estate, or whatever it was they were discussing.

"This is Leland A. Postil, the new president of the International Alliance of Stage and Theatrical Employees."

Shane reached out and shook hands with the thin, terrified man.

"How you doin'?"

Postil's face twitched, but he didn't speak.

"He's fine," Dennis answered for him. "Lee

finally gets it, don't ya, Lee?" No response from IATSE's new president. "Lee's a patriot. No kidding. He tells me about how film and TV sell American values to the world, right, Lee?"

"Uh . . . I . . ." Postil's voice was almost inaudible in the cold night.

"He told me that movies export the way we are, and how we behave, or some shit like that. How'd that go again, Lee?"

Now Postil seemed to focus. He found his voice, which, like his body, was thin and reedy. "What I told Mr. Valentine is that films are America's most important export. Not so much as an economic resource but because they export U.S. culture. Our film and TV entertainment make the rest of the countries on the planet, even Communist nations like China, covet our American lifestyle."

"Yeah, China. Tell him about the *Hunter* thing." Dennis grinned.

"Yes, well, the TV show *Hunter*, starring Fred Dryer, was on in China in the mid-eighties. First American TV show to ever play there. The producers didn't get much money for it, 'cause the TV business in China is small and government-owned. But that show had a huge cultural impact. After it ran, democracy gained a foothold. There is a good cause-and-effect case to be made that the rise of democratic thought in China paralleled the popularity of that show." Lee Postil was coming to life now.

"The Chinese people saw Hunter driving around in Bel-Air, saw the big homes, and it made them want democracy. After Tiananmen Square, the Chinese government threw the show off the national network, and it never played there again."

Shane smiled, but wondered why the hell were they standing on the lip of a dam in Pasadena in the middle of the night, talking about *Hunter* broadcasts in China?

"I love that story," Dennis said, smiling. "*The Neural Surfer* will export the shit outta American culture. That's why it's so important IATSE cuts us a deal to get it shot for short dollars. Right, Lee?"

"Yes. I think a similar case can be made, but —"

"No buts, Lee. Movies are power, man." Dennis was grinning broadly. His alabaster teeth gleamed dangerously. "*The Neural Surfer is* American culture," Dennis enthused. "It's about our psychological beginnings, our racial misunderstandings, our tortured journey out of darkness. And Lee knows that without his help, this testament to American values may never be seen by the Chinese or the emerging African nations. Am I right here, Lee?"

The narrow-shouldered man nodded, and now Shane could see where this was heading.

"We need IATSE's help to bring the budget down or else we can't shoot it," Dennis continued. "Lee has agreed to make a special arrangement with Cine-Roma. Right, Lee?"

"Yes, I guess," the IATSE president said tentatively, looking like a man trying to decide whether or not to jump over the rail to his death.

"Tell our producer here what you're prepared to do," Dennis prodded.

"Uh, even though this is a big-budget film, given its sociological values and definition of American culture, IATSE would be willing to work against our low-budget rate card to help get it green-lit."

Dennis was smiling. "If you do the math, on a fifty-million-dollar below-the-line budget, that would cut the union costs roughly in half. Am I correct, Lee?"

"In essence . . . if you . . . more or less," he croaked.

"This is great news," Dennis said, slapping the tall man on the back. "I've got the agreement letter right here, all drawn up and ready for signatures." He reached down, picked up his alligator briefcase, opened it, then withdrew three copies of a letter printed on IATSE stationery. Valentine closed the briefcase on the narrow railing and used it as a writing surface. He pulled a gold Mont Blanc out of his pocket, clicked it open, and handed it to Lee Postil, who signed all three copies of the document. Then Dennis handed the pen to Shane.

"Shane, you're a damn smart producer. You have just saved your production twenty-five million in below-the-line costs." Dennis beamed and handed the pen over.

Shane took the gold Mont Blanc and signed all three copies.

Valentine's friendly smile suddenly disappeared like smoke out an open window. It was replaced with a cold, hard, menacing stare. "Our deal was percent for percent. There's the signed paper I promised, guaranteeing the low rate card. I'm in. We'll call my end fifty-one percent of your end."

"We'll do the math once the budget is set," Shane countered. "The way Lubick is going, twenty-five million might not even cover our catering costs."

"Okay, but I'm holding you to the equation. That was our deal."

Shane nodded.

"As of right now, I'm coproducing a Michael Fallon movie," Valentine whispered reverently, testing the sound of that sentence.

"Film," Shane corrected.

Dennis was beaming. "This is an auspicious occasion. The coming together of a unique creative enterprise with an alliance of working-class unions, in the interest of spreading democracy around the world."

"Too bad nobody brought a camera," Shane quipped.

32

COMING HOME

Shane and the president of IATSE switched cars for the ride back from Devil's Gate Dam. Lee Postil looked terrified as he squeezed in with the American buffaloes, while Shane walked down the rutted dirt road with Dennis Valentine. He had another Rolls-Royce convertible parked on a slab of poured concrete by the spill-gates. This one was midnight blue with a tan interior.

"I see you got a new parade float," Shane observed.

"I lease these things. Can't drive a car full of bullet holes."

They got into the Corniche convertible and Shane inhaled the rich smell of English leather. Dennis drove out of the arroyo and found his way back onto the westbound 210.

"What's the story with Lee Postil?" Shane finally asked. "He was so scared, I thought he was about to jump."

"I used to think Postil was a democratic visionary, but it turned out he was just another slimeball extortionist. Guy takes our help to get elected — our money, our muscle — then after he wins the I.A. presidency, he starts half-steppin'. All of a sudden, it's like, 'Who's Dennis Valentine?' I had to give him a little flashlight therapy to put him back in line."

Shane touched the cell phone on his belt to make sure it was still warm and transmitting.

"You hear all that shit about film and TV exporting American culture to the world?" Dennis continued, shaking his head in disbelief. "He actually told me that when I was trying to line him up a year ago. That shitbird thinks *Hunter* is changing the course of democracy in China. I hear stuff like that, I know I'm gonna be huge out here, 'cause nobody is thinking straight."

"Probably all the carbs we're getting."

"You laugh, but that ain't far off."

By the time Dennis pulled up in front of North Chalon Road, it was already one a.m. He turned off the engine, then fixed Shane with a businesslike stare.

"Now that I'm a full-fledged partner and getting my percentage against cost, I think we need to rein in this out-of-control director you hired."

"And how do you think we can do that

without scaring off Rajindi Singh and Michael Fallon?"

"I was thinkin' maybe we pull him out of the office some night, find a quiet spot, give him a Louisville adjustment."

"You wanna beat Paul Lubick with a bat?"

Valentine shrugged. "Listen, Dennis, I admit he's a jerk, but if you beat him up, you better either kill him or take off running, 'cause he thinks he's invincible and he'll go right to the cops."

"Then how do we fireproof this asshole?" Dennis asked. "You see the way he's spending money and I can't even get a copy of the script!"

"Let me and Nicky handle it."

"Nicky? That little liar can't handle shit."

"He's good with Hollywood types. Let us deal with it."

Dennis frowned but finally nodded.

Shane got out of the car, walked around the back, then stopped at the driver's side and looked in at Valentine. "Tell Silvio I want my piece back. Tell him to put it in the mail slot over there. If it's not here in the morning, I'm gonna have Alexa write some paper on him."

"Jesus, calm down. I'll take care of it." Champagne Dennis Valentine started the Rolls. "Don't forget, we're flying to Jersey, eight a.m. on Saturday. Plane is leaving out of Burbank, hangar twenty-six. Don't be late."

Shane watched as the midnight-blue convertible drove up the street, then turned right at the end of the block.

Once Shane walked inside some sixth sense told him he wasn't alone. Somebody was in the house. Shane was unarmed, so he froze in the entry. Then he heard Chooch's voice.

"Dad, it's me."

Relief flooded through him. He hurried into the living room and found Chooch sitting in the beige club chair holding Franco on his lap. The cat jumped down as Chooch stood. Then Shane reached out and gave his son a hug.

"My God, I've been so worried."

"Dad, I need your help."

"Where were you? Why didn't you call?"

"I left messages —"

"That's a buncha bullshit." Anger swept in and took the place of fear. "I couldn't talk to a message machine and you knew it."

"Dad, I'm in trouble. Please, I came here to get help, not a lecture."

Shane stood in the room a few feet from Chooch, trying to push two days' worth of tension and emotion out of the way. "Okay. Okay, sure. Whatta you need?" he finally said, but his voice was trembling.

"Dad, I never told you about my girlfriend —"

"Wait a minute, not yet." Shane's eyes flicked toward the bug hidden in the lamp. "Follow me, I wanna show you something first." He turned and walked out of the house onto the pool deck.

Chooch followed him as Franco trailed behind, slipping out through the sliding glass door just before Chooch closed it.

Shane led the way around the pool. There were still a few ribbons and scraps of wrapping paper on the glass-topped table from Nora's shower. Shane and Chooch sat across from one another at the table.

"Why are we out here?" Chooch asked.

"The house is bugged. It's a long story. A lot's happened since you left. Go on . . ."

"Dad, I have a girlfriend. I met her when I was fourteen, on the streets."

"I know all about her, son. Delfina Delgado. Amac's second cousin." Chooch looked surprised. "After you left, I got in touch with American. He told me she was your *jiana,* and that she'd disappeared. He told me he didn't think she'd been kidnapped."

"Dad, he's lying. She was kidnapped by the black gangs, and he knows it. While he's been trying to arrange to buy her back, I think I found out where she is, but I can't go to Amac, because he'll try and take her by force. That's why I came to you."

"Where is she?"

"Before I tell you, I need your promise that you won't call LAPD and tell them. You can't even tell Mom."

"Both things I'm not going to agree to in the blind."

"Dad, this is really important to me. I love her. I love her as much as you love Mom."

"Then you're very lucky, but I can't make promises until I know what I'm agreeing to."

Chooch looked troubled, then spread his hands in some kind of gesture of defeat. "Can you at least promise me you'll listen to all my arguments?"

"I can do that."

They sat looking at each other across a no-man's-land of clear glass and torn wrapping paper. Finally Shane leaned forward in his chair. "Go on," he said. "Let's hear what you've got."

"Delfina was kidnapped by Crip gangsters. Guys from Kevin Cordell's set. Hardcore Hayes is in charge now but they're hooked up with the Compton Bloods on some huge drug deal."

"Where is she?"

"I think they're holding her out at Stone's old house in Westlake. It's a mansion on more than six acres. Three years ago Stone moved out of South Central into a millionaire's neighborhood. After the cops finished their murder investigation there, they padlocked the gate to his mansion. The place is supposed to be empty, but there's a guesthouse down by the artificial lake, and I think some G's slipped back in there with her. I saw one of their work cars parked nearby."

"And . . . ?"

"And I think I know how to rescue her, but I can't do it alone. I need your help."

Shane sat still for a long time, thinking, before finally shaking his head.

"Dad . . ."

"Whatta you take me for, huh?" Shane asked. "I'm your father. I have a responsibility to your dead mother, Sandy, and to your stepmother, Alexa. I'm supposed to look out for you. So what'd you have in mind here? We both strap up and go in shooting?"

"Dad, come on . . ."

"No, you come on; this isn't a TV show. I could end up getting you killed." Shane paused, then continued. "We call Alexa right now. We fill her in, then CRASH will set up a hostage retrieval."

"You promised . . ."

"The hell I did!"

"You promised to hear me out. You haven't even tried. You heard what you wanted, then made a cop decision without even listening to my reasons."

"Okay, go ahead. Let's hear 'em."

Chooch took a deep breath to calm himself down, then he stood and started pacing around on the other side of the glass-topped table. "According to American, when I talked to him earlier, he and the black gangs are setting up a transfer to trade Delfina, in return for one hundred thousand in cash. But I think they don't really care about Amac's money, and have no intention of giving her back. It's probably just a way to draw Amac into an ambush. She'll die and Amac will die with her. I can't let that happen."

Chooch's voice was hard with anger. Shane was frightened for his son, but also extremely proud. He knew in that moment that Chooch had become a man.

"That's all the more reason to go to Alexa," Shane said.

"Listen to me! Just please listen." Chooch was almost shouting.

"Don't yell at me."

"If we tell Mom you know exactly what she's gonna do. She's gonna take it straight to the Gang Squad."

"Right. Because that's the correct thing to do."

"Dad, it's a horrible idea. To begin with, CRASH is trying to shut this war down. There's lots of glass-house pressure on them, plus they're like frickin' commandos. They're only gonna want to take out the Crip and Blood shot-callers, and get Amac, too. That'll be their top priority. Delfina is just bait to them. It'll end up as some kind of SWAT operation with tear gas and street sweepers. Delfina will be expendable."

"So how would you play it?" Shane asked.

"You and me. We slip in there while they're

asleep. Pull a raid and get her the hell out of there."

"You and me. Butch and Sundance."

"Mom is by the book. That's why she's heading DSG. But you're more . . . creative."

"Creative . . . I see." Shane wasn't sure how to take that.

"I went out to Westlake and drove around Stone's property. There's a man-made lake with a runoff that goes under the fence to a culvert. We could get in through the runoff and —"

"Hold it. Back up a minute, okay?" Chooch stopped pacing and waited. "Where did you get the information that she's being held in Stone's Westlake estate?"

"What's it matter?"

"Because the source of that information could sell you out. You could be walking into something."

"Nobody cares about me."

"Wise up, Chooch! Your mom is head of DSG. You'd be a great trading card."

"I don't —" Then Chooch stopped. He obviously hadn't thought of that. "Okay, so . . ."

"So, who gave you the intel?"

"I overheard it. I was hanging out in one of Stone's strip clubs down in South Central. The guy I overheard talking was a crazy-looking light-skinned brother with a Senegalese twist. This braid was hangin' halfway down his back. He was bragging about how he and some other

Crips were holding American Macado's cousin, were gonna use her to get Amac. I was one table over, listening. When he left, I followed him all the way to the mansion out in Westlake. I asked around and found out the place was owned by Kevin Cordell."

"Jeez, you coulda gotten killed." Chooch shrugged. "But it fits. Amac told me some light-skinned brother with a braid did the hit on Stone."

"He's one of Hardcore's tights. That makes this all the more righteous."

"I don't trust it. Maybe they knew you were listening."

"These guys aren't that clever."

But Shane was frowning.

"Dad, you and I could do this. If Delfina's there in the guesthouse being held by a coupla Crips, we could crawl through that spillway, sneak up on the place, then break in and grab her."

"Look, I'm not gonna do this."

"Dad, I'm gonna rescue her with or without you."

"Wanna bet?" Shane looked up at Chooch, who, at six-three, two-twenty, would be damn hard to stop. It was a classic parental dilemma. In that moment he realized he could probably no longer physically control his son.

"Dad, this is exactly what you'd do if you were me."

"No, it —"

"Be fair," Chooch interrupted. "If this was Mom being held, would you go to the cops? Would you risk SWAT and tear gas and all the rest of it? Or would you try and sneak in there and pull her out?"

"That's different, and you know it. I'm an adult and an experienced police officer."

"This isn't about being a cop. It's about being a man. You always tell me that a man has to live with the consequences of his actions. Well, I can't live with the consequences of in-action. You told me on my birthday last year that from now on, you're going to treat me as an equal. But I guess that's just when nothing's at stake. Now that someone I really care about is in danger, you're telling me I'm a kid, that I don't really have a vote."

Shane sat still for a long minute. Dammit, he hated to be quoted against himself! But his son was right about one thing: Shane would never call SWAT if it was Alexa. He wouldn't trust an adrenaline squad of twenty-year-olds to go in, guns blazing, and hope they could pull her out alive.

"Dad, Amac is gonna try and set up the trade. If we pull her out tonight, *before* he meets with the Crips, then you'll have saved his life — paid him back for what he did for us three years ago."

Shane did owe Amac for his son's future, but still, how could he take part in a three a.m. raid on Stone's mansion using his seventeen-year-old son as backup?! If they survived, Alexa would kill him. If it went wrong, he would never be able to explain it.

"Dad, I came to you because you're my best friend, and the only person on earth I would trust with my life and Delfina's. You've got to do this with me."

33

BUTCH AND SUNDANCE

They were driving on the 101 toward Westlake Village. Shane was behind the wheel. Alexa's backup gun, a no-nonsense Colt Double Eagle, and a box of .45 ACP cartridges were on the seat beside him.

He reached into his pocket and handed Chooch two empty clips. "Why don't you load these — they take eight shots."

Chooch opened the box of ammo. The metallic snick of brass on lubricated steel rang softly inside the car as he thumbed cartridges into the clips.

They drove past Woodland Hills and Calabasas, then fifteen minutes later turned onto Westlake Village Road, which bordered ten acres of blue moonlit water on one side, and a string of multimillion-dollar homes on the other.

As they drove south, Chooch pointed out a huge colonial mansion hiding behind wrought-iron gates still festooned with yellow LAPD crime tape. The estate was one of the largest and, as Chooch had said, sat on at least six acres of manicured property. It was guarded by an eight-foot-high electric fence and lit with xenon lights. Kevin Cordell had come a long way from his bullet-scarred neighborhood in South Central to this millionaire's estate in Westlake. But Shane knew many had died so Stone could make the journey.

Following Chooch's directions, Shane drove around to the south end of the property, where they parked on a side street.

They sat quietly inside the black Acura, letting their nerves settle.

"Okay, you stay here. I'm gonna do some reconnaissance."

"I'm going with you," Chooch answered. "Don't try and talk me out of it."

Shane sighed, then grabbed the loaded Double Eagle with its spare clip and got out of the car as Chooch followed. They headed up the street away from the estate.

"Where're you going? The way in's back there."

"The police padlock is still on the gate. You said they parked on the street. I wanta check out the work car first."

A block away they found a blue '78 Charger with a busted-out taillight and a bullet hole in the right rear fender. Shane forced the window wing, unlocked the door, then found the registration in the glove box. "Darnel Sweet, with a bullet hole in the fender. This rig doesn't live around here." Shane opened the hood, removed the distributor cap and threw it in the bushes. "Only one car. If they all came together, that means four or five at the most," Shane said. "Now show me the way in."

His son led him back to the overflow spillway, a short distance down the street. When they got there, Chooch knelt down and pointed to an oblong pipe that ran under the electric security fence. Shane knelt down beside him, then leaned forward and peered into the opening. It was going to be tight squeezing through, but, fortunately, whoever put in the spillway hadn't safeguarded it with an iron grate.

"Except for this, security looks pretty good, so you can bet Stone has motion traps in there," Shane said softly.

"Yeah, probably."

Shane was determined to keep his son as far away from this as possible. "You're too big to get through. Go get the car and repark it back here. I'll go in. Keep the engine running. If I find her, and can bring her out, I'm gonna need a quick dust-off."

"I can get through there," Chooch responded.

"I need you out here."

"Dad, I'm going —"

"Not an option."

"She won't go with you. She doesn't know you."

"I met her up at her aunt's house in the Hills, three years ago."

"You're *chota*. She won't trust you." Emes called cops *la chota* and viewed them all as corrupt racists.

"Listen, Chooch, I'm not letting you —"

"I'm going. That's it. This was my idea." Chooch didn't wait for further argument, but dropped to his stomach and started to squeeze through the narrow spillway.

Shane was praying that his son wouldn't be able to fit. The teenager had broad shoulders, made even broader by all the weight lifting he'd done for football. Slowly, Chooch inched deeper and deeper into the enclosure, until only his tennis shoes were sticking out. Then he stopped.

Shane thought, *Good, he's stuck, the smartass.* But before he could grab Chooch's ankles and pull him out, his son was moving forward again, the tennis shoes slowly disappearing into the pipe. Shane waited. About two minutes later, he heard rustling on the far side of the fence.

"Okay, I'm through," his son whispered.

Shane followed Chooch through the spillway, slushing in two inches of water and slime that had collected on the bottom of the runoff.

Finally he reached the end and slithered out of the gooey mess.

Once he was through, he realized how Chooch had managed to make it. There was so much moss and mildew in the runoff pipe that it acted as a lubricant. Shane rolled to a sitting position. His clothes were soaked and stained with greenish-brown gunk. His son, looking just as funky, was crouched, staring off across a small man-made lake toward the guesthouse.

"What about guard dogs?" Chooch asked softly.

"If the Westlake PD secured this place, they'll be at Animal Rescue."

Chooch nodded. "Let's go."

"Hold it. What's the rush? Let's take a look around first."

"Dad, the guesthouse is right over there by the pool." He pointed at a low-roofed structure about two hundred yards away.

"Yeah, but Stone was a Crip legend with lots of enemies, so this place probably has better security than the White House." Shane began looking at the ground, checking the area around the spillway.

"What are you looking for?"

"Darnel Sweet was parked on this side of the house, so maybe we're not the only ones to use this drainpipe."

"Shit, you're right, lookit that. . . ." Chooch said, pointing to some moss and dried slime on the grass to the right of them.

"Darnel and his friends didn't want to toast their nuts on that electric fence either. If he knew about this runoff, he probably also knows where the motion traps are, so let's follow his footsteps."

"You're pretty good at this," Chooch admitted.

"Ain't my first roundup."

Shane found four sets of footprints. He held up four fingers. Chooch nodded and they moved along, following the tracks. Soon the trail led them out onto the lighted lawn, and Chooch stopped abruptly. "We go out there, they'll see us."

"They're probably asleep. Besides, they usually put motion traps in the dark places in the yard, not the lighted ones. If Darnel was avoiding the motion detectors, we need to stay in his tracks. We don't have a choice."

Nonetheless, Shane felt hopelessly exposed as they crept along, lit by powerful overhead xenon lights.

Finally they made it to the guesthouse. Shane motioned for Chooch to stay back, then crept up to the structure, inching slowly around the perimeter, checking the security on every screen door and window opening.

It was a class-A installation. The alarm wiring had all been punched through the walls and ran in copper conduit — no way to straight-wire or short it. He returned to where Chooch was waiting and knelt next to him.

"It's a good system," Shane whispered. "I don't wanna mess with it."

"We gotta get in there now," Chooch insisted.

"We could kick in a door and swarm the place, but we only have one gun, and they probably all have street sweepers. Furthermore, they have Delfina. Like you said, if we go in like SWAT, she could end up dead."

"So whatta we do?" Chooch sounded panicked.

"One of us has to set off one of these trap alarms while the other waits for them to come out."

"*One* of us . . . ?" Chooch was frowning. "You mean *me!*"

"I've got the gun, and if you think I'm turning it over, you're nuts."

"She won't go with you," Chooch stubbornly insisted.

"I'll deal with that when the time comes."

"Dad —"

"Dammit, Chooch, I'm trained in tactical planning. Lemme do the fucking tactics!" Shane snapped. He was buzzing like a power line. *Calm down,* he told himself, but doing a raid with his only son was almost more than he could handle. Shane remembered a dog-and-cat patrol team that had worked a basic car in South Central a few years back. They fell in love and ran off to Vegas to get married, but didn't tell anybody and kept working the Plain

Jane together — a nearly fatal mistake. The guy ended up getting shot and almost died because they were both so busy protecting each other, they didn't use good tactics. Shane had the same problem. He was more worried about Chooch than the killers inside the house.

"Let's try and get this done before the sun comes up," Shane said, pointing the gun in the direction of the footsteps they were following. "When I get into position, you veer off the path and trip an alarm."

Chooch moved off, as instructed, while Shane sprinted to a shadowy place he found next to the front door. He prayed the G's came out together so he could take them all at once.

Once Shane was in position, he quietly chambered the Double Eagle.

Suddenly all of the alarms in the yard went off. A hooting siren followed by a huge ten-inch ringer. It set up a clattering, whooping din in the once quiet neighborhood. Shane counted to twenty before the back door swung open and two black guys wearing nothing but boxer shorts ran out of the house carrying auto-mags. A second after exploding out of the door, they caught sight of him and spun. The first one triggered off a wild burst as Shane fired. The slug from his Double Eagle hit the G high on the hip, spinning him around. He screamed as he fell, his Tec-Nine wildly stitching holes in the brick pool decking. The second G spun in the opposite direction and was accidentally disarmed by a friendly lemon tree. The barrel of his auto-mag hit the trunk and it was knocked out of his hands. Shane stepped forward and clocked him hard with the broad side of the Double Eagle. The man's head chimed loudly against the steel breach. He fell onto his back and began snoring. Shane heaved the G's auto-mag into the dark.

The first g'ster was shrieking in pain as Shane grabbed his Tec-Nine and ran into the house.

Almost immediately, he saw a light-complexioned g'ster with a long tenza braid standing naked in the kitchen, a bad-looking, cut-down ArmaLite AR-10 machine gun in his right hand. He was swinging it toward Shane, who was off balance, skidding to a halt. He instantly knew that by the time he squared up and completed his pivot, he'd be dead, so he threw the Tec-Nine back-handed across the room toward the G.

"Catch!" he yelled. The light-skinned man attempted to catch the gun or dodge out of the way. In either case, he lost his grip on the AR-10. As he struggled to control the weapon, Shane finished his pivot, pulled the Double E, and fired. The automatic reared up in his outstretched hands and blew a hole in the G's chest.

The naked man flew backward spouting blood, then hit the wall and fell in a sprawl of arms and legs.

Shane stepped over his lifeless body and moved through the house, slower now, alert for more G's.

There were no more Crips in the house.

He found Delfina duct-taped to the bed in a guest bedroom. She was bruised and naked, with a sock stuffed in her mouth. A look of mindless terror filled her vacant eyes.

Shane pulled the sock out of her mouth and she immediately started screaming. Blood-curdling, insane screeches. God only knew what they had been doing to her.

Shane opened his pocket knife and cut the duct tape from her hands and feet, then grabbed the terrified girl, threw her over his shoulder, and ran from the house.

She never stopped screaming.

When he got outside, Chooch appeared next to him. They made the run across the yard, accompanied by Delfina's screeches and the whooping alarm sirens. Shane figured since this was Stone's house, the alarm probably didn't have a direct-dial to the police. It would just clatter and howl until the angry neighbors finally called 911.

As they reached the spillway, Shane pulled Delfina off his shoulder. Chooch stripped off his grass-stained Pendleton overshirt and put it on his naked, crazed girlfriend.

"Delfina, it's me! It's Chooch!" he pleaded, but her eyes were wild, nothing registered. "Please, Delfina, I'm here! You're safe now,"

Chooch begged, but the girl was delusional with terror.

Shane squeezed through the spillway and yelled for Chooch to wedge Delfina into the narrow opening. He crawled halfway back, then grabbed her wrists, pulling as hard as he could.

She was scratching and clawing. One of her fingernails cut a gouge in his face under his eye.

Finally Shane pulled her out of the narrow aqueduct and held her until Chooch scrambled through the opening.

They ran to the Acura, helped Delfina into the backseat, and pulled out. She never stopped screaming. It was as if her mind had snapped.

She screamed all the way out of Westlake Village, to the freeway, and all the way down the freeway to the emergency room at Sherman Oaks Community Hospital.

34

PTSD

It was four a.m. and Alexa had just arrived from Parker Center, where she had been sleeping on a cot when Shane called. "Why didn't you stay there at Stone's and wait for the police to arrive?" she said as she stood before him in the hospital waiting room. "According to Westlake P.D., you left one dead and two down at the scene."

Shane had come crashing down from his adrenaline rush of an hour ago. He felt irritable, tired, and wanted to change the subject even more than he wanted to change his moss-stained clothes. Chooch had lied, saying he was Delfina's brother, and was now upstairs with her in the psychiatric trauma ward.

"I didn't wait because Chooch was with me."

"You mean in spirit or something? 'Cause

I'm *sure* you're not trying to tell me you took our son to a shootout."

"He was in there with me. He helped me get her out. I didn't want the police to find him there. If this gets goofy, and we get some kind of backfire prosecution, I don't want Chooch named in it."

"How the hell could *that* happen? They were all armed, holding a sixteen-year-old girl at gunpoint."

"I just don't want him involved."

"How could he *not* be involved? You took him with you!" She seemed floored by all this.

"Well, theoretically, that's one way of looking at it."

"What's the other?"

"He took me with him. Matter of fact, honey, he was the one who found where they were holding her. He came to me for help. There was no way to stop him. He loves her. He was going whether I said so or not."

"That's absurd."

"You think?" He held her gaze and finally she sat on one of the vinyl-upholstered chairs. Her eyes were red from lack of sleep.

"I did the shooting," he continued. "All he did was handle the diversion and help me carry her out of there. So how 'bout we just pretend he was never there. Can we do that?"

"Now *I'm* supposed to lie." Her anger was escalating. "It would have been better if I didn't know. Why did you have to tell me?"

"I never lie to you."

"Bullshit."

"I trust your judgment then. It would mean a great deal to me if you would keep our son out of it," he said softly.

Suddenly her cell phone rang and she pulled it out of her purse and opened it. "Yeah . . . okay . . . Just gimme the headlines." She listened. "Okay . . . okay . . . sure. You can reach me on this phone." She hung up, looked up at Shane. "The Westlake P.D. is policing the crime scene. The paramedics have the two wounded Crips at USC on the lockdown floor."

"Who was the D.B.?"

"They're printing him, but one of the Westlake blues on the scene said he wrote him for a taillight infraction a few days ago when he was out at Stone's place — a gangster named Darnel Sweet. I know him. I've been studying Crip arrest sheets and F.I. cards all damn week. His street name is J Rock. His gang profile says he's Russell Hayes's first cousin."

"He's the one Amac thinks killed Stone."

"A lot of people killed Cordel. He had so much lead in him, we almost called a crane to lift him onto the coroner's gurney. Stone got it from so many directions, it's a miracle they didn't waste each other in the crossfire."

A half-hour later Chooch called from upstairs and asked Shane and Alexa to come up to the psych ward on the second floor. They rode up in the elevator, then sat on worn-out sofas behind a screened-off lounge. A few minutes after they arrived Chooch came out of the ward and joined them. Like Shane, he was filthy, tired, and drawn.

"They made me leave. Every time Delfina looked at me, she started crying." Then he faced Alexa. "Thanks for coming, Mom."

"Thank God you're all right. But what you two did was harebrained." Alexa took Chooch into her arms and hugged him. Shane thought he saw tears in his son's eyes.

Then Chooch pulled back. "Mom, don't be mad at Dad, okay? I made him do it."

"I'm not mad at him," Alexa said. "I'm just frustrated." She heaved a sigh. "But I guess if I ever really got him rewired, he'd be too normal to hang with."

Chooch said, "If SWAT had been called in, they would have —"

"Spare me your SWAT evaluations, okay?" Alexa interrupted. "You guys don't know what SWAT would have done. Maybe they could have actually rescued her without wasting anybody."

"Or maybe they would have killed the whole bunch," Chooch said softly. "Delfina included."

"We'll never know."

They were all so tired that it was impossible to continue the conversation. The sun was just coming over the San Bernardino Mountains, throwing shafts of orange light into the gray, sterile corridors of the psychiatric ward.

They waited for further word from either the Westlake police department or the doctors examining Delfina, but none came. They were all bone-tired so they stretched out on the sofas, and almost before his head hit the imitation leather, Shane was asleep.

The dream was as disturbing as it was bizarre. Shane, who was dark and Mediterranean in life, was blond and pale in the dream. He was wearing a three-piece light gray suit, standing in a wood-walled stable or stall of some kind, washing a huge brown animal with a soft brush. Strangely, with each stroke, Shane removed pieces of skin from the howling beast, the hide coming off in ugly, bloody strips. The animal sometimes looked like a buffalo, and sometimes more like a Clydesdale horse. It bucked and cried as he scrubbed its skin off. Shane was alarmed at the damage he was doing and kept checking the brush, trying it on himself to see how it was possible for it to do such damage. When he brushed his own skin, the bristles felt soft as velvet. Reassured, he continued washing the animal, and once again, would be skinning the shrieking beast. Occasionally, he would look up and see his reflection in a mirror hanging in the grooming stall. Was it really him in the mirror with this strange three-piece suit and weird blond hair? Shane was frightened by his unfamiliar appearance and by the damage he was doing, but knew it was important for him to finish. Then he would turn to the animal and begin the torturous task all over again.

Suddenly somebody was shaking him. He left his bizarre animal-washing project and drifted up into a world that was equally disturbing. Shane sat up and found himself looking into the probing eyes of a gray-haired woman who introduced herself as Dr. Elizabeth Sloan. She said she was a psychiatrist and looked the part: horn-rimmed glasses and a white hospital coat with her name and degree stitched over the pocket. "Could we have a little chat?" she asked as Alexa and Chooch sat up rubbing their eyes. "We might all be more comfortable in my office."

They followed her down a wide linoleum corridor lined with painted metal doors that had wire-reinforced glass observation windows cut in the center. Dr. Sloan turned the corner at the end of the hall and showed them into a cluttered office with an old sofa, a desk, and two pull-up chairs. She sat in one of the pull-ups; Chooch and Shane took the sofa, leaving Alexa the remaining chair.

"How is she?" Chooch blurted.

"It's very complicated, but I think you need to know what you're facing. Are you her mother?" Dr. Sloan asked Alexa.

Alexa reached into her purse, pulled out her

badge, and showed it to the psychiatrist.

"Lieutenant Scully?" Dr. Sloan furrowed her brow. "Do you know where her family is?"

"They're in Cuernavaca," Chooch answered. "She only has an aunt. Her parents are both dead."

"But you're her brother?"

"No, I'm sorry. I lied. I'm her boyfriend," Chooch confessed.

"Doctor, could you tell us what's going on? What's happened to her?" Alexa probed.

"She's a juvenile, only sixteen. I'm afraid I can only consult with the parents or a responsible member of her family."

"She was kidnapped," Alexa said, trying to control her frustration. "One of her kidnappers died in a shootout while police were effecting her rescue. This is a felony abduction case with an attendant homicide. Her parents are deceased and she doesn't have any relatives here except for a second cousin who is a Mexican Mafia gang leader and a fugitive. She's an essential witness to a long list of class-A felonies. So why don't you forget all this neat med school protocol and help us understand her condition."

Dr. Sloan smiled, then leaned back in her chair. "Does this in-your-face style work well at the LAPD?"

"Works great. Gonna work here, too. If I have to go over your head, I will. How's it going to help her to withhold information?"

"Please," Chooch pleaded.

Dr. Sloan saw the desperation on his face, then sighed and finally nodded. "I think your friend has severe post-traumatic stress disorder. I'm prohibited from making PTSD her official diagnosis until I can observe her for at least two weeks. But from what I can see, particularly since I now know she was kidnapped and raped —"

"Raped?" Chooch interrupted.

Shane reached out and put a hand on his arm. Now that Alexa had her talking, he didn't want to break the doctor's flow. "Keep going," he said.

"We've done some vaginal swabs and, from our preliminary examination, it looks like she was sexually assaulted, maybe by more than one person. The DNA tests will hopefully sort all that out." She paused to evaluate their reactions. "There are certain diagnostic criteria for PTSD, and she fits quite enough of them to warrant the preliminary diagnosis."

"What are they?" Shane prodded.

"When a person experiences a severe traumatic event outside the range of what we might call normal human experience, PTSD can occur. The kind of severe stressor I'm talking about might include the threat of violence, a deadly threat against a loved one, war experience, or abduction, and most certainly a multiple rape."

"And the symptoms . . . ?" Alexa asked.

"She doesn't remember much after last Tuesday, when she says she was walking near her aunt's house. This short-term memory loss is known as psychogenic amnesia. She's a little dazed and not focusing too clearly. She seems to have a feeling of detachment to events currently going on around her. Of course, we've sedated her, and that could be partially responsible, but she's also not falling asleep with tranquilizers or sleeping pills, which is very consistent with this condition. She has an exaggerated startle response — another supporting symptom. If you come up behind and surprise her, she almost jumps out of her skin. Once she finally falls asleep, she's most likely going to dream about the inciting traumatic event and, therefore, her subconscious fear of these dreams is keeping her awake. In short, since it walks like a duck and quacks like a duck, in two weeks I'm probably going to be able to label it a duck: post-traumatic stress disorder."

"I thought you only got that in combat," Shane said.

"Well, isn't that exactly where she's been? But aside from military combat, it hits when we're emotionally overridden by an experience we can't absorb, and our defenses start shutting systems down until we can deal with it."

"But she'll eventually be okay?" Chooch asked. He had flinched at the first mention of rape but was now focused on the more important issue of Delfina's recovery.

"She might; she might not. Sometimes things short-circuit in our heads when we're under too much stress. That's not a very medical way of putting it, but in essence, it's what can happen. All we can do now is wait and see."

"I want to stay with her," Chooch said.

"I don't have a problem with that," Dr. Sloan replied. "It might help to have a friend here."

"This girl was being held in connection with the gang violence that's taking place in L.A.," Alexa said. "She's probably still in some danger, so I'm going to assign a police officer to watch her room."

Dr. Sloan nodded. "Okay, but you'll have to set that up with the hospital administrator."

The three of them thanked her, then walked out of the office into the corridor.

"Chooch, if you stay here, I want the officer guarding her to keep an eye on you, too," Alexa said.

"Come on, Mom, I'm not in danger."

"No 'Come on, Mom.' Just call it a justifiable parental overreaction."

"I agree," Shane said. "I did what you asked, now you do this for us."

"Okay," Chooch finally relented. They left him in the waiting room and walked to the elevator.

"I've got to go back to North Chalon Road and change clothes, then make a conference at the studio at noon," Shane said. "Unless you want the LAPD Detective Services Group to end up owing millions, I better not miss that meeting. I'm sure you and Filosiani can clean up this little mess I made out in Westlake Village."

She smiled at him as the elevator arrived and they got aboard. "A little mess is when you drop a plate, Shane. When you drop three assholes, it's called a major incident." They rode down to the lobby, and after they exited Alexa took his hand.

They walked out into the sunshine and kissed in the parking lot, then headed to their separate cars.

The Acura was boiling hot, so he quickly rolled down the windows. It was ten-thirty, and the temperature was already in the high seventies. The Valley was headed toward another triple-digit day. The northern winds that had cleansed the city and kept it cool for the last half week had left as suddenly as they had arrived. Now the Basin was baking in one of its classic inversion layers. As Shane started his car, he looked up at the hospital windows on the second floor and wondered what would happen to Delfina. Would she carry these scars forever, or could she find the strength to bury the ugliness and leave it all behind? *Where there's no fault, there should be no guilt,* he thought. But then a soft voice argued from inside his head.

Some things can be true and, at the same time, have no meaning.

35

THE DENNIS HOPPER RULE

When Shane arrived at Hollywood General Studios, he couldn't drive onto the lot because a huge eighteen-wheel truck, with a gargantuan redwood log strapped onto the flatbed trailer, was maneuvering back and forth on Monitor Street, trying to back through the gate. Shane parked outside at the curb and walked onto the lot past the retired motor officer, who had a clipboard in one hand and his phone in the other. He saw Shane and waved him over. As Shane approached, he could hear one side of an angry conversation.

". . . no place to put another eighteen-wheeler. You're also gonna have t'find parking off the lot for the star dressing rooms, the honey wagons and two-holers. The wardrobe, prop, and camera trucks I'll try to squeeze in here for security reasons, but that's it. I only got two hundred parking spaces." The guard listened for a moment, making a face for Shane's benefit. "I don't care if you're pissed off! *I'm* pissed off! You're not the only film shooting here." He slammed down the phone.

"Problems?"

"Your director is an asshole. His rental trucks started moving in here this morning and knocked the shit outta the place." He looked up at the growling logging truck, which seemed to be getting itself hopelessly wedged in the studio driveway. "Lookit this asshole. He's never gonna get that thing through the gate."

"Is this all for *The Neural Surfer*?" Shane asked, looking past the guard shack into the lot, where a dozen rental trucks were parked with their back doors open and tailgates down. Twenty or more men were taking inventory, unloading camera equipment and grip and electrical packages.

"We're not equipped to make a hundred-million-dollar film here," the gate guard protested.

"A what?!"

"That's what the director said . . . Lubinski, or whatever his name is."

"Lubick . . . and this picture isn't gonna cost anywhere near a hundred million."

"Somebody better tell him. I never saw this much rolling stock."

Shane started toward the production office, but the guard grabbed his arm. "Reason I waved you over is Mr. Marcella wanted me to give you something." He ducked into the shack, then reappeared a second later and handed Shane a folded note.

Shane . . .
Meet me at the vomitorium before noon.
<u>Imperative</u>.
                                    Nicholas

The little grifter was wedged behind a tiny table in the dining car, drinking coffee. He had a copy of *The Neural Surfer* and looked up from it as Shane approached and slid into the empty seat across from him.

"Where the hell you been?" Nicky groused.

"You're not my only project." Shane looked down at the red-paged script. "You finally got it?"

"Yeah, I stole this from Rajindi's desk."

"Is it full of *ferae naturae?*" Shane deadpanned.

"Huh?"

"Untamed nature."

"This script is more confusing than a Palm Beach ballot," Nicky said solemnly. "It's like somebody threw it all over the room, randomly gathered up the pages, then bradded the fucker with everything out of order."

"But a bargain at any price."

"Not to quibble, but Lubick told me this morning, whatever the printed budget number is, cube it."

"He's crazy. Doesn't anybody know that but us?" Shane groused.

"There's an old rule in Hollywood, which we call the Dennis Hopper Rule. Dennis is a good citizen now, but this was written back in the seventies, when he was a fucking head case. The rule states that it's perfectly okay to hire crazy, creative people for a film, unless it's Dennis Hopper, who you should never hire, because he's not crazy, he's insane." Nicky closed the script and glared at Shane. "Lubick isn't insane, he's only crazy. I'm trying to slow him down by telling him we aren't funded for anything close to a hundred and fifty million dollars."

"A hundred and fifty million?! The gate guard said it was a hundred million."

"Now the gate guard's doing budgets?" Nicky sighed. "But what's it matter . . . a hundred million, a hundred fifty? We don't have it, anyway."

"Good point."

"This asshole, Lubick, tells me just this morning that it's his solemn *obligation* as a director to bring this film in as far over budget as humanly possible."

"Dennis Valentine wants to take him out and kick the shit out of him."

"Where do I sign up?" Nicky said, then leaned forward. "But all is not lost, *boychik*, because I have secured what we call in the biz 'major studio interest.' I told you my phone's been ringing off the hook with guys from the majors who all want to get in on this project. I've been fending them off, but I think the time is ripe to bring in a partner, which is a seven-letter word we use in the film biz that means sucker."

"Who?"

"There's a guy at Universal. Actually, he's the president of production, and I think he's perfect. Name's Steve Bergman, known around town as Stevie Wonder because he can't read."

"I'm sorry . . . ?"

"He can't read. He's illiterate."

"And he's head of a major studio? How can the head of a studio not be able to read? That's crazy."

"Right. It's also the *Dennis Hopper rule*. Besides, he doesn't have to read. He's not stupid, just seriously dyslexic. Actually, he's a smart son of a bitch and a killer when it comes to deal points. Besides, a studio only has to say yes to twelve or fifteen films a year, so when Steve's development execs are ready to punch one up, and need him to green-light the project, they just put together a little table read. They hire actors to perform all the characters, and Stevie just sits at the head of the table with his eyes closed and listens. Nobody talks about the fact that he's illiterate and probably has ADD to boot. All the players know, but nobody makes anything out of it. It's like *The Wizard of Oz* without the funny costumes."

"You're putting me on," Shane said. "If you can't read, how can you pick a good script?"

"Lookit us. Our script reads like it came apart in the Xerox machine, and we're already half a million into preproduction."

"Okay . . . okay, so tell me how we get Stevie on board." Shane was grasping at straws, dreading his next meeting with Filosiani.

"We've got a late lunch with him in" — Nicky looked at his Rolex; Shane wondered if it was rented — "one hour, in the private executive dining room at Universal. He's talking about putting up half the budget and all the P and A."

"On a script he hasn't read?"

"On a script he *can't* read."

"Which undoubtedly works to our advantage here."

"It doesn't matter, Shane. We've got so much momentum, this thing could be as hard to understand as a Salman Rushdie novel and nobody would care. Stevie sees this as a good commercial investment, a shared risk with Cine-Roma. By the way, you like that name? It's starting to sound way too ethnic to me. I was thinking maybe we should be Platinum Pictures — get a cool, interlocking P logo. . . ." He spread his hands in the air. "Platinum Pictures presents: a Nicholas Marcella film. . . ."

Nicky had parked his car around the corner

from the vomitorium and was anxiously looking over his shoulder as he scurried along toward it.

"Are you trying to avoid someone?" Shane
asked as he followed.

"You bet. Half this fucking town wants a
piece of this deal," the little grifter answered.
"As of right now, we're the hottest fucking producers in showbiz."

36

MAKING MOVIES

Universal was a big-time film company located on hundreds of acres with thirty or more soundstages and a huge back lot. You could fit all of Hollywood General Studios onto half of the east parking lot. Nicky docked the maroon Bentley in a space near the commissary. Shane got out and was gawking at ten scantily clad women dressed as space aliens, walking away from the kiosk eating candy bars.

Nicky joined him, pointing. "Probably extras on *Space Mission Earth*, the new Gene Roddenberry TV series spin-off."

"I thought Gene Roddenberry was dead."

"Death is relative in show business. In Roddenberry's case, he died physically but not professionally. Commercial viability transcends mortality. A confusing but meaningful concept. Okay, *boychik*, lemme do the talking."

"When you talk, are you gonna actually say anything this time?"

"I had a cough drop stuck in my throat at CAA. I'm fine now."

They entered the main commissary, where the hostess took their names and led them to the rear of the large dining room, which had been designed with curved walls. The tables were arranged in clusters.

"There's no east wall," Shane said to Nicky as they followed the attractive blond hostess through the crowded roomful of studio employees. "You said the room was a rectangle and the tables were in rows. That people tried to sit near Lew Wasserman by the east wall."

"The dumbass things you pick to worry about," Nicky said, brushing this useless remark aside. "After Seagram's bought the studio, they redesigned it, put in the S-curves and the seating clusters. Happy now? Try and focus on business, not bullshit."

They were led through a door into a private dining room that was very tastefully decorated with antiques. A man in a white coat stood at the far end of a twelve-seat rectangular table and smiled at them as they entered.

"Take any chair you like," the waiter said. "My name is Arthur."

"Thanks." Nicky picked the seat at the head of the table.

"I should have said, except that one," Arthur amended. "That's Mr. Bergman's place."

Nicky got up quickly, then picked a seat at the center of the table, while Shane took the chair beside him. Nicky smiled at Arthur. "How many people are attending this luncheon?"

"Mr. Bergman, Ms. Smart, Mr. Feltheim, Ms. Ansara, and Ms. Freeman."

Nicky was doing the math on his fingers as Arthur went back into the kitchen. "Five. Shane, move over there, take that one across from me."

"Why?"

"We're gonna get flanked if we sit like this. Emotionally, this room is his territory. He's also got the power chair at the head of the table. We don't want to be sitting side by side like a couple of *schmucks* on a park bench. Whatever you do, don't get pushed to the weak zone down there at the far end of the table."

Shane got up and moved around to the other side, but he was smiling. "The dumbass things *you* pick to worry about."

"This isn't lunch, it's war. You'd never catch Schwarzkopf with his battle groups side by side. Everything in a negotiation has intense subtextural meaning."

The doors opened and a Napoleonic curly-haired man wearing a Hawaiian shirt topped by a fancy leather vest with silver conchos walked into the room. He was followed by a group of Hollywood-chic executives. They were ethnically mixed but similarly dressed. Some wore

368

T-shirts and jeans with plain leather vests, others short-sleeved shirts, jeans, and plain leather vests. The vests seemed to be the preferred uniform on this side of the hill, but only Bergman got the one with cool silver conchos.

"I'm Stevie Bergman," the man said, smiling. He took off a pair of Nikon darks and hung them on the top button of his Hawaiian shirt.

Nicky stood and began moving his mouth like a beached flounder. This time Shane was ready and leaped forward. "I'm Shane Scully. May I present my associate and partner at Cine-Roma, Nicholas Marcella."

They both shook Stevie Bergman's hand; he had a soft but firm grip. Then he turned to the crowd behind him.

"These are my D's," he said. "This is Tammy Ansara and Bobby Feltheim."

Shane shook hands with them. Tammy was a strikingly beautiful woman in her late twenties with auburn hair. Feltheim was the same age, blond, and had aqua baby-blues — probably contacts. "Everybody calls me 'the Felt,' " he offered warmly as Arthur returned from the kitchen.

Bergman turned and introduced the African-Americans. Ms. Freeman was Denise; Ms. Smart was Sondra. They were trim, beautiful, and still professionally safe at under thirty.

They all shook hands, then found their favorite seats up by Bergman at the north end of the table, slickly moving Shane and Nicky out of their prepicked, strategic positions, forcing them into the weak zone at the far end of the table.

Nicky was so shell-shocked, he led the retreat.

"*Bueno,*" Bergman said, surveying the seating. "This is perfect, excellent-o. Unfortunately, boys and girls, I only have twenty or thirty minutes, so I asked Arturo to serve us immediament-o. I have a nice lunch planned. I hope you like Cordon Bleu."

"Isn't that chicken in cream sauce?" Shane asked.

"This is Bleu à la Bergman. It's been marinated for six hours and then basted in my mother's special recipe. She makes it in her own kitchen. And except for an odd case of botulism now and then, people seem to love it." He beat a rim shot on the tabletop with his hands. "Joke, boys and girls, just kidding." Everybody smiled.

Nicky nodded. He was still moving his lips, but no sound had yet come out.

"Okay, we talk while we eat. Arturo, sling the hash."

Arthur took off for the kitchen again.

"*Neural Surfer* . . ." Stevie Bergman said. "Brilliant. The Felt read an early draft and he's amped. Right, Bobby?"

"I didn't read the actual script, only coverage," the Felt confessed. "And I must admit, the coverage was a tad confusing, but the kids who write these synopses are just outta college." He grinned. "They want Britney Spears to star in everything. By the way, we have a first-look deal with her. She might be good casting as the slave master's concubine."

Shane didn't even know there was a role for a slave master's concubine, and if there was, he certainly didn't think the hip, teen bombshell would be right for it. But Shane was a cop. As far as he was concerned, good casting was something you did when you went trout fishing.

"I'd love to get the latest draft of the script," the Felt said.

"It's loaded with *ferae naturae*," Shane assured him.

"It's not so much the untamed nature that excites us," Bergman chimed in. "Because, frankly, we expect to get that from Paul and Michael. Right now, to be honest, we're more interested in your completion and delivery dates."

"Our completion dates?" Shane was puzzled.

"Shall we let our hair down, boys and girls?" Stevie was looking around the table with an impish grin. The D people, whoever or whatever they were, all nodded.

"We just had a huge Christmas movie fall out on us. Tom and Julia, with Francis helming. Leaves us with a gigantic hole-o-rama in our December release schedule, and I don't have to tell you what that means."

He did, but Shane was determined not to show his ignorance.

"What makes your project so tantalizing, aside from the beaucoup package, is it has blockbuster size, which is what we need to tent-pole our Christmas release schedule. The fact that you might be able to get it in the can and drop it into our empty release date makes it irresistible," Bergman said.

"At this point, you can see why it's not so much about the screenplay as the timing," Felt said. "I mean, we love what we're hearing, and the elements attached are certainly primo, but we've got five thousand screens reserved for the tenth of December, and if we don't have a big Christmas film to release, we're pretty much fucked."

"In the ass-o-rama," Bergman added.

"Well, gee, uh, Christmas . . . I don't see why not. Sounds good, doesn't it, Nick?" Shane was desperate to get this monster off the LAPD's budget.

Nothing from Nicky. He was locked up tighter than a pawnbroker's safe.

"What d'ya think, Nicky? Christmas sound doable?" Shane asked again.

More mouth movement, maybe some spittle.

Shane didn't have a clue whether they could get it done by then, especially with Lubick directing. "Christmas sounds makeable, right, Nick?" he repeated.

Then his vapor-locked partner opened his

mouth. "Christmas," Nicky finally sputtered.

"Yeah, Christmas." Shane was getting pissed.

"Christmas," Nicky repeated impotently.

Shane gave up and smiled at Stevie. "No problem on Christmas."

"Okay, good." Bergman leaned forward. "A word of caution. We love Paul Lubick, but we've found, over the years, that working with him can be challenging. He's going to have to sign on for this delivery date. No fucking around like he did last year on *Adam's Apple*. That picture missed two marketing and distribution slots while he played with himself in the editing room."

"And even then," the Felt added, "it was longer than a summer harvest. People grew old and died watching that thing. Took three hours and forty minutes to unspool."

"Good point. It's gotta have a running time of less than two hours," Bergman demanded.

"Paul is . . . he's —"

"Yeah, we know," Stevie said, cutting Shane off. "Our financing will be subject to contract-defined running-time restrictions and a finite delivery date. We're willing to fund half the project in return for fifty percent of the profits. Our standard distribution fee of fifteen percent is off the top; we're in first position on our initial investment, plus an additional fifty percent against final computed production and P and A costs. Per industry standards, P and A is in last but recoups first. All recoupment after break is *pari passu*. We'll put our half of the money in escrow, and you can borrow against it to get financing. But in the event you don't deliver for our December third preview screening, we're going to freeze the escrow account, assume total ownership of the film, tie you two guys to a stake at the Tour Center, and sell tickets to tourists to watch you burn," Bergman warned.

"Christmas," Nicky said flatly. He seemed to be focused now, but at these meetings, you could never tell.

"That's how we make movies around here. No bullshit-o. Simple and straight," Stevie said. "Of course, we'll have standard approvals on all front title cast and approvals on key crew people: D.P., A.D., the UPM, and like that. Finally, we want to post everything here on this lot. Do the CGI, Foley, the ADR, all the sound design, dubbing, everything."

"Sounds great," Shane said, not knowing what half of those letters and phrases stood for.

"Okay, then, in principle, we'll consider this a done deal." He turned to the Felt. "Let's get Legal Affairs to paper it."

Shane looked at Nicky, who nodded and smiled at everybody.

They had the Cordon Bleu à la Bergman, which was basically chicken in cream sauce but with a strange, tinny aftertaste. Nobody got botulism. They talked about the Lakers and Democratic politics. Throughout it all, everybody kept looking at their watches.

374

In less than half an hour they were all on their feet again, shaking hands and smiling.

"We'll have our people get in touch with your people," Stevie said. "Who does your gunfighting?"

"My what?"

"Who's your liar for hire? Your attorney?"

Shane couldn't tell him the LAPD Legal Affairs Department was going to cut the deal, so he smiled. "We're just in the midst of changing gunfighters. Our new liar will get in touch with your —"

"Have him call the Felt. He'll be the picture exec on this project," Bergman interrupted. Then they all swept out of the room, leaving Shane and Nicky looking across the empty table at Arthur.

Shane got Nicky to the door, then finally to the parking lot.

"Christmas. How we gonna get this done by Christmas?" Nicky was coming out of it.

"Shut up, Nicky. I could've used that criticism half an hour ago."

"But Christmas! Are you out of your fucking mind? We'll never make it," the little grifter wailed.

37

IN THE WIND

"Does the chief know about this?" asked Charlotte Brooks, who insisted on being called Charlie. They were in her cramped, windowless office in Legal Affairs at Parker Center.

"Yeah, kinda," Shane hedged, but in truth, he hadn't been able to get in to see the Day-Glo Dago. Four more gangsters had hit the sidewalk, and the escalating street warfare had Alexa and the chief in a frenzy.

"So I'm supposed to call this Mr. Feltheim at Universal, he'll put me in touch with their legal department, and then we're supposed to do what? Arrange for the LAPD to sell an interest in a movie that's being shot by a production company named Cine-Roma, that we supposedly own?" Her right eyebrow was cocked and she was looking sideways at him through thick octagonal glasses.

"Yeah, but you can't mention you work for the LAPD. Cine-Roma is a front company. All you have to do is take down their preliminary offer and make sure there're no loopholes."

"Sergeant, I don't know anything about movie deals. I wouldn't even recognize standard boilerplate."

"We'll . . . we . . ." He stopped and took stock of Charlie. She was only about twenty-six and looked frail and uncertain. She'd go down like Polish infantry in front of the leather-vested killers at Universal.

"Okay. I'll get a showbiz attorney to negotiate the general deal points, then you can go through it for the LAPD. 'Cause I need somebody from our legal department to approve the contract before I sign it."

"Why is the LAPD making a movie?" She pushed her glasses a little higher on her nose. "I don't think we should be doing that. I mean, we're a city service, a nonprofit agency."

"Wonderful observation, Charlie. And when I come up with an answer, I'll have my people call your people."

Shane left Parker Center and decided that he'd better get Nicky to call his entertainment attorney after all. He tried Cine-Roma from his cell phone and got Nicky's secretary.

"Cine-Roma, Mr. Lubick's office, Daphne Del Rey speaking."

"This is Shane, I'm trying to get in touch with Nicky."

"Well, I'm not that man's secretary anymore. I work for Mr. Lubick now." There was both disdain and relief in Daphne's voice. She had fended off her last bimbo in short-shorts.

"Hey, congratulations. But if you're with our esteemed director, throw away that computer, 'cause you're working with a shovel now."

"I know you think that's funny, but Mr. Lubick is a genius. His visions have creative magnitude. I didn't come to Hollywood to work on scams like *Boots and Bikinis*. Paul is actually trying to make a meaningful film here, so if you say one more smartass thing about him, I'll be forced to report it."

"As well you should." Shane shook his head; this wasn't getting him anywhere. "Look, Daphne, I apologize. You're right, of course. Paul Lubick is the best. He's tits. But right now I need to talk to Nicky. Think you could hook me up?"

"I'm not supposed to handle anything but Mr. Lubick's business. I'm his personal assistant."

"Could you make an exception just this once? Can you please just transfer me?"

"Nicky went home. He's at his apartment."

"Thanks. And congratulations on the promotion."

She didn't respond; instead she hung up on him. Shane dialed Nicky's apartment three times but kept getting a busy signal. The Hollywood Towers were only five minutes away, so he drove there, parked on the street out front, then went into the building. It was five-thirty, so he left the pizza box prop in the trunk. He was going to find the manager this time and just badge him. But his timing was perfect. Somebody was just getting off the elevator as he walked into the lobby. He sped up and caught the door before it closed. If he'd been a home invasion specialist, this building would be high up on his target list.

Shane exited on the twenty-fifth floor and walked down the hall to Nicky's apartment.

He pulled up a few feet away.

The door was ajar, the lock splintered.

Somebody had left a big, black boot mark up by the brass knob. This B&E was about as subtle as a gay pride parade.

Shane was still packing Alexa's Double Eagle in his belt, at the small of his back. He pulled the piece, chambered it, touched the door with his toe, and pushed it open. Then he dove into the apartment.

It wasn't pretty.

The place had been completely trashed. Tables and furniture were tipped over. The Japanese prints had been pulled off the wall and kicked to shreds. Shane rolled to his feet, and, not hearing any movement, began to creep carefully through the rooms. Just minutes ago, the phone had been busy, so he took no chances.

He slowly cleared the apartment. The destruction seemed gratuitous. This had been more than a search; there was anger here. It looked like whoever had done this came specifically to destroy things.

Nicky's personal effects were gone. The bathroom had been emptied.

Shane opened the closet door. Nicky's suits were all off the hangers and thrown on the floor. His jewelry box was crushed, his watches stomped on. The little grifter's tan Louis Vuitton overnight bag was missing. Shane reached up and found the shoe box that had contained the 9mm pistol and two clips. The minute he put his hand on it, he could tell the box was empty. He pulled it down anyway, carefully removing the top, using his thumbs to push it up and off.

He found a baggie in the kitchen and secured the box top for prints.

Nicky's trick book with all the girls' pictures in glassine envelopes had been removed from his sock drawer.

Then Shane's eyes fell on the telephone. It had been knocked off the hook, which explained the busy signal. This could have happened any time since Nicky left the apartment this morning.

Shane stood in the center of the ransacked living room trying to add this piece to the puzzle. Nicky was a small-time crook, a petty criminal. He was a, well, to be honest, a Pooh. Nicky the Pooh was the kind of guy you slapped around but probably didn't hit. This angry trashing of his apartment was a troubling, discordant note in the whimsical life of the little con man. So who had tossed this place? Who could get this mad at Little Nicky? It didn't figure. But either way, Nicky was in the wind.

Shane looked at his watch: six o'clock. He needed to be at the Jonathan Club in Santa Monica in an hour for Farrell's bachelor party. He decided he would try to piece it together on the drive there.

38

THE BACHELOR PARTY

The Santa Monica Freeway was a parking lot full of rush-hour hostility. Shane was cut off, flipped off, and pissed off. He tried to calm himself while averaging a snail-like six miles an hour. He inched along past Hoover, then La Brea. His car was creeping, but his mind was racing.

Despite the fact that many crimes appear to be disorganized and chaotic, inside that chaos is usually some kind of twisted criminal logic. If an investigator can adopt the right mind-set, he can often spot a pattern.

As Shane smogged along in a sea of potential violence, he let his mind zigzag across Nicky Marcella's involvement in this case. He could easily understand Nicky hanging out with Champagne Dennis Valentine, running his errands, even getting Shane to find Carol White for him. All of that fit into some kind of logical equation.

What didn't make sense was Nicky's relationship with a Hollywood heavy-hitter like Farrell Champion. Why would Farrell hang out and do deals with a small-time bullshit artist like Nicky the Pooh? Yet there he was at the famous producer's engagement party, in his two-tone suit and Cuban heels, bragging about the projects they had in development together. *Savages in the Midst*, a film about a girl destroyed by Hollywood . . . the Carol White Story.

Nicky was a pretender. So why would Farrell Champion, a.k.a. Daniel Zelso, have anything to do with him? With his WITSEC status, the last thing the producer or the U.S. Marshals office would want was for him to befriend a criminal loser like Nicky Marcella. It just didn't track.

Now Nicky was missing. He'd either been snatched or, as his missing suitcase suggested, had packed up and left in a hurry. Somebody had gotten pissed and trashed his place either during the snatch or after Nicky left. Shane didn't think whoever did it was searching for anything. They were sending a message.

After leaving the vomitorium this afternoon, Nicky had scurried along, looking over his shoulder as if somebody was after him. Now Shane wondered who that might be.

At seven-fifteen he finally arrived at the luxurious, private Jonathan Club. The massive brown building sat on the sand at Santa Monica Beach, with one windowless wall backing up against the four-lane Coast Highway. The sun was hovering just above the ocean, tinging everything with orange light. Shane made a left through the arch and drove toward the entrance. A man in a red jacket was valet-parking cars. As Shane pulled up and got out, he looked at the nearby parking area, trying to spot Nicky's maroon Bentley — it wasn't there. He gave up the Acura and headed inside the private club, where he was met by a tall, good-looking man about thirty, wearing a dark suit.

"I'm here for Farrell Champion's bachelor party."

"Yes, sir. Take a right down the stairs. It's in the Grill's private dining room."

Shane turned and walked across the magnificent wood-paneled lobby, down a few steps to ground level, then followed the corridor to the Beach Grill, where he found a set of green louvered doors fronting a small, private room that overlooked the sandy Santa Monica Beach. Several beach volleyball courts were in use. Very athletic games of mixed doubles were being played by tanned twenty-year-olds. Their hard, muscular bodies glistened as they leaped and spiked, giving high-fives after every winning point.

The room was only half full with about twenty well-dressed male guests. Shane stepped up to the small five-seat bar and started looking around for Farrell.

"Hey, bud, way to go, you made it," the handsome producer said as he made his way over and gave Shane a bear hug. It seemed they were "buds" now. Shane was again struck by the animal magnetism of the man. He was also struck by the fact that Farrell looked nothing like the faxed picture of Daniel Zelso, which was locked inside his briefcase in the Acura's trunk. Shane tried to spot surgical scars. He checked under Farrell's chin and behind the ears. Nothing.

Could it be that he'd been wrong? That somebody else's prints had been on that lighter?

"Nora said the bridal shower was amazing," Farrell said. "You guys really are the best."

"Well, you know how close Alexa and Nora are."

"I'll tell you, Shane, if it weren't for Alexa, I think Nora would have gone back to Michigan a long time ago. She told me once that she finds Hollywood people superficial. Where do you suppose she gets that?" He grinned and showed Shane that great set of pearlies. "Hollywood . . . superficial? We drink bottled water, wear nothing that ever grew fur, except for rabbits, which don't count. We all have personal trainers and maintain staffs that are gender neutral, with perfect ethnic balance. We support liberal politicians no matter how many hummers they get from their interns; we go to the White House religiously, on Air Force One — our definition of political activism. What's not to like?"

He'd done it again. Shane found himself liking the guy. He was self-effacing, funny, and smart — all gifts of a natural con man.

"I guess Nicky Marcella couldn't make it," Shane said.

"Who?"

"Nicholas Marcella? I met him at your engagement party. Real short guy, rail-thin, said he was coming tonight."

"Nicholas Marcella?" A puzzled frown wrinkled Farrell's forehead. "Oh, wait a minute, yeah, I guess that was his real name. I've blotted that unfortunate episode from my mind. When he worked for me he was calling himself Mark Nickles."

"He worked for you?"

"Used to be my studio limousine driver. He spent a lot of time waiting for me parked out in front of my house. I felt bad for him so I told him he could wait inside. Shortly after that a lot of stuff started disappearing. I had some friends in law enforcement run a check on him. Turns out Mark Nickles was Nicholas Marcella. Had a rap sheet with twenty priors, all kinds of sleazy bullshit. Last June I sent some people to his apartment to reacquire my possessions — mostly rings and watches, stuff like that. I still have a criminal case pending against the little thief."

"So what was he doing at your engagement party?"

"He wasn't at my party." Farrell was looking at Shane closely. "Are you serious? A little guy, always wore stacked heels, narrow face, eyes too close together?"

"That's the one. He said he had two pictures in development with you at Paramount."

"That guy couldn't develop Polaroids. I found out before he worked for me, he was doing deaf-and-dumb street-corner hustles."

Shane nodded. It was true. He'd busted Nicky twice for sitting on the sidewalk at Hollywood and Vine with a sign reading: DEAF AND DUMB, PLEASE HELP. "Well, he was at your party. Maybe when you get home, you oughta recheck your jewelry case."

"No kidding," Farrell said.

Later that evening Shane finally learned what D people did, because Farrell introduced him to three of them.

"These are my best D guys," he said, and Shane shook hands with an African-American named Colby, who should have been doing picture layouts in *Esquire*; a Mexican-American with horn-rims, named Rudy; and a white guy named Lance. *Perfect ethnic balance. What's not to like?*

"Exactly what is a D person?" Shane finally asked.

"*D* stands for development," Rudy said, clearing up the mystery. "We develop literary properties and then once we think they're ready, we pass the scripts along to Farrell."

"These two guys brought me some of my biggest popcorn hits," Farrell said, slapping Lance and Colby on the back.

"Popcorn hits?" Shane asked.

"Yeah, mindless action movies: pretty girls, guys with abs, gunfire, rock 'n' roll. It's not my fault America loves that shit." Farrell grinned, but Colby and Lance looked hurt.

"I'm trying to do the more emotionally involving, thematic material," Rudy Garcia brown-nosed. "I want to develop something Farrell can really be proud of for a change." It seemed Rudy was the sensitive, caring D guy, but judging from Lance and Colby's scowls, Farrell should probably hire somebody to start his car for a while.

"Emotional involvement is the easiest thing in the world to accomplish," Colby fired back, his ego still bruised. "Just get a little kitten and have Jack Palance wring its neck. Everybody cries. I think Farrell's next film should be transcendent."

Farrell smiled and nodded, happy to be at the center of the disagreement.

Shane didn't know what a transcendent film was, so he just nodded.

Then they had dinner. It wasn't creamed chicken, either. Farrell served them oysters Rockefeller as a starter, duck à l'orange as the entrée, and peach flambé for dessert.

After dinner, a senior vice president of Paramount Pictures ran an elaborate gag video. It was a salute to the end of Farrell's bachelorhood, complete with explosions, special effects, and outtakes from *Mission Impossible 2*. At least forty name stars of both sexes appeared. They all lamented Farrell's sexual prowess and Nora's dire mistake in marrying him. It was funny in some spots, crude in others.

At one point, Michael Fallon was onscreen grinning into the camera, his bad-boy curls hanging loosely on his tan forehead. "Farrell, old buddy," the actor joked, "you're getting a great girl. I oughta know, I've been fucking her for three and a half years." It was that kind of funny. But the room roared with laughter. Most of them probably hadn't dealt recently with Michael's chronomentrophobia — a comedy-killing ailment.

At ten o'clock the speeches started — mostly low blows and crude insults. One by one, Farrell's friends stood up and talked about the length of his penis, or his inability to maintain erections. It reminded Shane of a smoker in Hoboken.

After dessert was cleared, everybody stood and Shane made his move. He had been carefully watching Farrell's water glass, and nobody but Farrell had handled it. Shane waited until Farrell left his place at the head of the table, then beat the busboy to it. Grabbing the glass by the bottom, he hurried out of the room,

389

heading toward the parking lot. When he spotted his car, Shane asked the valet to give him his keys so he could get something out of it. He walked over to the Acura, opened the trunk and placed Farrell's water glass in a plastic evidence bag next to Nicky's shoe box top, then turned to go back inside.

Just as he was reentering the club, a white Cadillac convertible with Arizona plates pulled up. A tall, dark-haired, dark-skinned man in Western clothes got out holding a white Stetson. The man put on his cowboy hat, handed his keys to the valet, and moved inside, his footsteps making that heel-toe sound peculiar to people walking in Western boots.

Shane followed the man down the hall, right back into Farrell's party. When the producer saw the tall cowboy, he flung his arms wide. "Carlos, *mi amigo,* you made it!" he yelled.

Carlos gave Farrell a big hug, and after a lot of back-pounding, apologized for being late. "My damn flight got canceled." He had a slight Latin accent. "No flights out of Arizona 'cause a huge weather front hit the state. I had to charter a private jet, then pay the damn pilots extra to take off, 'cause of wind shears, which was probably bullshit."

"Whatta buddy." Farrell grinned. "Risked your life to get here."

Maybe it was because Carlos was from Arizona, and that's where Alexa said the drugs were headed. Maybe it was the bullshit about chartering a private jet when his car was parked right outside with Arizona plates on it. Maybe it was because Carlos had slicked-back hair and looked like a dirtbag. Who knows what made Shane suspicious, but the cowboy with the white Stetson had all of his alarm bells ringing. By asking around, he found out his last name was Martinez. Carlos Martinez was the Latin equivalent of John Smith.

Shane waited until the Cohibas came out, then handed Carlos a box of matches and watched while he held the box and struck a wooden match on its side. Then Shane took the box back and slipped it into his pocket.

"Whatta you do in Arizona?" Shane asked conversationally.

"This and that. Excuse me," the cowboy said, and walked away.

Ten minutes later, Shane said his good-byes to Farrell, thanking him for a great time. He retrieved his Acura from the valet, then drove out of the beach club and turned left.

The houses along the beach bordering the club were all expensive, and had private concrete strips adjoining the Coast Highway to handle overflow parking in front of their garages. Thirty or forty yards north of the entrance to the Jonathan Club Shane swung a U-turn and parked on one of the concrete pads just off the highway.

He had to wait for almost an hour, but a little after midnight the white Cadillac pulled out of the club drive and headed south down the Coast Highway to the Santa Monica Freeway. Shane pulled out and followed, carefully keeping two or three cars back.

The cowboy turned onto the 405, then exited on Sunset and headed out toward Pacific Palisades.

Then a strange thing happened.

Carlos Martinez turned onto Mandeville Canyon Road. Suddenly, Shane's heart began to pound. He decelerated, keeping the convertible's taillights in view while falling farther back.

The white Cadillac pulled up to some lighted gates. Shane turned off his headlights, parked half a block down, then watched in amazement as the gates opened and the cowboy disappeared onto the huge estate of Champagne Dennis Valentine.

39

OCCAM'S RAZOR

Shane sat in the dark, half a block down from Valentine's estate, trying to figure out why Carlos Martinez, a guest at Farrell Champion's bachelor party, would drive directly from the Jonathan Club to Dennis Valentine's estate on Mandeville Canyon Road. It destroyed all of Shane's theories about what was going on.

So he sat in the dark and ran through it all again, looking for his mistake. His investigation had started at Farrell Champion's engagement party, because the producer had made a bad joke about two dead ex-wives. That initial concern had led him down a path of inquiries that culminated in the discovery of Farrell's real identity — Danny Zelso — along with a drug background in Panama, two murdered wives, and his enrollment in WITSEC. Farrell Champion was the North Pole of one investigation.

Shane also reviewed the route that had led him to Dennis Valente a.k.a. "Champagne" Dennis Valentine. At Farrell's engagement party, Shane had run into Nicky Marcella, who had asked him to find Carol White. That investigation had led him down another completely separate line of inquiry. Shane was successful, turned Carol's location over to Nicky, and now believed that act led to Carol's murder. He'd grabbed Nicky, who quickly spit up Champagne Dennis Valentine. That put the New Jersey mobster at the South Pole of a completely separate investigation.

To that point, the only thing connecting Farrell Champion and Dennis Valentine was Nicky's attendance at Farrell's engagement party, and that was easily explained by Nicky's new career in show business.

But tonight, Farrell not only denied inviting Nicky to his party, he actually had a complaint pending against the little grifter for grand theft. Then in pops Farrell Champion's cowboy amigo, Carlos Martinez, who does "this and that" in Arizona. He leaves Farrell's party and drives to Valentine's estate, connecting the two poles of seemingly separate investigations.

The longer Shane thought about it, the less sense it made; unless he was willing to accept the connection as pure coincidence, which, as Alexa cautioned, you never did in police work.

Shane sat and pondered.

At the Police Academy, he had taken a class in criminal logic that included a theory called Occam's Razor. The essence of this principle stated that when things were extremely complicated, the simplest answer was usually the right one.

So Shane sat in the dark, searching for the simplest solution. He began by setting out all the basic points and separating them into three piles: facts, lies, and suppositions.

Then he started over, analyzing each piece.

Dennis Valentine had been attacked by La Eme. A fact. Because of this attack, Shane believed the mobster might be the one masterminding the importation of White Dragon heroin into L.A. A supposition. According to Alexa's street intel, the drugs were heading to Arizona, and Carlos was from Arizona — both still suppositions. That was all he had on Dennis Valentine's side of the equation, except for his mob history and current scam to organize the I.A. unions, which Shane didn't think was a part of this big drug smuggle.

Next he reexamined the Farrell Champion track, using the same three categories. Champion's real name was Daniel Zelso. A strong supposition that could turn into a fact if the prints on the water glass came back hot. According to the WITSEC computer, Zelso used to launder money for a Panamanian drug syndicate and Farrell Champion was one of WITSEC's assets — both facts. Farrell said

Nicky had been his studio driver. Probably true, but Shane would check it out. All the P.R. stuff on Farrell was probably bullshit, except maybe the gun-running story. Guns and drugs lived in the same criminal quadrant.

So how did this collection of facts, suppositions, and lies make a picture?

While Shane methodically let the sediment settle, one thing became increasingly clear to him: Nicky Marcella had to be the common denominator.

Nicky had been friends with Dennis Valentine at Teaneck High School in New Jersey. Once they were both in L.A., he had tried to help Valentine meet agents and showbiz players. Nicky had also used Shane to find Carol White, then Dennis probably had her killed. That covered Nicky the Pooh's connection to Dennis Valentine.

Next, Shane reexamined Nicky's connection to Farrell Champion.

Nicky had driven Farrell's studio limo and had stolen jewelry from the producer; an act that eventually got him fired. Moreover, Farrell had a criminal case pending against the little grifter. If Nicky had lied about his relationship with the famous producer, what the hell was he doing crashing Farrell's engagement party? If Farrell had seen him, and eventually he would have, Farrell would have simply called security, or the police, and Nicky would have been arrested on the spot. The more Shane thought about that, the less sense it all made.

Shane had been meaning to run Nicky Marcella through the police computer, but he'd been so busy, he'd forgotten. He would do that the first chance he got.

Shane also had some nagging questions: Who busted up Nicky's apartment, kicked the shit out of his Oriental paintings, and stomped on his expensive watches? It probably wasn't Valentine, who was still using Nicky. So who? Farrell? The U.S. Marshals? Tiger Woods?

His head was beginning to ache. He didn't know where the answer was hiding in this slew of facts, guesses, and questions. Shane needed help.

He had written down the Cadillac's license plate number so he now called it into the DMV. After he gave them his badge number, they came back immediately with the information. The car was registered to Hertz, in Flagstaff, Arizona. He took Carlos's residency in Arizona out of the maybe column and put it with the facts. The picture became a bit clearer.

Shane dialed Alexa's cell phone.

"Yes," she answered, her voice clipped.

"I need to see you and Chief Filosiani right now."

"Shane, I'm . . . we're —"

"I know . . . people are dying in South Central."

"All over town. I've had three more machine-gun shootings since yesterday. It's like the Gaza

Strip in some of these divisions."

"I think I might have some of the pieces on that."

"What pieces? You're working on Dennis Valentine. What does that have to do with this gang war?"

"I told you before, I think he may be the one moving the White Dragon into L.A. Now I think Farrell Champion may be involved, too."

"Come on, Shane . . ."

"Honey, I need forty minutes with you and the chief. It's gonna be worth your time. Send a detective car out to Valentine's house on Mandeville Canyon. I'm sitting on a Hispanic cowboy driving a white Caddy convertible with Arizona plates. His name is Carlos Martinez, but that's probably a bum handle. The car was rented from Hertz in Flagstaff, Arizona, wherever the hell that is. I'm going to ask R and I to contact Hertz and get me the name of whoever rented this car, and I'll bet you a weekend in Paradise it's not anyone named Carlos Martinez."

"Hertz doesn't even rent Cad convertibles — only Ford Mustangs, Buick LeBarons, Lincoln Towncars, and SUVs."

"Then it's got stolen plates. Honey, stop arguing and get a detective car out here — somebody who can tail this guy without being made. I need to get in there and run through this with you."

"All right. I'm on the sixth floor at DSG. The"

chief's sleeping in his office. He's in a horrible mood."

"Why should he be the exception?" Shane hung up.

Twenty minutes later a gray Plymouth plain wrap pulled up beside him. Two guys he'd never seen before, wearing windbreakers, were in the front seat.

"You Scully?" an Asian cop in the passenger seat asked.

"Yeah."

"Chen and Hibbs. We'll take over."

Twenty-five minutes later he was in Alexa's office at Parker Center.

They walked down the corridor together and woke up Chief Filosiani, who was angry, irritable, and tired. Shane had seen friendlier eyes on rattlesnakes.

40

HOSING DOWN TONY

"What the fuck d'you think you're doing?" Tony's angry question hung over Shane like a sword of reckoning.

"I'm just trying to . . . to tell you about a strange thing that happened at Farrell Champion's bachelor party. I'm . . ."

"I don't care about Farrell Champion's party, I wanta know what's going on with this damn movie. Somebody in our legal department, an attorney named Charlotte Brooks, says you talked to her today about some movie deal with Universal. Is that right?"

"Charlie? Yes, I did."

"She also says she talked to somebody over at Cine-Roma Productions who says they're on the hook for over a half a million dollars in preproduction costs, and in less than a week they're gonna owe twenty million on a hundred-million-dollar movie. Cine-Roma is half owned by us! What the fuck are you doing?! I only authorized a hundred and fifty thousand. I been tryin' to reach you all afternoon, but your cell's been off."

"Uh . . . yeah, well, the reason for that is, I got this cell from ESD, and it's got a bug in it. I keep it off unless I . . ." Shane froze in mid-sentence because of the exasperated expression on Tony's face.

"For the love of God, tell me we ain't really in that deep?" Tony looked tired in his rumpled suit. Wisps of fringe hair stuck up in back of his head where he'd slept on it. His round face and mostly bald scalp were turning pink with anger. "I can't believe this. How did it happen? I want the truth, Sergeant."

"Well, sir, in Hollywood, there are many truths," Shane began, "and those truths are generally dominated by soft facts, which are subject to constant reevaluation and revision."

"You sound just like one a them now," Tony accused.

"I'm sorry. It's just . . . to understand this, you have to realize how it works. Everything in Hollywood is upside down."

"Upside down? Are you kidding me? I want you to explain how this little sting I originally approved for a hundred and fifty thousand dollars got so fucking out of control."

"It's a little hard to explain, sir."

"Try."

"Okay, well, the first thing you have to understand is everybody in Hollywood *wants* films to be expensive."

The chief frowned. "Bullshit."

"It's not bullshit. It's a Hollywood truth."

The chief just glowered.

Shane's throat was dry. "Let's suppose you can make the exact same film for ten million dollars, or for a hundred million dollars . . . which would you choose?"

"And they're exactly the same? Same stars, same everything?"

Shane nodded. "Finished film is identical."

"Well, of course I'd make the one for ten million. Only a fool would spend ten times more."

"Well, in a normal business context you're right, but in Hollywood, you're wrong. Nobody at a major Hollywood studio wants to make a ten-million-dollar film. The industry average is thirty-mil, but that includes a lot of low-budget stuff made by independents. At minimum, the majors would rather spend something north of fifty. And why do you suppose that is?"

"You tell me."

"Because it doesn't make sense to them to make a film for ten million and then go out and spend fifty mil on thousands of theater prints and national advertising. That's about what it costs in P and A to support a wide domestic release these days — more than three thousand screens. Y'see, in their minds, it's foolhardy to put five times more money behind the bet than you've got riding on the film in the first place.

"The idea started to flourish in Hollywood that you're better off spending fifty million instead of ten to make the same movie, because now the fifty mil in releasing costs makes more sense. Then some genius says: 'What if we spend a hundred million on a film?' The cost of P and A basically doesn't change too much, so now we have a great deal. A hundred-mil blockbuster, and only fifty is backing the bet. Pretty soon everybody was buying into that."

Filosiani glowered at this weird logic.

"Okay, that's the complicated truth," Shane sighed. "Now comes a simple truth: A lot of directors think if you're making a forty-million-dollar film, you're nowhere near as important as the guy who's directing a hundred-million-dollar film. Some directors try to spend money on anything and everything to get the cost of production up. With directors trying to spend money and push the budget up, a lot of films spiral quickly out of control."

"That is the stupidest thing I've ever heard." The chief was smoldering.

"Egos conspire to cost money in show business. Like I said, the logic is upside down. But I've still got ten days." He glanced at the calendar on his watch. "Well, more like eight and a half now, before we get hammered with all those pay-or-play clauses. I'm going to New Jersey later this morning. We take off at eight a.m. Dennis Valentine is going to introduce me to his uncle. I think I've got a pretty good chance of hooking Don Carlo DeCesare to this union-fixing, police-bribery case. Then once I've got Little Caesar on tape, I'll either shut this film down or sell it outright to Universal, which should recoup all our money."

"And if Universal won't buy it? What then? How much have we spent?"

"Well, sir, uh . . . these figures are a little bit in flux. The soft costs are hard to compute, and hard costs are —"

"Goddammit! Answer the fucking question!" Filosiani's face was flushed; he was almost screaming.

"Around five hundred and fifty thousand. We could subtract Dennis Valentine's two hundred fifty thousand bribe from that, but we've only received a hundred so far. The total's either three hundred or four fifty . . . not counting the transportation and construction costs. I don't know where we are on that, how much it costs us to freight those redwoods in from Oregon, or how many extras we hired yesterday, or what kind of deal the director made with his brother to set up the Civil War school in Reseda —"

"The what?!"

"We're . . . uh . . ." He looked to Alexa for help. She jumped in fast and switched to damage control.

"Sir, I promise, Shane will have us out of this by the weekend. I know we're a little over budget, but he's going to nail Don Carlo

404

DeCesare. You've got to remember what a huge catch it would be to get Little Caesar on a RICO prosecution."

"He's not going to say shit. I know that guy — he won't incriminate himself," Filosiani growled, but the thought had calmed him slightly.

"Uh . . . sir . . . I know Shane will deliver," Alexa said weakly. "It's going to be huge. Then, once we have the goods, we'll shut the movie down."

At this point, Shane wasn't confident he could deliver a pizza.

"Let's go, Shane. You can give him the other information in a memo." She pulled him out of Filosiani's office without even letting him tell the chief why he'd come here in the first place.

He followed Alexa down the hall into her office.

"We're both gonna get fired. Jesus, five hundred and fifty thousand from my OCB detective budget," she lamented.

"I'll be lucky if I can hold it to that. You want to know the truth? This boat has left the dock. Our only real chance of bailing out is to get Universal to take it over."

"Are you telling me that the Los Angeles Police Department is actually producing a Michael Fallon high-budget action picture?"

"I wouldn't exactly call it an action picture. It's more of a spiritual thriller."

"Shane, don't fuck with me."

"Yes, we're producing the film. How do you want your credit to read?"

"I'm speechless."

"Listen, I think I need to get out of here."

"What was all that malarkey about Farrell Champion and Dennis Valentine both being involved with this drug deal and gang war?"

"Oh, that." He smiled. "I've gotta rethink some of that." He kissed Alexa, then gave her a hug.

"I'm out of here at eight a.m. to New Jersey. I'll keep the StarTAC on. They're monitoring the tapes at ESD."

"Shane, what was it you were going to tell us? You said it was important." She was leaning forward, insistent now.

"I'm not sure what's important and what's not anymore. I think I'm losing my perspective. I need sleep. At least five hours all in one snooze. I'm starting to ramble." He kissed her again, then left the sixth floor.

He took the water glass and box top out of his briefcase, tagged them, along with the matchbox, and dropped them all off at R&I, with instructions for an immediate print-run on all three items.

Shane drove back to North Chalon Drive and let himself in. It was 2:30 a.m. Chooch wasn't there — probably still at the hospital. His gun was in the mail slot and Franco was waiting for him. The cat followed Shane into the bedroom and watched while he set the alarm. Exhausted, Shane fell backwards on the bed without undressing. Franco jumped up, licked his face, and purred in his ear.

"I'm trying, Frank. I don't know who did it yet. The hole I'm in just keeps getting deeper and wider. I don't even know what the fuck I'm doing anymore."

The cat reached out and put a soft paw on his cheek. *Finally,* somebody cared how *he* felt. Shane fell asleep with Franco curled beside him. He didn't open his eyes until the alarm went off at six o'clock the next morning.

41

LITTLE CAESAR

The jet was a shiny new green-and-white four-teen-passenger Challenger. Shane sat across from Dennis Valentine, who had elected to shed his Hollywood plumage; no white on white for this visit. He was now in pinstripes. His tailor-made suit draped his scrupulously maintained body like a charcoal-gray paint job. His ruby cuff links danced and twinkled. Silvio Cardetti and Little Mo were decked out in Gotti-esque double-breasted black. They sat a few seats back, near the rear of the cabin, playing cards.

The cuisine was tofu and brown rice. Colonel Sanders and the Frito Bandito had missed the flight.

The plane thundered down the Burbank runway, lifting off toward the purplish mountains to the east. In a gesture that symbolized

408

the entire trip, Dennis threw his Hollywood trade papers aside and picked up the *Wall Street Journal*.

Conversations with Dennis, when they weren't on business, were usually on fitness. As soon as the wheels were up, he launched into a primo riff on vascular health.

"People don't know how important it is," he said. "You got guys walking around, their ankles all swollen, and you know what causes it?"

"Bad shoes?" Shane asked, trying to field an easy grounder but missing the ball.

"Fuck no. Lack of diosmin. It's a flavonoid. Flavonoids are microscopic water-soluble pigments and there are over four thousand kinds. Diosmin is the most important flavonoid 'cause it makes the veins in your lower limbs elastic. You find it mostly in rosemary leaves, but it's gotta be chemically micronized, so it's small enough for the body to process."

"I won't forget that," Shane said. "But scotch tastes better and does the exact same thing. Makes your lower limbs rubbery as hell."

"I know you're just fucking with me, but one day, some vascular surgeon is gonna be stripping your veins and you're gonna wish you'd listened."

Shane couldn't take this all the way to Jersey, so he told Dennis that he'd only had two hours sleep, lowered the seat on the comfortable jet, and closed his eyes. As he tried for unconsciousness, his mind kept circling the tragic memory of Carol White. Maybe it was the close proximity to the man he suspected of having her killed, or maybe it was because he was headed to Carol's hometown in Teaneck. Whatever the reason, the pictures and remembered sounds of her haunted him.

The beauty contest winner who came to Hollywood to be a star but ended up with a King Kong habit, turning tricks for a bunch of curb-crawlers on Adams Boulevard.

He thought about the slender thread that was binding all of them to their futures. Chooch had risked everything to save Delfina. She was still in psychological shock, choosing a world of soft shapes and blurry sounds over a more brutal set of memories that, if confronted, might destroy her. Delfina had done no wrong, a victim of nothing more sinister than her relationship to American Macado.

Unlike Delfina, Carol had made horrible choices. She had tried to drown the ache of her life's mistakes by shooting up. But she'd also been too vulnerable. Carol White had "loser" written in invisible ink on her forehead, in letters only predators could see. Sadly, her weakness had led her to the garage in Rampart as surely as this jet was taking them back to Teaneck where her tragic journey began.

Shane half-opened his eyes and peeked under his lids at the handsome mobster who worried about how much diosmin he was getting. Shane wondered if the thread holding Dennis to his future was as slender as the ones holding Carol and the rest of them. He wondered if there was too much lead in a 9mm bullet for a vegetarian.

Then Shane fell asleep. He dreamed about a lot of things, most of them aimless and jumbled. But as they were landing in Newark, one dream stuck with him. He was riding in a parade with Chooch and American. They'd been in a barrio bouncer, a low-rider splashed with a sparkle paint job. The car would rise up on its rear axle, then come down again, bouncing over and over. American Macado was driving, wearing a vest with beautiful silver conchos.

"Ain't this tits?" Amac said, grinning.

Suddenly, the Challenger's wheels touched down and they had landed.

A black limousine with two chase cars was waiting on the tarmac as the jet taxied up and they deplaned. It was cold in New Jersey. Frost clung stubbornly to the ground. Silvio and Little Mo got into the lead car as Shane and Dennis climbed into the Lincoln stretch.

"Only takes about ten minutes from here," Dennis said. "When I was a kid, I owned this county. Had a little Corvette, red with white seats. Bagged more pussy than a cat doctor."

"Didn't have a *número uno?*" Shane asked, thinking of Carol.

Dennis looked over at him, his eyes a little distant. "There were a few who thought so, but a guy like me, I've got to taste everything; gotta eat at all the restaurants. Know what I'm sayin'? Pussy is cuisine."

"But is it vegetarian?" Shane deadpanned.

"You love to bust my balls, don't you?"

"Hey, Dennis, you know how it is. A slow-moving target is always gonna draw fire."

Valentine looked over at him, and for a minute, Shane didn't know which way it was going to go. Most made guys and mob smart-heads had an instinct for who was an employee and who was a player. Once they had you down as an ass-kisser, you were never going to hear anything but orders. He needed to get Dennis on even ground, so he would eventually open up and say something meaningful for the little mike hidden in the cell phone on Shane's belt.

He thought it was significant that Silvio hadn't run the wand over him before they boarded the plane in Burbank. Maybe that meant he was gaining some trust and respect. By verbally jabbing Valentine, Shane was hoping to set up the feeling that they were equals. Of course, the downside to that was he could go too far and truly piss Dennis off. Then, instead of equal ground, he'd be getting hallowed ground.

Shane watched as a slow smile broke on Dennis Valentine's face. "I like you," the handsome mobster said.

Don Carlo DeCesare lived on a ten-acre estate at the foot of the Saddleback Mountains. As they pulled up, Dennis told Shane that the houses located at all the strategic spots surrounding the property had been bought by the DeCesare family, and that only confirmed or made soldiers lived in these homes. These DeCesare wiseguys got beautiful bargain housing, but in return, they had a responsibility to protect the estate. Dennis explained that nobody could get close to the Don or his family without the soldiers getting plenty of advance warning.

Standing at the large security gates, stamping their feet to ward off the cold, were two unmade DeCesare wanna-bes — *cugini*. The limo's windows were lowered so the two young guards could see that it was Dennis, then the caravan was waved through. They drove up a long, manicured drive, where several men in coveralls were busy planting spring flowers. Even though the afternoon April temperature was still in the mid-forties, the gardeners were kneeling, digging holes in freezing ground, putting hundreds of multicolored impatiens in the sculptured flower beds that adjoined the driveway.

The house was architecturally magnificent; a castlelike structure of gray stone. Turret towers guarded all four corners. A massive arched door with carved panels dominated the front porch. The only thing missing was a drawbridge, but the array of auto-mags in the hands of four young Mafia hitters on the porch had eliminated the need for a moat.

There were two older men standing with the others, both in their fifties, both wearing boxy suits. One of these capos walked down the gray stone steps and opened the door of the limo.

"Uncle Pietro . . ." Dennis grinned as the man stuck his fleshy, cologne-drenched face into the car.

"You look like you got a suntan out on da Coast," Uncle Pietro said, smiling.

"Nobody should lay in the sun — ages the skin and causes cancer. I use an indoor tanning product." After delivering this health warning, Dennis piled out of the limo with his briefcase, followed by Shane. Once they were standing beside the car, Dennis turned to his uncle and introduced Shane. "Uncle Pietro, this is the man I told you about, Shane Scully." Dennis turned to Shane: "Uncle Pietro was my baby-sitter growing up. His job was to follow me around, make sure I stayed healthy and out of trouble, right, Pete?"

"You took some serious looking after, bambino." Pietro grinned. "Chased his ass all up and down the state fixing messes."

"God knows how many illegitimate babies he buried." Dennis was enjoying the memory.

"Hey, all I did was ditch the evidence."

They were both grinning and laughing. Shane pasted a smile on his face, but he really wanted to slug both of them.

Suddenly, Dennis switched the subject. "How's Uncle Carlo?"

"Y'know, I guess he's doing good as can be expected. He's through with his chemo, but with all the other stuff he takes he's sick a lotta the time. He's having lotsa trouble with his legs now, clots and shit. Doctor's got him on blood thinners." Shane wondered if the Don was getting enough flavonoids.

They moved into the house and stood in the large entry hall. There were half a dozen fifteenth-century suits of armor lining the parquet floor. An arched window at the end of the hall looked out on the rolling hills and the Saddleback Mountains beyond.

"Sorry, but we gotta check for bugs," Pietro said to Shane. He motioned to another *cugino* standing nearby, wearing slacks and a polo shirt. He had short, dark hair and huge biceps. In his right hand was another 2300 Frequency Finder. The feds must have been having a sale on the damned things. Shane spread his arms and let the machine run over him.

"Nothing," the *cugino* said. "He's clean."

"I think we should take a closer look, Frankie," Pietro cautioned.

"Guy's okay, Uncle Pete," Dennis said, but the capo shook his head.

"He's still a cop, Denny. Is it okay, Mr. Scully? You don't mind, do you?"

Shane shrugged. "Fine with me." But it wasn't; it pissed him off.

Frankie led the way to a bathroom off the entry hall. Once they were inside, the wanna-be wiseguy closed the door. "Mind stripping down?"

"Yeah, I mind. But I'll do it." Shane took the StarTAC phone off his belt and handed it to Frankie, then removed his coat, shirt, and pants. Finally, he was standing in his shoes, socks, and underwear, feeling ridiculous.

"Turn around please," Frankie said, holding the StarTAC, which contained the very thing he was searching for. Frankie inspected him for a wire and finally nodded. "Okay, thanks. You can get dressed."

Shane put on his clothes, then held out his hand for the phone.

Frankie returned it, and as Shane clipped it on his belt, he turned it back on.

"You don't pack?" Frankie asked, referring to the fact that Shane had no weapon.

"Not outta state. Besides, I figured you wouldn't let me bring one in here anyway."

"Good thinking . . ."

Shane followed Frankie into the entry hall, where they rejoined Dennis and Pietro.

"My uncle is waiting to see you. Come on," Dennis said.

They walked down a beautiful flag-draped hall, passing under an ornate stone archway. Dennis stopped at a pair of carved oak doors and hesitated for a second before knocking. The doors opened immediately, and they were facing another steroid-fed side of beef in a painted-on suit.

"How ya doin', Kerry?" Dennis said.

"Hangin' in. You look good. L.A. must agree with ya."

"Yeah, but Lynette is breakin' my chops out there. She shops all day."

"Broads." Kerry smiled, motioning them inside a large dark den.

It took Shane's eyes a minute to adjust to the low light. The room was lined with bookshelves and was underfurnished. A huge antique desk and chair sat against one wall. An oxblood-colored sofa and two club chairs were positioned across the room. In several spaces on each book-lined wall, magnificent oil paintings hung in dimly lit alcoves. All were of elderly men in various kinds of period-dress. Two of the more recent paintings depicted stern-faced characters in expensive suits from the twenties and forties. Shane didn't have to ask; he knew he was looking at the criminal bloodline of the DeCesare family. Seated by the window in a wheelchair, with his back to them, was a small, frail old man: Don Carlo DeCesare — Little Caesar.

"Uncle Carlo, it's Dennis."

The old man slowly pivoted the chair to face them. Shane tried not to gasp, but half the Don's face had been surgically altered. Welts and scar tissue dominated everything below his nose.

Dennis moved across the room to his uncle's wheelchair and whispered something to him;

417

the old man nodded. Then Dennis turned and motioned for Shane to approach.

"He wants to meet you."

As Shane walked toward them he became aware that someone else was in the room; a slender, dark-haired young woman with glasses, who looked to be about twenty.

"This is Don Carlo's daughter, Celia," Dennis said. "She talks for my uncle. He signs."

"She does what?"

"My uncle lost most of his tongue and vocal cords to cancer."

Shane looked at the scarred face of the Don and tried to deal with this new fact. It appeared he would be forced to converse with this girl, instead of the Don, himself. *Would recordings containing only Celia's voice hold up in court?*

Shane crossed the room and stood in front of the wheelchair. Up close, Don DeCesare's destroyed lower jaw and the deep scars on his neck were ghastly and disfiguring. Shane was trying to collect his thoughts. This changed everything.

Amac's wisdom rang in his ear. *Así es, así será . . . Just keep going,* he told himself. He nodded to the old man, who returned the gesture.

"Uncle Carlo, this is L.A. detective Shane Scully, who I told you about."

Suddenly, Don Carlo began signing with his fingers. Celia, who was sitting a few feet away, next to the window, translated for him.

"He says he is glad to meet you." Her voice was soft and whispery, echoing strangely in the high-ceilinged room.

"It's my pleasure," Shane replied.

The Don nodded. He looked at Shane with sharp, piercing eyes, while he signed at his daughter.

"I am pleased that you and your wife have agreed to help my nephew with his new venture in Los Angeles," Celia's sweet voice translated.

"Alexa is the head of Detective Services Group. DSG supervises all the detectives on the LAPD, so she's in a terrific place to handle any investigation if someone in that union complains," Shane replied.

The Don signed again and Celia spoke:

"What Dennis has accomplished in Los Angeles is remarkable. I have convinced the brotherhoods in D.C. to stand aside, and not make trouble once special deals are cut with the IATSE unions. I am pleased you and your wife have accepted my payment, and will guarantee that Dennis is never prosecuted."

What payment? Shane thought. *We could sure use the rest of the fucking money.* But rather than bring that up, he said, "Whatever happens, we'll make certain that your nephew is safe."

The Don signed slowly, forcing them to stand patiently in silence.

"It is important for you to understand that since money has changed hands, our deal is now sealed. It cannot be undone. Any failure to perform services as agreed will result in your death, and the death of your family." It was strange to listen as this slender girl's soft voice conveyed a death threat against his loved ones. Celia continued. "This is not only a threat, but a necessary part of the agreement. Dennis will soon be taking over for the family and all efforts must be made to protect him."

"I understand," Shane replied.

Don DeCesare held out a frail hand, palm down. It was a strange gesture and Shane wasn't sure what the old man wanted.

"He wants you to kiss his hand," Celia said. "It is our custom to seal an agreement."

So, feeling foolish, Shane bowed his head and kissed the old man's hand. As his lips brushed against the cold, papery skin, he wondered at the evil the Godfather had done in his lifetime. He stepped back and the Don made a few more trembling hand gestures.

"Thank you. I must talk to my nephew alone," Celia translated.

Shane turned and left the room.

He walked back to the entry hall where he stood alone, listening to voices coming from a side room. Shane wondered if the crafty old Don had really lost his vocal cords or if he had learned sign language just so he could hold sensitive meetings with a family interpreter doing the talking so as to avoid the risk of being caught on tape.

The StarTAC unit had shot their conversation into space and back to the monitoring room at ESD in L.A. But could Shane prove that it had really been the Don who had said those things? He had only recorded his own voice and Celia's. Hell, he probably couldn't even prove Don Carlo had been there. It would be Shane's word against theirs.

He was angry and depressed as laughter swelled in the adjoining area, so he walked in that direction and soon entered a large living room with turn-of-the-century furniture and a fifteen-foot-high vaulted ceiling.

Pete, Paulie, and Frank were seated around a marble-topped table, next to a large plate-glass window, playing some kind of European card game. On the other side of the glass, Shane could see more rolling lawns and even a few white-coated animals that, from a distance, looked like sheep or even llamas.

Shane sat on the arm of a nearby chair, watching the game.

"Is the Don gonna be okay?" he finally said, breaking the ice.

"He's not doin' too hot, but he's a tough old man. Surprises us all the time," Pietro said.

"This is beautiful here. I understand Dennis went to high school out in Teaneck."

"Yep, sure did," Pietro said, smiling. "He was some kinda hot shit back then. Captain of the football team, good shortstop in baseball, pretty much had his way with the ladies." Then he turned to another old capo whom Shane hadn't noticed, sitting in a wing chair by the fireplace. "Hey, Norm, remember that girl from Trenton, came down here, camped out in front of the driveway? Jesus, she was so stuck on Denny, she slept there for two days . . . wouldn't go away." Norm laughed and just nodded. "I went down and threatened this bitch, but she still wouldn't leave. She was willing to die to get in here and see him."

"Yeah," Shane smiled. "Nicholas said Dennis always had lotsa girls." Shane was fishing, hoping one of these *goombas* would hit the line.

"Who's Nicholas?" Pietro said as he laid down some cards and said *"Banco."* Then scraped a pile of chips off the table.

"Nicholas was a real good friend of Dennis's in high school."

"I don't think so. I spent mosta my time sweeping up after the kid back then. I don't remember no friend named Nicholas. What's his last name?"

"Marcella."

Pietro was now shaking his head and smiling as he stacked his winnings.

"Something funny?"

"Ya mean *Nicky?* That pathetic little prick was never friends with Dennis. Who told you that? Dennis used to terrorize him, made him eat his lunch off the floor in the school cafeteria. Shit like that. They called him Nicky the

Pooh 'cause the guy was so pathetic. Denny fucked him over constantly while all the kids laughed. I told Dennis back then that he should cool it. You never know with people. You can push 'em too far. Some little nothing guy will snap, come off hot, get a gun, *ka-boom*, you're in the obits."

"Nicky wasn't his friend?" Shane asked.

"That little *schmuck* was so piss-in-his-pants scared a Dennis, he used to shake when he was around, y'know? And Dennis just thought it was funny. Used t'make him wash his car and shine his shoes. Sometimes forced Nicky t'follow him around at school on his hands and knees barking like a dog. Everybody thought it was funny, but I seen the look in that little guy's eyes. You should never push anybody that far 'less you're gonna clip him after. Course, Dennis, he was only seventeen then. He thought nothing could ever happen to him. You grow up, you learn." Now Pietro was dealing again, flipping cards onto the table. "Last I heard, Nicky Marcella went out to L.A. to live with his married sister. Just goes t'show ya. What kinda limp dick moves in with his sister?" The talkative capo took some chips and tossed them into the center of the table.

Shane picked up a magazine and sat on the sofa a few feet away to wait for Dennis while the card game continued.

Why was Nicholas Marcella out in L.A. throwing parties for a man who had once made

423

him crawl on his hands and knees and bark like a dog? Shane tried to concentrate on the magazine, but his mind wouldn't stop circling this strange new fact.

42

GUESSWORK

They all slept on the flight back to the West Coast. When the jet touched down in Burbank, it was ten-thirty that same night. They deplaned and headed to their cars. Champagne Dennis Valentine paused by his blue Rolls and looked over at Shane. "That was good. Uncle Carlo is very happy you came."

"I'm very happy he's very happy."

They agreed to talk in the morning.

Shane called Alexa as soon as he pulled away from the airport.

After expressing relief that he was back safely, she shifted to disappointment: "I listened to the tapes at ESD. All they had on them was you and some girl. That's never gonna work in court."

"We have my sworn statement that the Don was there. I witnessed it."

425

"But Shane —"

"What was I supposed to do? The guy's claiming his tongue and vocal cords are gone."

"I know, but . . . It's just . . . We can't." Her angry broken sentences snapped, like wet laundry on a backyard line.

"I've gotta see you right away," she finally said. "Everything is happening at once; it's all gaining speed and the chief wants a meeting. He went to Santa Monica tonight — two Crip shooters are being interrogated out there — but he should be back soon."

"I'll shut down the damn film deal, okay? But I can't go through another meeting with Tony pounding on me."

"It's not just about the film, Shane. Your print runs came back. Farrell *is* Danny Zelso. The prints on the shoe box top were Nicky's."

"What about the Arizona cowboy?"

"That's where it gets confusing. The matchbox prints belong to General Miguel Fernando Ruiz, a Panamanian drug kingpin who disappeared after Zelso was arrested."

"Alexa, I told you these cases were interlocked."

"Yeah, but I don't know what's holding them together."

"I do," Shane said. "Since Filosiani's in Santa Monica, it's closer if we all meet at our Venice house in twenty minutes."

"Good idea, I'll call him," she said, then hung up.

★ ★ ★

When Shane opened the door, it was musty inside — the kind of thick atmosphere that only lives in a closed-up beach house. He walked through the place, opening windows and doors. Although he was back where he had once thought he belonged, now, after living in the big house on North Chalon, his little castle in Venice looked small. He had only been gone a few days, but it seemed as if he'd never really lived here at all, like he didn't belong here any longer. He had always seen himself as a dedicated fighter for values he believed in. His goals were modest. He wanted good to prevail over evil; he wanted justice for victims; he longed for a society that valued fairness over profit. But his short stint in Hollywood had begun to convince him that their upside-down value system actually seemed to work better. In its own hedonistic way, it was more efficient. The system he had pledged his life to valued criminals over victims. Murderers were often portrayed as battered children in court, while rape victims were vilified. Tim McVeigh preached his madness from the cover of *Time* magazine. Even the Dennis Hopper Rule made sense. Why shouldn't his family live in a house like the one on North Chalon Road? Shane looked around his small, threadbare home in Venice and wondered if these new ambitions were temporary, or if his values forged over a lifetime could change so quickly.

Just then the phone rang.

It was Alexa. "Shane, Nora just called. She's hysterical. I'm going out to Malibu to pick her up."

"What's wrong?"

"I couldn't get much of it. She was sobbing. Something about Farrell missing . . . getting forced into a boat during his nightly swim. I'll get there as quickly as I can."

Tony Filosiani arrived twenty minutes later. He came through the door with his head down and shoulders hunched — a tired man dragging a huge weight. He trudged across the carpet in the entry hall.

"This is nice," he said with no particular enthusiasm. Shane led him out to the lawn, then gave him a beer, a rusting lawn chair, and a moonlit view of some stagnant water.

"You look bushed," Shane said.

"Yeah, this is more frontline detective work than I like at one time."

They quickly ran through Shane's trip to New Jersey. Filosiani hadn't heard the StarTAC tapes, but Alexa had filled him in on what happened.

"If the Don *can* talk, this is the best piece a mob bullshit since Vinnie 'The Chin' Gigante wandered the streets of New York in his bathrobe, mumbling, singing, and pretending to be insane," Tony sighed.

"He looked pretty cut up. I think it's legit."

The disparate facts Shane had absorbed

these last two days were rolling around in his head like marbles in a tin box, driving him crazy. He had a theory that strung them all together in a sequence that was logically possible, although somewhat far-fetched.

"I think Nicky Marcella is at the center of this," Shane said. Then he told Filosiani everything he knew about Nicky and his connection to Farrell Champion a.k.a. Danny Zelso and his connection to Dennis Valentine a.k.a. Dennis Valente. He briefed the chief thoroughly, including Nicky's disappearance the previous day.

"I read his yellow sheet," Filosiani countered after Shane finished. "Marcella's just a street barker . . . did a flat bit in county jail for block hustles on Sunset Boulevard. Guy is strictly a short-timer."

"I'll admit that he's a grifter, but I've been with him a lot this past week, and one thing he's not is stupid."

"If somebody snatched him, then he's probably dust," Tony reasoned. "We should move on. He can't be the focal point of something this complex."

"I don't think he got snatched. I searched his place and his suitcase was gone, along with his cosmetics, his hair dye, and toothbrush. Also, since his prints were on the shoe box, I figure it was Nicky who took the nine outta the closet. I think he packed up and split."

"Who wrecked his place?"

"I think Nicky did. Busted up everything, kicked his silk-screen Japanese art to pieces, turned over the furniture and left."

"Why?" The chief was frustrated, exhausted, and on a short fuse.

"Because that way it looks like he's been kidnapped or murdered. He wants everyone to think he's out of the mix, at least for a few days. I think you may be wrong about Nicky not planning something this complex. I think he might have rigged this whole drug deal, even put Dennis and Farrell together. Now he's sitting back and waiting for his two worst enemies to hit the wall together."

"I don't get it."

"It took me some time to 'duce it out, but here's the way I see it now. At first I thought Nicky the Pooh idolized Dennis Valentine, but back in Jersey I learned I was completely wrong about that. According to a capo who knew them all back in high school, Nicky hated him so much he used to vibrate when Dennis was nearby. The capo thought Nicky would do anything to give Dennis payback. But Dennis Valente is a *goomba* prince, heir to the DeCesare family throne. Nicky can't just step up and give him flying lessons. He'd never survive. So instead he sets up a situation where somebody else does it for him."

"Who?"

"I'm not sure yet — La Eme, the Arizona State Police, the feds, us . . . lotta good candidates. I thought Nicky and Champion were in the movie business together, but I was wrong about that, too. Turns out Nicky's got a shitty personal history with Farrell Champion, too, including a four fifty-seven complaint against him for stealing jewelry out of Farrell's house six months ago."

The chief frowned. "What does *any* of this have to do with *anything?*"

"Please be patient, Chief, it's essential background. The rest is guesswork, but it kinda fits. I think Nicky found out who Farrell really was. He used to drive Farrell's limo, which means he was probably sitting in the front seat listening to his phone calls. He musta been able to figure out what was going on. Marshals in dark suits with crew cuts checking on Farrell every few days. How hard would it be to figure he was in WITSEC, then pay someone to run that down? Nicky has connections at LAPD; he was always kicking down street info to cops like me. I found out who Farrell was; Nicky could have made that same connection — discovered that Farrell Champion was Danny Zelso. Knowing Nicky, he then sold that info to the highest bidder."

"Who would that be?"

"It's pretty obvious, isn't it?"

"I'm tired, so why don't you just tell me."

"The highest bidder is always the guy with the biggest bankroll and the most to lose. Farrell Champion."

"So Nicky Marcella's blackmailing Farrell Champion."

"You got it. I checked on the way over here, and Farrell dropped the grand-theft jewelry beef against Nicky two weeks ago. Farrell lied to me about that, and I think he also lied about not knowing Nicky was at his engagement party. That never made any sense to me. If Nicky knew Farrell's real identity, he could force Farrell to invite him. Nicky's a grifter. Grifters love hanging around in expensive crowds. It makes a lot more sense that way. I'm guessing that Nicky talked Farrell into lining up the Mexican heroin, using this missing Panamanian general and all his old drug connections. Then Nicky introduces Farrell to Dennis Valentine, who is setting up shop in L.A. Valentine would want to control the drug trade, so he pays for the product and gets rid of Stone, which allows him to organize the Crips and Bloods to distribute it for him. I think Nicky put the two guys he despised most in the world into the same doomed drug deal and intends to push the whole burning mess over a cliff." Shane asked the chief if the two undercover cops he'd left at Valentine's were still following the Mexican in the white Caddy.

"No," Filosiani said sourly. "I was frustrated with all the money we were spending. The prints hadn't come back yet, so I pulled the surveillance."

The chief was angry at himself and biting his

lip, so Shane pushed past that and continued: "Nicky's got all these people heading to the same place in Arizona. Crips, Bloods, La Eme, and mobsters. He times it and dimes it. Everybody arrives out in the desert at the same time, loaded with rage, testosterone, and automatic weapons. When they get there they run into a wall of cops instead. It's a recipe for a bloodbath."

The chief rubbed his forehead. He looked like he was actually in pain. "That's a lot of ifs, buts, and maybes," Filosiani finally said.

"I know. But it sorta fits all the facts. I might have one or two pieces out of place, but if I were you, I'd get in touch with your friend at the FBI . . . see if any of the local feds knows what happened to Farrell. If he's one of WITSEC's assets, they probably have some kind of ongoing surveillance on him. Nora says he's missing. I'm not so sure. Whatever happened to him, I'll bet he turns up in the Arizona desert."

Tony sat quietly in the metal chair, rolling the cold can of beer across his forehead. "Shit. I'm so tired I could fall asleep getting a blow job."

"I'm not too interested in watching that," Shane moaned.

Twenty minutes later Alexa showed up with Nora. Her former baby-sitter's face was streaked with tears. Nora told them that Farrell had been doing his evening swim out in the ocean and that she watched through binoculars as a boatful of young Hispanic-looking men motored up, then forced him to get inside.

"You're sure he was forced?" Shane asked.

"He had to be," Nora said, breaking into tears again. "He isn't capable of leaving without telling me. He knows how terrified I'd be."

Alexa squeezed Nora's hand, but Shane wondered if Nora had any idea what Farrell Champion was really capable of.

43

WHERE'S NICKY?

Chooch called to say he was on his way home, so Tony took Nora back to Malibu while Shane and Alexa waited.

An hour later his son walked into the kitchen through the back door, looking tired and dispirited as he slumped down in a chair at the kitchen table and shoved his hands deep into his pants pockets.

"Dad, she doesn't even know I'm there," he said. "She looks right through me. The doctors say it's part of the PTSD, but I'm worried. She's not getting any better."

"Honey, you can't hope for too much, too soon," Alexa counseled.

"I don't know what else to do." Chooch's voice was so low, Shane had to lean forward to hear him.

"You want me to call and talk to the psychiatrist?" Shane offered.

"No. Dr. Sloan's been great. She said exactly what Mom just said . . . that it's going to take time. But I can't stand to see Delfina that way. It's killing me." Chooch told them he was going to spend the night at home, then go back first thing in the morning. He got up and headed toward his room to take a shower.

Shane and Alexa remained in the kitchen, looking after him.

"Hard lessons," Alexa finally said.

Shane nodded. "Life can be a bitch."

"I've got to get back to the office. I'm running a briefing at nine a.m. so I'll probably sleep down there."

Shane reached out and took her hand. "No, you will not," he said. "You're going to leave it alone for eight hours and sleep right here, in our bed, with me."

She looked at him for a long moment. "God, wouldn't that be great for a change?"

"You're not leaving. You can't be much help down there, half-conscious like you are. I'll set the alarm for six."

So they had a scotch in the backyard and watched the moonlight ripple on the still canal. Then they got up and went inside to their bedroom.

Shane watched from the bed as she undressed, marveling again at how blessed he'd been to win her. His early life as a child had been so filled with disappointment and darkness, maybe the Grand Pooh-Bah of Karma had decided he was finally due for a psychic paycheck. God knows, Alexa and Chooch had more than balanced the scale.

She turned and caught him looking at her. "Whatta you leering at, buddy?" She smiled.

"Just checkin' out your booty," Shane admitted, then he reached out and she came to him.

They made love for almost an hour. Afterward they lay in each other's arms. He kissed her and felt her heart beating against his chest. Finally they both found comfort in sleep.

When he awoke the next morning, it was eight a.m. He had not heard the alarm ring, and after he checked, he discovered that Alexa and Chooch had already left the house. He showered, dressed, then drove down to Parker Center. Alexa's Crown Vic was in her assigned space. The hood was already cold, so she'd been there for hours.

By nine-thirty he was standing with Lee Fineburg in the Records Services Division, watching the wiry geek make notes while he talked.

"My target's name is Nicholas Marcella. He has an apartment at the Hollywood Towers, but he's gone. I think he may be with his married sister, but I don't have a clue what her first or last name is. They were both originally from Teaneck, New Jersey."

Lee finished writing all of this down, then, without speaking, spun toward his computer and went to work.

First he tried the New Jersey DMV. There were twenty Marcellas listed in Teaneck, ten more in the burbs. Twelve were women, so he wrote their names down.

Next he searched the L.A. County Marriage Records database looking for women with one of those maiden names. He found one match: Elizabeth Marcella.

Fineburg studied the information on the screen. He found that Elizabeth Marcella had been wed on June 12, 1998, to Lawrence "Butch" Finta.

"I think I found her," the computer geek said. "Her married name is Elizabeth Finta." Then he went to the Unified Phone Listings, punched in the name Lawrence Finta, and presto . . . out came the address: 2358 Coast Highway, Torrance, California.

The guy was a magician.

The house was on the corner of PCH and Higuera, two blocks from the ocean. Shane parked a short distance up the street and took stock of the place. Butch and Elizabeth Finta weren't spending much time or money on maintenance. The yard was overgrown, the house needed paint, and there was an old, slant-nose silver van parked in the driveway, which looked like a giant rusting suppository.

Shane decided that the best and quickest way was the most direct. Since he could probably run little Nicky down in a footrace, he got out of the car and walked to the front door. Shane tried to peek in a window, but the shades were drawn. He knocked, and after a minute heard Nicky calling through the door, "Go away!"

Shane pitched his voice an octave higher. "UPS, I need a signature!"

The door opened and, for a moment, Nicky Marcella was standing there, looking ridiculous in tennis shorts and a green Hawaiian shirt with huge red and yellow flowers. But this riotous vision was only temporary because Nicky immediately spun and bolted through the house.

Shane shot after him and almost caught him in the first five steps — reached out and missed by inches, coming up with a fistful of air.

Like a slippery rat, Nicky was out the back door, zigzagging across a yard strewn with old auto parts and rusting junk. He hit and jackknifed over the six-foot grape stake, agile as a spider monkey, landing on the other side.

Unfortunately, Shane hit the fence like a walrus, oofing loudly, dragging himself up, getting splinters in his palms, finally lurching over, landing in a heap next door.

What happened next was sort of embarrassing. Nicky the Pooh left Shane in the dust.

Maybe it was all that barking like a dog, or running away from bullies in high school that had made him so fast. Nicky flew down a space between the adjoining houses, using his diminutive size to slip through an opening in the neighbor's fence.

Shane hit the same hole like a linebacker, knocking the shit out of himself in the process. By then Nicky was down the street, around the corner.

Nicky was widening the lead, while Shane was beginning to wheeze and growl. The sounds coming out of his throat sounded like a low chord on an accordion. His lungs were heaving, his footsteps slowing.

Salvation finally arrived in the form of a little Yamaha crotch-rocket. The yellow-and-white motorcycle buzzed around the corner going too fast. Nicky was running in the middle of the street, looking back over his shoulder at Shane, when the Yamaha sideswiped him and knocked the little grifter into the gutter.

Shane hoofed up to him, bent down with his hands on his knees, sucking air, while he tried to catch his breath. Nicky the Pooh was still conscious, but lying on his side moaning. Miraculously, he wasn't bleeding. Shane put a hand down on Nicky's shoulder. "Gotcha," he finally wheezed.

The motorcyclist was a geeky teenager with a pubescent goatee, growing in unevenly like wispy plugs of sage. "Hey, dude, like I didn't see ya."

"I'm suing," Nicky managed between groans.

"Asshole, you were in the middle of the

fucking street," Shane angrily exclaimed.

"You willing t'be my witness?" the boy asked Shane.

"Not gonna be any lawsuit." Shane flashed his badge. "You can take off."

The kid was gone before Shane finished the sentence.

Nicky pulled himself up. "Jesus, whatta you doin' here?" he whined.

"Selling life insurance. You gotta lot of explaining to do." Shane took the little grifter by his shirt collar, dragged him back to his sister's house, and shoved him down on the sofa in a cluttered living room that smelled of air freshener.

"Okay, Nicky, I've got most of it. I figure it was you who introduced Valentine to Champion. That's the only way it makes sense. But this thing keeps growing and I'm not sure I can see the edges anymore. So here's your choice. Start talking or start bleeding."

"Shane, I think I broke something here. . . ."

"I'm gonna break everything 'less you open up."

"I don't know what you're talking about."

Shane slapped him.

Actually, he didn't mean to hit him as hard as he did, but just as he swung, Nicky exploded upward, attempting a second escape, and he walked right into it. The sound was like a rifle crack. Nicky flew backwards into the faded upholstery, whining again.

441

"Nicky, I want to know exactly where this drug deal is going down. Arizona is a big state."

"I don't know, Shane. You think those two arrogant pricks would tell me anything?"

"How are you gonna dime 'em out if you don't know where they are?"

"Who said I'm gonna —"

"I did. You hate these two guys. You're setting them both up."

"Oh, that . . . Yeah," Nicky answered, rubbing the side of his face, which was red where Shane had smacked him.

"Let's go. I'm out of patience here."

"I know a huge Mexican from the one short bit I did in County. Guy was an Eme named Julian Hernandez — Tortilla Fats — weighed over four hundred pounds. He's a *veterano* in the Eighteenth Street Sureños. I called him, told him what Farrell and Valentine were doing, how they were working with the black gangs to take over the drug trade in L.A."

"So that's why Amac tried to hit Dennis Valentine in front of Ciro's Pompadoro. Without Valentine, there'd be no White Dragon — the Emes wouldn't have to compete on that new line of drugs."

Nicky slowly nodded.

"It was probably Amac who scooped Farrell out of the water in front of his Malibu house," Shane said, thinking aloud. "Amac will get Farrell to talk, then he'll be in Arizona when the black gangs and Valentine meet to close the deal. I need to know where that meeting is, Nicky."

"I told you: I don't have a clue. But believe me, Shane, everything those two pricks got coming, it ain't enough."

"Nicky, I'm caught up in this. My son got caught up in it. His girlfriend is in the hospital because of it."

"Much as I hate to say it, bunky, that's kinda your problem, not mine."

"Only I'm making it yours."

"I swear, Shane. You can beat me till my ears bleed. I got no more info. I told Tortilla Fats. He told his Eme brothers, end of story. I'm out of it."

"And you're just gonna hide out here till the shooting stops?"

"Yep. My sister went on a camping trip with Butch, so I'm just watching TV, waiting to hear those two *gonifs* are dead."

Shane pulled Nicky off the sofa, but the little grifter dug his heels in. "I ain't goin' nowhere, Shane, so don't try and make me."

Shane pushed him hard, driving him toward the door.

"Okay, I'm goin' then. But I'm not very good at this. In fact, I'm a —"

"Coward . . . I know. I'll show ya how to get over that."

Shane dragged Nicky the Pooh out of his sister's house and took him for a long-overdue meeting with Chief Filosiani.

44

JURISDICTIONAL WARFARE

The Day-Glo Dago's office was full of men in suits wearing cheap cologne. The room was starting to smell like a flower shop. There were two suits from the DEA, narrow-faced, sallow-complected attitude cases dressed in identical off-the-rack black numbers. They said they had picked up on this White Dragon smuggle from a street source, and were claiming jurisdiction. Shane had their business cards in his pocket but had already forgotten their names. The only way he could tell them apart was that one of them was chewing on a toothpick. There was another suit from the local FBI field office, Burt Semus, the special agent in charge for L.A. For some unknown reason everyone called him Shavo. He didn't look like a Shavo. He looked like an underachieving Burt.

Although Shavo was round-faced and ruddy-cheeked, he had expressionless eyes that belonged in a taxidermy shop, dark and hard as marbles. Of course, he was claiming jurisdiction for the FBI. He had no legitimate criminal standing in the case, but that didn't seem to bother him. The Frisbees were notorious claim-jumpers.

Also present were a few Brooks Brothers jobs from WITSEC, most likely the entire L.A. office. Carl was the one in charge, but he looked like a sales rep from Gold's Gym, with wall-busting shoulders and the pissed-off expression of a steroid jockey. He couldn't admit Farrell was in the program, but WITSEC wanted to manage this case anyway.

The roomful of hungry feds kept circulating around the office, hunting for a place they liked, but since Filosiani had no chairs, they simply looked unsettled and frustrated.

Shane, Alexa, and the chief represented the LAPD.

After Nicky the Pooh reported what he knew, he backed up and stood off to the side, trying to blend into the wall — a difficult task while wearing a flowered Hawaiian shirt and tennis shoes. Shane brought them all up to date on what he suspected. Then Filosiani took control of the meeting — or at least tried to. Problem was, nobody had much use for anyone else in the room. The DEA hated the FBI, and vice versa. They all hated the Marshals, who hated them back. Information was proving to be a scarce commodity. Adding to the confusion, everybody's beeper kept going off. They would glance at their little screens, then step out into the hall to return their calls in private. With all the paging going on, it was no secret that everyone's office was on Red Alert.

"You guys over at WITSEC must have some kinda ongoing management of your assets," Filosiani said.

"What assets?" Carl, the wide-body head marshal, deadpanned. "We don't control anybody named Zelso or Champion. Furthermore, even if he *was* on our list, which he isn't, WITSEC is constitutionally exempt from cooperating with other investigations in regard to our clients."

"Then why is the guy in your fucking computer?" Shane asked hotly.

"That's enough a that, Sergeant," Filosiani reprimanded, then turned back to Carl. "Then why's the guy in your fucking computer?"

"You telling me the LAPD has been hacking into a secure WITSEC computer and lifting confidential information?" Carl was glaring at Tony; then his beeper went off. He glanced at it, then handed it to another marshal, who left the office to return the call.

"Why can't we share what we have?" Alexa said, somewhat naively. But she had lost control of her gang war and was getting desperate. "This is red-ball. If American Macado abducted Farrell Champion, and the dope

446

coming into Arizona is being supplied by Valentine, we could be headed for a bloodbath. So let's cut all this interoffice bullshit and try to work together."

"Are you somebody's secretary or something?" Shavo asked, looking appalled at her suggestion.

"This is Lieutenant Scully, the head of my Detective Services Group," Filosiani said angrily.

"Obviously, Lieutenant Scully has not worked on many cross-jurisdictional cases," the DEA suit said around his toothpick. "We're tasked out of Treasury, the FBI is outta Justice, and the Marshals here report to some intergalactic war council in outer space. I have serious jurisdictional issues. I have people above me who ask hard questions when I give up jurisdiction." His beeper went off. "Excuse me." He stepped out, passing the deputy marshal, who was just coming back.

"Listen," Filosiani said, spreading his hands in supplication, still addressing Carl from the Marshal's office. "I know you guys watch your assets. You've got video surveillance or bugs — something. You can't tell me you don't have a clue what happened to Farrell, that you weren't watching him when he was put in that boat in front a his house, that you haven't got a tail working."

"Farrell? Who is Farrell, again? Was he Zelso, or Champion? I'm confused," Carl asked, impatiently looking at his watch.

"I guess the meeting's over," Filosiani announced. "It's every man for himself." Tony walked to his office door and opened it. As they all headed out, another beeper went off, but in the crowd, it was impossible to tell whose it was.

Before he left, Shavo stopped and gave Tony a stern warning: "You are instructed to stay out of what is clearly an FBI situation. Don't get involved."

"What situation you talking about?" Tony asked. "Since there ain't no Danny Zelso, or Farrell Champion, why don't you buncha territorial assholes just eat me?"

"It would be a big mistake if you pursued this," the toothpick from the DEA said.

"Yeah, well, I'll live with mine if you live with yours," Tony replied. "See ya, boys." He was in the threshold of his office as the crowd finally left.

"What a waste of time," Tony said, closing the door. "They're all lyin'. They know a lot more than they're sayin'. But in the meantime, we're left standing in the rain here. We got no way to track this. It could be goin' down anywhere in Arizona."

"Well, bunky," Nicky said to Shane, "having done my civic duty, I think I'll just hit the road." Nicky started toward the door, but Shane pushed him back.

"You're not going anywhere yet." Then

Shane's beeper went off. He looked at it and turned to Alexa. "Chooch." He pulled out his cell phone and hit a preprogrammed number.

Chooch answered immediately.

"You okay?" Shane asked. "Where are you?"

"I'm fine. I'm at the hospital with Delfina. She's talking again . . . making sense."

"That's great."

"Dad, you gotta get over here. She knows most of what's going on."

45

THE DAIRY

"His name isn't Carlos Martinez, it's Juan Ruiz," Delfina said, her voice a whisper. She looked like a delicate, dark-skinned, black-eyed doll lying in the hospital bed, her glossy black hair fanned out on the pillow around her.

Chooch was sitting next to her, holding her hand.

"They thought I wasn't listening, but I was. They had me taped to the bed. I was . . . I was without clothes . . . they . . ." She shut her eyes.

Chooch looked at Shane, silently pleading with him not to pursue Delfina's darkest memories.

Shane and Alexa were standing across from the bed. Dr. Sloan had suggested they keep the group small and was waiting in the hall with the chief and Nicky.

"It's okay," Alexa said. "We don't have to discuss that."

"No, no . . . I have to say it." Delfina looked up at Chooch. "I'm so ashamed," she said. "But if I can't talk about it, it will live inside me. I will not get past it. I won't get better." Surprising wisdom from a sixteen-year-old.

"You did nothing, *querida*," Chooch whispered. "It was them."

She had tears rimming her eyes as she smiled up at him. "Thank God you are here with me, *querido*."

"What else did they say?" Shane asked.

"They said this man Ruiz has a dairy in Arizona, that they use his hay trucks, which come up from Sinaloa, Mexico, where he owns a hay farm. Juan Ruiz ships the Mexican hay across the border to feed his cows in Arizona, but the real reason is the *chiva*. The *mayates* said the drugs make it through the border checks because Customs dogs cannot smell it hidden in the hay."

"Did they say when this was going to happen? When the shipment of heroin was coming in?" Shane asked.

"My cousin thinks soon."

"American," Shane said.

She nodded. "*Señor* . . ." Delfina was looking only at Shane now, her eyes boring into him while choosing her words with care. "My cousin is *rifa*. You know this word? He is special — the very best. But he fights for things so

451

big, he has made bad choices to win. He worries about the *movimiento* and our *clica*. He fights for his people, but his weapons are wrong. He uses drugs and guns. These things give him money, and money gives him power, but they also enslave the children he hopes one day to free. He knows this and it tortures him. He cannot sleep. He is up half the night pacing. He wants to be a force for good. He wants to change the laws, to effect the politics here in *El Norte,* but without the drugs he has no leverage. This dilemma is destroying him. He carries it all on his back. It is making him desperate, and one day soon it will cause his death."

She was saying a lot of what Chooch had said two days ago in the kitchen in Venice. "You are the police, but he trusts you. If you can find him, maybe he will listen to you or to Chooch. Deep down he knows that to make a difference he must fight using the right weapons, and must be able to survive. He understands that the real solution is education. Soon our people will be the majority in California. Amac told me about a new plan he has to try to get elected to Congress, maybe go to Washington one day and become a great leader. But to do this he must not be a criminal. Please help him." When she was finished, her eyes remained locked on Shane.

"The blacks who held you, are they going to Arizona?" he asked.

"*Sí*, Arizona. They said they were going soon. Maybe they have left already."

"But you don't know where?"

"No, but wherever Juan Ruiz's dairy is, that is where they go."

"Thank you," Shane said. "I hope you feel better soon."

She nodded. "I will feel better when my cousin is safe."

Shane and Alexa left the room and found Chief Filosiani and Nicky down the hall. Dr. Sloan had gone to attend to another patient.

"What'd you get?" Filosiani asked.

"Somebody named Juan Ruiz, which could be another alias for General Fernando Miguel Ruiz, or possibly he's a relative." Then Shane told him about the dairy in Arizona and the heroin that was coming in on hay trucks from Mexico. "We need to get into the state tax records and run a cross-check, see if we can tie somebody named Juan Ruiz to a milk business anywhere in the state of Arizona. It's probably near Flagstaff, because that's where the stolen Hertz plate came from. If that doesn't work, I'd check to see if there are any Arizona dairies owned by anybody with a Spanish surname, starting with Martinez and going on from there."

"Maybe we're about to get back in this thing after all." Filosiani opened his cell phone and moved down the hall, stopping next to a window for better reception.

"Pretty remarkable girl," Alexa said softly.

"Muy rifa." Shane nodded.

"Whatever the hell that means," Nicky commented.

Chooch exited the room and walked over to them, a fiercely determined look on his face. "Dad, I want to go with you."

"Jesus, if we're gonna keep having this argument, you better get over to the Police Academy and grab yourself a badge."

"Dad, please, what she said about American is true. He could make a difference one day. He could change things, but he's out of control right now. He'll try and avenge what they did to her. But I can get to him, talk him out of it. I know his heart. I'll be able to reach him."

"Son, we can't keep doing this. *I can't.* If this drug deal is going down, and American has gotten Farrell to spit up the location, then believe me, it's gonna be bad theater. I can't have you there."

"I owe Amac. It was *my* life and future he saved in that park two years ago. If we can keep him alive, someday he could really help our people."

"Our people?"

"I can't pretend I'm not Hispanic, that people don't look at me and see my dark skin. Sandy took chances to try and get a new life. She had brains and beauty, but here in *El Norte*, she had to sell her body to get ahead. If Amac's dreams had been true back then, she wouldn't have had to do that. If things were different, she could have had a different life."

As always when Shane was stuck, he looked over at Alexa, who just stared back at him.

"Don't you dare," she said softly.

46

TOP COW

Nicky the Pooh escaped from them at the long stoplight, two blocks north of Parker Center. He simply opened the door, bolted out of the chief's Crown Vic, and took off running. The last thing Shane saw was a glimpse of riotous green silk billowing off the little grifter's back as he dashed around the front bumper of a van.

"Let him go," Shane said to Alexa and Tony, refusing to humiliate himself again by trying to run Nicky down.

They arrived at Burbank Airport's Police Air Unit a little after one p.m. Shane and Alexa followed Filosiani over to a small, black twin-engine King Air that had been flying drugs up from Mexico until last March, when the pilot had lost power and landed on the Ventura Freeway in the middle of the night. The LAPD had arrested him, confiscated the King Air, and now used it to fly high-ranking officers to different law enforcement conventions around the state. The little plane was a turboprop with a top speed of around three hundred mph without headwinds.

The police department had a fleet of choppers, but only one fixed-wing airplane. The pilot was a grizzly bear of a man who was standing by the boarding ladder as Shane, Alexa, and Tony climbed the steps and settled into the comfortable dove-gray seats. Soon the propellers were spinning and the plane was taxiing down the runway.

They hadn't heard back yet on their computer tax search of dairies in Arizona. Their plan was to get moving anyway, fly in the general direction of Flagstaff, which was north of Phoenix, and hope that the search yielded results before they got too far off course.

They lifted off, climbed over the San Gabriel Mountains, and in ten minutes, were flying east over the California desert. The flat, dry landscape was endless, stretching below them like a sandy brown carpet.

The chief was working the phone, trying not to sound like a pissed-off commander kicking ass, but he was demanding results. "Put a few more people on it! Use the guys over at Computer Management Division."

"Try Lee Fineburg," Shane suggested. "He's in Records and Services, Special Duties. Guy's a genius."

"Get Lee Fineburg on the fourth floor," the chief said. "I want half-hour updates and don't hang me up here doing figure-eights over the fuckin' Arizona border."

After he hung up, they all remained quiet, looking down at the relentless desert. They were flying into a hundred-mile-an-hour head-wind, which was scrubbing precious minutes off their ETA.

Finally the air-phone in the plane buzzed; the chief snatched it up, listened for a moment, then grabbed a pen from his coat pocket and started scribbling. "Got it," he said, then hung up and smiled at Shane. "Fineburg . . . White Cow Dairy. Registered owner is Juan Ruiz, Scottsdale, Arizona, on Happy Valley Road."

They landed at Deer Valley Airport, on the east side of Phoenix, near Scottsdale, and rented a Lincoln Town Car from the Executive Jet Terminal.

As they stood in refracted heat bouncing off the tarmac, Tony's eyes went warily toward three executive jets parked a short distance away. Two Gulfstreams and a Challenger — big iron. When the ramp agent delivered their car, Tony badged him. "Who came in on those three birds?" he asked.

"Buncha' feds . . . landed twenty minutes apart, couple of hours ago."

"Figures," Tony said. He took the keys, climbed into the Town Car, got the air-conditioning going, then started driving. "Get a map outta the glove box," he barked at Alexa, now in the front seat beside him. "Find 2676 Happy Valley," he said as she spread the map across her knees and started studying it.

"Turn right on Deer Valley Road," Alexa directed, "take it to Cave Creek, go left on Pinnacle, then right . . ."

"Jeez, Lieutenant, I'm from Brooklyn. Keep it simple. Tell me where to turn when I'm gettin' close."

"Sorry, sir."

They rode in silence for a while, but Tony was frowning, his forehead gathered up in folds below his hairline. Finally he spoke. "Okay, look. This buncha eggbeaters from Washington got their own game going, and it's not called law enforcement, it's called politics. I don't trust any a them. More important, I want to take these people alive, without bloodshed, but there's just three of us and we're outta state with no jurisdiction."

"What're you suggesting?" Shane asked.

"I ain't *suggesting* nothing, Sergeant. I'm looking at operational alternatives and assigning risk co-efficients. We could call the Scottsdale cops, try an' get 'em to back our play, but I don't know this department. We could end up with a buncha toothpick-chewin' gunslingers, wearing RayBans and straw hats. I don't wanta add to the confusion."

"I agree," Shane said. "We oughta be able to handle it alone."

"You fuckin' nuts?" Tony said. "We probably got a mess a Crip and Blood shot-callers plus the Mexican and Italian Mafia, and God knows who else. We need backup, but we gotta get a look at the landscape first. If the feds are already at White Cow, then that's it. I ain't gonna fuck with 'em. But if they're not, then we'll case the place, get an idea where the shooters are, how many guys we're facing. Then we call in the Scottsdale P.D. Once I have the layout, I think I can control the outcome."

"Sounds *much* more sensible," Alexa said, sending Shane a withering look.

Tony pulled a gun out of his hip holster and checked the cylinder, snapped it closed, and reholstered it. The gun was pure Tony. A no-nonsense .38-caliber Smith & Wesson round wheel with a blue-steel finish. Tony had wrapped hundreds of rubber bands around the handle to make the grip larger and softer. The only place Shane had ever seen that modification was in Chicago. A lot of Chicago cops rubber-banded their grips. Tony, as usual, was an unorthodox mixture of good ideas and proven methodologies.

They made a left on Pinnacle, then went for about six miles before Alexa instructed Tony to turn right on Scottsdale Road, another mile and a half to Happy Valley. They made a right and started following the numbers.

Scottsdale was not geographically located in one place. It was spread out in population clusters. Land was not a pricey commodity in the desert, so people built low-level buildings in places that suited them. Only a few buildings at intersections and around business centers were three stories or taller.

The three LAPD interlopers continued down Happy Valley Road, eventually passing through a residential area and entering an open stretch of vegetative desert with no buildings. It was magnificent, arid country with Joshua trees dotting the landscape. Palms and bougainvillea bordered the roadside. Beyond, the desert seemed to stretch endlessly.

White Cow Dairy turned out to be a few hundred acres near some low rock outcroppings. A line of trees and a white split-rail fence that ran along the road bordered the dairy. There were at least two hundred Herefords grazing in the surrounding fields. A huge WHITE COW DAIRY arch spanned the entrance to the main center drive. Barns and milking sheds were located at the end of this long road. A white Colonial house with a covered porch and slate roof stood off to one side.

Tony drove by at the posted thirty-mile-an-hour speed limit. Alexa pulled a digital camera out of her purse and began taking pictures.

There were no cars, no trucks, and no people. Shane was worried they'd made a mistake because the farm appeared to be completely deserted.

47

HANGIN' WITH HEREFORDS

"We meet back here in ten minutes," Tony ordered.

They were standing next to the rented Lincoln, parked off the road several hundred yards from the main gate. They had popped the hood up, to make the car look abandoned.

"Shane, you take the east end of the place. Go in through the field, try and get close enough to the buildings to see if anybody's in there. I'll do the same from the west." He turned to Alexa. "Lieutenant, find a position out front. If anybody comes down the driveway, you hold the front door and contact us on the pager. Nine-one-one means trouble. Here's my number." He handed it to Alexa.

Shane didn't have his pager, but he did have his new satellite phone with the bug from ESD. He turned it on and set it to vibrate, then handed Alexa the number, which he had written on the back of one of his business cards.

"Okay, ten minutes," Tony repeated. "Then we're back here with whatever we find out."

They all took off. Shane went with Alexa, up the road alongside the line of cypress trees and the white split-rail fence. They reached a group of low rocks across from the front gate and ducked behind them.

"This looks like a good spot," Shane said as Alexa settled down and took a chrome-plated .38 Smith & Wesson out of her purse and laid it on the rock in front of her.

"Listen, Shane, just so we've got this straight. No John Wayne bullshit, okay?"

"The Duke's dead. Hit the slab almost twenty-five years ago," he said, remembering Nicky's line.

"Shane . . ."

"Okay, okay. I'm just gonna go hang out with a buncha Herefords. John Wayne would've never hid under a cow." He kissed the end of her nose, and before she could pursue it, moved out.

"Don't start a stampede!" he heard her whisper as he sprinted past the front of the dairy, ducking under the split-rail fence into the field. He made a dash across the pasture, then hunkered down with the closest herd of grazing milk cows. It wasn't quite a herd — there were only three white-faced Herefords —

more like a small gathering. They probably didn't wash these dairy cows, because Shane was immediately engulfed in their heavy, pungent musk. He knelt down between two of the animals and peered underneath at the barn and milking sheds, which were now only about two hundred yards away.

From here the dairy still looked deserted.

Shane watched the front of the farmhouse from beneath the swollen udder of Flossy or Bessie or whatever, but regardless, she didn't like him down there and kept moving and pivoting away to keep him out from under her. Shane had to duck-walk the Dance of the Toreadors to keep from being trampled.

After being stepped on once or twice, he finally managed to get a hand on the cow's neck and hold her still. She mooed, stamped her feet, then urinated. A yellow stream splashed on the ground, splattering him. "I guess you're trying to tell me something," he grumbled, then got out from under her, moving on to another cow.

When Shane looked over at the farm from this new angle, he could see the front end of an eighteen-wheeler parked behind the hay barn. The flatbed tractor wasn't attached, just a cab with some writing on the door.

He tried to make out what it said, but it was too far away, so he attempted to push his new cow in the general direction of the milking sheds to get closer. But she had also tired of him. Her udder was red. Shane was no farmer, but it looked like she'd already been milked once today and didn't want to give it up again. She mooed loudly and looked like she was about to head-butt him.

Suddenly, she turned her head and gave Shane the angriest look he could ever remember seeing on either man or beast.

"Okay, okay have it your way. I'm leaving," he whispered. Then he left her, sprinting across some open ground to the next cluster of grazing Herefords.

He was now about fifty yards away from the milking sheds and hay barns. He squatted again, looking underneath a new cow.

From this distance he could read the writing on the side door of the truck cab: *Sinaloa Farms*.

Sinaloa was where Delfina said Ruiz's hay farm was in Mexico. The new cow Shane was hiding under slowly turned her head and looked down at him with sleepy, slutty eyes.

"I'm married," Shane whispered as he began to herd her gently toward the barn. She moved slowly at first, but then started to get into it . . . or maybe she was just trying to get away from him. At any rate, the cow kept picking up speed, until she was almost cantering toward the barns. Shane was running beside her, awkwardly stumbling in weeds and rocks, trying to stay upright, when he abruptly lost his footing and fell, facedown, in the dirt. The cow moved on for a few paces, then stopped, and looked back at him. She stretched her lips in what Shane was almost certain was a grin.

He stayed low, surveying the terrain, wondering what to do next. Then in the distance he heard two flat pops. *Gunfire.*

It was coming from the west end of the property.

He heard two more flat, popping sounds. Then everything went quiet. Shane clawed for his phone, pulled it off his belt, and dialed Alexa. She answered on the first ring.

"You hear that?"

"Yeah."

"Sounds like Tony. It came from his direction."

"It's blown," Alexa said. "Pull back."

"You're breaking up . . ."

"Goddammit, Shane! Don't pull this shit on me. Save it for Tony."

"Didn't get all of that. Only heard 'Save Tony,' so I'm moving up. Get in touch with Scottsdale P.D. We need backup."

"Shane, cut the bullshit. I know you can hear me. Pull back! That's a direct order!"

"Hello . . . Hello?" Shane said, then closed the phone.

He could see a plume of dust rolling down the road on the west side of the property, heading toward the barns. Seconds later he heard the high whine of an engine wound tight, then, finally, he could make out a tan Land

Rover racing ahead of the billowing cloud of dirt. He wasn't sure if Tony was in that vehicle, but it finally skidded to a stop in front of the hay barn, throwing dust that began swirling and drifting with the breeze.

Shane inched closer on his stomach. His phone was vibrating on his hip — Alexa trying to get back to him. He ignored it and kept going.

When he was about twenty-five yards away, he could see two black men open the back door of the Land Rover and yank out Tony Filosiani. He was bleeding badly from two wounds, one in the shoulder area, another near the stomach. The Day-Glo Dago was doubled over, unable to walk. His toes cut a line in the dust as two African-American gangbangers with Crip blue headbands pulled him across the front yard of the dairy and into the barn.

Suddenly something wet and cold touched Shane's leg. He exploded upright onto his feet, his heart pounding. He turned and saw that the friendly cow with the bedroom eyes had just nuzzled his ankle.

Shane took a deep breath, kneeled down again, and got his jackhammering heart under control. He decided to make a run for it across open ground, try to reach cover on the near side of the barn. He had to admit, the plan *was* a little John Wayne, but his position was out in the open, and he sure as hell didn't like the looks of Tony's wounds. Despite the chief's in-your-face M.O., he was becoming very fond of the Day-Glo Dago. Or maybe he was just becoming another in a long line of department suck-ups. He shook off the thought, gathered his knees under him, said a quick prayer, then took off.

Sprinting on the sandy dirt wearing loafers reminded Shane of the slow-motion running he often did when he was being chased by overwhelming evil in his nightmares. This twenty-five-yard adrenaline dash was so dismal he could have timed it with a sundial. He finally reached the side of the barn and flattened himself against the weathered wood. Somehow, miraculously, his sluggish sprint had gone unobserved. He tried to catch his breath as he resurveyed the dairy.

Shane could now see half a dozen Crip and Blood work cars parked behind the Colonial-style house, out of view of the main road. His cell vibrated again on his hip; he cursed Alexa's stubbornness, but this time he answered.

He whispered angrily, "They got Tony. He's been wounded."

"I called for backup. Now get out of there," she said resolutely. "That's an order."

"I'm *trying* to get him out of there," he said. "Call you when it's done." As he hung up, he could hear her angry protest. Shane crept slowly around the barn. When he reached the corner, he stopped. From this angle he could see several more cars parked behind the milking sheds. Mercedes and BMWs, probably motherships. Dennis Valentine's blue Rolls-Royce was a ways off, under a tree. Shane pulled the Beretta off his ankle and chambered it. From the look of all the rolling stock hidden from the road, Shane figured there were at least twenty gangbangers out here.

He edged around the corner of the barn, then started to make his way toward a standard-sized door cut in the center of the side wall. As he got closer, Shane dropped to his stomach. With the barrel of his gun, he gently touched the door. It was unlatched, so he pushed it open a crack wider and looked inside. Through the slit, he could see only half the barn, but that area was deserted. He listened for voices; nothing but silence, so he carefully pushed the door wider, craning his neck in for a better look.

He had just seen five men, including Tony, enter this barn seconds ago, but now it was absolutely empty.

Shane held his breath, then wiggled the rest of the way through the opening, staying on his stomach with the Beretta out in front of him until he could see the entire room. The hay trailer had been pulled inside the barn and was parked next to the east wall. From his prone position on the floor, he could see under the still-loaded trailer. Nobody was there, but several bales of hay had been removed from the center of the load. Shane assumed that was where the shipment of White Dragon had been stashed. Suddenly he heard voices. They were distant, sounding as if they were echoing through a tunnel. Then silence. Shane slowly got to his feet and began to move deeper into the barn. He stopped, stood very still, and listened. The voices started again. Shane cautiously followed the direction of the sound and soon found a metal door. It was on the far end of the barn, partially hidden behind a riding blanket. The door had been left slightly ajar, so the voices were leaking through the opening. He reached out and slowly pulled the door wider. It creaked loudly on rusted hinges. Shane froze, then tried again, pulling it an anxious inch at a time. Once he had a few feet clearance, he quickly swung his gun through the opening, pivoted, and followed it in.

He was looking down a dimly lit, short flight of stairs that led to a narrow concrete passageway. Shane kicked off his loafers. In his stocking feet, he crept down the steps until he got to the floor of the tunnel. He was standing in a long, curving concrete corridor. There were a few dim lights hanging from exposed fixtures. Moisture glistened from the walls. He could make out muffled laughter. Then he heard Tony cry out in pain.

Shane moved slowly along the hallway, putting one foot carefully before the other, his gun extended firmly in both hands. He was hugging the far wall to get the longest visual reach down the curving tunnel. He crept forward until, finally, he saw a bright light reflecting off the glistening walls ahead. As he drew closer, he saw another set of stairs leading to a lit area above.

Suddenly, more talk . . . Shane couldn't make out all that was being said because it was distorted by echo. Tony's voice sounded weak, but he thought he heard the chief say, "Fuck you, asshole."

Shane was now at the foot of the concrete steps. Desperately trying not to make any noise, he began to creep silently up the stairs in his socks, his Beretta out in front of him.

Just as he was almost at the top, a gunshot thundered through the echoing silence, followed immediately by a screaming ricochet. A slug chipped the wall beside his head, stinging his cheek with flying concrete before it whined away, thunking into a riser at the top of the stairs. Shane dropped to one knee and spun around, squinting back into the dark passageway. He saw two vague shapes wearing blue headbands. Huge chrome Colts glinted in their outstretched hands. Both had stopped and had him in their sights. Shane was raising his Beretta, ready to fire, but he was already too late.

48

WAR IN THE DESERT

Two more shots thundered in the tunnel. Instantly, Shane plastered himself against the cold, curved wall, as both Crip gangsters flew forward, landing facedown on the concrete floor. Miraculously, Shane wasn't bleeding.

A second later, Shane heard several weapons trombone behind him. A shotgun racked. Alexa was moving up the corridor, the smoking Smith in her right hand. Suddenly Shane felt cold steel on the back of his head, then somebody behind him yanked the Beretta out of his grip.

"Drop the piece!" Dennis Valentine shouted at Alexa.

She froze, caught out in the open with her gun up. Shane was between his wife and Dennis, who was backed by armed g'sters. It was why she hadn't fired again. She was afraid she'd hit him. Alexa held her breath, powerless

472

in the narrow corridor, her eyes wide, her .38 glinting impotently.

Shane felt an icy fear for his beautiful wife.

"Drop it!" Valentine demanded.

"Hey, dirtbag, no LAPD officer ever gives up a weapon." Alexa's voice was a low, adrenalized hiss.

"I've got no more use for your guy here," Dennis said. "Put it down or I'm gonna paint this place red with him."

She looked at Valentine, trying to gauge the threat. "I don't think so," she said. "Not your style."

"I'm not the one's gonna do it." He motioned to a tall, muscular African American. "He is." One of the Crips stepped forward. From the corner of his eye Shane caught a glimpse of Russell Hayes, the man Amac credited with arranging Stone's murder. Without hesitation, Hardcore Hayes put his cut-down .12 gauge to Shane's head. Fear and indecision flickered in Alexa's eyes. There was no doubt in anybody's mind that Hardcore would pull the trigger.

"Okay," Alexa said, lowering her gun.

The rest was just housekeeping.

Two more Crips ran into the corridor, grabbed Alexa, and threw her on the floor. Dennis stepped back and another two gangbangers took Shane down in exactly the same fashion. Once subdued, they were both pulled up the stairs into a windowless neon-lit room

473

about twenty feet long and ten feet wide. Across the end of the chamber were five tables with hammered metal tops. They looked as if they had perhaps once been milking shed tables, but now they were piled high with Baggies of powder, each one displaying White Dragon logos stenciled on the sides.

There were a dozen Crip and Blood bangers in the room with Dennis Valentine, all packing street sweepers or cut-down shotguns.

Farrell Champion and General Ruiz were not there.

Shane was shoved forward and saw Tony slumped in the corner, his shirt drenched in blood. His normally round, cherubic face had gone pale and damp. He looked like he was going into shock. Two Crip gunmen were standing over him, but the chief wasn't going to be causing any trouble. He was hanging by a thread, bleeding out.

"You gotta get him medical attention," Alexa said anxiously. She was being held by a muscular banger whom Shane remembered from gang briefings: a dangerous Crip murderer known as Insane Wayne.

"You don't get it. All a you motherfuckas 'bout t'get taken off d'count," Hardcore Hayes said in a deep Barry White-type voice.

Then, as if to prove the point, Tony started coughing — deep, rattling, dangerous sounds that scared Shane more than Hardcore's threats.

"It's not gonna go down that easy, Hayes," Alexa said softly.

"Git your ass down offa your shoulder, bitch," Hardcore growled. "This is over."

"I got troops rolling," Alexa said. "In a few minutes, this place is gonna look like a federal law enforcement convention."

"Shut up, Alexa," Shane growled. "Don't give these jerkoffs anything."

She looked over at him and glowered. It was bad acting — *Dragnet* theater — but it seemed to work. Dennis and Hardcore looked worried, like they suddenly didn't know how to play it.

"Put 'em in the container truck and get 'em outta here," Valentine ordered. "Rest a you guys load up the powder in the other tanker, then follow in the SUVs. Let's move outta here," Dennis said, sudden urgency in his voice.

Alexa and Shane were dragged across the room toward another metal door, then pushed out into a large automated milking shed.

Shane could see that the sorting room they had just left had been partitioned off from the main building. The entire setup was pretty slick: Juan Ruiz, or whoever controlled White Cow Dairy, had dug an underground tunnel from the hay barn to the windowless room. The *chiva* was unloaded in the barn, brought through the tunnel to the sorting room, then walked through the milking shed into waiting tanker trucks and driven off the property to be distributed all over the State of California. The operation was invisible from the road and from the air.

Shane and Alexa were forced out of the milking shed into a covered distribution center where several twelve-wheel, shiny, aluminum refrigerated tanker trucks were parked. They all had White Cow logos on the cab doors.

Shane was dragged to the nearest truck.

"Up," Dennis ordered. "Climb." He pushed Shane to the metal ladder that led to the top of the large aluminum tank.

"Can't . . . I'm lactose intolerant. Allergic to dairy," Shane said. Dennis put his gun to the back of Shane's head and cocked it.

"Funny . . . case you haven't figured this out, you're already dead, asshole. I gave you and your lady a chance to get rich. You coulda had a piece of a sixty-billion-dollar business, but instead you turn into a fucking Boy Scout. You made your choice. I can waste you right now, but then I gotta drag your leakin' corpse up that ladder and ruin this great Armani suit. You wanna live another twenty minutes, you climb. Otherwise, you're on the ark right now."

So Shane grabbed the metal ladder and started up to the top of the tanker. Two g'sters were waiting above. They were balanced on the shiny aluminum cask with their guns drawn. One of the Bloods was a fat, sweating O.G. in federated colors, a bright red running suit and matching head rag. Shane also recognized him from LAPD gang briefings — a Compton Blood named Li'l Hunchie.

"Don't make no jack move, mothafucka," the O.G. said, training his auto-mag.

Shane went to the raised hatch and climbed in, lowering himself down. He held on to the opening for a while, but Li'l Hunchie got impatient and started stomping on his fingers. Shane yelled out in pain, then let go, and dropped the last three feet into the shiny cylindrical interior. His scream echoed in the hollow container, and as it diminished, he saw Alexa being lowered. He grabbed her legs, helping her down.

"Total cluster fuck," she said once she was inside the cask.

"Where's our backup?" Shane demanded.

"I called SPD. Claimed they knew where this place was, but the better question is, what happened to the feds? They got here two hours ahead of us. Where the fuck are they? Did they stop for doughnuts?"

"You were supposed to hold the front," Shane complained. "You're sure not doing us much good in here, are ya!" There was anger in his voice, but he was frightened for her safety and that's how it manifested itself.

Tony was lowered down next. He was unconscious and his pants were soaked with blood. Shane could feel the coldness of the chief's body as he grabbed him, then laid him on the floor of the tanker.

The hatch was slammed shut and they were plunged into inky blackness.

"Shit, we gotta get a tourniquet on him, but I can't see a damned thing. You see where they hit him?" Alexa asked.

"Looked like he took one in the shoulder, another in the stomach or abdomen," Shane answered.

He heard Alexa ripping fabric, tearing her jacket into strips. "Make me some compresses," she said. "I'll find the bullet holes with my fingers. Jam this cloth in. We gotta stop this bleeding."

Using his teeth, Shane started tearing his own jacket. He could feel her moving beside him, but could see absolutely nothing.

"Fuck you doing?" Tony growled.

"You're awake! Thank God," she answered.

Tony started coughing. They were wet, racking coughs and Shane didn't like the sound of them.

Alexa was trying to find Tony's wounds by touch, stuff them with torn pieces of her jacket, then bind them up. Suddenly the truck lurched forward, throwing them all into a pile in the back.

The inside of the milk tank was slick, and Shane, still in his socks, was sliding around like a dog on ice. He stripped them off to get better traction, then tried to stand. The truck was rocking badly as it left the loading dock, so he couldn't keep his balance and was being thrown all over the place.

"Where are you?" he said as he felt the truck turn onto the dairy's main drive.

"Down here, on the right," Alexa answered.

"When they open the hatch to take us out and kill us . . . that's when we have to —"

"I don't think we're getting out of here," she said. "If it was me, I'd crash this thing and set fire to it. Burn the evidence."

"That's not very fucking encouraging," Shane said.

Then Tony moaned and started coughing again.

He had only been inside the tanker for a few minutes, but already Shane was beginning to sweat profusely inside the airless tanker. He concentrated on balancing against the side, trying not to fall. But as the truck accelerated up the drive, they were both off balance, trying not to land on Tony.

Then the driver missed a shift and the engine screamed. The gears ground, then engaged, as they jerked hard and were picking up more speed. The truck turned sharply, then bounced and careened along, rocking badly. It felt as if the tanker had left the dairy's main road and was bouncing out into the field, out of control, going too fast.

"Something's wrong!" Shane shouted as he was being thrown around in the dark.

"Yeah?" Alexa quipped. "How can you tell?"

Tony continued to moan.

From outside, a machine gun started clattering. Bullets pierced the top of the tanker, puncturing pinholes of light through the metal just a few feet above their heads. Shane and Alexa threw themselves down on the floor, just as another burst of deadly automatic gunfire let loose. The milk truck swerved sharply, and Shane could feel it begin to tip. It teetered on its right-side wheels for a second, then began to turn over.

The tanker rolled once . . . twice . . . then a third time. They were all flipping around inside the metal cylinder like laundry on tumble-dry. Finally the truck came to a shuddering stop, resting on its side.

Shane crawled to the hatch and tried to push it open, but it wouldn't budge. He turned, and lying on his back, tried to kick the airtight seal loose with his bare feet — his ankles ached with each lunging kick. The sound inside was like a steel drum, echoing with each blow. But the hatch wouldn't budge.

Suddenly they heard more gunfire outside, more bullet holes riddled the metal tank. Most of the rounds punched through one side and out the other, but a few ricocheted around dangerously inside. Soon Shane heard someone working on the hatch — probably one of the Crip or Blood gangsters. He quickly got his feet under him, ready to fight for their lives.

They held their breaths as the hatch was pulled back, and somebody's face was looking in, backlit by the bright desert sunshine. Shane couldn't see who it was, so he balled up his fist and let fly.

"Dad, no!" Chooch yelled, just as Shane connected, knocking his son back through the hole.

"Shit, Chooch!" Shane shouted, then scrambled out through the hatch into bright light. When his eyes finally adjusted, he saw his son lying on the sand at his feet. Chooch's mouth was bleeding and one of his front teeth was missing. Simultaneously, machine guns started firing in the distance.

"Sorry, Chooch. I'm sorry . . . Jesus, whatta you doing here?" Shane demanded.

"Where's Mom?" Chooch asked, holding his jaw.

"Inside the tanker." Shane stuck his head through the hatch. "Alexa, it's Chooch. You both stay here with Tony." He looked in the direction of the machine-gun fire and asked his son, "Who's doing the shooting?"

"Amac," Chooch said. "He was out by the milking sheds trying to get the layout when he saw them put you guys in the truck. When it left the farm, he chased it, then shot out some tires and ran it off the driveway. The other Emes chased the escort cars away and dropped me off. Amac's over there trying to take the rest of them out, but he's only got five guys left. Here, take this." Chooch handed his father Alexa's backup gun — the Double Eagle.

"Stay here," Shane ordered.

"I'm not staying here."

"You packing?"

Chooch pulled his coat back and showed Shane one of Alexa's purse guns: the little Spanish Astra.

"Okay, but if you don't do *exactly* what I say, I'm gonna clock you."

"Okay."

"For starters, lemme look at that tooth."

"Why?"

"No arguments, remember?"

Chooch frowned, but turned to show him, and as he did, Shane hit him with his best right hook . . . putting everything into the shot. As he connected, Shane felt the blow all the way up to his elbow. Chooch went down on one knee, then he toppled over and was soon breathing deeply, with his eyes closed.

Shane took his son's pulse, pulled back an eyelid, and looked at the pupil. "Alexa, get out here. I had to clock Chooch. He's out. I think I gave him a concussion."

Alexa, with Tony's blood all over her, scrambled out of the overturned tanker. Shane moved around and looked into the cab of the truck. Li'l Hunchie was behind the wheel, his red Nike running suit stained maroon with deep arterial ooze. Half a dozen bullet holes riddled the g'ster's chest. Li'l Hunchie had his eyes open, but his lights were out.

Shane jumped up onto the overturned cab,

reached down inside, and pulled Hunchie's MAC-10 off the floor. Then he turned and started sprinting in the direction of the gunfire. He was running pretty well across the sand in his bare feet — until he started picking up thorns. He hopped and brushed at the bottoms of his feet as he ran. Soon he came to a low rise. Shane threw himself down on the sand and edged up to the lip, peeking over.

What he saw was pure Sam Peckinpah; no horses or wagons, but it was still right out of *The Wild Bunch*. Three low-riders were stalled on one side of the field next to the dairy, the gangsters now out of them, taking cover behind the fenders. Two of the abandoned Crip SUVs were tire-shot and riddled with bullet holes.

The second tanker truck, which was loaded with the bags of White Dragon, was tipped over and on fire. It had rolled just like the one Shane, Alexa, and the chief had been in, but one of its gas tanks had ruptured, and flames were now licking at the shiny aluminum. Half a dozen Crips and Bloods with auto-mags were getting heat rash hiding behind the burning truck, rising up occasionally and triggering off long bursts of 9mm ordnance, firing at the pinned-down Emes.

Shane was directly behind the tanker, in a great position to start picking the black gangsters off. He could also see that Amac and his men were in trouble. Badly outnumbered, they were hiding behind their disabled low-riders.

Several Crips in blue headbands were crawling away from the burning truck, toward a wash. Blood shooters behind the truck rose up periodically, laying down a barrage of cover fire, their burping machine guns strafing the lowriders with 9mm rounds, keeping the Emes from moving and allowing the Crips to continue sneaking up the wash, unobserved. Within minutes, they would be able to set up a lethal crossfire.

Shane decided his best and most critical shot was Hardcore Hayes, who was only twenty yards away, crouched down behind the burning truck. The problem was, Shane didn't want to back-shoot him. These guys were killers, and sniper fire was part of the package in war, but just triggering Hayes off from behind seemed so cowardly and cold-blooded, Shane didn't think he could do it. Nevertheless, he slowly pulled up Li'l Hunchie's MAC-10 and put the retractable stock on his shoulder. "Meet your maker, asshole," Shane whispered as he sighted down the barrel.

But he couldn't do it — couldn't pull the trigger.

He took a deep breath, hardened his resolve, then refocused on Hardcore Hayes.

Shane squeezed off a short burst.

And missed.

Seconds later all hell broke loose. The Crips and Bloods who were hiding behind the truck with Hardcore turned and fired back at Shane, raking the top of the ridge where he was with hollow points. Sand flew in all directions. Shane dropped the MAC-10 by mistake and started zigzagging along the ridge, desperately trying to find cover. Slugs tugged at his sleeves and ripped holes in the dirt beneath his feet. He dove into a rain-wash and dug his head into the sand. After a second, the bullets stopped, so he picked his head up for a peek.

The Emes had used the diversion to abandon their bullet-riddled low-riders and charge the tanker. Shane could see five Mexicans in blue headbands running across the open terrain. American Macado was leading the charge. Suddenly, the Crips and Bloods all turned away from Shane back toward the charging Emes, who were caught out in the open. Twenty ejector slides began clattering as the Crips opened up in force. Within seconds, half the Emes were down and bleeding in the sand.

Shane couldn't believe his eyes — the mindless violence — but now he had no choice. He started to pick off the Crips and Bloods with the Double Eagle, sighting carefully before each shot. He dropped Hardcore Hayes first, then got the Blood closest to Hayes. Now he had the advantage and was dividing their attention. The remaining Crip and Blood bangers turned away from Amac and started firing at Shane. Bullets thudded in the dirt inches from him. He took off running again, sprinting along in the open looking for better cover. But the ridge was quickly disappearing and soon he was going to end up with no cover at all. So he threw himself down, proned out in the sand, and the second he hit the ground, a flock of nines went overhead, stirring his short hair.

He heard shouting. When Shane looked up, Amac had managed to get all the way to the overturned tanker. He seemed like the only Eme still on his feet. Amac stepped around the back of the truck and fired on the remaining two Bloods now cringing behind the burning tanker. As Amac crept farther around for a better shot, the flames reached their second gas tank, and suddenly it exploded. Both Blood g'sters and Amac were hurled away from the fiery truck by the explosion, airborne and screaming; they landed twenty feet away, bleeding in the sand.

From the corner of his eye, Shane caught Dennis Valentine's midnight blue Rolls-Royce speeding up the drive toward the front gate of the dairy. Shane stood and fired the Double Eagle, emptying the clip, but he was out of range. It seemed as if after all this, Champagne Dennis Valentine was going to escape.

Shane's tax dollars finally arrived. Three fully loaded gray sedans swung into view from the highway and blocked the front of the dairy, forcing Dennis to skid his Rolls to a stop to avoid hitting them.

Shane didn't wait to watch the arrest. He ran down the hill toward the burning tanker, checking the two Bloods on the way. They were both alive but unconscious. He grabbed their machine guns and heaved them as far as he could into the desert. Then he ran to Amac.

American was on his back with a huge piece of shiny aluminum tanker shrapnel lodged in his stomach. It was at least two feet long and looked like it had knifed all the way through, pinning him to the hard desert ground like a bug on a board.

As he leaned over, Shane could see the life in American's eyes leaving, like light on a fast-dimming rheostat.

"Amac . . ."

American's lips were caked with dirt and dried saliva. "You . . . you take care of him?" he croaked softly.

"Of Chooch . . ."

Amac nodded, then coughed. "And Delfina . . . she has nobody now."

"I'll be there."

"She could be the one, Scully. She could live the dream."

Shane nodded and took his hand.

"See, I was right," Amac whispered. "No freedom yet. Maybe next time . . ." He closed his eyes.

Shane knelt in the sand beside him as the sound of incoming sirens filled the desert. He leaned down and listened for a heartbeat, but there was none. Shane held Amac's lifeless hand, watching the blood pour out of him, staining the desert sand. Oddly, the crimson fanned out symmetrically underneath him, like angel's wings. A brown angel.

But this guy was a drug lord. He killed people, Shane thought.

Then Amac's voice echoed in his memory: *Así es, así será . . . This is how it is. How it's going to be.*

49

RIO BRAVO

In the dream, Amac was standing on the far bank of a raging river, smiling. He looked much younger, much happier — or maybe it was just pure relief. Shane couldn't tell.

"This is some river, *gabacho*," Amac shouted as the water screamed in their ears. "They call it Rio Bravo, the Great Divide, no? Although it runs between Mexico and the United States, it really runs between you and me. We had to shout across this river, *ese,* but somehow we could always hear each other. Perhaps someday this river will dry up and there will be no more Great Divide."

Shane called across the river. "You died saving Chooch and me, Alexa and Tony. I can never pay you back."

"*Que caballo, ese*. You see these things through Anglo eyes. But I am where I belong.

489

There is honor in death . . . honor more precious than mortality. Do you know the Tarahumara Indians?"

Shane had never heard of them, so he shook his head.

"Their home was in the mountain ranges of Chihuahua. They were one of the tribes that never succumbed to the Spanish. They lived in poverty, but they were proud people, Scully. Proud and happy because they had honor, and never lost their heritage. I am one of those Indians. It is not so hard to die when you believe in what you die for. So remember what I said about Delfina. Make sure she does not forget about her people. Let her live the dream, *ese*."

When Shane woke up he was in Phoenix Memorial Hospital on a couch in the waiting room. As he wiped the sleep from his eyes, he felt tears.

He looked over and saw Alexa and Chooch sleeping on couches nearby. Then he remembered: A few hours ago they had brought Tony to the hospital by ambulance, along with the surviving bangers.

In the car, Chooch had explained to Alexa that a black-skinned Eme, a *prieto* named Midnight, had been left behind in L.A. to guard Delfina. Chooch had come to Delfina's hospital room and had managed to get him to confide that Amac was going to the White Cow Dairy in Scottsdale. Chooch had flown there on Delta and hooked up with the Emes.

490

When they arrived at the E.R., Tony, hovering near death, was sent to surgery.

Time would tell.

The Panamanian general never showed up. But Dennis Valentine was now in custody, demanding his lawyers.

Farrell Champion had been found in the trunk of one of Amac's low-riders, bound and gagged. Once they got the tape off his mouth, he made a phone call, and wide-shouldered Carl from WITSEC showed up an hour later. He still claimed to know nothing about anything, but whisked Farrell off anyway, placing the producer in protective custody. Carl had a federal warrant, so there was nothing Shane or Alexa could do to stop it. Farrell was back among the missing. Who knew where he would turn up next? Maybe as an anchor on CNN, or wired to one in Long Beach Harbor. Either way, Farrell was going to be a no-show at Nora's wedding.

Tony was moved out of surgery into ICU at six that evening, in critical condition. His wife, Mary, had arrived from L.A., so Shane, Alexa, and Chooch ducked out of the hospital through a side door to avoid the growing collection of local and national media.

They drove to the Deer Valley Airport. The federal asset-seizure jets had all left. They climbed aboard the King Air and flew back to L.A. Chooch was sitting in the front of the airplane, in the right-hand seat next to the pilot, his lip swollen where Shane had hit him. After the wheels were up, Shane went forward and kneeled in the aisle.

"You okay?" he asked, wishing his son would discuss what had happened in the desert, talk about Amac's death. Chooch's brooding silence seemed ominous.

His son didn't look at him but said, "I'm fine."

"If you hadn't shown up out there, gotten me and Mom out of that truck . . ." Shane offered.

"I'm fine, Dad," he said again, turning to look at the instruments, then out the side window of the small two-engine prop plane. Anywhere but at Shane.

When they got back to the canal house in Venice, Chooch went straight to his room. Shane was standing in the hallway, looking at his son's closed door, trying to decide what to do. Alexa took his arm and led him to the backyard.

Their metal chairs were waiting. A heavy fog had descended. In L.A., fog was always called a "marine layer," but it was really just fog — as heavy and gray as Shane's spirit.

They sat looking at gray water reflecting a gray sky. The buildings in the distance went up three stories and disappeared in the mist. It was that dense.

"It's not you, Shane," she said softly. "It's Amac. Chooch can't deal with the death. He's angry. He needs to put that anger somewhere.

You're handy. He'll get over it."

"Yeah," he said, softly. "I know how close they were." Shane could feel the fog's moisture, which had settled on the chair, seeping up through his pants, dampening his underwear. "You ever heard of the Tarahumara Indians, in Chihuahua?" Shane asked.

"No. Why?"

"I had a strange dream at the hospital. Amac was telling me he was one of those Indians, so I wondered if you'd ever heard of them."

She shook her head. "They're probably just a figment of your dream."

Shane lunged out of his chair and lumbered into the house. In his den, he pulled the *Encyclopaedia Britannica* off the shelf and looked them up. In a moment, he could smell Alexa behind him, fragrant as lilacs, could feel her looking at the book over his shoulder.

"Here they are," Shane said. "Page five seventeen. 'One of the few Aztec tribes of Mexico who never surrendered to the Spanish.' Just like Amac said."

"Maybe you studied them in school a long time ago," she said. "You didn't just vibe it out of thin air."

"Right . . ." He turned and walked back out to the lawn to again sit on the old metal chair looking out at the canals.

Their Venice house had started to feel like home again. Shane was determined not to return to the asset-seizure house on North

Chalon Road except to pick up his things and get Franco. Something told him there was hidden danger for him there. Hubris and ambition lived in that house. It had started to creep inside and poison him. More and more, he worried about his soul. Some would probably call that growth, but Shane suspected that the barrier that held back his psychic demons was crumbling.

Like Carol White, he also had some dangerous flaws. Carol's flaw had been her foolish dream. Her drug was heroin. His flaw was foolish pride. His drug was self-deception. Alexa returned with a beer for him. He pulled the tab, contemplating his family's future.

"What is it? You have something else you need to tell me," she said softly. When he didn't answer, she pressed on. "C'mon, Shane, in your dream, Amac didn't just tell you about courageous Aztec Indians."

"You're right." His resolution silently forming, he turned to face her. "Alexa, I want to make a place here for Delfina when she gets out of the hospital."

"You're kidding. . . ."

"No, I mean it. She has nobody left here in California. With Amac gone, she's all alone —"

"You're right. It's okay, honey."

"You don't mind?"

"Take 'yes' for an answer." She was smiling at him.

"I was thinking we could make a room out of

the garage for Chooch. Give her Chooch's room. We could all park our cars in the alley."

"No problem."

God, he loved her.

They sat in silence. Night finally descended, swallowing the heavy gray mist in the process.

While Alexa locked up, Shane walked into their bedroom, bone tired. He sat on the bed, then took off his shoes and socks. That's when he noticed a paper on his pillow.

It was Chooch's college essay, with a note clipped onto the front.

Dad,
It's finally ready for you to read.

Love,
Chooch

HEROES
by
Charles Sandoval Scully

I am six years old, and I am standing in a large room full of toys. I've been told by my teacher that I can only have one, but it is a terribly difficult choice because often I think I want something, but once I have it, I tire of it quickly. I know I must choose, so I study the shelves carefully. Do I want the policeman set, or the tin soldiers? The fire engine, or the doctor set?

I spend almost an hour vacillating — taking one thing off the shelf and almost deciding, be-

fore putting it back and choosing another.

I stand looking at the toys, but I cannot choose.

I am fifteen, looking down at my mother's grave, trying to understand my thoughts. She never let me see inside her, never let me know who she really was. I hated her for most of my life . . . hated her for what she did, for the way she made her living. She sold herself for money, but in the end, she died trying to save me.

I never really knew her, and now that she's gone, I don't know how I feel. Do I hate her? Do I pity her? Do I wish she was alive? Is she better off where she is? Am I better off because she's gone? I do not know. I cannot choose.

I am fifteen and a half, and I'm in a Mexican street gang.

I'm standing with my carnal, a powerful leader. We are brothers and I worship him, but there are guns on the bed. We are planning a payback shooting — a drive-by.

I feel I don't belong here, but I have made so many bad choices in my life that I'm trapped. Do I say no? Do I walk away, and disappoint my brothers? Will they kill me if I leave? Do I pick up a gun and kill a stranger? My big brother says we are fighting to free our people, but is that true? Could it possibly be right to kill, even for a cause?

I do not know . . . I cannot choose.

But now I am afraid and frightened for my soul.

I am seventeen, standing in my father's den. My new life's choices, like that roomful of toys long ago, are spread out in front of me.

Do I want to be a policeman like my father, or a soldier? Do I want to be a doctor or a fireman?

I have come a long way, and I know I must finally choose. My father is strong and fair. I love and trust him enough to be afraid in front of him. But he cannot help me. The choice is mine alone.

When I was six, my idols were Batman and Superman. I thought I would never find somebody real to look up to. But now I know I was searching for my heroes too high up and too far away. My heroes were always right there in front of me: my mother, who died to save me; my big brother Amac, who tried to achieve an impossible dream to set me free against all odds; my strong, courageous father, who risks everything for me every day.

From him, I have finally learned that to be truly happy, I must live my life for others. I must not take joy from status or power, but from my accomplishments, and the way I chose to accomplish them.

The problem is not what I will become but how I will become it.

I finally have made my decision . . . I know what I want to be.

I want to be exactly like my dad.

50

STRAYS

The deal was signed at eleven a.m. in the main conference room on the twelfth floor of the Black Tower at Universal. Stevie Bergman was presiding over a roomful of even tans and perfect teeth. There was precise ethnic and gender balance.

Nicky Marcella arrived just as the meeting was convening. He waved at Shane but never looked directly at him. Nicky was wearing another two-tone number — green and blue this time. The fabric changed colors as he moved. He shined and shimmered like New Year's bunting.

The D people held the perimeter of the room, standing with their backs against the wall, looking proud. The Felt was grinning; so was Tammy Ansara. The African-American Ds looked foxy and cool. Jerry Wireman was there, looking, well, wiry. He was representing CAA's back-end points. Also present were Mike Fallon, Paul Lubick, and Rajindi Singh. Wireman had come with a head crammed full of Latin phrases, ready to kick some loquacious ass.

Along with Shane was Charlotte "Call me Charlie" Brooks, from LAPD Legal Affairs, who was representing the department. Charlie was nervous and overdressed.

Earlier that morning, Shane had been told by the chief, who was still in the Phoenix hospital, that the federal attorney wasn't going to file charges against Don Carlo DeCesare. The feds had listened to the tape and said it would be useless in court. So the New Jersey Don would just have to finish his life on Earth sentenced to a wheelchair parked in front of a plate-glass window, watching llamas eat grass while his deadly cancer spread.

The Day-Glo Dago must have been feeling better, because at the end of the conversation he implored Shane to "Get us da fuck outta d'movie business!" Which, at this moment, Shane was desperately trying to accomplish.

"*Bueno,*" Stevie Bergman said, hosting the event with trilingual charisma. "This is excellent-o." He glanced at his watch. "I only have thirty minutes, boys and girls, so let's cha-cha-cha."

Shane was having déjà vu.

As far as the LAPD was concerned, the deal

was pretty straightforward. They sold their half of *The Neural Surfer* for four hundred thousand dollars, which was the accrued cost of pre-production up to nine o'clock that morning, less Dennis's hundred grand. Shane argued with the chief that the LAPD should retain some upside back-end points, just in case Paul and Michael actually managed to prove that turkeys really could fly. But Filosiani wanted out.

"Since this is now a major studio picture, Michael Fallon and Rajindi Singh should no longer be deferring salary. We want their contracted amounts up front, upon signing. *Mutus consensus.*" Wireman smiled.

"Be smart and fair," Steve Bergman said. *"Mens regnum bona possidet."*

"Huh?" Charlie said, wrinkling her freckled nose. Apparently nobody spoke Latin in the LAPD Legal Affairs Department.

"Means 'A good mind will win the day,' " Wireman grinned, eager to translate for the dummies in the room.

"Actually, it means, 'A good mind will possess the kingdom,' " Stevie Bergman corrected.

Wireman pushed up the glasses on his nose, then smiled and nodded. "I stand corrected."

"Mentiri splendide," Stevie said.

Shane was getting another headache.

Despite all the posturing and bullshit, the deal was finally signed. The LAPD got its cashier's check for four hundred thousand dollars, which Shane handed to Charlie. She snapped it up into her worn leather briefcase like a fly down a frog's throat.

Soon they were out the door and in the elevator.

As Shane was unlocking his car in the Universal parking lot, he heard his name being called. He looked around and saw Nicky hustling toward him across the asphalt, teetering along on his stacked Cuban heels. Shane waited until the little grifter got there.

"Nice going, Nicky. Twenty-five percent of a major studio picture. Congratulations."

"The pricks reduced me down to ten, but, hey, who's complaining? I'm getting a producer credit, got a housekeeping deal here at Uni, complete with a development fund, and a great office in Building Nineteen. Got a neat little patio. If I go out there and stand on my furniture, I can actually see Steven Spielberg's tile roof over at Amblin Entertainment."

"Sounds like you're well positioned," Shane said as he turned and popped the lock on his Acura, then took off his coat because it was a hot day.

Nicky was shifting back and forth, looking a little like a seal, waiting for his trainer to throw the ball.

"Something on your mind?"

Nicky stopped rocking. "Yeah . . ." He squinted at Shane, using his doe-eyed expression, the one he used to con old ladies on

Sunset Boulevard back in the nineties. "I feel kinda funny about all this. I mean, if it hadn't been for you, I would've never got the front money to get this movie going, hire all these A-listers. Now I got a major studio movie, and you got nothin'."

"I got what I wanted, Nicky. You got what you wanted. We're square, okay? Don't worry about it."

"Yeah, okay." But his ferret eyes looked puzzled, his narrow face scrunched up with worry. It wasn't hard to read his thoughts: *Had Shane scored a piece of this deal that he didn't know about? Was he being screwed?* "What did you get that you wanted?" Nicky asked suspiciously.

"I got the D.A. to indict Dennis for Carol's murder. Insane Wayne was in on the hit. He's downtown, singing like Pavarotti. Dennis is gonna go down. The full twenty-five with an L."

"Oh, that," he said. Now he seemed recalcitrant. "Y'know, Shane, that wasn't my fault she got killed."

"Yes, it was. Yours and mine."

"But I didn't know he was gonna clip her."

"You knew she was using heroin when she auditioned for you."

The little grifter looked down in embarrassment.

"And you knew Dennis had something more than friendship on his mind when he asked you to find her. You must have guessed she was

502

threatening to go to the cops and expose Dennis's movie scam if he didn't give her money for her heroin habit. You had to know it wasn't going to be good once he found her."

Nicky slowly looked up. Shane saw deep pain and guilt on his narrow face.

"Nicky, we were careless, and we set her up for him. Admit it, 'cause if you don't own up to your mistakes, you'll just keep making them. It's how you grow. It's how you reach out and finally come to Jesus. Say hallelujah."

"I know you're making fun of me, but I did find Jesus. And I do pray for her, Shane. I pray for her every day." He was close to tears.

"Me, too."

They stood uncomfortably in the parking lot, bathed in hot sun and shared guilt.

Suddenly Nicky leaned forward, lowering his voice. "Shane . . ." he said softly, looking like a man on the edge of a confession. Then his resolve hardened and he said, "You were right. . . ."

"About what?"

"I knew she was on drugs. When she came in for that reading a few years back, she was pretty seriously tweaked. She looked like shit and tried to borrow money and I didn't do anything . . . not a damned thing. I just . . . I kinda . . . I got her out of the office because she . . ." He stopped, tears welling up.

"She embarrassed you," Shane finished.

"I had to get her out. My investors were

shocked at her appearance." Now the tears were flowing.

"It's okay, Nicky. . . . In the long run, you'll feel better if you own up to it."

"It's not okay, Shane. . . . It's not. I owed her much more. She was my friend in school when nobody else was willing to be. I didn't protect her when she needed me." He pulled out a silk handkerchief and wiped his eyes.

"Neither did I," Shane said softly.

They looked at each other across this big ugly fact.

Finally, Nicky seemed to shake out of it. He put the handkerchief away, reached into his pocket, pulled out an envelope, and handed it to Shane.

"What's this?"

"Well, it's probably not worth anything, but I'm giving you a point and a half outta my back-end of *The Neural Surfer.* Course, by the time Universal gets through bookkeeping the profit participants, net points are usually worth *bubkes.* But who knows? Stranger things have happened."

Shane nodded and put the envelope in his pocket.

"I really did love her, Shane," Nicky said softly.

"I know," Shane said sadly, then got into his car and pulled away.

As he turned the corner on Lankersheim, he looked back and saw Nicky was still standing in the Universal parking lot . . . a tiny little man in an iridescent suit. Thinking. Rocking. Looking down at the pavement.

Carol's funeral was at five o'clock at the New Calvary Cemetery. Besides the minister, there was just Shane, Alexa, Chooch, and Franco. Delfina couldn't make it because she was still in the hospital. But she was being discharged the next day, and moving in with them.

Nicky called at the last minute to say he had to go into a budget meeting and wouldn't be able to make it. Apparently somebody in Universal's auditing department had discovered a line-item for five Oregon redwoods, which were cut and shipped at fifty thousand per tree. Nicky conceded to Shane over the phone that they should have used papier-mâché. Just before the service began, a flower truck arrived with a wreath from Nicky that would have held its own at Gotti's funeral.

Alexa cradled Carol's cat in her arms while the minister read the service.

Chooch had donated the casket, his mahogany Heaven Rider, as well as his pre-selected, prepaid burial plot — all courtesy of American Macado and the 18th Street Sureños. Carol was being laid to rest surrounded by the graves of dead Emes. Amac's funeral wasn't scheduled yet, because the Scottsdale P.D. hadn't released his body. Once they did, Shane, Alexa, Chooch, and Delfina would be back here, standing two plots away, while a hundred Mexican bangers, wearing their trademark Eme blue, stood on the graves of their fallen brothers, nodding wisely, saying that Amac was *con safos* — one hundred proof — *rifa*. It was an endless, useless cycle of death that showed no sign of ever ending.

After the minister finished with the "dust to dust" part of his ceremony, Shane walked him to the road. They stood next to his two-year-old station wagon while Shane paid him.

"Not much of a turnout," the minister said.

"What it lacks in size it makes up for in quality."

The man nodded, got into his Chevy, and pulled out. As Shane watched him go, he thought it was ironic how things happened. He had never had a family growing up, and now that he finally had one, he seemed to have an overpowering desire to take in every stray that touched his heart. First Franco . . . now Delfina. He wondered who would be next.

After the service ended, they walked over to the mortuary building to check on the brass headstone that Shane had ordered. Once completed, it had been waiting for the grave to be filled. Now the headstone could be placed in cement over Carol's earthly remains. The man behind the counter handed it to them, then he turned and went into the back room. The plaque was heavy in Shane's hands, almost twenty pounds. He set it on the floor and they all looked down at it.

Shane often thought that guilt was like poison, that each person had only a limited amount they could absorb. Once you hit your saturation point, guilt got its shot at you. It would knock you down and feed on you, weakening you until you could no longer stand the consequences of your actions. Guilt could drive you in dangerous directions, push you up against defining prerogatives and ugly realities. It seemed to him that cops were especially susceptible. They saw the worst of society and often got the worst. They wore thin armor constructed out of cynicism and disdain, but often got pushed into dark emotional corners where they ended the struggle by chewing on their own gun barrels. Carol had pushed Shane slightly closer to his own psychological and emotional edge. Pushed him there because, since Alexa and Chooch had come into his life, he had started to feel. He had started to care. But feelings were sloppy, untidy emotions that, in law enforcement, were a terrible liability.

For the hundredth time, Shane wondered about changing careers. This time, maybe something shiny and fun. He had tried being a Blue Knight, had tried living up to a higher vision of himself. But when Carol White needed a hero, there were none around — only a confused cop who had badly misplayed his hand.

If he quit the job, what would he do? Run a fishing boat? Work with kids? Open a sporting goods store? Fireman . . . lawyer . . . teacher?

He could not choose.

Franco began to squirm in Alexa's arms, so she put him down. He sniffed at the corner of the brass headstone.

Then he looked up at them, and cried.

Shane stared at the plaque and wondered if he had chosen the right inscription. He didn't know. Maybe it was okay, or maybe it was just stupid and corny. It probably didn't say what she would have wanted. Shane barely knew Carol White, but she had affected him in ways he found hard to understand. Yet if life was going to be about anything, maybe it should be about hope.

Shane picked up Franco and read the inscription one last time . . .

CAROLYN WHITE
1965–2003
The Prettiest Girl in Teaneck, New Jersey
She came that close

Acknowledgments

Writing is a solitary profession. Because of my dyslexia, it is also a very sloppy one. Cleaning up after me is the best mop-and-pail team in the business:

Grace Curcio, my assistant and old friend, who for more than twenty years has been fielding the messy, badly spelled first drafts: "Stephen, I can't read this. You really just fell on the keys today." Without her I would be lost.

Kathy Ezso, my assistant and special line of defense. A good friend who does my countless rewrites as well as first-draft material. Kathy gets a lot of pencil revisions: "What the hell does this say, Stephen? You've got to stop writing so close to the bottom of the page. It's not coming through the fax." Without your dedication and patience, I would be lost.

510

Christine Trepczyk, who is always there for me in a pinch, handling overflow and wondering what the hell is scribbled in the margins. "Stephen, send the pages upside down so I can read the right-side margin. How many times do I have to tell you this?" Christine, I would be lost without you.

Also, Jo Swerling, who reads all my first drafts with a sharp eye for logic and story, and has perfected his ability to tell me when something is not right without crushing my spirit.

All of my friends at St. Martin's Press: Charlie Spicer, how can I thank you for all of your enthusiasm and dedication to my work? You are a great friend and editor. Sally Richardson, who sticks to her guns and makes everything at St. Martin's go. Sally, you're a wise and gentle hand on our tiller. Thank you for contributing your enthusiasm and energy to my process. You're hands on, and I wouldn't trade you for anything.

To my agents, Eric Simenoff and Mort Janklow. I am blessed by your contributions to my career. Eric, your support over the years has been unflinching. I can always count on you for fair advice and savvy thinking. You are a treasured friend. Mort, thanks for adding your wisdom and council to the mix.

My thanks to Matthew Shear of St. Martin's Paperbacks, as well as Joe Cleemann and John Murphy.

To my children, Tawnia, Chelsea, and Cody:

You guys make me proud to be a dad.

And finally, Marcia . . . I met you in eighth grade. You wore my ring around your neck. I married you when we graduated from college. You have supported my writing career from the beginning, when there was no reason to believe I could ever succeed. Without you I would still be in the furniture business, looking at the clock, waiting for the day to be over. I owe all this to you, babe.

9/28